continued . . .

Others Books by Simone St. James

The Haunting of Maddy Clare

An
Inquiry into

Love
and
Death

Simone St. James

 New American Library

New American Library
Published by the Penguin Group
Penguin Group (USA) Inc., 375 Hudson Street,
New York, New York 10014, USA
Penguin Group (Canada), 90 Eglinton Avenue East, Suite 700, Toronto
Ontario M4P 2Y3, Canada (a division of Pearson Penguin Canada Inc.)
Penguin Books Ltd., 80 Strand, London WC2R 0RL, England
Penguin Ireland, 25 St. Stephen's Green, Dublin 2,
Ireland (a division of Penguin Books Ltd.)
Penguin Group (Australia), 707 Collins Street, Melbourne, Victoria 3008,
Australia (a division of Pearson Australia Group Pty. Ltd.)
Penguin Books India Pvt. Ltd., 11 Community Centre, Panchsheel Park,
New Delhi–110 017, India
Penguin Group (NZ), 67 Apollo Drive, Rosedale, Auckland 0632,
New Zealand (a division of Pearson New Zealand Ltd.)
Penguin Books (South Africa), Rosebank Office Park, 181 Jan Smuts Avenue,
Parktown North 2193, South Africa
Penguin China, B7 Jiaming Center, 27 East Third Ring Road North,
Chaoyang District, Beijing 100020, China

Penguin Books Ltd., Registered Offices:
80 Strand, London WC2R 0RL, England

First published by New American Library,
a division of Penguin Group (USA) Inc.

First Printing, March 2013
10 9 8 7 6 5 4 3 2 1

 REGISTERED TRADEMARK—MARCA REGISTRADA

LIBRARY OF CONGRESS CATALOGING-IN-PUBLICATION DATA:

St. James, Simone.
    An inquiry into love and death/Simone St. James.
        p. cm.
    ISBN 978-0-451-23925-9
    I. Title.
    PR9199.4.S726I57 2013
    813'.6—dc23
    2012027265

Set in Adobe Garamond
Designed by Spring Hoteling

Printed in the United States of America

PUBLISHER'S NOTE
This is a work of fiction. Names, characters, places, and incidents either are the product
of the author's imagination or are used fictitiously, and any resemblance to actual per-
sons, living or dead, business establishments, events, or locales is entirely coincidental.
    The publisher does not have any control over and does not assume any responsibility
for author or third-party Web sites or their content.

For my mother

Acknowledgments

My sincerest gratitude goes to my editor, Ellen Edwards, for her tireless work on this book. It would not be nearly the same story without her input and advice. Thanks to my wonderful agent, Pam Hopkins, for her partnership and friendship. Thanks also go to the publicity department at NAL for their support and to the art department for my beautiful covers.

My friends—specifically Tiffany Clare, Michelle Rowen, Molly O'Keefe, Maureen McGowan, Juliana Stone, and Eve Silver—were incredibly generous with their friendship and advice. Thanks, guys. I'm grateful to my family—my mother and sister for cheering me on, and my brother, David, for helping me with my Web site. And as always, every day, thank you, Adam, for everything.

An
Inquiry into
Love
and *Death*

One

My uncle Toby died of a broken neck in the autumn of 1924, just as I was starting the Michaelmas term at Oxford. I was pulled from the back of the lecture hall by a pimpled assistant in thick Mary Janes and an ill-fitting skirt who hissed that I had a confidential summons and must go to the administrative office at once. She even led me there, though it was just across the quad, so agog was she at the mystery of it.

When I learned what had happened, it was a mystery to me as well, for my uncle had not been spoken of in my family in nearly eight years.

I was shown into an unused office where the solicitor from London gave me the news. He was a compact man in a neat vest, out of place against the scored and mismatched furniture and stacks of books. Still, he bade me sit and spoke to me with quiet courtesy, as if we were not in a damp, borrowed room whose drafty windows barely kept out the mist from the commons outside.

"I'm sorry," he said, after he had told me. He reached into his pocket and pulled out a clean handkerchief. "Do you need a moment before we proceed?"

I looked at the handkerchief, apparently a spare, and the only thought I could muster was that he had come terribly well prepared. "You must give news like this often," I said.

Surprise flickered across his face, and he folded the handker-chief again.

"I'm sorry," I said, realizing how I sounded. "It's just that I don't know what to say. I really don't. I didn't know Toby very well. And I don't—That is, I've never dealt with . . ." I trailed off. How stupid for a philosophy student, who had safely debated the concept of death and the immortality of the soul with her fellows, to admit she had never known anyone to actually die.

"It will take some time," the solicitor, who was called Mr. Reed, said kindly. "And yes, I do give such news from time to time. Usually in situations in which the deceased does not have much family."

I nearly opened my mouth to protest: *But Toby has family*. He had his brother, my father. But perhaps Mr. Reed meant a wife, children. Toby had never had those. And why count family one didn't speak to? "Does my father know?" I asked.

"Yes. I cabled him yesterday." Mr. Reed gave me a calm, law-yerly regard, stern but not without gentleness. It was well perfected for a man under forty. "I've come, Miss Leigh, to tell you there is a great deal to be done. Do you understand?"

I nodded, awash with relief. "Yes, yes, of course I understand. My parents will come home."

There was an awkward silence as he straightened the papers in front of him, running his finger along the edges. "I'm afraid that's not quite what I mean. I received the reply by cable this morning. It's why I came up here from London on the first train directly. Your parents are not coming home. They have sent me to you."

"To me? What can I do?"

"His personal effects will require taking care of. But as your uncle carried no identification on him, no legal issues can be ad-dressed before someone identifies the body."

I stared at him for a long moment, aghast. "You must be joking."

He shook his head. "I wish I were."

"I can't do that. Identify a body. Are you mad? I simply can't."

Again he ran his finger along the edge of his papers. "Miss Leigh, I realize the idea is unpleasant. I admit these aren't the exact circumstances I would have chosen. But it seems these are the circumstances we've been given. Your uncle's body is currently housed in a magistrate's office in Devonshire. The coroner has not yet submitted his ruling, but I expect it will be classified an accident. In any case, we can't move forward with Toby's final wishes until the identification is done."

I tried to picture it—my uncle lying on a table in a shabby room somewhere, under a sheet—and failed. Toby had always been kind to me, bringing me sweets when I was a child, even though he was shy and unused to children. I pressed my hands to my temples. I felt ill, but I tried to buck myself up. I'd go to Devonshire, get this hideous experience over with, and come straight back to school. That was all.

Then Mr. Reed continued on about wills, and finances, and cremation arrangements—it seemed my uncle did not want a funeral or a burial plot—and I felt a sickening twist in my stomach as everything suddenly got worse. A headache began to form beneath my temples.

I was twenty-two, and a college student; a worse candidate for these tasks could hardly be found. I interrupted him midsentence. "Are you certain this is what my parents instructed? I'd think it is something they would want to handle themselves."

"It's unorthodox," he admitted. "But I don't know your parents, Miss Leigh. I only knew your uncle, and, well"—he smiled,

as if he had gathered I wouldn't take offense at the implication—
"some families are less orthodox than others."

I nearly groaned. *Unorthodox* only began to describe my
parents—or Uncle Toby, for that matter. I possessed only enough
courage to tell the girls at school a much-edited version of the
truth. "What did you mean about his belongings?"

"Yes, that. Miss Leigh, I gather you are aware of what your
uncle did for a living."

I forced my lips to move. Mention of Toby's occupation always gave me a chill of fear, mixed with bewilderment I had
never untangled. "Yes."

"He was staying in a small town called Rothewell. In Devonshire, as I say. I believe he was on one of his unusual projects. He
had taken rooms, which need to be emptied, and his things sorted
and packed."

One of his unusual projects. Oh, God. "Travel to Devonshire?
It's the start of the term. Can't it wait?"

"According to the landlady, I'm afraid not."

I stared down into my tweed-skirted lap. Somerville was the
most prestigious women's college in the country. Girls prepared
for years to get in. As it was, I worked day and night to keep up
with the workload; I was, quite simply, expected to succeed. To
leave at the beginning of term was ludicrous. And yet, it seemed
my unorthodox family would conspire to have me do just that.

He was on one of his unusual projects.

Perhaps someone could be hired. . . . But no. Even at my
most selfish, I wouldn't hire a stranger to go through my uncle's
things.

"Miss Leigh," Mr. Reed said, as if reading my mind. "I would
not be here if there were another option."

My glance caught his hands, resting on the desk. He wore a

wedding ring. He would take the London train home tonight to his wife, and possibly his children, in a warm, happy home. He had family; so, in a fashion, did I. Toby had no one.

I sighed and raised my head.

Mr. Reed looked into my eyes and smiled. "Let me get the map," he said.

⁕

"That's simply horrible," my flatmate, Caroline, said when I told her the news. She leaned back against the dusty radiator and watched as I put the valise on my bed and opened it. "Did he really fall from a cliff?"

"Yes, in the town where he'd been staying."

"But what happened to the poor man?"

"I don't know."

"Didn't they say? Do you think he . . ." Her eyes widened.

I kept my voice calm. "They think it was an accident."

"But you don't *know*," she said as I tossed dresses into the valise. She was blond, rounded, pretty behind the glasses she wore. "It's utterly gothic, like a novel. Perhaps he was a millionaire and has left you everything. Perhaps he was a spy on a secret mission."

I was glad she didn't know the truth. "Caro, he was none of those things."

"Well, you needn't be sensitive. You said you hardly knew him. You're the only person I've met who has had a mysterious uncle die. It's the most excitement we'll see here for weeks."

She wasn't entirely wrong. To the outside world, Somerville girls—females with the gall to want an actual Oxford education—were a novelty, an insult, a threat, or sometimes a laughingstock.

We were wild, marauding womanhood, making off with civiliza-
tion and traditional values with our thoughtless modern ways. In
reality we were well-bred, well-behaved girls who spent all our evenings studying and trying not to think about the male students we
weren't allowed anywhere near.

Somerville didn't have housing, so I stayed in an all-girls'
boardinghouse, overseen by a landlady who strictly regulated every girl's comings and goings, as well as everything we ate and
wore. The house had but one radio, placed in the main sitting
room for better supervision; lights went out at exactly ten thirty,
and any girl who disobeyed was promptly told to leave. My father's international reputation as a chemist, as well as his money,
had gained my admittance. It was my good behavior—as well as
my failure to mention my eccentric, disreputable uncle to anyone
I knew—that kept me there.

"We'll see," I said. "Is that my telegram?"

"Oh, God—yes, I forgot." Caroline took the paper I'd seen
on the dressing table and handed it to me. "It just came. I'm sorry."

I tore it open. It was from my mother.

Mr. Reed will be contacting you, Mother wrote, belatedly.
*Please do as he asks. Toby likely left his affairs a mess. I don't think
there's any money. Your father and I cannot leave Paris. The work
here is too important. It's only for a few days, darling, I promise.
Please do this for us. We simply cannot handle it. Toby should be laid
to rest by family.*

Family meant, in this case, me.

I had a sudden memory of a seaside vacation we'd all taken
when I was a small child. A hotel with a wooden veranda painted
white, a hot summer sky, a dark sand beach. My parents lazing
late into the morning, mixing cocktails in the afternoon, talking
through the night. And Toby taking me out to the water's edge as

the sun came up, before anyone else awoke, crouching down and smiling at me from under the brim of his straw boater. He had shown me the shells in the sand, naming each of them for me, explaining where they had come from and what creatures had owned them, answering my endless questions until the sun was high and we had gone in to breakfast.

"Jillian, are you all right?"

I folded the paper, tossed it in my valise, and resumed packing. "Mother says they're not coming home. I already knew that from the solicitor."

"So you really must go yourself." Caroline took a cigarette case from her pocket and extracted one. "I don't know whether to be sorry for you or horribly jealous."

"Jealous? I have to see a *body*, Caro. Then I have to pack up his dusty old things. I'll be working nights for weeks after to make up for it, if I make it up at all. This will practically ruin my term. What is there to be jealous of?"

"But you get to go do something," she said, as she watched me stuff in yet another pair of stockings. "I get to stay in a girls-only boardinghouse and listen to Mary Spatsby complain for the hundredth time that she's homesick for her old nanny, while I try to study twelfth-century ethics." She lit her cigarette and inhaled shallowly, arranging it between two fingers for best effect.

"Mary Spatsby is everyone's burden to bear," I said. "You must try to be noble about it."

"What was your uncle doing by the seaside?"

I shut the valise, closed the latches, and quickly thought up an answer. "He was researching some sort of project."

"Mysterious." She righted her tilting cigarette in her fingers and took another careful drag. She seemed to accept the scenario without question. Like me, Caroline came from a long line of academics, and everyone was always researching *something*. "You must tell me everything when you get back. Will there be men?"

I sighed. "There won't be men."

"There must be men. There are men everywhere in England, or so I hear, except here at Somerville. If you even spot a milkman or a vicar, I want every detail."

I shook my head. I said friendly good-byes to Caro and the other girls, my voice casual—*oh, just an uncle I barely knew, that's all*. But as I sat on the omnibus that ran to the outskirts of town, my shoulders sagged. I had not allowed myself to think too much about Toby, dying alone in a strange place, falling from a cliff.

Or jumping.

I stared out the window as Oxford receded, until I could see only the roofs of the chapels and libraries punctuated with spires, and the green squares filled with undergraduates chatting in the cold autumn sunshine were gone from view.

I thought of that man in the straw boater, his kind, attentive gaze. What had happened?

I got off the omnibus at the edge of town and walked half a mile to a small coaching inn. The landlord here, seeing an opportunity, had dismantled the stalls in half his barn and cleared it out. For a fee, the empty half now housed motorcars—including mine.

The remaining horses whickered curiously as I pulled the canvas storage sheet from the motor and folded it. An aged groom smoked a cigarette and leaned against the wall, staring at me through pouched eyes with a look that dared me to ask him for help. I gave him a look back and said nothing.

The car was called an Alvis, though I knew nothing about motorcars and did not know what that meant. It had been a gift from my father; he'd taught me to drive it one warm morning in early summer, the two of us jolting over the roads, my mother watching from the front stoop, declaring herself fit for a nervous breakdown, though she'd laughed and sipped a gin as she said it.

I knew no other girls who had been taught how to drive. Even among the unconventional set at Oxford, it was a rather dashing skill for a girl to have. The car—and the lessons—had been a reward for gaining admission to Somerville, with disregard for the fact that motorcars were not allowed within Oxford proper, and therefore I'd have no place to use it. That was typical thinking of my parents. The world conformed to them, not the other way 'round. I now wondered whether there had been guilt in the extravagant gesture, as they'd gone to Paris a month later.

So I had parked the Alvis and left it. I stared at it now, as it gleamed in the dim light of the barn, with trepidation and not a little fear. I'd never driven anywhere but the roads around my parents' house, and I'd never driven alone.

I was leaving the familiar confines of Oxford behind, and the fear mixed deep in my stomach with sour, shamed excitement. I loved life at school—the quiet, the perfect alignment of the hours of each day. I was truly grieved by the death of my uncle. And yet, a small voice inside me admitted that I wanted to, as Caro had said, *do* something.

I stowed my valise and heavy books I'd carried, and took a deep breath. There was nothing for it, then, but to go. I removed my hat and tied on a scarf, as my earlobe-length hair tended to curl when given its way, and the wind would have a heyday with it. I pulled on a pair of driving gloves and looked at the groom again. To my surprise, he gave me a nod.

I got in the motorcar and drove away.

TWO

T he roadster was sleek and picked up speed quickly. I had
a long drive ahead.

The town of Rothewell wasn't in my Baedeker's, but
the maps provided by Mr. Reed showed it somewhere on the
north coast of Devonshire. I made my painstaking way past Bris-
tol as the familiar countryside vanished, stopping every hour to
recheck my way. This was nothing like sitting back in a train
compartment, waiting to get off at your destination. In adverts,
I'd seen drawings of drivers flying down the road, carefree and
easy. Instead I gripped the wheel, my back aching, straining my
eyes at rare road signs as I passed fields of grazing sheep and tidy
hedgerows.

At first, other motorcars passed me or came the other way—
men in overcoats and goggles, a smart-looking fellow and his
pretty blond girlfriend, a few rowdy boys waving at me and
shouting quips I couldn't hear—but as I got closer to the seacoast
and turned along its quiet roads, the other cars all but disappeared, leaving me the lanes to myself.

Somewhere in the fourth hour, along the coast toward Ex-
moor, it began to rain, a light sprinkling through the heavy, wet
air of the sea, and I was glad I had pulled the roof up during one
of my many stops. By then I would gladly have pulled over to

wait out the weather, or even to spend the night, but I wanted to make Barnstaple if I could, and there was no hotel to be seen. I trundled on as the roads got wetter, trying my best to see through the roadster's windscreen.

By dark my hands were shaking and my head throbbed with pain. I no longer felt adventurous. I longed for my familiar rooms at Oxford, but of course I couldn't go back. I had reached Barnstaple at last, and in the morning it would be time to see the magistrate.

Barnstaple was pretty enough, though of course not as beautiful as Oxford to my eye. I found an old hotel near the River Taw (EXCEPTIONAL ACCOMMODATION—MODERN CONS INSTALLED—REASONABLE RATES), which seemed to house a small but eclectic mix of tourists, couples, and traveling businessmen. If I was an unusual sort of guest as a woman traveling alone, no one had the bad grace to remark on it, and I was too tired to care. I had gone straight to my room and slept fitfully despite my exhaustion, visions of the rainy road and memories of Toby flitting behind my closed eyes.

Now, in the bright, chilled sunshine of the following morning, I sat in the magistrate's office on the second floor of a centuries-old building in the center of town, wearing my most formal skirt and jacket, itchy stockings, and high heels, trying not to twist my gloves to ruin in my damp hands.

"Rothewell, you see, is far too small to have a magistrate or a coroner in residence, so your uncle's case was brought here," said the magistrate, whose name was Mr. Hindhead. He was about fiftyish, sported thinning blond hair, and was ensconced from head to toe in soft, pillowy fat. "The coroner has examined the body. Do you understand?"

I nodded, for the second time in two days sitting before a man who sat behind a desk and attempted to explain the world to me. "Is there to be . . . an autopsy, then?"

He shook his head. "No, my dear, unless of course you request one. But even so . . ." He sighed, as if burdened. "The coroner has already ruled, you see."

"What do you mean?"

"Well, that is, he examined your uncle's body. You just missed him—he was here last night. As the circumstances were a little unusual, the coroner has to rule one way or the other, and if he sees evidence of foul play, we call in the police and go from there." Mr. Hindhead pulled a small tin from his desk drawer and extracted a mint from it, which he popped between his thin lips. "But the coroner's already been, my dear, and he's ruled it an accident."

"An accident? You mean my uncle fell?"

"Yes, so it would seem. Though I assure you"—he waved a placating hand at me, as if I'd managed to move—"there was no evidence of drunkenness."

The thought of my uncle Toby drunk was so jarring that it took me a moment to refocus. "I don't understand. Are you saying I'm not needed here?"

"Yes, Miss Leigh, you are, but only for the formality of the identification. It's just the last bit of paperwork, and then your family can put this tragedy behind you. In a way it's good news, you see. No lingering. It's bad enough for a girl alone. I've never seen such a thing. You haven't a cousin, a brother-in-law, anyone who could have come? Well. You mustn't worry about the rest of it, calling the undertaker's man or such. Mr. Leigh's solicitor will take care of all of that."

I swallowed. I hadn't thought about arranging the cremation. I would call Mr. Reed as soon as I could find a telephone. "I see. Well." I swallowed again. "All right, then."

Mr. Hindhead summoned a constable, and we left the office for a warren of hallways and stairs. I followed, numb, not noting where we were going, thinking of Toby slipping over a cliff's edge. What had he been doing? Taking a walk, perhaps? Searching for something? Was it something to do with his profession? I pictured him going too far to the land's edge, not noting how close he was, and that endless moment when his feet slipped from under him. . . .

The old building housing the magistrate's office seemed to be connected via corridor to another, larger building. I realized we had come to a paneled hall in a basement. Mr. Hindhead stopped in front of a set of thick double doors. He set his hand on the knob of one and turned to me, his face serious.

"Miss Leigh. Are you ready?"

I managed to nod.

"Very well, then. Constable Jenkins, you are witness. We'll do this quickly."

He pushed open the door. I could see nothing within but a bare floor, a few shelves, the corner of a table. I didn't realize I had not moved until I felt the constable touch my elbow. I glanced up into his ruddy face and he nodded at me, his eyes pitying me from over the large brush of his mustache.

I stepped forward. The table held a body under a thick canvas sheet. I forced my legs to take me closer, and Mr. Hindhead folded back the canvas.

I had been picturing Toby in my mind on that day at the beach, years ago. He'd been young then, and if never exactly handsome, he'd had the buoyancy of youth about him in the morning sunlight, a shy, fleeting smile, and eyes that lit on me with pleasure. Even the last time I'd seen him, some eight years ago, he'd been trim, clean-shaven, well-groomed, if weighed down by some sadness I didn't understand. He'd barely looked at me then, and his visit had been brief, something I'd taken no note of, as I'd had no idea he would disappear from my life.

He looked older, now, than his forty-three years. His mouth was pulled into a grim line, his cheeks and brows slack as if with despair. Death, I realized, had aged him. Down the left side of his face was a swath of angry purple-red contusions, and his nose was set crookedly in his face. His brown hair was uncombed, matted with something dark. His shoulders, under the sheet, were bare. I had never seen my uncle in anything other than a shirt, collar, waistcoat, and tie.

Wrong. This is wrong.

"Miss Leigh," said Mr. Hindhead. "Do you identify this man as your uncle, Tobias Leigh?"

"I do," I said.

The magistrate nodded, and Constable Jenkins moved forward and pulled the sheet back over my uncle's face. I lifted my eyes and saw Mr. Hindhead watching me from across the table.

"A girl alone," he said, and shook his head. "Such a shame. I'll order up some tea. It's almost over, my dear. It's almost over."

By afternoon it began to rain again and I was driving through a landscape of thick woods, the leaves brittle on the trees in the long afternoon light, some of the branches beginning to lose their foliage altogether. As I stopped at a crossing and waited for a farmer to move his cow from the road—he was most apologetic, and the cow most reluctant—I heard a sharp pattering over my head. I leaned out the window and looked up to see rain dripping from the undersides of the canopy of leaves, woven over the road, the branches bowing under the lowered wet sky.

I hadn't wept for Toby. I couldn't. My eyes burned and my throat was choked closed, but nothing would come. Instead I had moved through the hours mechanically, somehow doing what needed doing—nodding when the magistrate spoke, placing the call through to the solicitor, checking out of the inn—as my brain gratefully surrendered to a thick fog. I barely remembered driving from Barnstaple and could not recall any of the scenery I'd passed since.

Now, as I looked up at the leafy canopy and felt cool rain on my face, I began to awaken. I realized I was lost. Most of the day had slipped away from me as I took wrong turn after wrong turn on the roads. I had not rechecked the maps. I had simply driven, the memory of Toby's battered face the only thing I could see before my eyes.

But Rothewell was on the sea, and even in my blindness I had pointed the car in that direction. I could hear the sea now, a low roar complementing the light patter of rain. I could smell salt in the air. There is something about the smell of the sea that has an effect on every human living, and always will. My sluggish mind began to move.

I leaned into the passenger seat and pulled up the map, wondering how far off course I was. The map was nearly useless; how to know whether the narrow inked line on a piece of paper corresponded with the two-track lane of mud I was currently following? I turned it this way and that as the cow and its owner made their way off the road. I should try to keep the sea to my right, I thought. That was the best way to stay in the right direction. I was pleased with this thought until I realized, too late, that I could have asked the farmer for directions.

An hour later, the rain was coming down harder, and dusk fell. I was tired. I came to a crossroads and pulled over.

I got out of the Alvis, pulled up my coat collar, and looked around me. The road each way was deserted. It had been so long since I had seen another car, I might have been transported to fairyland, or backward in time. The air was purplish gray, the only sound the rush of raindrops in the trees overhead and the crunch of my shoes on the gravel. Somewhere far off, a lark called. I could no longer hear the sound of the sea over the rain.

I huddled deeper into my coat. Here, in this desolate spot, the thoughts I'd been pushing away began to overtake me. Toby had come this way. He hadn't been researching a project, as I'd told Caroline, and he hadn't been on holiday. It was time to admit to myself what Toby had done for a living, and that it frightened me.

Toby had hunted ghosts.

Your uncle was working on one of his unusual projects.

Ghosts—the pursuit of them, the study of them—had been my uncle's profession. He'd made a living being called upon by the haunted and the desperate. He'd traveled all over the country, chasing specters of the dead. *Toby's foolishness*, my father had called it—for my father, the scientist, most certainly did not believe in the afterlife. *Have a little sympathy for your brother*, had been my mother's words to my father. *After all, he truly believes he can see them.*

Toby was dead himself now, where I had left him in that silent basement room. Again I felt the nagging tug that something was wrong. Perhaps it was the shock I'd sustained, or the violence I'd seen done to my uncle's body, but I couldn't shake my unease.

A drunk man would have slipped from a cliff, perhaps, or a man outside in a blinding storm. But Toby hadn't been in

Rothewell to take the air or to exercise himself with constitution-
als. If he had been on Rothewell's cliffs, I couldn't help but think it
had been for a purpose connected with his lifelong search for the
dead.

What ghost had he followed to this place?

I closed my eyes, listened to the rain, felt my nose grow cold
in the chill air. I hadn't known much about Toby's profession. I'd
never asked him about it. I'd never really wanted to think about
it, in truth. I saw now that all my life, I'd separated the gruesome
idea of Toby's ghost hunting from the kind man I knew, as if they
were two different people. And now, in this horrible situation, I
was following him to his final case.

I opened my eyes again, and my glance caught something by
the side of the road. I approached it, pushing aside some under-
brush with my damp, gloved fingers, and revealed a sign, long
neglected and fallen over. I pulled it upright and cleared it off.

ROTHEWELL, it said.

This was the way, then. I held the sign a moment longer, its
dirt crumbling over my sleeve.

Something rustled in the tall brush behind me. I dropped
the sign and whirled, peering into the gloom. The brambles and
dead honeysuckle bobbed where something had brushed by, but
no other sound came. It had been only a rabbit, perhaps, or a
mole, running from a predator.

Still, my back prickled as I walked back to the motorcar, and
as I drove off as quickly as I could, I imagined something silent
watching me from far back in the trees.

Three

Rothewell showed itself in drifting silence as I emerged from the woods. First came a worn track, the edges of which were overgrown with bushes and the dead heads of wild flowering shrubs. A few lonely cottages peered from within the greenery. Behind these cottages was only a shocking wall of white-gray sky, as if the structures were positioned on the edge of the earth. As I crawled the motorcar along the bumpy road, I saw that I was in fact on a high ridge. Far ahead, I could see that the road fell away and twisted, dotted with more houses as it made its complex way down toward the sea.

The water itself, here, was vast and beautiful. This was not the calm, clear blue water of a tropical paradise, but choppy and cold, with whitecaps frothing on the tops of the restless waves as they were driven toward a rocky beach. At the bottom of the hillside road were more buildings, set on a rise over the empty shore. Past these there was only the sea and the sky, blending with the soft touch of blurred chalk at the horizon.

Ahead of me, something came out of the rainy gloom. As it drew closer, I realized it was none other than an old-fashioned donkey cart, driven by a man hunched into his coat and cap. The donkey plodded, its tail flicking, unconcerned about the weather.

The driver reined in as he saw me, and I stopped as I pulled

alongside him and leaned out the window. "Excuse me; I wonder
if you could help me?"

The man leaned toward me, and I saw that he was thirtyish,
with a reddish beard that likely indicated red hair under his cap.
"I suppose I could do that," he said amicably, his eyes lit with curiosity he was too polite to speak of. "What can I help you with?"

"I'm looking for a place called Barrow House. Perhaps you
know it?"

Now his look was tempered with genuine surprise and a quick
hint of wariness. "I do. You're to do with the fellow who lived there,
then?"

"I'm his niece, yes."

"You do look a little like him. I'm very sorry for your loss."
He removed his cloth cap for a moment, indeed revealing a head
of red hair, and replaced it again. "My name is Edward Bruton.
I'm the deliveryman in these parts. If I can help, please let me
know."

He seemed in no hurry to answer my question, though it
meant he had to sit in the rain. "Jillian Leigh," I replied. "A deliveryman?" I could not help glancing at the donkey, which stood
good-naturedly in its traces.

Edward Bruton smiled, glancing at my beautiful motor. "A
bit old-fashioned, I suppose. But the fact is, she handles the climb
better than any other animal or vehicle. It isn't easy getting into
Rothewell proper"—he nodded in the direction of the buildings
at the bottom of the road, by the water—"so they use me. I'm
postman, milkman, messenger boy—whatever is needed, I do it."

"You must know everything, then. Which way is Barrow
House?"

"Just down the track, take the bend to the left, and you'll see
it. Go all the way to the end of the road—it's the farthest house

by the woods." He peered past me into the car. "But surely you're not going there alone, are you?"

"I am." I looked at his expression. "Is that a problem?"

"Well, no. No, of course not. We just don't get many young ladies here alone, that's all."

"My uncle was alone."

He nodded, but his eyes were thinking of something else. "So he was."

"I'm sorry," I said, holding my hand out to him. "I've got you standing in the rain. I won't keep you any longer. Good night."

He looked at my hand, then shook it with a wry look that said I'd just amused him. "Good night, miss. I'll check on you in the morning and see if you need anything; how is that?"

I thanked him and drove on into the descending darkness, my wheels bumping over the road.

Barrow House was exactly where Edward Bruton had said it would be—at least, there was only one house there, far past all the others. It was dark and unlit. I pulled up next to the low wrought-iron gate and got out of the car.

It was a stone building, obviously old. A triangular gable rose from the first-story roof, on the left; and the second story, added to the main structure on some long-ago date, had a second triangular gable on the right. The effect was lopsided but somehow impressive. Behind the house was the tree line, an extension of the woods I had just come out of, and the lane here did a gentle curve, presumably toward more neighbors not in view.

I could strongly smell the sea; in fact, I could nearly taste it on the back of my tongue, the way one can taste thick fog when walking in it. The air was lowering and damp, the rain trickling down the glass panes of Barrow House and running off the edges of the gables. It was growing darker and colder by the moment; the house, as odd and lonely as it was, would at least be dry inside.

Far away, a man whistled for his dog. There was no other human sound.

I pulled my valise from the motorcar and took my pocketbook and the key ring with a single key the solicitor had given me from the front seat. I unlatched the gate and hurried up the front steps to the house, unlocking the door and setting everything down in the dark just inside. Then I trotted back to the car and took out my stack of schoolbooks, hurrying back so the books would not get too wet. There was still time for studying tonight.

I had been hoping against hope for a modern installation of electric light, but I was disappointed. I fumbled in the gloomy foyer and found an old oil lamp and a box of matches. I lit the lamp and opened the wick as far as I could, seeing only a dusty, cluttered hall, a door to the left, and a set of stairs before me. The place smelled just a little unused, as if the occupant had been gone only a little while. Toby had died three days ago.

A quick look through the main floor showed a few rooms full of mismatched furniture, a sign of a succession of renters over the years. I couldn't see any belongings sitting on tables or draped over chairs. At the back of the house, in the bare kitchen, I found the first evidence that Toby had even been there—a single ceramic bowl stood on the washboard, cleaned out and left next to a single, equally clean spoon.

I sighed. A bachelor's kitchen, and the long drive had made me hungry. Well, I'd been feeding myself for as long as I could remember; my mother could barely prepare toast. I'd have to make do.

But as I swung my lamp in the direction of the larder, something in the light caught my eye. I leaned closer.

In the middle of the wooden kitchen table—precisely in the middle—was a pocket watch. It gleamed dully, the lamplight reflecting from its glass face. I picked it up and turned it over, my fingers taking in the familiar surface. This was Toby's pocket watch; I had played with it as a child. And suddenly, the weight of remembrance was on me again.

Toby had often visited during my childhood. He had been a plain-looking man whose face gave nothing away, a man one would never notice in a crowd: of average height, neither slender nor fat. He had short dark hair and his suits were never new, less from poverty—though there may have been that—than from simple bachelor carelessness. He spoke little and seemed particularly tongue-tied around children.

I suppose he was hardly the dashing, heroic type of uncle who told war stories at bedtime, or the kind of uncle whose visits delighted children, laughing and full of fun. Toby spent most of his visits reading and writing, talking with my parents about grown-up subjects, or pottering about our house and gardens, fixing things on his own. After my mother found he had unclogged a backed-up sink drain in the kitchen unasked, she declared him a gentleman and nearly kissed him; he blushed, shook his head, and said nothing.

And yet, in his unguarded moments, like that morning on the beach—moments very rare in a man of Toby's shyness—he was the best sort of uncle, the attentive kind who never made a child feel foolish or unwanted.

I had a vivid memory of sitting on the floor of my father's study, quietly reading my picture books, as Toby sat at the desk and worked. I had the same memory of reading chapter books next to him as I got older; we must have shared this ritual of quiet companionship for years. Most adults require something when in a room with a child: a peppered series of questions, usually, that seem like conversation to the adult but to the child are a test they cannot know the answers to. Toby had a gift for silence. He could simply sit with a child in peace and accept her companionship as something of value in itself.

We had never exchanged gifts, but the pocket watch was utterly familiar in my hands, dredged up from an old, half-forgotten memory. Perhaps he had let his little niece play with his watch, for in my mind the watch had been larger and heavier, my hands smaller.

None of this fit the idea of a ghost hunter. My parents had never hidden Toby's occupation from me; I had no recollection now of how I learned of it, only that the idea made me so deeply uneasy I never spoke of it. Was it shame that had made me willfully pretend Toby's profession didn't exist? A little, yes. I wanted the girls at Somerville to think I was normal, to like me. My academic pedigree through my parents was something my fellow students understood.

But mostly, the reason was fear. I'd never been able to piece together the man I knew with the pursuit of the dead. I'd never seen a ghost myself, but Toby had believed in them. Either Toby had been a lifelong madman, or he'd truly seen spirits. I didn't want to contemplate either possibility.

Sometime after I turned fourteen, Toby stopped coming, and he never visited again. At the mention of him, my mother's lips grew tense, and a tired look came into my father's eyes. I was never told why. I slid the watch into my pocket.

I took my valise up the narrow stairs to the second floor, abandoning the idea of food. I was too exhausted to do anything else tonight, and the morning's gruesome appointment had left me depressed. The first bedroom I found was Toby's. I couldn't bear to go in, to sleep on his pillow, there among his sweaters and underthings. I found a second bedroom across the hall instead, furnished with only a bed and dresser.

I rummaged through a nearby closet for linens, which were vaguely musty-smelling, and made up the narrow bed. When I finished I peeked out the window past the yellowed lace curtains, wondering whether I'd see any other sign of life in Rothewell.

Nothing presented itself. There were no neighbors in this direction, only the back garden, surrounded by a stone wall, and beyond that, the darker ink of the line of trees. I was beginning to miss the familiar, if incessant, sounds of my small student flat: the shouts and laughter from the square outside, the chatter of other girls in the halls, the whistle of a teakettle in the communal kitchen. Someone was always awake, even late into the night after curfew, and one could always find the yellow under-door light of a midnight study session.

That night, as I slept, I had vague, uneasy dreams. I seemed to be awake, though I knew I was asleep; there was cold sweat on my neck, and my hair was damp. My neck hurt from the tight clench of my jaw, and my shoulders ached as I lay on my side on the hard bed. I wanted to move, but in the unbearable logic of dreams I could not, and lay frozen where I was, panting in panic.

I may have dozed uneasily again, but in the next dream something scratched at the window behind my turned back. *A tree branch*, I said to myself in the dream, and I tried again to move. I was still stuck, listening to the sound behind me—a long sound, inexorable, like something being dragged slowly across the glass from one side to the other. I ground my teeth and flinched in my frozen place, listening to it go on and on.

When dawn came, I awoke stiff and more exhausted than when I'd gone to bed. My nightgown was damp with sweat. I lay staring at the ceiling and felt the vivid details of the night wash over me. For a long time, the fear stayed with me, even in the morning sun. But as dreams do, it began to fade, and eventually I pulled myself out of bed.

The dream had seemed real, but as I stretched my shoulders and rubbed my aching neck, I knew it was all a fiction. For through the lace curtains, I could see that there was no tree outside the bedroom window. There was nothing there at all.

Four

I washed and dressed, scrubbing away the sweat and grogginess of the night, the floors cold and dusty beneath my feet. From my valise I pulled a comfortable shirtwaist dress and an old dark brown cashmere cardigan, a favorite garment I'd bought at a men's shop. It fell to midthigh, and the cuffs were rolled. After a moment's consideration, I left off stockings and shoes. This was the outfit I usually chose for studying; it was unfashionable and a little scandalous, but most of the girls in my boardinghouse had something similar they wore when hard at work, with no chance of one's mother or any member of the male sex laying eyes on it.

I hurried down to the kitchen to light the stove. I was relieved to see that Toby had laid by a good stock of wood, if he had not bothered with much else; I could at least make tea and warm a few rooms in the house. We'd had few servants as I grew up, just a daily cook and a weekly washerwoman and maid, though we could have well afforded more—one of my parents' many eccentricities. It meant I could lay a fire as quickly and neatly as any girl I knew.

I pulled open the stove door and stared.

Lying squarely in the cold stove, carefully placed in its grimy, unlit darkness, was a book. It lay open to a place in the middle, its pages flat and unruffled. It was thick, its binding of brown leather.

I stared at it for a long moment. It seemed to mock me, lying there. There was no reason for it—and yet, there it was.

I reached in and slid it out, careful not to flip the pages. A glance at the title page revealed *A History of Incurable Visitations*, by someone named Charles Vizier. I read the page where the book had been left open.

> . . . A second translation of *De Spirituum Apparitione*, produced in Cologne in 1747, terms the most disturbing manifestations as *grappione*, or nearly demoniac in nature, though the specific demonic influence has not been classified. Certainly such accounts have been disputed over the years, though there is little doubt that the Abbey of Sénanque experienced one such visitation, consisting of thrown crockery, overturned rain barrels, and even ghostly slaps and pinches assaulting nighttime guests— which persisted over the course of several decades.

I stood reading, my body paralyzed by a strange sort of fear. It was only a book. I forced myself to read on.

> Though possibly demonic, the account of the *grappione* at Sénanque also bears resemblance to the traditional Scottish haunt called a *boggart*, or sometimes *bogey*, a mischievous—sometimes vicious—manifestation tied to a single place, and often terrifying the inhabitants of any area in which it takes up residence. . . .

I closed the book and placed it on the table. I took out the watch from last night, which I had put in the pocket of my sweater, and looked at it. A watch on the table. A book in the stove.

I put the watch next to the book and strode out the kitchen door to the back garden. The sun was up now, the sky turning a crisp autumn blue. The cobblestones were cold and rough on my bare feet. I turned and looked up at my bedroom window. Just as I'd seen this morning, there was nothing there, nothing that could have scratched the glass. I stepped closer, peered into the remains of the dead garden that bordered the house. There were no footprints or telltale points of a ladder. I swept my gaze farther, into the dried weeds and nettles, looking for trampled spaces. There was nothing.

You could have dreamed it, I told myself. *You must have dreamed it. You must have.* Still, I backed farther into the garden, away from the house, stepping around a heavy ceramic vase full of soil and dead flowers, and directed my gaze upward. Could someone have climbed down from the roof? Somehow scaled the other gable to get to my window? An animal, perhaps? I shaded my eyes against the sun and squinted. Had it all been in my mind?

"Excuse me!"

I jumped and turned, nearly overbalancing. Standing beyond the stone wall of the garden were two women, an older and a younger. Though they were dressed differently, their faces marked them as mother and daughter. The mother gave me an apologetic wave. "I'm so sorry to have startled you. We were passing on our morning walk and couldn't resist stopping to say hello."

I let out a breath. The fence wall was nearly shoulder-high, which made conversation awkward, so I walked to the gate and unlatched it. "Of course," I managed. "Do come in. I'm Jillian Leigh."

"Diana Kates," the woman said as she approached and held out her hand. "And this is my daughter, Julia."

Both women were dressed for walking; and indeed, with the gate open, I noticed a path behind the property that skirted the woods. Mrs. Kates was perhaps thirty-five, her hair cropped very short and fashionably marcelled. Over this she had placed a cloche with a wide ribbon, under the brim of which only the well-placed ends of her hair could be seen. She wore a dress of faded blue silk, decorated with beads along the neckline, under a coat with a worn fur collar. The daughter, a step behind her, was no more than sixteen, in large shoes and a tweed coat that went to her knees. She had elected to wear her long hair in a braid down her back, from which wisps of frizz escaped.

As I greeted them, I realized I must look a perfect fright. My hair was wild, my man's sweater was wrapped around me, and my legs and feet were bare. I'd never thought anyone would see my studying outfit. "I'm sorry," I said, looking down at myself and up again. "I was just out here a moment—I didn't realize—"

"Of course," said Mrs. Kates, smiling. "We've intruded. But I couldn't help but introduce myself. I'm the landlady here, you see."

"Oh." I looked back at Barrow House, then turned to her again. "I'm Toby Leigh's niece. I'm here to clean out his things."

"Yes, I had a letter from the solicitor. I'm so sorry about what happened to your uncle. Such a kind man."

This was said with such cheer I could only stare for a second. "Yes, well, thank you."

"Though he was rather a hermit," she went on as if I hadn't spoken. "I barely saw him. He prepaid the rent for the month, so you mustn't worry about that, truly. Though I did have to write the solicitors when I sent them the key, to mention that he is paid only to the end of the month. I must admit, when they wrote me that his niece was coming, I pictured a married woman. Are you alone?"

My mind spun with the changes of subject. I glanced at the daughter, but she was no help; she merely looked at me and waited for an answer. "I'm alone," I admitted. "My parents could not come."

That stopped Mrs. Kates, but only for a moment; the daughter's jaw dropped visibly, as if I'd just shed my clothes.

"Why, how very modern!" Mrs. Kates exclaimed. "We don't get much of that here. Are your parents ill, perhaps?"

It was well-meant, but both Mr. Hindhead and Edward Bruton had already commented on my single status. I was beginning to feel like a two-headed cow or a bearded lady. Was a girl alone so very freakish? My parents had always been too busy or preoccupied to coddle me. "They're not ill. I'm twenty-two; I can care for myself, I assure you."

"Well, I certainly wouldn't know." Mrs. Kates lifted her shoulders in a shrug. "I went straight from my father's house to my husband's when I was seventeen, and then I had Julia. People say we look more like sisters than mother and daughter."

"You do," I said politely, though it was altogether true. Mrs. Kates wore a great deal of makeup, skillfully applied, but under it she was blessed with unlined skin, as if she'd never had a worry or a day in the sun. Julia, with her unvarnished face and ungroomed brows, looked like an alternate version of her mother.

"I don't know much about modern girls," Mrs. Kates was saying. "Marry and have children, that's what's always worked just fine, as far as I know. Is that motorcar yours? Are you married?"

"No," I said, rubbing the bottom of one bare, cold foot over the top of the other and contemplating the chilled air on my knees. "I'm a student at Oxford."

This was greeted with a thunderous, surprised silence, as if I'd announced my intention to run as MP. I plunged ahead into the gap. "Look, I'd ask you in for tea, only the stove's not lit, and I haven't looked at the supplies. Perhaps—"

"Oh, no, dear." Mrs. Kates regained her voice. "You mustn't worry. What brings you into the garden on such a morning, anyway?"

"The window," I replied, motioning up toward the bedroom. "I thought I heard something there last night. You don't know anything about rodents or birds on the roof, do you?"

"Heavens, no. Though the house belonged to my husband, and I've only taken it over since he died. I don't know much of anything about those sorts of things at all. I don't even come out here often, as it's so far at the end of the road. Was it very bad?"

"Halloo!" came another voice over the wall.

We all turned. Edward Bruton came through the gate carrying a paper sack in each hand. "I knocked at the front, miss," he said to me, "but no one answered, and when I heard voices, I came 'round. I thought you could do with some supplies from town."

I tried to decline, but he waved me away and said he had a few things in his cart anyway, which he may as well give to me, as they were entirely extra and he had no idea what he would do with them otherwise. I could do nothing but accept in the end, as he would have it no other way, though I did manage to convince him that I could light the stove myself. No, he hadn't heard of any rodents on the roof, though if I needed him to do so, he could check in a jiffy. He'd done some light work around Barrow House when Mrs. Kates needed it, hadn't he?

Mrs. Kates agreed with this, though she had notably ceased talking. Julia, predictably, said nothing. And after Edward Bruton had gone—kindly without mention of my horrid appearance—Mrs. Kates turned to me with a new look in her eye, that of the gossip who had been waiting for her subject to leave.

"And how did you meet Edward already?" she asked me.

"Last night, on the road into town. He gave me directions."

"I see. He's had a hard time since the war, you know. His father left the business in a terrible state—he had health problems, and he got taken in by some sort of phony investment scheme, not that I understand such things. In any case, poor Edward came home to financial ruin. But he's been working hard since then, and I think things have turned around. He hasn't taken a wife yet, but I believe he has an eye on my Julia."

"Mother!" Julia cried in anguish, the first word I'd heard her say.

"I see," I said, wondering madly what was expected. "He seems very kind."

"Yes, he is. My dear, we simply must be on our way. It's been a pleasure. Julia, come with me."

I watched them go, the girl slouching with embarrassment as she followed her mother. Mrs. Kates stopped and turned. "By the way, it's a strange thing. I don't have a key to the house. I set it down when I was in the house last, and I forgot it. Have you seen it lying about?"

"I'm afraid I haven't," I said. "I have the one given me by the solicitor."

"Yes, that was your uncle's. I kept my own—until I misplaced it, that is. You haven't seen it?"

"Sorry, no."

"Well. Do keep an eye for it, if you would. I really will need both sets of keys back at the end of the month."

"I understand."

Inside, I finally lit the stove and put on tea—Edward Bruton, bless him, had brought some—grateful for the silence again. As kind as they were, I could see how small-town neighbors could be exhausting.

As I poured the tea, I looked at the watch and the book on the table again. In the mundane light of day, they were less unsettling. It was strange to find the book in the stove, certainly—but it wasn't inexplicable. Toby could have put it there in an absent moment. As for the watch, it had been left on the table; that was all. The sounds outside my window last night were made by some sort of rodent, and I'd turned the sounds into night-mares because of my grim, depressed mood. The experience in Barnstaple had made me see things, feel things that weren't there. *An accident. It was an accident; that was all.*

I took my cup and wandered through the hall to the front rooms, which I'd seen only in the dark last night. I'd start over as if last night hadn't happened. I'd collect Toby's things and pack them up, and then I'd return to Oxford.

I poked my head into the library and saw no personal effects there. I moved into the mismatched front parlor at the front of the house, taking in the worn rug, the spindly chairs, and the ugly fire-place. There were no personal effects there either, and no wonder; I couldn't imagine anyone using such an uncomfortable room.

I was about to move on to the stairs when a movement out-side the parlor window caught my eye. I pulled back the curtain and peeked out.

A large, dark brown sedan was pulling up in front of Barrow House, coming to a stop behind my parked Alvis. The driver's door opened and a man got out—a long-legged, dark-cloaked man. As I watched, he shut the door of the motorcar and strode toward the house, his chin tilted down, the brim of his hat shad-ing his eyes from view.

He moved easily, powerfully, clad in a slate gray suit under an overcoat of deep, almost velvety black. There was something almost sinister about the black of that coat and the sharp, low brim of his hat; he made an incongruous figure on a sunny morn-ing in a small English town. As if in answer to this, a cloud dimmed the sun and a gust of wind blew up, swirling the dead leaves in the garden behind him.

I felt my well-being fade away. The man slowed and raised his head, and the hat brim lifted, revealing a square jaw, a well-shaped mouth, high cheekbones. His eyes were dark, and though he was handsome, there was nothing comforting about that face. It was grave, intelligent, perhaps a little weary, his gaze taking in the house with mechanical precision.

He's from the solicitor's office, my mind scrambled. But no, he didn't look the lawyerly type. *The undertaker's man, then, come to the wrong place.*

Then he saw me watching from the window, and his gaze stopped on me. I felt a flush of awareness and an inexorable drop of dread. The cloud thickened over the sun, the sky darkened further, and he silently touched his hat, then lowered his hand to point at the front door, a request for me to let him in.

I set down my cup and obeyed, my feet moving before I was even aware of it. As I opened the door, he was coming up the steps, taking them with effortless grace. He reached up and removed his hat as he approached. "Miss Leigh, I presume?"

"What is it?" I managed. "Just tell me, please."

He read my expression and frowned. "I'm sorry. I didn't mean to frighten you."

I shook my head. "It's too late for that. Yes, I am Jillian Leigh. I've already worked out that you're not a solicitor or an undertaker, and that it's something terribly bad. So just tell me what it is, then, if you would."

I had surprised him; he thought this through for a moment, and I realized he was incredibly handsome, and that I was viscerally, almost painfully aware of it.

"Very well then," he said at last. "I need to speak to you, if you have a few moments. I'm Inspector Merriken, of Scotland Yard."

Five

Scotland Yard?" I stared at him in horror. "What does Scotland Yard want with me?"

"Perhaps we could discuss that inside."

If I slammed the door in his face, perhaps all of this would go away. I bit my lip and looked at him. He waited patiently, his hat in his hand. His gaze traveled over me casually, but I wasn't fooled.

"Miss Leigh?"

I stepped back from the door. "All right. All right then. Please come in."

He moved forward and I closed the door behind him. Up close, I could see that his suit was well tailored, his shirt crisp, the tie knotted flawlessly at his throat. A man who dressed with care, then, on whatever an inspector's salary was. It was easy for him to be sartorially perfect, as he had a frame that would give most men's tailors fits of joy: tall, broad shouldered, slim hipped, sleekly muscled. He wore both the suit and the coat with an ease that bespoke a man who took his physique for granted. He smelled of chill fall air and wool.

I stepped back and thumped into the wall of the tiny hall. I knew what he saw when he looked at me—a raw, inexperienced girl, barely dressed. *Take hold of the situation, Jillian.* I'd spent too long in a girls' school, the only men of my acquaintance aged professors and fellow students in home-knitted jumpers. Old men and boys, really.

"I'm sorry," I managed. "That wasn't much of a greeting. I'm not usually so rude."

"It's quite all right," he said.

"Would you, ah, would you like tea?"

"If you have some, yes."

I nodded. "Follow me."

I led him down the hall, conscious of the fact that I'd been caught in my studying clothes yet again. I was aware of my bare legs and feet, of the hem of my dress brushing the backs of my knees, in a way I hadn't been in the presence of Mrs. Kates or even Edward Bruton. Likely Inspector Merriken considered me slovenly and unkempt. I wrapped my cardigan more closely around myself as I walked.

If the inspector thought anything of my appearance, his expression gave nothing away. When we reached the kitchen, he took a seat at the table as I put the kettle back on the hob and found more cups.

"I'm sorry about your uncle," he said.

His tone was quiet and sincere, and I turned my back to him, busying myself with the tea things. "Thank you."

"I was in Barnstaple yesterday," the inspector continued. "I got there shortly after you did, as it happens. I met with the magistrate."

"He told me my uncle's case was an accident," I said to the dishes I was arranging. "He said it was official."

"Yes. He told me the same thing."

I set the tea on the table and looked at him. "Then I'm sorry for asking, but why are you here?"

He had not removed the dark coat, and it folded around him where he sat at the table, the edges of the fine wool spilling off his chair. He had placed his hat on one long thigh, and his hand rested atop it, the fingers spread and graceful. He tipped his head just the slightest degree as he watched me. "Mr. Hindhead was rather concerned about you," he said by way of reply. "He said you didn't weep or, indeed, appear the least bit upset. He told me he could only conclude that instilling education in women produces in them a decided lack of natural feeling."

I was shocked for only a second, until anger took over. I crossed my arms. "I didn't realize that viewing my uncle's body was a test of my decorum," I said tightly. "I mistakenly thought it was the most horrible experience of my life."

The inspector's gaze held mine. I thought I saw something flicker across it—a flash of approval, perhaps, though I was too angry to care. "Then we are of the same mind about Mr. Hindhead's opinions."

It took me a second to understand what he was saying. Before I could gather myself to form a reply, the inspector tapped the cover of *A History of Incurable Visitations*, which lay alongside the watch on the table before him. "Were these your uncle's?"

"Yes."

He picked up the book, read the title on the spine. He lowered it again and leaned toward me across the table. "All right, Miss Leigh, let's be clear. Forget about the magistrate for a moment. Your uncle was an unusual man."

I swallowed. "Yes, he was."

"Most people, you see, fit some sort of pattern at the heart of it. Your uncle was not one of those people. He was a stranger here, and he had no reason to be on those cliffs. No one knows, or will admit to knowing, who hired him to come here. I cannot quite see the pattern, and it bothers me."

My heart pounded in my chest. I had assumed Toby had been here on a job, called here by someone as usual. "But the coroner . . ."

"The coroner at Barnstaple," the inspector said, "knows more about foxhunting and trout fishing than he knows about death. He likely made a ruling so he could go home to supper. I don't particularly care what he wrote on that piece of paper. I don't answer to the coroner."

I lowered myself into the chair opposite him. "I don't think I can help. I don't have any of the answers. To tell the truth, I barely knew my uncle."

"When was the last time you saw him?"

"Eight years ago."

"Were you close before that?"

I thought of the afternoons reading, of the day on the beach. "He was kind to me."

"Why hadn't you seen him in so long?"

I shook my head. "I can't answer that. He had some kind of rift with my parents. I never knew what it was about. He just disappeared one day; that was all."

"And your parents are in Paris."

"Yes."

He looked away, calculating. He had a face of constant clear yet subtle expression, somber, inquisitive, suspicious. Already I was fascinated by it. In repose, he was handsome, but it was the play of thoughts behind his eyes that made him almost searing to look at.

He turned back to me. For a long moment his gaze took me in, unmistakably assessing me, as if for that moment I were the only person in existence. The force of it was unsettling, but I kept my chin up and stared back. *Take hold of the situation, Jillian.*

He seemed to make a decision. "Your uncle," he said without further preamble, "was found on the beach at the foot of the cliffs. A fisherman in a passing boat spotted him from the water. It's an open spot, but hard to see from land. We're lucky someone saw him when he did. It was ten o'clock in the morning, and your uncle had been dead for three to five hours."

I swallowed. The tea sat untouched between us on the table.

"I ask myself the question," he continued, "whether a healthy, sober man simply slipped off a cliff in daylight. Don't you?"

"Yes." My voice was barely more than a whisper.

"Did your uncle have any enemies?"

I shook my head. Inspector Merriken, I realized, was taking advantage of my shock and pressing me. He was very skilled at it. "You forget that he may have killed himself."

He leaned forward again. "That's why I'm here. You knew him. Do you think he killed himself?"

I looked down at the table. I had set my hands flat, and I stared at the backs of them, at the spread of my fingers. "I don't— I can't picture—" I tried again. "He was alone; I do know that. He'd never married or had children. He was considered eccentric. He was estranged from my parents, who were his only family." It felt traitorous even to be saying these things. "Still, the idea that he would . . . just *do* that—I don't think I believe it." I looked back up and watched the expressions on Inspector Merriken's face—skepticism, disappointment perhaps. "I suppose the family members never believe it, do they?"

"It's an understandable reaction."

Anger rose in my throat again, surprising me. "There's nothing understandable about this. Nothing."

He only nodded, and took a small notebook and pen from the breast pocket of his jacket. "Now you see why I'm here."

He bent to the notebook and wrote, obviously some kind of notes for himself. I waited during a moment of silence, the only sound the scratching pen. I looked at his handsome face and realized I was still angry at his calculated manipulation of me, at his effortless control, at my own attraction that tempted me to give in. I wanted to shake him.

"Why not me?" I said at last.

"Beg your pardon?"

"Why not suspect me of murder? Perhaps I had a motive."

He did not look up. "Because you were in school at the time he died, in a tutorial with three other students and a professor named Martha Mackenzie. I've talked to the professor already."

I was speechless. He finished writing, closed the notebook with a snap, and looked up at me.

"You suspected me of murder?" I said.

"I suspect everyone of murder," he replied. "Where was your uncle's room?"

Toby had taken the master bedroom, which featured a double bed of unpolished brass, a few thin blankets, a dresser, and an old writing desk. The bed was made, a few of Toby's clothes tossed carelessly on it. A shaving mirror was propped on the dresser, next to a tray containing his other shaving items. A toothbrush, a comb. None of this was remarkable.

The window and the suitcases were remarkable.

The window, by my calculation, looked over the front of the house. But there was no view through it, for behind the heavy, drawn curtains we could see that the glass was blocked. The inspector pulled one of the curtains back. Someone—Toby—had taken a wool blanket from the linen cupboard and nailed it into the four corners of the wooden window frame. Then he had covered the dark square with the heavy curtains, which he had fastened shut.

The effect was one of sinister gloom. The sunlight only barely penetrated, and the details of the room were hard to see, as if we were in a watercolor painting.

"Hmm," said the inspector. "Perhaps your uncle had insomnia. There are people who can't sleep unless they're in total darkness."

I said nothing. I stared at the window, my stomach sinking. It seemed to stare back at me. It made me think of the scratching at my window last night, that long, slow sound, and I pushed the thought away.

Inspector Merriken moved on to two large suitcases that were stacked against the wall. They looked heavy; the smaller one was on top of the larger one, and the writing desk had been pushed out of the way to make room. The suitcases were far too big to contain clothing, unless Toby had a wardrobe that would put a Hollywood actor to shame.

I moved over to the inspector's shoulder as he unlatched the top one and lifted the lid. We both stared down into the case. Then the inspector picked up the carefully packed objects there one by one, removing them from their dark velvet lining.

"A clock," he said. "No, two clocks—one is a stopwatch. A thermometer. An electric torch and a spare. A compass. A measuring tape. Canisters of film . . ."

"Ghost-hunting tools," I said. "This is my uncle's ghost-hunting kit."

His eyes caught mine for a second. "Are you certain?"

"It must be," I said. I pointed to the items one by one. "A clock to note when the sightings appear. A stopwatch to time them. A thermometer to measure air temperature changes. A torch for nighttime work, and a spare in case the first is broken. As for the film . . ." I looked around us. "The camera is in a case next to the bed, over there. To try to capture the ghosts on film, of course."

He looked back down into the case, perplexed. "I've never seen anything like this before. You have a rather interesting family."

"Thank you."

He touched some of the items again, brushing his hand over them as if they could tell him something, as absorbed as a dog on a scent. Then he shut the lid. "Has anyone else been through the house since your uncle died?"

I shook my head. "The landlady told me she doesn't even have a key. She's lost her copy."

"And have you touched anything? Gone through his belongings?"

"No."

He hauled the smaller of the two cases off the larger one and onto the bed, then opened the larger case. This one we stared at for even longer, trying to figure out—at least on my part—what the thing could be.

It was a single object, carefully placed in a case that was obviously custom-made to transport it. There seemed to be a large metal base, a battery, knobs. Protruding from the top of the inexplicable thing was a metal gauge etched with numbers, measured by a long, narrow needle.

"What in the world is it?" I said.

"It's hard to tell in this light." He opened the smaller case again and pulled out one of the electric torches, which he shone on the etched metal numbers as he leaned close to read them. The light spilled over his profile, making him into a black-and-white photograph, like the pictures of film stars they put in magazines.

"I believe it's a galvanoscope," he said.

"And what is that?"

He shut off the torch and replaced it. "It measures electro-magnetic energy fluctuations. We used them in the war to detect submarines."

I shook my head. "This is nothing like I thought it would be."

"What do you mean?"

I gestured at the cases. "It's all so scientific. Electromagnetic fluctuations? I think I imagined him doing séances, or something similar. But this equipment—the galvanoscope alone must have been expensive. He must have had it custom-made, unless he was secretly in the navy."

"The navy doesn't give them out, no. At least, not that I'm aware of."

I stopped, realizing he was a few years older than me, the right age to have been in the war. "Were you in the navy?"

He turned away, closed the lid to the case containing the clocks and torches. "No. RAF."

"You were a pilot?"

"Yes."

I could picture him as a pilot. The RAF was celebrated for its fearless fighters with nerves of steel. The newspapers and newsreels had had a heyday with them during the war. "It sounds heroic."

He raised his head and looked at me, his eyes glinting in the dim light, shadows smudged under his cheekbones. He gave a sort of grim laugh, a sound that was pure darkness. "Not exactly."

I hadn't met many soldiers; I had no brothers or cousins, and I'd been too young to volunteer myself. My father had done some kind of job for the War Office that kept him in London; Toby hadn't served that I knew of, and as he'd left our lives, what Toby had done during wartime was now one of his many mysteries. I knew of the butcher's son who had come home missing a hand, and my tutor's grandson who hadn't come home at all. At Somer-ville, I knew girls who had lost brothers and cousins, and it was a common refrain among all the girls that there was a lack of marriageable men.

Inspector Merriken closed the case containing the galvanoscope with his strong arms and powerful hands, the dim light casting him in shadow.

"I'm sorry," I said.

"It's all right." His voice held something tightly leashed. "It just isn't much of a talent, killing people. No matter how good one gets to be at it. And it seems I was awfully good." He frowned. "For God's sake, I shouldn't have said that. Forget I said it."

"Of course."

The air seemed to have gone out of the room. He raised a hand and rubbed his forehead. I watched him. "All right," I said after a moment. "You aren't heroic. I'll make a note of it."

He glanced at me sharply, then shook his head. "Please forget it. What were we talking about?"

"The galvanoscope. And you were questioning me."

"Thank you. I'll continue, then. Did your parents approve of Toby's ghost hunting?"

"Not at all," I replied, glad to change the subject. "They hated it. I think it embarrassed them. My father is a chemist; he's rather renowned, and he has to look out for his reputation. In any case, he's devoted his life to the pursuit of science, and my mother assists him." My mother had been my father's assistant when they became involved; they had made quite a scandal in their day. "They see ghost hunting as charlatanism, not science."

"Is that the reason for their disagreement?"

"I don't see how it could be. Toby was always a ghost hunter, since before I was born. I don't see what could have changed."

"And yet, when Toby died, neither of your parents came home to bury him."

I ran a hand through my hair, looking helplessly around at all the belongings I was somehow supposed to dispose of. "They would have come. But my father is teaching in Paris."

Recovered now, Inspector Merriken put his hands in his pockets and regarded me in the gloom. "They left you to deal with the body on your own. I find that interesting."

"I don't think they realized," I said, the defense automatic from my mouth.

"And if they had?"

That stopped me. For if they had, they would still have stayed in Paris. The work always came first.

"Right," he said in reply to my silence.

It was a shot, meant to reestablish his authority over me, and it was a well-aimed one. "Are you asking me to admit I'm angry at my parents? Very well, I am—a little. But you haven't met them. They just jolly you out of it and pour a drink. Anger isn't something we do in our family."

"Perhaps you should start."

"Thank you for the advice." My cheeks were burning. I turned and made for the door.

"Miss Leigh."

I looked down. His hand was on my arm. Something made my breath stop in my throat. I raised my eyes to his.

And just like that, something arced between us. My body flushed hot. His hand on me felt almost familiar, as if he'd touched me before. His gaze darkened as he looked at me, his grip flexed, and for just a second I felt a pull—so brief I thought I'd imagined it—as if he were about to draw me toward him. In that second, I would have gone, my body understanding before my mind could protest.

Then he let me go.

He stepped back into the shadows, put his hands in his pockets again.

"Should I forget about that, too?" I asked.

He was quiet. I couldn't see his face in the dark, but I knew mine was burning. My heart wouldn't slow down. I could still feel his touch on my arm.

"I'll see myself out," he said after a moment, his voice composed. "I'm at a hotel called the White Lion in St. Thomas' Gate, if you need me. It's just a mile up the road through the woods." He turned toward the door.

I found my voice. "What should I do?" I asked him.

He paused. "You can pack his things now," he said. "I've seen what I need. And if you're adept at research, you may want to dig up what you can about the local ghost."

The moment broke. "The what?"

"The local ghost," he repeated. "There's a legendary one hereabouts. I believe his name is Walking John." Inspector Merriken nodded toward the equipment behind me. "I'll wager that's who your uncle was hunting. I'll be in touch, Miss Leigh."

And with that, he was gone.

Six

An hour later, I was behind the wheel of my little motorcar, carefully navigating into town. I was restless and
unable to stay in Barrow House. I kept thinking about
Inspector Merriken, and my mind would not settle. I decided to
go into Rothewell proper for supplies.

What had just happened between us? He'd touched only my
arm, but I'd felt the reverberations of that touch through my
body like an echo. I could still feel them now.

I knew what happened between men and women. My parents had never seen any reason not to educate me, and they'd
been permissive in letting me read anything I wanted. Still, for a
girl going from her parents' home to a women's college, opportunities with men were few. I'd had a handful of evenings out and
exactly two clumsy, awkward kisses—all of which convinced me
there was something the books were not quite telling me. I'd
spent some long, lonely nights wondering exactly what it was.

That raw moment with Inspector Merriken had stirred me. It
had been strange, thrilling, and unfamiliar. Part of my mind—
the rational part—jangled in alarm. Inspector Merriken would
not be a safe man to tangle with.

As I drove, I soon saw why Edward Bruton preferred transport by donkey. I gripped the wheel as the motorcar jolted down

the hill, following the road back and forth through one switch-back turn after another. The day had become cool and gray, the sun hiding behind the brisk, solid clouds of midautumn. Before me, at the foot of the hill, the vast expanse of the sea approached, pearlescent and swirling, dotted with a handful of boats.

There were houses even on the steep slope here, built bravely on a slant, giving the appearance of being ready to tumble into the sea. One or two housewives swept porches; an old man smoked his pipe in his front doorway and watched me with unbroken con-centration as I passed. I kept my eyes on the narrow road.

On the last plateau before the final drop to the sea, Rothewell had built its High Street. The buildings were set in a tidy row overlooking the ocean, protected from the wind and the drop to the beach by a low stone wall. Below this, the beach was a large expanse sliding out to the turbulent sea. An old wooden pier stood in the water, battered and wet, with only a few fishing boats tethered along one side. There was no activity anywhere along the pier; at this time of day, I assumed, the fishermen were already out working, and wouldn't come back until sundown.

I parked in a stony clearing at the end of the road. My hands were cramped from clenching the wheel on the hairpin drive. High Street contained a few stores, a post office, an old church at one end, and a few citizens who looked at me curiously as they went about their business. A man sitting in the window of a pub watched me as I passed; he was youngish, his hair wheat blond, dressed in an open-throated shirt and jacket, a plate of food un-touched on the table before him.

Perhaps it was the motorcar, which was obviously unusual, that had people staring. Perhaps it was simply the presence of a stranger. I had put on a silk dress, overcoat, stockings, patent-leather pumps, and a hat with a dark blue ribbon.

I ducked into a shop with a hand-lettered sign offering MARKET—SUNDRIES—GOODS. It was small and a little musty, but someone had taken great care with each shelf, tidying it and stocking it just so. To my surprise, the only person in the shop was a boy of about nine, with blue eyes and thick blond hair, who sat on a high stool behind the counter. When he saw me, he slid from his seat without a word and ducked into a back room, presumably to fetch a grown-up.

I selected some sausage, bread, cheese, and cocoa to bring back to Barrow House. A woman appeared from the back room and took her place behind the counter. She was slender, her hair tied carelessly at the back of her neck. She appeared to be over thirty, with dark-lashed hazel eyes and a narrow chin, and her boxy dress and out-of-fashion collar did little to mar how pretty she was. She arranged my purchases with long, precise fingers adorned with a narrow gold wedding ring.

I smiled at her. "Was that your boy?"

Motherly pride broke through her reserve, and she smiled back, though I thought her eyes were sad. "Yes. That was Sam. He likes to help, though normally he has better manners. I'm afraid he's rather shy."

I assured her the boy's manners were impeccable, of course, as I paid for the food. As I left the store, I glanced at the pub again. The blond man was gone.

I stowed my basket in the motor and, unwilling to leave yet, I directed my steps down the cobbled path to the wall that paralleled the beach. Here I found a walking path, where one could stroll and take the air, or sit on the low wall and rest. It was the kind of thoroughfare built in resort towns, though there were no tourists to be seen on this chilled, dreary day, and I stood utterly alone.

I stopped and looked about me. The sea was beautiful, if rather desolate from here. Only a few boats, signified by smudged, lonely dots, traveled the water. To my left, rocky cliffs rose from the beach, crowned in dense woodland, beautiful in their frowning majesty.

I realized with a shock that I must be looking at the cliffs where my uncle had died. Inspector Merriken had said Toby had been seen from the water. He must have landed on the rocky outcrop at the foot of the cliffs. My stomach turned as I stared. It was a long, harrowing drop. I heard the inspector's voice. *It was ten o'clock in the morning, and your uncle had been dead for three to five hours.*

The scrape of footsteps came behind me, and I turned to see the woman from the shop. She had put on a wool coat against the chill wind and was pulling a small cigarette case from her pocket.

"Do you like the view?" she asked, as she took out her matchbook. "The fishing isn't good just here, so the boats all go to the other side of the bay, where it's better. It leaves the sea nice and quiet during the day. I like to have a cigarette out here from time to time. I find it soothing."

I glanced at the cruel stone cliffs, the water thrashing at the bottom. "It's terrifying."

She had struck a light to her cigarette, and her eyes regarded me inquisitively as she inhaled. She took the cigarette from her lips and her expression fell. "Oh, I've just realized. Toby Leigh."

"I'm his niece, yes."

"Yes, I see it now." She shook her head. "Well, what a blunder that was. I'm sorry." She moved to the stone wall and sat on it, her back to the water, several feet from me—giving me the option of ignoring her existence if I so chose without appearing rude.

I moved closer to her and held out my hand. "You mustn't worry about it, please. I'm Jillian Leigh."

She looked at my hand with a brief pause—hand shaking was apparently eccentric here, though the girls at Somerville did it all the time—and took it in her gloved fingers, squeezing gingerly. She gave me a small smile. "Rachel Moorcock."

"You own the market store?"

"My father does." She offered me a cigarette but I shook my head, never having enjoyed the habit. "He's ill, so I manage the store most days."

I wanted to ask where her husband was, but it seemed rude. The boy looked nearly old enough to have been born before the war, so perhaps I could guess. "It seems a lot of responsibility."

She shrugged. "I could get into worse trouble, I suppose." Her eyes flickered to me and she took another drag on her cigarette. "I didn't know Toby Leigh had a niece."

"My father was his only brother."

"And you've come here to handle things?" Her eyes flicked over me again, and I realized I was seeing curiosity, politely contained.

"Yes. You speak of my uncle as if you knew him."

"He came to the store for supplies. Papa liked him."

I felt a low hum of excitement at finding someone who could tell me about Toby, who could perhaps help me fill in the gaps. "Did he talk to you about what he was working on?"

She tapped the ash from her cigarette. "I'm not certain I know what you mean."

"Well, there's no other way to say it, I suppose. I'm not sure if he mentioned it, but my uncle was interested in ghosts." Inspector Merriken had told me to do research, so I may as well try. "I think he was here looking for your local ghost, Walking John."

She looked at me. Her eyes were a lovely hazel color, gray and green in the shifting light. Her expression was carefully contained and hard to read—suspicion, amusement, world-weary tolerance, and a touch of fear. "Looking for Walking John?" She put a slight emphasis on the word *looking*, as if it were something no normal person would do.

"Yes." I was rather embarrassed. "He was . . . that is, some would call him a ghost hunter. I think it's why he was here. Did he ever talk to you about it?"

"I see. No. He didn't talk to me very much. He came by one day when I'd put Papa outside in his chair to get some sunshine. He did sit with my father for a while, chatting, which I thought was kind. If your uncle came looking for ghosts, he came to the right place."

"Are you saying Rothewell is haunted?"

"Not the town proper." She gestured with her cigarette. "The woods, and the bay over the other side of the cliffs. People in the farthest houses by the woods hear things. Are you staying at Barrow House?"

I was suddenly cold. "Yes."

"They say no one stays there long, though I think it's a bit of claptrap, and I've lived here all my life." She took a drag. "People don't stay there long because it's a boardinghouse."

"I see," I said faintly.

"My father says Walking John was an old smuggler; that's why he haunts the cove. That there are strange lights in the woods from the old smugglers' lanterns. It's why the sailors haven't gone into the bay in centuries, because Walking John overturns the boats. Especially at this time of year."

I leaned toward her, interested despite myself. "This time of year?"

"Autumn. October. Coming up to All Souls' night, when the dead walk among the living."

I remembered something of the folktales, of leaving food and drink on the table for the dead when they came in the night. "And have you ever seen the lights? The ones in the woods?"

She shook her head, not in a negative, but to indicate the conversation was over. She had finished her cigarette and she tossed the butt to the ground, stepped on it. "Every child in Rothewell grows up with Walking John," she said. "'Behave, because Walking John carries off naughty children. If you lie or steal, Walking John will know.' I've used it on my own son, I admit." She gave me a tired smile. "I wouldn't go looking for lights in the woods for all the gold in the treasury, and then some."

"Who else might my uncle have spoken to?" I asked.

"The vicar, perhaps. He's our local historian in Rothewell. If your uncle wanted to know about Walking John, he'd likely start there."

"I see. Is there anyone else?"

"William Moorcock, I suppose. He fancies himself an expert." I noted the name was the same as her own, but I didn't ask, as a note of bitterness entered her voice as she spoke it. "He lives at the top of the hill—near Barrow House."

I thanked her, but my uncertainty must have shown on my face, because she gave me a sympathetic look as she turned to go.

"Don't worry," she said. "He doesn't usually bother strangers. Good luck, but I must get back to the store."

Seven

I did not believe in ghosts. Of course I didn't—no sane person believed in ghosts.

I believed in Oxford, and cobblestoned squares, and old bricks thick with ivy, and rainy days curled up reading books. I believed in my mother's strong coffee and in the lonely, aching scent of early dawn before anyone else in my boardinghouse was awake. I believed in my favorite men's cardigan and the way the wind felt on the back of my neck. I believed in life as it lay before me, spinning out slowly, day after day of warm springs and thunderstorms and laughter. These were the things I believed in.

And yet, for a few long moments as I'd talked to Rachel Moorcock, sitting on the stone wall, looking at the cliffs as the clouds lowered over the water, Rothewell had seemed just the place where ghosts would dwell.

I returned to Barrow House as the clouds threatened rain. I had just finished putting away the extra food when a commotion sounded in the back garden—the bark of a dog, deep and heavy, but pitched with excitement; the shouts of a man; and a wild, outraged screech that could only have come from a cat. I opened the back door to see what was going on.

The barking was coming from the other side of the garden wall. I had made my way only partway toward it when something streaked past me, fast and low to the ground. A stripe of orange, black, and white disappeared through the open kitchen door behind me and into the house.

The barking had not ceased; a large, shaggy brown and white head appeared over the garden wall, accompanied by two massive front paws larger—and much muddier—than my own hands. The head barked again, and slobbered like a predator, but its eyes were the soft, dark brown of a beast who, in the excitement of the hunt, is used to being more hopeful than vicious.

"Poseidon!" came the man's voice from behind the slobbering head. "Down, boy! Down!"

I approached the back gate, and at once the dog's head and paws disappeared. I nudged the gate open to find a great black nose pressed optimistically in the gap, hopeful of pursuing its quarry through the garden and into my kitchen.

"Oh, no, you don't." The nose pulled back, and I leaned out to see that the dog was leashed, and its owner—the man whose voice I heard—had finally gotten it under control.

The dog's owner was slender, not overly tall, and not above thirty. He wore a peaked cap, the brim of which he touched in greeting; under it I could see dark brown hair. He had a narrow face, unremarkable though not unhandsome, and his gray eyes regarded me with amusement. He wore a plain jacket and trousers, and had obviously been walking his dog along the trail that skirted the woods.

"I'm sorry to disturb you, miss." His accent said he'd had some education. "I lost hold of Poseidon's lead for a moment. He doesn't bite; I promise."

I looked doubtfully down at the dog, which was sitting next to its master, its head higher than the man's waist. "Poseidon?"

The man gave a rueful smile. "A dignified name for such a ridiculous specimen, I know. I'm afraid I had high hopes when I named him." He took a step forward and held out his hand. "William Moorcock."

I shook his hand, thinking the name sounded familiar. Rachel Moorcock had mentioned it, though I hadn't missed her intonation. *He fancies himself an expert*, she had said. "Jillian Leigh. I'm very glad to have run into you, in fact."

"Oh? And why is that?"

"I had heard—that is, someone mentioned that you may have met my uncle. Toby Leigh."

"I did. I'm terribly sorry about what happened to him. Are you all right?"

The question was a little touching in its directness. "Yes, I think so. Thank you."

"It's awful; it truly is. I live just down the road a way—the one with the sloped roof, just at the fork of the road toward town. You likely passed me on your way in. Did your uncle mention me?"

I paused, embarrassed. "We weren't close, I'm afraid. I'm just here cleaning up his things. Did he perhaps tell you what he was working on—why exactly he was in Rothewell?"

"Ah." William Moorcock petted his dog's head and smiled. "You're asking whether he confided in me about being a ghost hunter."

I was embarrassed again, but relieved as well. "It must seem eccentric."

"In some places, perhaps. Not here." He looked at me for a moment and smiled again. "Let me guess—you've never been to Rothewell before, and you're not quite sure what to make of this place." He shook his head as I tried to speak. "You needn't explain. Since it seems I've unintentionally saddled you with a cat,

I'll tell you what I can. Poseidon needs to stretch his legs. Can we walk?"

"Yes, of course." I shut the kitchen door, then the gate. "Lead the way."

"Your uncle was rather fascinating," said William as we took the path to the woods. "He came to my door, wanting to know about our local ghosts. I'm always happy to oblige. Though I thought Toby was particularly troubled, myself. Do you know whether he was ever a subject of psychotherapy?"

"Er—no, I don't know, I'm afraid."

"Well, that's too bad. I read a book about psychotherapy last week, and it made me think your uncle would have been a crack subject." He saw my surprise, and his shoulders sagged a little. "I'm sorry. I don't mean these things as I say them. My sister tells me I'm terrible for saying just the wrong thing. I don't mean to put you off."

"No—no, it's quite all right." We were taking the path through the trees now, the shade dappling and growing thicker. "It's just that I really wasn't very close to him, you know." The ground sloped here, and I felt myself growing warmer with the walk. "And now he's died, and I feel torn about it, as if I've left something terrible undone. As if I could somehow have done something more." It felt good to say the words aloud to someone, though I didn't mention the coroner's findings, or Inspector Merriken's suspicions. I wondered where the inspector was now, and what, if anything, he had learned.

"That's likely very common," William said. "I felt something similar when my parents died."

"Oh, I'm sorry."

"No, you mustn't say anything. There I go again. It was years ago, while I was at war. I just felt a similar way, that's all. Who was mentioning me, may I ask?"

"It was Rachel Moorcock, who runs the sundries shop."

"A ringing endorsement, I'm sure." His smile was wry. "Ah, now, you needn't be embarrassed. There are a lot of tangled connections in a small town like ours. Rachel is my sister-in-law, and she's never liked me."

"Oh?"

"She married my brother, Raymond. She disliked me from the start, and now that Raymond is gone, she has as little to do with me as she can. I wouldn't mind, except I don't get to see my nephew very much."

"Sam," I said. "I met him. I would never have guessed. He looks nothing like you."

"Ah, no. He looks like Raymond." William's gaze grew wistful as he led me down the path. "Raymond and I were very different."

I didn't miss the note of pain in his voice. "What happened to him?" I asked gently.

William shrugged. "Belleau Wood."

"I'm sorry."

"Now I've made you say that a second time." He managed a smile, one that wished to please. "Can we start again?"

I smiled back. "Of course."

We had turned along the curve of the woods now, and from the sight of the unbroken sky through the trees I could tell we were at a high vantage point. "Can we see the water from here?" I asked.

"We can. Just this way." William turned from the path and we cut through the woods, Poseidon bounding with excitement over the departure. "Calm, you great fool," William told his pet with obvious affection. "Show a little dignity in front of the lady." Poseidon barked happily, undeterred.

Soon we broke through the trees, and I looked around in amazement. We were at the top of the cliffs I had seen from town,

but we were not looking down the south coast toward Rothewell. We were on the other side, looking north down a long,
tangled, wooded slope to sea level, and the view was just as breath-
taking. The woods ended at a long sweep of beach, rocky, dark
sanded, and wet, battered by relentless water in a bay that curved
like a large, perfect shell. Through the mouth of the bay we could
see the open expanse of whitecapped ocean; inside the bay the
water surged choppily, like a bowl of water that was being gently
sloshed. There was not a soul, not a single building to be seen, only
the green of the tangled woods and the unbroken water.

"Blood Moon Bay," William Moorcock said, indicating the
curved cup of beach.

I hunched my shoulders against the biting wind, remembering what Rachel Moorcock had said. "These are the woods haunted
by Walking John," I said. "These woods and the bay."

"Oh, yes—our famous haunted woods."

"Who was he?"

"A smuggler," William replied. "In the seventeenth century,
when smuggling was everywhere in England."

"He was a ship's captain?"

"Actually no. He worked the land side of things—arranging
with the sailors when the boats would come in, unloading, hiding the goods, transporting them. If you go farther down this
path and over to the east—you see that promontory, just there?—
you'll find a signal house, where John kept his lantern. He'd light
it on nights when a ship was due to come in, signaling that the
coast was clear and it was safe to land. The structure is still there,
though of course it's very old now."

"Fascinating," I said. "He must have been rich."

"Not quite, though he wasn't poor either. A lot of men grew
rich, though not in this part of the country."

"Why not?"

"Well, we're on the wrong side of England for an easy trip from France. And with the currents, and these waters, and the rocks . . . there are easier places to land a boat in the middle of the night. Still, there was enough money to be made that the risk was worth it, at least some of the time. Am I boring you?"

"Not at all," I said truthfully. "Go on."

"Very well. Even with the risks, John Barrow did rather well, and he never got caught."

"Wait." My skin had gone cold. "Did you just say *John Barrow*?"

He regarded me with a twinkle of amusement. "You're staying at Barrow House, aren't you? Yes, that was his name, and that's his house you're in, in easy reach of the cliffs. It's actually modern; the original burned down in the 1740s, the site was left alone for a good long while, and what's there now was merely built onto the foundation. The house isn't haunted that I'm aware of, but it is close to the woods, and there are stories of strange sounds."

"Yes, so I've heard."

"You mustn't look so worried. It's a strange thing, having a local ghost—every time an animal pulls down a clothesline or a bird gets caught in a chimney, it gets blamed on the poor spirit. But Blood Moon Bay at night . . . that's a different matter." He gazed out over the water. "No one comes out here after dark. The bay is where he died, you see, rather tragically."

"What happened?"

"A shipment came in one night," William said. "Barrow's wife had died and they had one child, a boy of about seven, whom he doted on. On this night, after his father had left, the boy slipped out of his room and out of the house to follow his father to the bay. He was probably curious; most boys are. He would have come right by where we're standing, I think, and gone on down the path through the woods."

He was deep into the telling of the tale now, and I could tell he was relishing it. I could do nothing but give in and follow where it was going.

"Barrow knew nothing about it, of course," William went on. "No one knows quite what happened, but somehow the boy ended up slipping in the water as the men unloaded the ship, hitting his head in the dark, and drowning."

"Oh, no," I said.

"It gets worse. When Barrow saw what had happened, he lost his mind with grief. He pulled the boy's body from the water and held it. He wouldn't let go. He crouched over the body and wouldn't be moved, making horrible sounds.

"Now, the operation depended completely on speed and stealth, as you can imagine. Barrow's madness threatened to bring down the entire plan. They tried to talk to him, but he was having none of it. Finally, the rest of the crew decided he had to be moved. But when one of the men tried to take the body from him, Barrow pulled his pistol and shot the man in the head. Then he took the dead man's pistol from his belt and turned it on himself as he knelt over his son's body."

"My God! This is horrible."

"Yes, and there's more. They buried the boy in the churchyard, but they buried John Barrow just outside it. They'd never had a murder here, you see, and they didn't want to put him in with the other good citizens of Rothewell.

"Within a few days, Barrow's grave was found dug up, his body lying sprawled a few feet away. They buried him again, and it happened again. And again. Those who saw it said it looked like he had been crawling, trying to get to the churchyard and his son."

I crossed my arms. "Now you're pulling my leg."

"That's the legend, Miss Leigh. I'm just repeating it."

"My name is Jillian, please. And do tell—what happened next?"

"All right, I'm William then. The citizens of Rothewell used plain common sense, of course, for those days. They dug John Barrow up, beheaded him, burned him, and reburied him somewhere in the woods so he'd be away from the village. He stayed buried this time, but his spirit started walking. That's why he's called Walking John, by the way—because he was dead, and then he was walking. He can't rest, you see, having been buried so far from his beloved child, and now it can never be put right.

"There have been legends about him ever since. Sometimes it's the woods, sometimes along the beach in Blood Moon Bay. The smugglers kept landing here for a while, but eventually they stopped. There were stories of overturned cargoes, of strange footprints and sounds, of John Barrow and his ghostly crew coming to help the crews unload."

"That can't be true!" I said.

"Perhaps not, but it was enough to make the trade stop entirely in Rothewell. No one wanted to land a boat here in the middle of the night anymore." A cold, harsh wind had begun to blow up as he was talking, and he looked up at the sky. "It isn't a very nice story, I think. I've probably talked about the wrong thing again, and for too long."

I smiled to reassure him. "I'm used to history lectures. I'm a student at Oxford."

"Are you, then?" He looked at me, raised his eyebrows in surprise.

"If you're going to say something about educated women, I've heard it ad nauseam, I assure you. I already feel like a bit of a circus sideshow here."

"Ah. No," he said gently. "Not quite a sideshow. More like a unicorn, perhaps—something we've heard of, but never quite believed existed."

If it was a compliment, it had a bit of a sting to it, and yet I found I was strangely pleased. He hadn't lectured me about traveling alone or finding a husband, at least.

"It looks like a storm is blowing up," he said now. "Shall we head back?"

"I liked it," I said as he looped Poseidon's leash around his wrist, and we turned back to the woods. "The story, that is. It was rather good. Did you tell it to my uncle?"

"I didn't have to," he said. "He already knew it. Someone told it to him the last time he was here."

I stopped walking and stared at him. "I beg your pardon?"

He stopped and turned as well. "Toby was here before, years ago. Hunting Walking John. He said he'd come back a second time, this time because he'd left unfinished business."

"What was it?"

He shrugged. "I don't know. Your uncle wasn't very talkative."

I stared for another moment, then started walking again. "This makes less and less sense the more I learn of it," I said. "I don't understand."

"I wouldn't worry about it. It was probably nothing. We'll say good night, then, shall we?"

I thanked him and wished him good night. As he turned away, I hugged myself, the wind flapping my coat about my legs. Night was falling, and I turned to go inside. William was right, and a storm was coming.

Eight

There was no sign of the cat, though it must still have been in the house. I tried calling it—"Kitty, kitty"—but there was no response. It was likely hidden somewhere, still terrified by its encounter with Poseidon.

I started a pot of tea as the sky darkened outside the kitchen window and the wind began to moan in the eaves. A few spatters of rain pelted the glass. When my tea was ready I took a cup, a tin of biscuits, and a piece of the sausage I'd bought at Rachel Moorcock's store with me into the library.

The library was just off the front parlor, through a pair of French doors. It featured a battered desk and a few bookshelves, mostly empty. A window looked out the back garden and toward the woods. I had noticed this room before, and it seemed perfect now for what I wanted to do, for the desk had a large surface and the rest of the room was rather empty. I lit the lamps, built a fire in the fireplace, and put a few pieces of sausage on the floor in front of the flames. Then I went upstairs.

The two cases were where Inspector Merriken and I had left them, in Toby's bedroom. I carried them, one at a time, down to the library. I was ready to take a closer look at Toby Leigh's ghost-hunting kit.

I pulled the pieces from the first kit and laid them out on the desk. Clock, stopwatch, thermometer, two torches, measuring tape, film canisters, a spool of string and another of wire, a small metal box with a needle. This last seemed to measure sound; I snapped my fingers and watched the needle move.

A sound came behind me and for a second I froze, my blood chilled; then the sound came again, a soft padding, and I turned.

The cat had come out of hiding to get at the sausage. It was black, orange, and white, thin and ragged, its fur muddy. It crouched on the floor and looked up at me with suspicious brown eyes. Curled around its back legs was a disproportionately long tail blooming with thick fur, matted down with something apparently sticky. As I watched, the cat inched closer to the bites of meat, never taking its eyes from me.

I crouched on my haunches and hugged my knees, watching the cat's progress. It looked female, in my opinion; no self-respecting male cat would have such exquisite features or such a flagrantly pretty tail. As I watched her devour the sausage I couldn't help but feel a childish thrill, the excitement of a girl who had always wished for a kitten but never was given one because it would interfere with her studies.

"Do you have a name?" I asked her. The cat's ears swiveled, but she didn't stop eating.

"I can give you a name," I said conversationally, liking the way her ears followed my voice. On the desk, I could see the needle move on the sound monitor.

I knew what her name should be. It was the name I had always picked for my imaginary kitten. A foolish, dramatic name, but I would give it to her anyway. "Sultana," I said.

The cat had finished eating and was licking her paws. She gave only the barest indication she had heard me. I smiled to myself and went back to my work.

I wasn't sure, entirely, what I was after by going through Toby's equipment. I only knew that the mismatched parts of the end of Toby's life were like pieces from different puzzles put side by side, revealing little. I touched each item and turned it over, hoping it could tell me something.

I pulled the galvanoscope from the second case. It was heavy. I had no idea how it was to be set up; I put the main unit on the table and pulled out the battery next, wondering how it attached. Finally I figured out how the wires wrapped around the battery's nodes and connected them.

The needle moved at first as I connected the battery, then was still. Outside, the storm had blown to a feverish pitch, the eaves beginning to groan over my head, rain spattering the window. Sultana, finished with her bath, dozed by the fire, one half-opened eye watching me. "You should be grateful you're indoors," I chided her.

My eye caught something else in the galvanoscope's case, and I pulled it out: A small notebook, well-worn. I sat at the desk and opened it:

23 January 1919. Third night, Cotters' house, Shepham. Location, attic—

10:00 p.m. Temperature stable, no noises heard.

11:00 p.m. All gauges stable, nothing heard or seen.

11:37 p.m. Cold felt briefly, possible draft—no fluctuation noted on thermometer.

12:00 a.m., 24 January 1919. Still nothing seen . . .

It was a logbook—a ghost-hunter's logbook. I was fascinated. Many of the nights were spent like the night on the first page. I imagined hundreds of such nights over a span of years—for this was obviously just the latest of many notebooks—my uncle sitting hour after hour, noting the time going by with dutiful entries.

But not all of the vigils went so. Several pages later, I read:

2 August 1920. First night, Bakers' house, York. Location, copse of trees, from which the children claim they have seen translucent figures from the house.

8:00 p.m. Sunset. Nothing seen.

9:00 p.m. Many sounds; difficult to track properly. I watch the meter but nothing seems extraordinary.

9:11 p.m. Fluctuation on the galvanoscope. Needle moved three degrees, possibly four. Now returned to base position. No other readings.

9:13 p.m. Galvanoscope fluctuation again.

9:14 p.m. Again. The feeling has come to me. Something certainly here.

9:30 p.m. It has retreated; no readings. But it has not gone away.

9:41 p.m. Galvanoscope fluctuating to a much greater degree; continuous, without stopping. Something very certainly here. Temperature has lowered by 2.5 degrees. Sound meter shows no difference.

9:42 p.m. It is a woman.

9:49 p.m. Woman again, very near.

9:51 p.m. Galvanoscope very volatile—

9:53 p.m. She looks like—

10:17 p.m. I have seen it and spoken to it. A woman, twenty to twenty-five years old, hair cropped, in a dress of homespun. She saw me and made such sounds. She would not or could not give her name.

Her baby is buried here, in these trees. I will tell the Bakers. Perhaps the sexton will help.

I stared at the page before me, disbelieving. The language was so simple, the words so devastating. *She saw me and made such sounds. Her baby is buried here, in these trees.* Impossible, and yet what had Toby seen?

And, drawing my eye again: *The feeling has come to me. Something certainly here.*

Had Toby had—or believed he had—a sixth sense? An ability to see and speak with the dead? Was that even possible?

I looked around me. I was sitting at the desk, the various instruments around me, the notebook in front of me. It was night. I was sitting exactly as Toby would have sat, I realized, on one of his expeditions. Suddenly I could picture him very clearly in my mind, sitting at a table much like this one in a stranger's house at some ungodly hour of the morning, wearing one of his worn-out suits and scratching quietly with his pen. Check the time; check the instruments; make a note. I could almost see the faint glow of the moonlight on his face, the way his body would stiffen and his eyes raise as he suddenly felt something—something. . . .

Something crashed.

I jumped. The fire wavered, as if a cold breath had blown over it. The lamps went out. Sultana bolted from the room, leaving me alone in the firelight.

Another crash. I jumped again, my blood skittering in my veins. The sound came from the window—heavy and sharp, as if something were being slammed with great force. The wind gusted outside. Through the gap in the curtains I could see the trees bowing and flashing in the force of it, the tall grasses past the garden wall bending flat in ripples that gleamed silvery in the dark.

I pushed the chair back and got up, feeling my way. I could see little in the firelight, yet something about the window made me feel suddenly exposed. I had the same strange feeling as if I'd been jolted with electricity, the hair on the back of my neck standing nearly on end, my hands unsteady. I moved stealthily to the library door, and when I stopped I noticed that I had silently slipped my feet out of my shoes.

I had just begun to take a breath when the crash sounded again, followed quickly by another. This time I saw movement at the window, a shape looming across it, then gone again. I stared stupidly for a moment before my brain recognized the shape of a shutter. A shutter had come loose in the wind and was banging on the window frame.

Fix the shutter, then. I should have been relieved, but instead I wished fiercely for Inspector Merriken, for my father, for anyone. Even Sultana would do. The shutter banged again.

I swallowed, left the library, and moved down the hall. I could hear every noise the old house made in the wind: the howling eaves, the rattling windows, the creak of old wood, the harsh gusts of rain. *Just a windstorm.*

The kitchen was still and dark. The crash came again, and I couldn't help a mad, shuddering jump. If I went out the back door here and to my left along the house, I'd be at the library window in a few long steps. All I had to do was open the door.

Quickly, then.

I opened the door and a gust of wind hit me, cold and startling, spitting with rain. The hem of my dress flapped against my legs. In the wild whorls of air my hair flew almost upward, and I pressed my hands to my head, pushing strands from my eyes. The black vista behind the house was alive with movement, the grasses and weeds shaking with hissing wind, and the line of trees violently tossing their treetops. The clay flowerpot, containing only brown flower stems this time of year, was overturned, the earth in it scattered. I had the feeling, almost as a physical touch up my spine, that something had just left as I opened the door, and for a cowardly second I wanted to retreat, close the door again, and never look out for the rest of the night.

The shutter dangled from a single broken hinge. As I watched, the wind caught it and waved it heavily, irregularly, and threw it back to crash against the side of the house.

This, then, was the noise, as I had thought. All I had to do was step outside, pull the shutters closed, and latch them together. In the morning I'd look more closely at fixing the hinge.

Step outside. Latch the shutters. Step back in. Eight steps, perhaps ten. In the dark.

Cold needles of rain hit me, and the wind pressed my dress to my body. I plunged out into the darkness. The ground was damp and icy—I had completely forgotten that I had removed my shoes. I dashed to the window, grasped the shutter, wrestled with it. It bucked in my hands as the wind gusted again, and I lost my grip; I stretched and grasped it again before it could land a blow to my forehead. I closed it, then had to let it go to collect the other shutter; the first one dangled, then blew away again.

Behind me came another bang: the kitchen door, taking its turn in the wind. With my back to the garden, grasping first one shutter and then the other, my back tingled. Something—whatever it was that had just left—could be returning. It could, in fact, be directly behind me, and I could turn around and see—

The kitchen door banged again. I had hold of both shutters now, and I fumbled with the latch with numb fingers, stretching up on my toes in the relentless wind.

The rain plastered a lock of hair over my eye, but I could not release a hand to brush it away. I had nearly gotten the latch fastened when my hand slipped and the metal sliced under my thumbnail, sending a shock of pain up my arm. Still, I did not let go. I fastened the latch, feeling the warm wetness of blood under my fingers, and ran back to the house. My blood spattering in red drops on the cobblestones, I grasped for the door.

From behind me came a sound, and I turned to see the garden gate fly open as if thrown by an unseen hand. The hair on the back of my neck stood on end. There was no mistaking it for the wind; the gate, somehow unlatched, moved as if someone strong had pushed it in fury. I could see nothing, but I was overcome, in slick certainty, with sheer terror.

I slammed and bolted the kitchen door behind me as I flung myself into the safety of the house. I gasped for air, my back to the closed door, and tried to come back to myself. My thumb throbbed and bled. I cradled it in my other hand. My hair was tangled, my feet chilled and dirty; my wet dress stuck to my freezing skin. In a rush of weakness, I sank to the floor, my knees up, my back against the door.

Something moved in the kitchen with a soft sound, and from my seat on the floor I saw the cat, Sultana, crouched under the wooden dish cabinet. Her ears were flattened to her skull, and she looked at me with large, fear-wild eyes, her pupils dark slits of angry wariness. She was frozen still.

Instinct made me hold my breath: the thought of that gate

bursting open, perhaps, or the utter stillness and watchful eyes of Sultana. Without thinking I sat unmoving, trying for silence, like a small creature who hopes not to be noticed by a predator.

Something thumped against the door.

My hands flew to my mouth, clamping down the sound in my throat. That had not been the wild, sharp sound of something unmoored in the wind. It had not been the bony rapping of knuckles, of a human asking to come in. It had been a softer sound, more muffled. A single thump, inquisitive, almost exploratory. The sound of something testing to see whether the door, so recently open, would open again.

I felt as if someone had put an electric wire through me; I was unable to move, my arms and legs rigid, my breath frozen, like a body in the throes of shock. I stared at Sultana, whose tail had blossomed out, her body lowered to the ground, ears back, lips drawn up in a rictus of instinctive fear. I tried to stay silent as I waited for the sound to come again.

The terror I felt in that moment was something I had never thought possible. The thing outside the door was not human, I knew; it was a thing that had come through the garden gate— *toward me*—and was now only inches away, through the wood of the door, pressing where my backbone was. Looking for me. The world in that moment was not the place I had lived in all my life; it was as if a door had opened and I glimpsed how large reality was. I was a very small, very vulnerable creature in that second, unguarded flesh, my hubris the purest idiocy. Because if it found me, it could come. And I would not be able to stop it.

The sound did not come again. I sat there for what felt like hours, my bloody hands pressed to my mouth, trying not to move or breathe. I watched only Sultana, who stared back at me, and we waited in the darkness in silent understanding.

Little by little, eventually the terror began to recede. I took my hands from my mouth. I could feel blood running down my arm from the cut in my thumb, feel blood on my face. I moved one stiff limb, then another. My back ached. The feeling of electricity ebbed, and I thought the thing, whatever it was, had gone.

Sultana felt it, too. Her snarl relaxed, and her ears twitched in interest as she watched me move. Eventually, I pulled myself away from the door and crawled across the floor toward her, trying under my breath to call her to me. She was having none of it; she retreated farther under the cabinet, out of reach. More than anything I wanted the reassurance of another living creature, but I backed away and stood up on my cramped legs.

I limped to the stairs, the relentless wind growing louder in the eaves as I ascended. I briefly considered going to the library to retrieve one of the lamps, but the thought of the library window, even shuttered, was too much to contemplate. So I moved softly in the dark, my hands waving before me like a blind man, and found my way to my room.

There I washed with shaking hands, wrapped my thumb, took off my dirtied stockings and dress. In my underslip I wearily contemplated the bed, and its situation next to the window. Toby's blocked window came to mind again. I wouldn't sleep next to a window tonight, listening to those unearthly scratches.

I retrieved an extra blanket from the linen closet—again in the dark—and wound it over the curtain rod, covering the flimsy lace curtains. I had no tools with which to nail it to the window frame, but this would do. The sound of the rain became somewhat muffled as the window disappeared from sight.

Next I took hold of the end of the bed and dragged it along the wall to the other side of the room, away from the window. I put yet another spare blanket on the bed. There: With the window covered, and the bed blanketed and tucked in the corner, I could almost feel safe. Numb with exhaustion now, I pulled my aching limbs onto the bed and lay down.

I had barely arranged myself when, to my tired delight, Sultana joined me. She must have followed me upstairs and watched me ready everything, unseen, and now she leaped onto the bed next to me, fastidiously selected a spot, and curled up. I ran my hand over her matted, gnarled fur, her body heat rising into my palm. She did not purr, but only sighed, as if tolerating me well enough. She smelled of dirt and dead leaves and cat. I had never been so happy to smell anything in my life.

I awoke only once that night. Some sound had roused me, and I saw Sultana's head raised, her ears twitching as she listened. It may have been a scratch at the window. I waited for a long moment, my limbs still burning from the earlier terror, as if I'd done some great exertion, but no sound came. Sultana put her head back down and clenched her paws open and closed, relaxing again. Keeping my arm around her, I closed my eyes.

Nine

In the cold damp of morning, I drove through the woods to the neighboring town of St. Thomas' Gate. The storm had left its mark everywhere, in downed branches, scattered debris, and icy wet puddles that struggled to reflect the thin sunlight. It was as quiet as a place abandoned.

I'm at a hotel called the White Lion in St. Thomas' Gate, Inspector Merriken had said, *if you need me.*

I had stopped shaking, at least. I had managed to dress myself, in a blue-gray frock, double-breasted with buttons on the front, and stockings to replace last night's filthy ones; I had found my hat, my coat and its belt, a pair of matching shoes, and my driving gloves. I could pass for a normal young woman on a morning drive. It would have to do.

I was still awash with last night's experience. I felt what had happened in my nerve endings, as when one first awakens from a nightmare and stares at the ceiling, wondering what is real. Sultana, unconcerned, had forgotten her companionable nature come morning and ran from the house as soon as I opened the door. Perhaps it was for the best; otherwise I would have been tempted to take her with me everywhere I went in smothering affection, for in a way I felt she had saved my sanity.

You were born with good common sense, my father always said to me. *It's why we trust you on your own at Oxford.* I wondered now whether he would take back the sentiment. I'd spent the night cowering from ghosts, and my first destination the next morning was straight to a man I instinctively knew was dangerous. Already I could see his face clearly in my mind: the line of his jaw, the angle of his cheekbones, the inquisitive eyes that missed nothing. The image both calmed and excited me, a mix of feelings that had alarmingly little to do with common sense.

I found the White Lion easily, as St. Thomas' Gate was not much larger than Rothewell. The town was inland, so it did not have Rothewell's beautiful views, or its steep descent to the water. It did not have Rothewell's deadly cliffs or, I would wager, its resident ghost. It was a town of a short main street lined with oak and birch trees, and tidy farming cottages tucked on well-kept parcels of land.

A fortyish woman in spectacles greeted me as I entered the inn, but when I told her I was looking for Inspector Merriken, her welcoming smile faded.

"Well, then," she said with decided ill nature. "Which one would you be?"

"I beg your pardon?"

"Let's see." She pulled several slips of paper from the pocket of her apron and sorted them one by one. "Are you Edith, Genevieve, or Mary Ann?" She looked me over critically. "You don't look like any one of those. Cheap, they sounded, and I don't mind saying so."

I shook my head, confused. "I don't follow."

"So you're another one, then." She thrust the slips of paper at me. "Don't think an in-person visit is going to get you any further than the others. You can give these to him when you see him, and tell him he's made me sorry I ever installed a telephone."

"Oh." I helplessly took the papers. The first one was addressed along the top of the page, *For Inspector Drew Merriken.* I looked away before my curious eyes could go further. "Look, Mrs.—"

"Ebury, but don't you mind me. It's that inspector you need to mind, and that's my advice. Good day."

She turned away, headed back toward the inn's small dining room, in which a handful of locals were eating breakfast. I stood abandoned by the door, unsure of what to do. She hadn't even told me whether the inspector was in.

A few people at scattered tables had turned my way. I was still holding the papers; I must look like a lovesick girl, one of— apparently—many other lovesick girls acquainted with Inspector Merriken. *Cheap*, the landlady had said. I shoved the papers in the pocket of my skirt. To go upstairs and look for the man myself was unthinkably embarrassing. I'd have to find him another time. I pushed the door open and fled outside.

A figure was coming up the walk from the direction of the old carriage house. I recognized the black overcoat and long-legged gait immediately. Inspector Merriken was looking down as he walked, the brim of his hat low as it had been when I first saw him, and I realized he was deep in thought. There was no-where to go, so I stood where I was, waiting for him to notice me.

He was almost upon me before he did. I had a long moment unobserved to take in the pensive cast of his features, to wonder why he seemed so very solitary. Then he was standing before me, his gaze locked on mine.

"Miss Leigh," he said, frowning in surprise. "Is everything all right?"

Up close, I could see that his coat was unbuttoned, his tie loosened, his collar open at the throat. I could follow the line of his white shirt down his chest and stomach to his waist. The effect wasn't sloppy, only a little rumpled. Had he dressed quickly early this morning, or had he not been to bed at all? Embarrassed to even be thinking about it, I snapped my eyes back upward.

"These are yours," I said, holding the slips of paper out to him.

He took them from me and glanced at them one at a time before putting them in a breast pocket. "I see."

"You're rather popular."

He took a breath through his nose. "I wouldn't exactly say that."

"Wouldn't you? The landlady said—"

"Yes, all right."

"Is Drew short for Andrew?"

Now he was glaring. "Perhaps."

I tugged off my gloves. For some reason, the thought of the inspector as a ladies' man needled me, though of course it made sense. He was rather an attractive man. "It's none of my business, of course."

"I need to talk to you," he said. "I was about to go to you myself, as it happens. Miss Leigh—what happened to your hand?"

I had uncovered the makeshift bandage I'd ripped from an old towel and wound over my bleeding thumb. "I had something of a mishap."

"You've bandaged it all wrong."

"Probably. I had no supplies, and I had to do it one-handed. I'm not much of a nurse."

He took my wrist and unwound the strip of cloth. "Do I even want to know the story behind this?" he said, talking almost to himself. "Never mind. I have proper bandages in my room. Come with me."

"I can't do that!"

"Are you serious? Miss Leigh, you're bleeding."

"My name is Jillian." Since I knew his name, it seemed only

fair. "Everyone in there already thinks I'm one of your girlfriends. And I'm bleeding, not dying. It just started up again when you took off the bandage."

He seemed to grit his teeth. "All right. There is a sitting room upstairs. Will you consent to sit in it while I fetch a bandage?"

He had not let go of my wrist, and I felt that warm grip again through my sleeve, though I did my best not to be affected by it. "Yes," I managed.

After only the smallest of pauses—I may have imagined it— he let me go, and I followed him back into the inn and up the stairs. There was indeed a small private sitting room, where he deposited me; then he disappeared. In a few moments he returned with a roll of bandages and a pair of scissors. He had removed his hat, overcoat, and jacket, and without the extra layers, in only his shirtsleeves and trousers, he had a particular animal grace. He pulled a chair up to mine and rolled up his cuffs, revealing wrists with dark hair on them. He pulled my hand toward him without ceremony and inspected the bleeding thumb, his dark head bent low.

I sat, crackling with impatience and some kind of wild, excited energy as he deftly wrapped the thumb in a bandage and tied it off. His fingertips on my skin sent jolts up my arm. He seemed not to notice. He smelled of soap and the autumn air he'd brought from outside. His shoulders, under the white shirt, looked impossibly strong.

"You'll live," he said as he finished.

"That's a relief." I bit my lip as he straightened. "So, who is going to go first? You or me?"

"I will," he said easily. "I've ordered some food to be brought, and some tea."

"Do I need food for this conversation?"

"You may, yes." He crossed his arms and slouched back in his chair. He took a leisurely moment to look at me, as I sat with my legs crossed, my spine straight, my hands in my lap. His gaze traveled me as if searching for an answer, and though his expression was carefully impersonal, I felt its warmth.

"What is it?" I said.

He frowned a little. "You look different with clothes on."

My blush was hot. "I had clothes on when we met!"

"Not many." He raised his eyes to mine and shrugged. "You puzzle me. When I met you yesterday, you looked like a bohemian type who had just gotten out of bed."

I could have protested that it had been nine o'clock in the morning, and I *had* just gotten out of bed—but some blessed remnant of common sense made me keep my mouth shut. I also didn't argue that I had hardly been naked. My legs had been bare, but I'd been wearing my oversize men's sweater. I kept quiet and let him go on.

"However," he continued, "when we spoke, I realized that wasn't quite right. You may not quite be proper, but you aren't lax in your morals." He ignored my glare of outrage and continued. "A student, then. A buttoned-up intellectual type, perhaps. But you aren't that either. You're neither fish nor fowl."

"I see. And today?"

"Today you are dressed much like any other young woman, albeit with a bit of money. And you almost pull it off."

I choked. *"Almost?"*

"It's what I can't put my finger on," he admitted. "You wear the clothes of any other girl of your class, as if you're off to an afternoon of teas and husband hunting. But with you, it's quite obviously an act. You're something very different underneath, and I don't know exactly what that is."

"So you are simply attempting to put me into a pat little category."

"Most diligently, yes. And not succeeding."

"If that is the game, then I could categorize you as a womanizer."

"You wouldn't be exactly wrong," he said, "but you wouldn't be exactly right, either."

The barmaid came in and set down a tray of tea and toast. When she had gone, the inspector leaned forward without another word and pulled a small square of newsprint from his pocket. He unfolded it to reveal a white cigarette butt, smoked most of the way to the end.

"What is this?" I asked.

"I found it on the top of the cliffs this morning," he said. "And this one"—he pulled a second square from his pocket, and showed me an identical cigarette—"was found in the same spot by a local PC the day your uncle died. It was right at the top of the cliffs, where your uncle must have fallen."

I stared at the cigarette. My uncle had never smoked in any of my memories; I had seen no evidence of it in the house, not a cigarette or ashtray.

"I can see you calculating it," Drew said to me. "No, your uncle did not smoke. And if he had smoked the first cigarette, then who smoked the second one?"

"But the first one could be weeks old, could it not?"

"It could not. It rained heavily the night before your uncle died. This cigarette was found on the same morning as the body, perfectly dry."

I felt that sink in with a sick numbness. "Someone was there."

"It's a possibility, yes."

"You knew about this," I said, angry. "I know what you're saying. Why didn't you just tell me my uncle was murdered?"

"Because I don't know it, not really. This isn't much to go on. It isn't proof. But when I went back to the site again this morning and found the second one . . ." He looked tired. "If someone killed him, they may have gone back to the same place. It's a reasonably common pattern."

"Oh, my God," I said. "We have to do something. You need to call your headquarters at Scotland Yard."

"And give them what?" he said. "I have two cigarettes and a gut feeling. They won't think it's enough."

I stood. I was mindlessly agitated. It felt as if something were physically tearing at me, and I began to pace in an attempt to stop it. "So you need to find something else," I said, more sharply than I intended. I pointed at the second cigarette. "That one is just as dry as the first."

"And there was a storm last night, yes. So someone dropped it this morning."

I wondered whether the person had gone right by my back door on his or her way to the cliffs, taking the same path I had walked with William Moorcock. Did William smoke? I didn't think so. I thought of Rachel Moorcock, dropping her cigarette and grinding it out.

"You need to find out who smokes in Rothewell," I said.

He watched me as I paced, his look a little wary. "Perhaps. But not only Rothewell. The person could have come from another town."

"They would have required a motorcar. That would have been noticed."

"Not if they parked it a distance away. And they could have traveled by bicycle, or motorcycle. They could have walked."

Or traveled by donkey cart. I blew out a breath. "The cigarette has no lipstick on it. That means it was a man."

"Does it? You wore no lipstick yesterday."

He was right. Rachel had worn lipstick, as had Diana Kates, but Diana's daughter, Julia, had not. "You said my uncle's body was found at ten o'clock, and he had been dead three to five hours. That means he died sometime between five and seven o'clock in the morning."

"That's correct."

"Daylight, then." I turned to him. "Or at least dawn. The sun was coming up. Someone could have seen something."

"I spent much of yesterday afternoon canvassing town," he said. "It's why I didn't get to the cliffs until this morning. No one I've talked to saw anything at all."

"Please," I said in exasperation. "There must be something you can do!"

"Jillian." He said my name, softly, for the first time. "He could have jumped."

I put my hands to my eyes and pressed them. I was not weeping. My eyes were as dry and hot as they'd been the day I'd seen the body, my breath ragged in my chest. "He didn't jump," I managed to say from the darkness behind my hands. "You know that, and so do I. I was going to leave today, and never come back to this place again." The implications were only fully hitting me, and I could barely stand them. *"He didn't jump."*

We were quiet for a moment, me taking deep breaths to control myself, and Inspector Merriken in his chair, waiting. He offered no comfort, and I wanted none from him. If I remained in Rothewell, I'd be staying with that thing, whatever it had been. Whatever it had wanted. But if I left . . .

It was the cigarette that haunted me. That damned cigarette.

If I left, I'd know that someone had done something, known something, and I had done nothing about it. Someone had walked the cliffs just this morning, smoking and thinking of how they'd gotten away with it, and I had turned my back.

Toby should be laid to rest by family.

"Jillian?" said the inspector.

"Hush," I said. "I'm doing the right thing, and I have to say it's horribly difficult."

He gave me only a few seconds. "Why were you going to leave?"

I dropped my hands and managed a weak smile. "You told me to research Walking John, the ghost my uncle was likely here to see," I said. "Well, prepare yourself. I've done more than that— I've encountered him. Walking John is real."

Ten

Drew Merriken sat quiet, his tea cooling, as I told my story. He did not interrupt. I could not help but think this to his credit, for the more I spoke, the more insane and outlandish I sounded. Still, there was no help for it, as all of it was true.

When I finished, he stood and paced, his arms crossed. "I'd like to come to Barrow House," he said in the blunt way I was beginning to recognize. "There may be some evidence there to tell me what happened."

"I just told you what happened," I said quietly.

"Jillian." He looked at me. "You did not encounter a ghost last night."

"I very much disagree."

"It may have been nothing. You may have imagined it." He ignored my flush of anger and continued. "But what concerns me is that someone may have been trying to scare you."

I was incredulous. "Someone trying to *scare* me?"

"There's already a legend of a ghost in Rothewell. What if someone was trying to frighten you off?"

"I can't believe you're saying this. Are you suggesting that one of my neighbors came to my house last night and pretended to be a ghost, so I would run away?"

"It nearly worked, did it not?"

"Inspector, the gate *flew open*. There was nothing there. I *saw* it."

"It was the middle of a windstorm."

"A storm that opens latches?"

"It may not have been closed correctly in the first place. Did you open that gate at any point during the day?"

I was silent, thinking of my visit from Mrs. Kates and her daughter, my walk with William Moorcock.

"Admit it, Jillian," he said. "Everything you encountered has a logical explanation."

I stood and picked up my hat and gloves with a jerky motion. I was strangely, deeply hurt and suddenly felt very alone. "I thought . . . I don't know what I thought. I suppose Sultana is my only witness."

"Who is Sultana?"

"The cat."

"Well, as I can't interview a cat, I'll settle for looking around Barrow House. Let me get my things."

We left a few moments later, passing the disapproving Mrs. Ebury in the front foyer. We drove in our separate motorcars back to Rothewell. The look in the inspector's eyes as I'd spoken of the ghost, one of wariness and a sort of pity, had struck me, and I thought that Toby must have seen that look from other people a great many times in his life.

I entered Barrow House through the front door, but he didn't follow. When I opened the kitchen door, I found he'd already gone 'round the house to the garden. "Stand where you are, if you would," he said through the doorway. "I need to see any footprints back here."

The back garden was now lit with the thinning autumn sun,

but the evidence of last night was everywhere. The gate was opened, the flowerpot spilled and overturned, the shutters over the library crookedly fastened. I stood in the kitchen and felt the eeriness wash over me again.

Drew called a question to me, and I managed to reply. We went over everything in my story, step by step, the two of us shouting back and forth: the crash, my steps out the door to the shutter, the cut on my thumb, the steps back.

At the doorway again he bent to examine the stoop, and I stepped outside to peer over his shoulder.

"I told you to stay still," he said without looking at me.

I didn't bother to answer. For a moment I was distracted by the sight of him, his wrists braced casually over his bent knees, the line of his dark back. Then I saw what he was looking at.

Just outside the kitchen door, there was blood smeared heavily into the cobblestones.

My thumb throbbed. I took a step back. I remembered the shock and pain of the cut, the blood hitting the cobbles with a flat, wet sound.

The blood had been shining and wet last night, but something had pressed it into a long, rusty smear.

Drew looked up at me from his crouched position on the ground. "You don't remember hearing anything else?" he said gravely. "Footsteps? Any other noise?"

I shook my head.

He rose in one graceful, effortless motion. "Stay here." He strode to the back garden gate, which still stood open, and disappeared.

I stepped out onto the cobbles, avoiding the blood. Birds called to one another lazily. The sea was a distant rush, almost indistinguishable from the wind. The air smelled fresh, washed clean after the storm. I stared at the overturned flowerpot. It had been upright yesterday afternoon, when I had met William Moorcock and his dog; it must have been overturned by Walking John last night, but I had not heard it. Suddenly I understood, or thought I did, with a sickening chill. It began to make an awful kind of sense.

Drew returned, his jaw set in frustration. I didn't need to ask whether he had found any illuminating tracks. He approached me and looked down at me from under the elegant brim of his hat.

"If it was a ghost," he said, "then why are you staying here? Why not leave?"

"You can't be serious. My uncle was murdered."

"Yes, and that's what I'm here for. To find out who did it. You can go. You *should* go."

"I'm not leaving," I said.

His face was set in hard lines. "Well, what if this thing"—he gestured vaguely with a hand toward the garden, the woods—"whatever it is, comes again tonight?"

I swallowed. "It may. But I've figured something out. The flowerpot." I nodded toward it. "The wind could not have knocked that over, no matter how strong. It's far too heavy."

A muscle in his jaw twitched. "I know."

"It turned the pot over," I said. "Deliberately, while I was in the library. But it was storming, and I didn't hear. So it broke the shutter, and then he—it—left the garden. Do you see?"

"See what?"

"It was luring me. It waited until I came outside, and then it came back. It lured me deliberately. Because it can't come in. It wanted me to come out, because it can't get in the house."

A grim sort of horror overcame his expression, and for a

second—just that second—I saw him teeter on the brink of believing. "You're talking about some kind of intelligence."

"Yes, I think I am. I think the local ghost is more than just a legend. And I think my uncle knew it as well."

He looked back at the gate, seeming to consider this. I thought I'd get another lecture on the impossibility of it all, or the precarious state of my psyche, but when he turned to me again his demeanor had started to change. He had a spark of interest about him, instinctive and unthinking, like a well-trained dog who hears the flap of wings in the bushes.

"All right, I'll admit it's interesting," he said. "You're a hellishly impossible girl, and I could get laughed out of Scotland Yard, but for some reason—God knows why—I'm game. What do we do next, then?"

I remembered my conversation with Rachel Moorcock. She'd mentioned her brother-in-law, William, but she'd also said something else about the vicar: *He's our local historian. If your uncle wanted to know about Walking John, he'd likely start there.*

"I'd like to introduce myself to the vicar," I said to Inspector Merriken. "Would you like to come?"

Eleven

The front door of the vicarage was answered by a woman of striking height and spareness, with short-cropped hair. She was over forty, and her dress of the current style—flat in front, with a sash circling below the waist—accentuated her wide, boyish physique. While correct according to the fashion magazines, it was not flattering.

"He's around back, most likely," she said when we had introduced ourselves and asked for the vicar. She smiled at us, her eyes crinkling. "In the greenhouse, I think. I'm his wife, Mrs. Thorne. How do you do. I'm sorry, I'd let you in, but I was just heading out to do the shopping."

Inspector Merriken removed his hat. "We'll find him, thank you. We're sorry to interrupt."

She shrugged good-naturedly. "It's nothing, believe me. A vicar's wife gets used to it. Aubrey gets called on at the strangest times. He warned me when I married him, and I've found he's right."

She directed us to the greenhouse behind the vicarage, explaining that her husband spent his rare free afternoons there. We found a glass structure, added onto the house in the space between the vicarage and the church proper; it was homemade, though well built and neat. Inspector Merriken knocked on the painted door, and when a voice called to us, we went inside.

It was a small space, full of gardening tools and smelling of fresh, humid soil. It was lined with two long tables nearly the length of the room, cluttered with pots producing all sorts of greenery. I knew next to nothing about gardens, but I recognized primroses, though they had no blooms, and sowbread; in one corner was a larger pot containing a bush of lush pink roses.

Sitting on one of the benches, bending over a clay pot into which he was gingerly pressing a bulb, was a tall, long-legged man. He straightened at our approach, and replaced the view of his balding head with that of a long, bony, kindly face. It was not unhandsome in its way, with a strong brow, high cheekbones, and a prominent jaw.

"Good day," he said in a deep voice. "May I help you?"

"I'm sorry to disturb," the inspector said. "Your wife said we could come 'round."

"Of course, of course." The man tugged off his gardening gloves and stood as loose black soil tumbled back into the pot. "I'm Aubrey Thorne, the vicar here."

"Inspector Merriken, Scotland Yard. This is Miss Jillian Leigh."

The vicar looked from one to the other of us, comprehending. "I take it this is to do with Toby Leigh."

"Yes."

Thorne gathered two rickety chairs for us, and politely motioned us to sit. I noticed he was several years younger than his wife. It must have been a challenge, I thought, for the lady to find a husband taller than she was.

"Pardon the mess," said Thorne, lowering himself on his bench again as we sat. "I'm not allowed back in the house until I've thoroughly cleaned myself off."

"This is fine," said Drew.

Thorne looked at me. "I'm terribly sorry about Toby," he said with sincerity that only a vicar could express. "He never mentioned he had any children."

"I'm his niece, actually."

"Oh, pardon me. Well, in any case I'm glad to hear he had some family, someone to wrap things up for him. When I heard he'd died, I thought I'd be performing his funeral service, but seems he decreed against one."

"He requested cremation with no service at all. Toby was, ah, not very religious."

Thorne smiled. "I gathered as much," he said with good humor. "His views were, shall we say, irreverent?"

"You seem to have known him rather well," said Drew.

"Not as well as I would have liked, in truth," Thorne replied. "Toby was a hard man to get to know. He seemed preoccupied; at first I was concerned, but I think that was just his way."

"I assume you know what he did for a living?" I asked.

Thorne bent back down to his pot and smoothed the soil over the planted bulb, though his hand was now bare. "Ghost hunting? Yes, I knew. He was here in search of Walking John. We don't get many ghost hunters here, and I was wary at first. We don't really like to talk about Walking John in Rothewell." He glanced up at us and smiled, then turned back to his pot, as if smoothing the soil helped him think. "He had to tell me, because he wanted to go through the archives, and I wouldn't let him do that until I knew what he wanted. But Toby wasn't a thrill seeker or a charlatan. He was a scholar, probably a better one than I am."

"Did Toby find him?" I asked, leaning forward. Drew gave me a look; doubtless he would have liked to lead the conversation himself. "Walking John, I mean. Did he find him?"

Thorne straightened and smiled at me. "Goodness, I have no

idea. He never told me about it, and I never asked. I never go into the woods, myself."

"You mention these archives," the inspector said, taking over again. "What are they?"

"Oh, that's a grand word for it, I suppose. I collect bits of Rothewell's history. It's always fascinated me, so I keep my eye out for interesting pieces. I keep all of it in an archive, though of course I'm not a historian, just an amateur."

"What did Toby want to look at?"

Thorne almost scratched his forehead, then noticed the dirt on his hand and dropped it again. "Well, he wanted whatever he could find on John Barrow, of course." Drew nodded; I had told him the story of John Barrow's death as we drove down the hill. "I have a few letters that mention him, dating back to 1799. There are also accounts that mention the smuggling trade here in Devon, and in Rothewell specifically—histories, you know. There is an eyewitness account of Barrow's ghost that I've kept, though I can't be certain it's legitimate. A few other sources mentioning our local legend. Whatever I can pick up, you know. Toby went through it all. That was the first time."

"He came a second time?"

"Yes. I confess that I don't know exactly what he wanted the second time. I was called away that day and I left him to his own devices, to look at whatever he wanted. By then I knew he'd treat my archives properly, and I had no problem trusting him alone."

"What about the very first time Toby was here?" I said. "Years ago. Wouldn't he have gone through the archives then?"

Thorne frowned, not noticing the unpleasantly shocked look on Drew's face; I hadn't told him what William Moorcock had told me about Toby's previous visit. "If he was here years ago, then no. The archives didn't exist at all. I only started collecting after the war. After I gained the living here."

"You haven't been the vicar long?" asked Drew.

"Only a few years, though I grew up here. I began the training when I was young, but then the war came. When I came back I was angry and reckless. Rebellious. I lost God for a time; I think many of us did. But when the calling returned, it was stronger than ever." He smiled. "That was the same year I met my wife, and I've never looked back."

Drew's jaw was set. He pulled out his notebook and wrote in it. "Would Toby Leigh have signed anything out when he was here? Left any record?"

"I don't have such a sophisticated system." Thorne's eyes followed the inspector's pen, obviously wondering what was being written down. "I maintain the archive alone, on top of my duties here."

The inspector looked up at him. "How did you serve in the war?"

"Artillery, 'fifteen and 'sixteen, until an unexploded shell broke my arm in three places and they sent me home. My shoulder still freezes up on me, and I've never had the same hearing since. Unless I'm very much mistaken, you fought as well."

Some kind of knowledge I didn't understand passed between the two men. "RAF," Drew said.

"Ah," said Aubrey Thorne, not unkindly. "We didn't see much of you fellows."

Drew cleared his throat. "No, I suppose not."

"I shot at a lot of German planes. I don't know whether I hit any of them myself, but I saw a few of them go down. On fire, mostly, and they kept burning when they hit the ground. No way for a pilot to get out of that. Not a very good way to die. A quick bullet to the head, we always said; that's all we wanted if we had to go."

"We got those, too," the inspector said.

"Yes, I guess you did. At the time, I thought it exciting, a grand adventure. A way to thumb my nose at my family and their expectations of me. I was impulsive, as so many young people are. That's what I mean when I say I lost God."

"I don't remember feeling adventurous," Drew said. "I remember wondering if I'd live through another few hours. And seeing a lot of men who didn't. I remember looking around in the evenings and noting who hadn't come back, looking at all the faces wondering which of them would disappear tomorrow."

Aubrey Thorne shook his head. "I was sheltered and foolish. This is a small town, and not much happens here. I joined up with Will—that's William Moorcock, whom I've known all my life—and we went off to have a grand, glamorous lark. So did most of the young men of Rothewell. Only three of us who joined from Rothewell came back—me, Will, and Edward Bruton. This town has never been the same."

"William told me," I said. "He lost his brother, Raymond."

"You've met William, have you?" Thorne looked at me, and his gaze took me in carefully. "I think he'd quite like you."

Before I could answer this strange statement, Drew took over again. "Just a few more questions, if you would."

"Of course."

"Where were you on Thursday morning?"

Thorne blinked. "This past Thursday I was in the church, perhaps, opening it up, or here in the greenhouse. I couldn't rightly say."

"Did you see or hear anything unusual that morning? Think carefully."

"No . . . no, I don't believe I did."

"Did Toby Leigh ever talk to you about being afraid of anyone? Of anything out of the ordinary going on? Of any kind of trouble he was in?"

"Well." The vicar scratched his head, forgetting about the dirt this time. "That's difficult, as I didn't know him well, so I'm not sure what's ordinary. But no, he didn't mention anything. No."

Drew made another note. "And where were you last night?"

This surprised Thorne. "Why, home with Enid, of course. There was a frightful storm last night."

"Are you quite certain?"

There was a long pause, and the two men looked at each other again. "Yes," Thorne said at last, and the warmth had gone from his voice. "I am."

"Right, then." Drew closed his notebook. "We'll be in touch."

Twelve

You didn't have to antagonize him, you know," I said.

I was sitting on the stone wall in Rothewell again, looking out over the sea. Drew joined me, handing me a newspaper-wrapped piece of fish he'd fetched from the pub down the way. He unwrapped his own piece and began eating it with unconcern. "I don't know what you're talking about."

"Liar. All of that 'where were you' business. It completely put him off. What was all that about?"

"Jillian, as a private citizen, don't question the motives or methods of the police. We know what we're doing."

"I don't think you do. I highly doubt that man pushed my uncle to his death."

"Do you? That explains why you're you, and I'm me. I suggest you eat your fish before it gets cold."

I took a bite. It was delicious. I thought perhaps Aubrey Thorne had touched a nerve when he talked of the war, and that was why Drew had reacted. "And do you really think the local vicar was prowling around my house last night, pretending to be a ghost?"

"I think that something is rotten in Rothewell, and it doesn't hurt if I put it into the local wires that I'm here to rattle some cages. By the way, what was that about Toby having been here before? And what else haven't you told me?"

"I didn't think of it," I admitted. "There's been too much going on." I told him quickly of my meeting with William Moorcock and everything we'd said. "William was the one who told me the history of Walking John."

"Interesting," said the inspector. "What else do you know about this Moorcock fellow?"

"What do you mean?"

"Thorne said he's a veteran. Is he injured?"

"He didn't look it. But neither do you."

"What does he do for a living?"

I frowned. "Do you know, I have no idea. He didn't mention anything."

"A veteran of independent means," he mused. "You don't see too many of those."

I stopped eating and stared at him. "You really do suspect everyone of murder, don't you?"

"Did you think I was lying? Suspecting people of murder is my job."

"And do you like it? Unsettling people with questions and suspecting everyone you meet?"

For a second, his features relaxed into quiet humor. "The questions, yes, sometimes. The rest of it—well." He lowered his fish and looked away, serious again. "I'm not sure I chose this job. Most days, it seems it chose me."

"I don't understand."

He considered his words. "I never thought I'd join the police. My father is a barrister, a rather successful one, and I'm his only son. He wanted me to be ambitious, to reach even further than he had—perhaps even to be an MP someday. So I set myself on the course to do the opposite."

I raised my eyebrows. "What does that mean?"

"I did nothing with myself," he replied. "Nothing at all. I loafed; I borrowed money; I got in fights with the other boys at school; I mouthed off to my betters. I barely passed my courses. My father was so disgusted he could barely stand to speak to me. Then I made the mistake of actually stealing money from his billfold, and he caught me at it. He told me I either got myself some sort of employment, or he'd report me to the police himself."

"Goodness," I said, trying to picture the scene.

He glanced at me, then away again. "So I joined the regular police force. I picked the police partly because it horrified my father—it's far too low-class for his like—and partly because, for whatever reason, they agreed to take me. So I went. I did all right, I suppose; I didn't get sacked, anyway. Then I went to war.

"The next thing I knew, I was flying planes. Thorne was right—it was a horrible way to die. You learned quickly not to get attached to anyone, not to ask their last name or where they were from or whether they were married, because most of the men ended up dead. The lucky ones went down behind enemy lines, never to be seen again. The unlucky ones . . ." His gaze dulled. "After a while you went numb to it, and it became a relief."

He looked down at his fish wrapper, crumpled in his hands. He seemed inclined to keep talking, and I didn't interrupt. "When I got home, the police were short men everywhere. I got promoted to Scotland Yard; I wouldn't have had a ghost of a chance before the war. My first case on the job, the body of a man was left in the road, shot through the eye. He was lying exactly in the middle of the roadway in the country, as if he'd been pushed from a motorcar. But from the blood spatters, we knew he'd been killed on the spot. So someone had pushed him from the motorcar, shot him in the left eye, and driven on." He looked at me again. "That was my first week."

"My goodness," I said.

"Indeed. It taught me two things. First of all, that the detachment I'd learned in the war was perfect for a career in Scotland Yard. And second, that despite myself I'd found the only thing I'd ever want to do."

I shifted in my seat, disquieted. "You can't mean that. About the numbness from battle helping you at Scotland Yard."

"Why not? I do mean it. Being numb has aided me, I think, in every single case I've been a part of."

What about your life? I wondered. *Your parents? Those girls who left messages at the inn?* But instead I asked, "Did you solve it? The man on the road?"

"Oh, yes," he said, a smile lifting the corner of his mouth. "The wife did it. Or, more specifically, she hired a fellow."

I stared at him, my hand lowered to my lap, loosely clasping the last of my fish, which was forgotten and cold.

He looked at my expression, and his gaze slowly closed up, the smile evaporating, the lines of his face growing hard again. He took my fish wrapper from my hands and balled it up with his own. "I've never told anyone any of that," he said. "Your uncle found that ghost, you know. And Thorne knew it."

"What do you mean? He said he didn't know what my uncle found."

"Certainly. And he was lying."

"How do you know that?"

He seemed surprised by the question. "He simply was."

"But you don't *know* it. You don't *know* when someone is lying."

His gaze narrowed on me. "You don't *know* there was something at your door last night."

Very well. "But it makes no sense. Who would want to lie about a centuries-old ghost?"

"That's an excellent question. Now you're thinking like Scotland Yard."

He wandered off to find a trash can. It was noon, the sun high, the wind clear and cool across the rocky beach, the surf pounding in a hypnotic, overwhelming wash of sound. I watched the water, my mind turning over everything Drew had said. I felt I should get up, that we should be moving forward and doing something, but for the moment I wanted only to sit there and breathe the salted air, looking over the water at nothing.

He returned, and I sensed him as he sat next to me, the large dark bulk of him in the corner of my eye, the faint scent of him on the wind.

I found, after all, that there was one topic I could not quite leave alone. "Are you going to answer your messages?" I asked him.

He had taken off his hat, and I could see the tips of his ears grow red, though perhaps it was from the wind. "I wish you hadn't seen that."

"That isn't an answer."

He shrugged after a moment. "I don't like too many connections. I don't ask questions; I don't get details. It's easier that way."

"Inspector—"

"My name is Drew," he said.

Just like that, there it was again, the awareness between us. It ran up my spine, tensed all my muscles. I looked down to my lap. I wondered, to my shame, what it would feel like if he touched me—a man who would want nothing more from me than the feel of my skin.

"I wanted to go, you know," I said. "To war."

He paused for a moment, following me. "You were far too young."

"Yes, I was. I was only twelve when the war started. After the first Battle of the Somme I begged my parents to falsify my age so I could go and nurse. Of course they said no. We had a raging battle; you've no idea how dramatic a teenaged girl can be. But in the end I stayed home, read the newspapers, and studied."

"I'm glad you didn't go," he said.

He was looking out over the beach, over the water. His hair was short, dark brown, and ruffled softly in the wind. He looked at my face, and something in his eyes turned desolate. "Don't," he said. "Don't romanticize it. Just don't. It was nothing like you thought, you know. Nothing. If you romanticize it, you'll just be like all the other girls, and you're not."

Edith, Genevieve, Mary Ann. I studied him, impolite, unashamed. "You're lonely," I said.

He nearly flinched, but didn't. "You haven't been listening."

"You are."

"Aren't you? An intellectual girl, at Oxford?"

It was a fair enough question, but he'd struck a mark, and I felt myself heat. "I have a very good life."

"Perhaps. But I'm not blind. You're an intelligent girl in a world that still thinks intelligent girls are unnatural. You may be at university, but I'll wager you know very few people who truly understand."

My anger and hurt surprised even myself. "I am going to graduate Oxford," I said fiercely, "and the rest of the world can go to hell."

"Yes, you will. And then?"

"And then I'll become a don, with chin whiskers and mannish suits, and I'll teach the next generation of girls to be as smart as I am."

He had turned toward me, and for a long, quiet moment, he did nothing but look at me. He was unreadable, unfathomable; I could see a struggle in his eyes and a flicker of feeling, gone before I could analyze it. Then, with ruthless ease and practice, he leaned in toward me.

He touched my face, his fingertips brushing my cheek. He ran his thumb reverently along my lower lip. My skin sparked and I sat frozen, trapped by the scent of him, the nearness of his breath. The rest of the world fell away.

His gaze devoured me, fascinated; it lingered on my mouth. My lips parted by instinct, and his eyes darkened, their expression shifting to one of deep, sensual anticipation, mixed with something else I didn't recognize. His hand moved to cup the back of my neck and my entire body responded; I felt the warmth of his palm with perfect clarity, as if he'd already touched me everywhere. I could see on his face that he was picturing the same thing.

He leaned closer. I thought he would kiss me. I had been kissed before, but the thought of those kisses now was only embarrassing. Drew Merriken, instinct told me, would know very well how to kiss; he would do it with slow, perfect deliberation, like a man who takes utter pleasure in his work. In that second, I wanted nothing more than to feel it.

He leaned past my mouth, to my ear. "If there's one thing I know," he said softly, his breath warm on me, his lips brushing my skin, "it's that life doesn't always turn out as you expect it to."

He paused for a moment, as if breathing me in, savoring me. Then he stood, and I was alone in the cold again.

Thirteen

17 November 1922. Bains' house, Southampton. Claims to be haunted by the ghost of a child bleeding from the mouth. Onset of the manifestation recent, within one to two months; appears bedside, making pitiful sounds. No wife to corroborate. When asked about recent deaths of children in the area, he recoils, does not answer; I will set up the instruments and see if I can communicate. . . .

I put down Toby's notebook. I was sitting in the library again, with the curtains drawn and the shutters tightly closed outside, as the afternoon drew on. I had opened the book to try to distract myself from the thought of Drew, and so far, it was working.

Sultana sat before the fireplace, cleaning herself. She had reappeared at my door as I came home and eaten more of my sausage. I had retrieved my silver-backed brush from my bedroom, and she had allowed me to attempt to remove the thistles in her tail; I worked them out as gently as I could, telling her in a soothing voice how wonderful she was. She reversed her ears on her head in endurance and silently agreed, until she informed me with a hiss that the session was finished. She then lapped the bowl of cream I gave her as I quietly stroked her shoulder blades.

Now she regarded me calmly, the comfort of her beautiful eyes countering the terrible things I read in the notebook. I didn't want to read any more, but I had to; it must contain the key to Toby's last days.

I turned to the last few entries.

16 October 1924. I have arrived in Rothewell. There is a well-known ghost here that is a local legend: one of the most persistent apparitions I have ever encountered; the legend is rather tragic. I have ever regretted that I was not able to do something for him twenty-three years ago. I am, perhaps, on a fool's quest to try to rectify this, but if it were not for my memories of this place, I would have come sooner.

This place looks the same, though I am much older.

I rubbed my forehead. So, Toby had not been hired, then; he had come here on his own. There was that question answered. I turned the page.

17 October 1924, Barrow House, Rothewell. Uneasy dreams last night, and scratching at the window. Already something is here. It has not lessened in power in twenty-three years. Seems to be focused on this house as the closest one to the woods. I wonder if it recognizes me?

11:20 p.m. I have set up the instruments on the desk in the library. All quiet.

11:50 p.m. All quiet, instruments still. But I am aware of something. Very strong.

18 October 1924, Barrow House, 12:15 a.m. Galvano-scope acting strangely; cannot understand the readings.

12:30 a.m. Sounds from the back door; something is in the garden.

12:45 a.m. Quiet again. I have the feeling I have just been investigated, and it has now gone away. . . .

I shivered. *Something is in the garden.* I turned to the next entry.

19 October 1924, Barrow House. Rothewell has hardly changed since I left it; it is still a quiet fishing town that dozes its way through the days as it has done for centuries, except that now many of its young men have been lost in the war. I have spoken to some of the locals, trying to collect background, including a visit to the vicar's archives. Though most are very friendly, they tend to avoid the subject unless pushed. I am getting a strange feeling, though perhaps it's my imagination.

Yesterday I set up a small table with a bowl of water on it in the back garden, as water has great power over spirits. I also took a ladder and attached several threads around the upper windows. This morning the table was in the same place, turned exactly upside down; the threads were ripped from the windows, though nothing else was disturbed. The bowl of water was missing entirely until I climbed the ladder to look for the threads and found it tucked in the crook of one of the gables, right in my line of sight as I climbed. It was still full.

Mischievous, I think, and a little hostile.

This is the Walking John I remember, and he knows I am here.

20 October 1924, Barrow House. I have blocked off my bedroom windows in an attempt to get some sleep. There is no point in setting up the instruments again, as I already know what they will record. There are sounds, but I sleep through them, though I have bursts of awful dreams. He has overturned the table again, and moved the bowl. I am well aware of him now.

There were words in my dreams last night, though I don't know whether they were from the window or from the depths of my own mind. *Come out, come out.*

I must be ready.

21 October 1924, Barrow House. I spent almost the whole of the night outdoors. I set the instruments up in eight different locations, and took readings in each one. Twice I heard sounds that I did not think could be explained by local nighttime wildlife; both times the instruments showed nothing. I wonder if John Barrow's strength waxes and wanes; or does it strengthen only in certain areas? Did I imagine the taunting in my dreams last night? I must find my research on these kinds of manifestations.

I have marked each location and will return tomorrow night again.

22 October 1924, Barrow House. Another night spent in the woods. I have only just come home.

I saw—

I cannot write what I saw.

What do I do?

It does not escape me that if it were a ghost I had seen, I would have a better idea. I am already familiar with the dead. But it was no ghost. It was a person. A person . . . What does one do about a person?

There is not enough evidence to tell anyone. At least I was not seen, crouched in the dark, my torch switched off, the galvanoscope shoved in the bushes. But I did not see enough to be sure. My only option is to watch and wait.

Walking John made no appearance.

Later. I cannot sleep, so I have distracted myself with research.

I believe this manifestation is a *boggart* of a particularly powerful genus, tied to this location, mischievous and mean. These hauntings are unpleasant and difficult to remove. I must find a method. If only this were a simple ghost hunt. . . .

I have Vizier's book here. I will read until I fall asleep.

23 October 1924, Barrow House. Last night the flat of a palm slapped my bedroom window, which of course is on the second floor. The sound did not come again. He wants something of me.

I did not go back to the woods, but stayed in the house. I wonder if I shall go mad. I should never have come.

It is time to admit that Walking John is not the only reason I came here.

Elizabeth . . .

24 October 1924, Barrow House. The woods are quiet tonight, though something is watching, waiting for me. I believe I have the answer, though I now wonder whether I will ever get to try it.

As for the other, it was easier than I thought to get information. Perhaps I should have been a spy. I believe I can stop this. I do believe it. I have to believe it. If I could just find it—just find it—it could be stopped.

It's growing dark. I have no choice. I am ready—

I flipped through the pages, but there was no more writing. Here the journal ended.

I stood and paced. It was all there—the search for the ghost, the blocking of the windows, the use of the instruments—just as I had surmised. But I still had more questions than I had answers.

What had he seen? Who was Elizabeth? What had he been searching for? What needed to be stopped?

A knock came. I jumped, tried to calm myself. I opened the front door to find Drew. Behind him, night was falling from purplish darkness into black.

He'd changed out of his suit, and now he wore trousers and a wool sweater of dark brown. He was hatless, his hair tousled, and the air around him sparked with purpose. The sight of him brought back memories of earlier, and it was only as I came out of my confused jumble that I saw he carried an overnight bag.

"What are you doing?" I said.

He brushed past me into the parlor, his face set with intent. "I had a few things to do and a few telephone calls to make. But I'm finished, and it's all set."

"And what, exactly, are you talking about?"

He set down the bag. "Why, I'm staying here tonight, of course. With you."

I searched his face for a sign he was joking. I found none. Panic bloomed irrationally in my chest. "You can't. You're staying at your hotel."

"I've checked out of my hotel."

"You've what?"

He took a step toward me. "You didn't think I'd leave you alone, did you, after you were attacked last night?" He quirked an eyebrow. "I don't think the innkeeper liked me much, anyway. Don't worry; I've parked my motor away up the laneway and around the curve, so no one can impugn your honor. I've got to go back to London tomorrow. Scotland Yard has called me back, and I've got a few things to follow up on my own. But tonight . . ." His eyes gleamed. "Tonight I'll do some ghost hunting."

Standing in the shabby parlor, changed out of his formal clothes, he looked like a rough seaman, a dockworker. A pilot. There seemed to be no room for him. He was staying here alone. With me.

"You can't—" I tried. "That is . . . where you will be . . . you aren't—"

He paced toward the library. "Do I take it from the hash you're making that you're worried about where I'm going to sleep?" he said over his shoulder.

I flushed. "You wouldn't dare."

"Um. I'm planning to sleep in Toby's room, if it makes you feel any better." He caught sight of the instruments laid out on the desk, the open cases by the library door. "You've unpacked the equipment, I see."

"Yes."

"Good, I'll try some of it out. I'd like to see this thing for myself. And what is that?"

I followed his gaze to the spot before the fireplace. "Not what, *who*. That is Sultana, the cat."

"It needs a bath."

"If you've a wish for death, you can try to give her one."

Sultana raised her head and gave him a narrow-eyed look, which he returned with suspicion. "I think I'll keep my distance."

He picked up one of the torches from the desk and turned it on and off, testing it. He was toying with me. I stepped toward him, took it from his hand, and put it down again. "You can't stay the night," I said, panicked, thinking of my reputation, of Somerville, of my parents. "I'm not—"

"That kind of girl?" He watched me flush with embarrassment, and his expression hardened. This close, I could see the dusk of stubble on his chin. "I assure you," he said in a tone that was suddenly soft and dangerous, "I take this very seriously indeed. Something or someone was here last night, threatening you. I have no plans to lay a hand on you, but I have a case to solve. I'm going to do this, Jillian."

I was starting to get the impression that Drew Merriken was a far cry from the indolent child of privilege he'd once been. Something had changed him—the war, for one; the accidental discovery of a calling at Scotland Yard, for another. He was a man driven, who did not stop until he got what he wanted.

And as for me, what was I? An alien in this place, a unicorn.

Far from home. Why was I so worried about my reputation when my uncle's murder was at issue?

I stood back. "Very well, then. Would you like something to eat?"

∼⋞✕⋟∽

In the kitchen, Drew took one of the wooden chairs and watched me as I got food from the pantry. "You've stocked up," he said.

"Edward Bruton brought supplies." I'd been gone from the house since dawn, and I'd found the food left by the kitchen door; he must have been by while I was out.

"Ah, yes, the donkey-cart man. I've been looking for him. Seems I should be searching in your pantry."

I began to slice some bread. "He's only come by twice."

"And you've only been here two days."

"What are you getting at?"

He didn't answer. I arranged the slices of bread and some cheese on a plate and set it before him. He tilted his chair back and regarded me, standing there in my printed dress of white and dark green, still holding the knife in my hand. His gaze grew very still.

"It's the eyes, I think," he said finally. "And the hair—the curls. They're quite deadly. And beyond that, the legs."

I went instantly hot, my breasts and my stomach and my thighs. I couldn't move. I just let it wash through me, shock and a fierce sort of joy. Our gazes locked, and I knew he could see desire in my eyes. I let him see it. I had only ever known boys in my life, and suddenly all I wanted was to pull up the hem of his sweater and slide my hands under it. He knew it.

"So you've categorized me at last," I managed to say.

His eyes never left mine. "Not at all. You're different."

"Am I?"

"Completely."

I could hardly breathe. "I thought you didn't plan to lay a hand on me."

"I don't, damn it to hell. I don't."

"You don't like connections."

"No. Especially with inexperienced girls. Which, I admit, is why you present a problem."

I lifted my chin, stung. "Perhaps I'm not as innocent as you think."

He smiled a little, though it wasn't unkind. "With me, you're innocent. Believe me."

I flushed even harder and sat at the table, trying to hide my weakened knees. I took a piece of bread and cheese, busying my hands. "I'll ignore your boorish remarks for now. What do you mean about going to London?"

He tilted his chair forward again and took a piece for himself. "I've been called back. The Yard doesn't think there's enough here to open a murder investigation."

"What?" I stared at him. "I thought you were here to investigate."

"No, I was here to assess whether Toby Leigh's death was suspicious. I happen to think it is. My superiors happen to disagree with me."

"How can they?"

He tore into the bread. "Jillian, all I have are two cigarettes and a hunch. Rothewell is hardly a center of crime. Your uncle was a loner. The coroner's report contradicts me."

"And that's all?" I cried. "After all you told me about knowing something was wrong? You're just going to walk away?"

"Ah, well," he said, his voice tired, "I've told you, you mustn't question the police. We always know what we're doing."

"And what does that mean?"

"It means I'm going to London, just as they tell me to. But I have a partner, a man named Easterbrook. I think he might see things my way. I have a few ideas, and there are loose ends I want to look into if I can."

I had gone cold, listening to him. "You didn't tell me you had a theory. You didn't tell me."

"I don't. Just a hunch or two."

"You have to tell me," I said, not believing him. "Please."

"Jillian." He leaned over the table toward me. In his face I could see sympathy, but also the usual steely determination. "I'm the police here, not you. You have to trust me."

"Trust you? And what do I do while you're gone?" I asked. "Wait for whoever it is to come after me next?"

"Just do what you came to do," he said. "Pack your uncle's things. Keep your eyes open. Use common sense and that big brain of yours. Don't trust anyone. Don't take risks. And wait for me to come back."

"That's a tall order," I breathed.

"I know."

I opened my mouth to say something else, but suddenly it was gone from my mind. The hair prickled on the back of my neck. And something, loud and hollow, thumped in the library.

Fourteen

Our eyes met only briefly before Drew was out of his chair, moving quietly down the hall toward the library. I followed, keeping behind him.

In the library, nothing moved. The fire still flickered in the fireplace, and the lamps I had lit cast their own yellowed light. I glanced uneasily toward the window, but it didn't look like the curtains had been disturbed.

Drew pivoted, his gaze traveling the room. "What was it? Do you see anything?"

"No." It had been a distinct sound. A thump like a book being dropped or a drawer slammed closed.

"Maybe it was the cat," he said, but Sultana lay just where we'd left her, licking her matted fur with unconcern. Whatever it was, it hadn't frightened her.

I looked at the desk, and froze. "Look," I managed.

The needle of the galvanoscope had moved all the way to the upper end of its scale; as we watched, it lowered slowly, as if whatever had set it off were receding. Next to it, the thermometer had gone down.

Drew bent close to the galvanoscope and watched it. He put his hand on the desk next to the thermometer. "It's cold."

But my eyes were on the notebook. I had left Toby's journal on

the edge of the desk, open to the last page. The book had been ro-
tated ninety degrees, and now it was closed, facedown on the desk.
This, then, was the sound we had heard, the thump of the journal
closing. I reached out and touched the book with my fingertips. It
was cold as ice.

"Oh," I said.

A dim sort of electricity was going through me, as if I were
on the edge of a lightning storm: the charge that the galvanoscope was picking up. My heart thumped slow and hard in my
chest. It was a curious feeling, frightening, yet strangely alive.
Drew reached around from behind me and touched the journal
himself, and we froze there for a long moment, his body behind
mine, his arm coming 'round me, his breath in my ear.

His hand was large and wide next to mine, the knuckles
strong. I could see his forearm flex under the sleeve of his sweater.

With slow deliberation he lifted his other hand and touched
it to the back of my neck, under the ends of my hair. His warm
fingers slid up the line of my spine, as if tracing something he'd
looked at closely again and again. He was feeling the same electricity I was, I thought, the same breathless charge, and it made
him reckless. I couldn't speak as pleasure moved through my
whole body at that single touch.

I turned in place. He didn't move. We were face-to-face now,
my body against his. His hand was still on the back of my neck.
I looked up at him. His eyes were dark and wild.

"Oh, hell," he said, and kissed me.

I had been waiting for it. He kissed me deeply, unapologeti-
cally, attempting to be considerate, though his touch was rough.
I leaned into him, lost my balance, put my hands on his chest; it
burned under my fingers through the wool. I slid my hands
down, exploring, as I pressed further into him, up on my toes.
His hand on my jaw guided me gently, and he opened my mouth.

Something urgent and hot flushed through me as he ran his tongue expertly along the inside of my upper lip. This was Drew, then, when he gave up his precious control; this was the man underneath the careful exterior. Passionate, insistent. I was utterly out of my depth, and I didn't care. All I wanted was to taste him.

His hand left my jaw and moved down my back, as his other arm came around my waist, pressing me hard into him. I put my arms around his neck and pulled him closer. He obliged; he had me pushed into the desk now, his body covering mine, and he aligned me flush to him and kissed me more deeply with his tongue.

I let him do it. I more than let him—I kissed him back, inexpert perhaps, but greedy and eager to learn. I realized now that part of me had wanted to kiss him since the first time I saw him. And now I reveled in it, his stubbled skin rough against me, his arms holding me up. I made some sort of sound deep in my throat and he broke the kiss, leaving me raw and wanting.

"My God." He was hoarse.

"Do that again," I said, mindless.

He leaned close to me again, and again his hand came up and brushed my cheek, his thumb along my lower lip. He brushed his lips against me, a feather touch, and every part of me burned.

"Drew," I said.

He dropped his hands from me and braced himself on the edge of the desk, his hands on either side of my body. He closed his eyes briefly, his arms humming with tension, and I saw his control begin to fall back into place. "We need to stop this. Now."

I had forgotten about the cold book, the cold desk. I had forgotten everything but the smell of him, spicy and woolly and a little like bergamot. "I don't see—"

"Sssh."

His eyes had opened again, and he turned his head, distracted.

Suddenly he wore the expression I was beginning to recognize, the one of a dog on the hunt.

"Do you hear something?" he asked.

We listened, his arms still braced on the desk around me.

Upstairs, something moved.

He straightened, and we separated. The thing upstairs thumped again, a furtive sound. He pushed me behind him.

"What is it?" I hissed.

Before he could answer, the thump came from the top of the stairs. Standing in the library, we had no view of the staircase; we stood in the only light in the house, for as night had fallen, I'd lit lamps only in the library, and the rest of the house was dark.

Drew turned to the desk to grab one of the torches from the ghost-hunting kit; that was when we both noticed that the torches were gone. And at the same time, the sound from the stairs came again, distinctly metallic.

It was too quick to calculate, but somehow I knew. Drew grabbed one of the oil lamps and, motioning me behind him again, walked toward the stairs. "Come out," he said in a voice clear and even. "Police. Come out."

Something was rolling down the stairs now. I followed him and looked past him and saw none other than one of the missing torches, rolling down step by step in the dim lamplight. It came to the bottom of the stairs and rested.

Drew stooped and picked it up. We glanced at each other. He handed me the oil lamp, then moved the switch and turned on the beam of light.

With a cold breath of air, the lamp blew out.

Drew moved the torch; for a moment, as my eyes adjusted, I saw only glimpses of the floor, the wall, the steps in the circle of the beam. The light moved up the staircase, showing the worn runner, the cracked baseboards, the dust in the creases and seams. The beam came to the top of the steps and landed on thin air, motes of dust spinning in nothingness.

"Stay here," said Drew, and before I could stop him he moved up the steps.

I felt beside me for a hallway table and put down the dark lamp. My eyes began to adjust, and there was low, yellow light coming from the fireplace, which was still lit in the library. I could see gray, humped shapes, the square of the doorway, a glow on the floor of the hall. With a stab of panic I realized that, even with my adjusted sight, I wouldn't know until it was too late if something—if anything—came toward me. I followed Drew's dark shape up the stairs.

Drew turned as he heard my steps, and spoke over his shoulder. "I told you to stay there."

"I'm coming."

I couldn't see his face in the dark, but I imagined his jaw clenched. But perhaps he realized that I was no safer at the bottom of the stairs, for he turned away again without a word.

Upstairs, the beam of Drew's torch was the only beacon. I followed it, tentative, as we reached the landing.

"Is anyone here?" Drew's voice never quavered. "If you're here, you must come out. I'm the police."

The words fell into the answering silence like stones.

Rooms opened off the cramped hall: my little bedroom to the right, Toby's to the left. Farther down was the linen cupboard, the lavatory, and a spare room I had opened only briefly before closing the door on its dusty emptiness. As Drew turned the light on this last door, I could see it was ajar.

"Were you in here?" he asked me.

"No," I said, cold with dread.

"All right. Stay here."

He went through the door. I hugged myself; I was suddenly freezing. The cold came down my back, as if I were backed into an icebox. Icy, bone-chilling cold.

I knew I should turn.

I didn't want to. But somehow, slowly, I did. Perhaps it was the soft sound I heard that made me do it, one I recognized well: the padding sound of a cat's paws.

I turned. The cold crept over my face now, down my neck, over the tops of my arms. My blood roared in my ears.

There was only dark hallway behind me. But on the landing, where I had just come up, Sultana sat in the gloom. She was sitting on the floor, her tail curled over her feet, her head up, her ears perked. She wasn't looking at me, but at the empty space at the head of the hallway, her big eyes staring intently into the darkness. She cocked her head and moved her ears, as if following something. Her gaze moved; her focus stayed intent, fascinated.

Where she looked I saw nothing but darkness, a floor and the corner of two empty walls. Utter blackness.

I stood a long moment, not daring to breathe.

Behind me, I heard Drew come out of the spare room. The light of his torch shone over my shoulder. "There's nothing in there. What is it?"

"There's something here," I managed, my voice a rasp.

He moved the beam over the space at the top of the stairs. I nearly flinched; I realized in a flash that I didn't want to see whatever it was, whatever it looked like. But the light only illuminated Sultana, who flattened her ears and turned to pad back down the stairs.

"There's nothing," said Drew. "It's just the cat."

"No." The cold was dispersing, my face and neck tingling as it receded. "There was something—just now. Something was *there*."

"Jillian, it's all right. There's nothing."

I was shaking. Something was in the house. I had thought myself safe in here, fool that I had been. But there was something here, inside with us.

"I didn't see anything in the other room," Drew was saying. "It looks unused. Hard to tell in this light if anything's been disturbed, but I don't think so. I wonder where that other torch has gotten to."

He stopped. There came a creaking sound from outside. From the doorway to my little bedroom, I moved like a sleepwalker to the window I'd covered and pulled aside the blanket. I looked out into the garden below.

The garden gate was creaking open, slowly and deliberately, on its own.

"Drew," I said, for he had followed me and watched over my shoulder out the window. "That isn't the wind."

"What the hell," he said softly.

"Walking John," I whispered.

He didn't answer. The gate finished its slow arc and stood open. It didn't move again. The garden was still.

"What the bloody hell," he said again, and his voice sounded a little strangled. After a moment, he added: "The hinge could be broken."

"It isn't."

"It could be. There could be something jamming it. I'll just go down and check it out."

My throat closed. "Drew, you mustn't!"

"Of course I must. Look, it's a little eerie; I admit that. It isn't so strange that you got frightened, and the missing torch bothers me. But you can't assume ghosts are everywhere you look, when there could be an easy explanation. I'll check out this hinge and we'll see—"

The overturned flowerpot in the garden exploded as if hit with a rifle shot. The shutter over the library windows began to rattle. At the same time, there came a sharp rapping on the kitchen door.

We stared down at the empty expanse of the garden. The tapping on the door below came again—*rap, rap, rap.*

I jolted backward into Drew, who grasped my shoulders. He hesitated only the briefest instant. "All right, then," I thought I heard him say through my panic. "All right." He dropped his hands from me and left the room, shining the torch.

I stumbled down the stairs after him, as the shutters continued to rattle on a windless night. The knocking had not come again, and the kitchen was still. I saw the bursting flowerpot again before my eyes, the bits of pottery showering upward, the dirt spilling onto the stones. I grabbed Drew's arm as he headed for the kitchen door. "Please! Don't go out there."

He turned to me. Again I found it hard to see his face in the dark. He may have seen mine, though, for he only said softly, "I won't open the door—all right? Just let me try something."

I released my grip. He approached the kitchen door on quiet feet, leaned toward it, pressed his ear to the wood. No sound came from the other side, though from the library the shutter continued to make its unnerving noise. Drew listened for a long second; then he straightened and knocked on the door himself—*rap, rap, rap.*

A long moment of silence. Then a response: *Rap, rap, RAP!*

I may have screamed a little. My brain thought wildly of the words in Toby's journal: *Come out, come out.* Drew stood back, his face pale.

There was a workmanlike thump on the door, followed by a scrabbling sound that shot straight into my brain and skittered down my spine in jangling terror. The sound seemed to move across the wall toward the library window, like the clicking of a bird's feet but deep and heavy.

Drew and I moved in tandem. We dashed from the kitchen as one and down the hall to the library. There was a groaning sound from the window, and a high creaking; it sounded as if one of the shutters had come off its hinges. The fire was still lit in there, and Sultana was long gone, hiding somewhere, no doubt, her fur on end. She knew Walking John as well as I did.

I reached out to one of the heavy curtains I'd closed over the window, and paused. "I don't think I can do this."

"You have to," he said.

I sweated, and my hand shook. My arm felt like vibrating wire. All I would have to do was just lean in and open the curtain—like so—

One of the shutters was indeed off its hinge. It dangled and banged. Past it was the empty dark garden, the opened gate, the ruined flowerpot.

At the top of the window—the very top—a hand was pressed to the glass.

The hand was reaching *down*—from God knew where—and flattened to the glass. It was grayish white, damp. The pads of its fingers were rotted black. I glimpsed blackened fingernails and a ripped, ruined thumbnail. As we watched, the hand pressed harder into the window glass—as if being used to launch the body—and disappeared. It left behind no mark.

"Drew," I said. *"It's climbing up the wall."*

We heard the sounds move upward over the side of the house. Somewhere around the roof they stopped, and all was silence.

Both of us rasped ragged breaths into the darkness. The shutter dangled. The garden was quiet. The trees beyond the garden were leafy and still. The gate did not move, and the wind did not blow. From the top of the house to the bottom, there was now absolute quiet, as if none of it had happened.

Drew sounded as if he had just run a sprint. He stood tensed, looking at the ceiling, as if expecting to see something there. "What," he said finally, "what *the fuck* was that?"

"It's gone up," I said, ignoring the profanity. "Only up." I bit my lip. "It hasn't come down."

He swore again, creatively and shockingly, and I had to remember he'd been in the army. "Did it do this last night?"

"No—not exactly." I couldn't help adding, "I *told* you."

He didn't acknowledge this, but only looked down at his torch. "And how the hell did this come down the stairs? It wasn't that thing on your roof. What was it?"

"I don't know." My voice quavered. "I didn't know there was any—anything—in here. In the house."

"I'm going out." He looked at me, and with the light of both the fire and the torch I could see him now, his chiseled face like a charcoal sketch. "I have to go out there. You know that, don't you?"

I was shaking my head. "Please don't. That's what it *wants*."

"Jillian. I'm not just going to go to bed now and have sweet dreams. I'm going out there to take a look. Maybe I'll draw that thing off the roof while I'm at it."

"And then what?" I cried.

"I'll deal with that when I come to it." He shook his head. "A ghost. For God's sake, a ghost. I came here because a man fell off a cliff, and now I have a bloody ghost. Why wasn't a murder enough to deal with?"

I followed him to the kitchen door, still pleading. "Drew, please. Please don't." In the extremity of my terror, it was the only thing I could manage.

But he was unmoved. He was an RAF pilot, and when men

like him saw danger they walked toward it, not away. "I'll be right back."

"You won't. Please don't go. Please!"

He stopped before the kitchen door. For a second I thought he was hesitating, but I knew better. He merely squared his shoulders.

Then, in a single movement, he turned to me, tilted my head up to his, and kissed me fiercely.

"I'll be right back," he said again. Then he opened the door and went out into the night.

Fifteen

I watched him through the library window, past the broken shutter. He studied the smashed flowerpot and the cobbles, the light of his torch moving to and fro. Then he moved to the back gate and swiveled it, examining the hinges. He stood there for what seemed like ages, as my nails dug into my palms, but no sound came from the roof—or from anywhere.

Come back, come back. . . .

Drew straightened, as if hearing something; he turned in the direction of the woods, his torch down by his side. He froze for a long moment. Then, as I watched in horror, he switched off the torch, moved through the gate, and disappeared among the trees.

I shouted, but there was no answer. I had no idea what to do. He'd told me to stay; perhaps he'd just gone a short way into the woods. Perhaps he'd be back directly, and all I had to do was wait.

I couldn't look through the window anymore—the memory of that sickening hand kept coming back, and I had no desire to see anything lower itself back down—so I went to the kitchen. I couldn't make tea. I couldn't even pace. I sat at the kitchen table, staring at nothing, and waited.

Nothing moved in the house. Whatever had teased us with the torches had disappeared or was quiet; still, I couldn't bear to leave the kitchen table to find a lamp and light it. And so I sat.

After an hour, I had to admit Drew wasn't coming back. I had a very large problem—whether to wait, or whether to go out after him. I pressed my hands to my face and rubbed my eyes with my fingertips. That thing was hunting me—it wanted something of me, just as it had wanted something of Toby. It was trying to lure me outside; it had already succeeded with Drew. To go out there could well be the last piece of foolishness I would ever perform.

I thought of the way Drew had straightened, listening, then walked away. What better way to lure me outside than to draw Drew where I would follow? To use him as bait? It was a hunter's trick, was it not?

Mischievous, and a little hostile.

Still, I stood. I wanted my coat, but there was no way I was going to feel my way through the dark to the front hall to find it. I had no time to lose, anyway. The seconds were going by. My dress and shoes would have to do.

I closed my eyes. I would have to be quick and quiet. I would have to be aware. I would have to be clever. I opened the kitchen door.

The night was chilled and crisp, the air clear, as if everything were etched in ink. I ran lightly across the cobbles and out the opened gate, taking the path that Drew had taken, by my nearest guess. I had no idea which direction he had gone once he left my sight, but I kept going as the trees got thicker and thicker, roughly the same way William Moorcock had taken me on our walk. I heard no sound behind me.

After a moment, I could do nothing but stop and get my bearings, silently catching my breath. Barrow House was behind me, past the dark edge of the trees; beyond it was the steep descent to Rothewell. To my left, the woods skirting the cliff made the descent toward Blood Moon Bay—the tangled, impenetrable green I'd seen from the vantage point William had shown me. I plunged ahead.

Far to my left, a light came as a pinpoint through the trees. It waxed, as if someone had turned up a wick or opened a lantern gate, and then it waned again.

I stood frozen. After a moment, the light came again, steady, from the same place. So it wasn't a lantern being carried; it was sitting somewhere, stationary. I remembered William's words—*a signal house, where John kept his lantern. He'd light it on nights when a ship was due to come in.* That must be it. If Drew had seen it, he would have gone toward it.

But he could not have seen the light all the way from the back garden. I hesitated, wondering what to do.

From far behind me came a furtive sound. It came quietly, through the trees, and was still again. The familiar creak of my back garden gate.

I ran. I plunged headlong through the trees, unheeding of where I was going, just trying to get away. My feet found a narrow path, and I followed it. It rose as I ran, taking me on an incline, and the sound of the crashing sea came louder.

The trees thinned, then vanished. And I stopped.

I was at the crest of the cliff where it thrust up from the sea. Below me, the buildings of Rothewell's High Street were laid out like children's toys. The water was vast and dark far below, churning.

This was the place where my uncle had gone over the cliff.

I took a step back. The wind stung my cheeks, pulled my hair. Toby had died here; someone had pushed him. He had gone over the edge, and down, down. . . .

If something had lured Drew to the cliff . . . If he hadn't been careful—

I backed into the trees again and changed direction. This time I ran toward the light, by some unthinking instinct. The trees thickened around me again, the green world damp with the onset of an English autumn night. I could barely see my own feet, and at first I flailed clumsily, my feet slipping; then I fell into a rhythm, focused on the light through the trees, on my breathing, on not falling. I briefly thought I could have used a torch—but of course, the light would have given me dead away. I thought of Drew, deliberately turning his torch off when he went into the woods.

Now I came to the same clearing William and I had come to in our walk, looking down the slope toward Blood Moon Bay. I couldn't see the beach in the dark, but I could hear the heavy sound of the water, and I inhaled the salty air down my throat. The light came and went again, more clearly now, set on a promontory where it could be easily seen from the water. I had to find my way around to it without descending to the beach, and I had no bearings in the dark.

I wasted precious minutes fighting my way through a thick patch of bush, then moving up and down, trying to see a way through. There seemed to be no path. I got caught in thorns, had to extricate myself, and made a horrible amount of noise; I paused, gasping. Behind me, a branch cracked—far away, but unmistakable.

I bent, grasped my knees. He was coming. My mind blanked, as a mouse's must when the shadow of an owl flies overhead. I had no ideas. I had no thoughts. I could only think to run, to hide, and I did not know where.

In the dimness, as I began to sink into helpless panic, I spotted a path. It was cut deep into the earth, the slope crumbling and rocky, and it was going the wrong way, but I took it.

And suddenly, as I moved, I was silent. There must be some buried instinct deep inside the human mind that understands the hunter and the hunted. Mine awoke now, and my mind and body were in perfect tandem, my feet slipping quietly over the gravelly stones of the path, stepping past roots, my legs tireless, my eyes trained on the ground. I slid through the night like a shadow.

The path was taking me down the slope, toward Blood Moon Bay. I had no thought past that, no thought past getting away from the predator behind me. I had made it nearly halfway down the long, steep wooded slope when I heard the crumble of gravel far behind me. So he was at the head of the path, then, and following me down.

Again, my instinct flew. I ducked off the path and jagged sideways into the trees for cover.

This slowed my progress, but this way, he didn't know which direction I was going, and he would have to find me in the woods. I moved softly from tree to tree, my steps light on the mossy ground. I paused at times, hidden by a particularly large trunk, listening, getting my bearings. I was not in full-out flight now. I was an animal in stealthy retreat, trying to outwit its hunter.

And at each pause, I listened for Drew. A voice, a footstep, a shout—anything. Nothing came.

I found I was making my way, slowly and by zigzag, down toward the water of Blood Moon Bay. The sound of the surf was unmistakable, the sea air becoming thicker. I could get my bearings there, find another way up toward the signal house, and maybe look for a sign of Drew. My pace was slow and steady, silent and clear. There was no way anyone—anything—could track me.

In the end, I got nearly to the bottom.

The trees thinned, and I could now see dim light from the bright, full moon overhead. And I suddenly realized my mistake. If I moved out of my cover, I'd be exposed in the moonlight. There was nowhere else to go.

I stopped and nearly stumbled; I grabbed a nearby branch, and it snapped. Behind me, something began to crash through the trees.

I ran. I threw all caution and silence to the wind and ran, my feet flying, making careless sounds, the brambles scratching my legs. I screamed Drew's name, then screamed it again. There was no answer.

I came to the ragged edge of the trees and broke through toward the beach, heedless. The ground here was littered with broken branches and driftwood, overgrown with low weeds and vines. I wove and leaped obstacle after obstacle. "Drew!" I screamed.

The beach opened before me, the water dark as oil, the horizon suddenly wide and undulating in the sea's endless motion. A cold wind tore at my hair, smarted on my cheeks. I ran down the beach, toward the water. "Drew!"

My body went cold; my jaw froze; my spine seized. I was gripped with the terror from the night before in the kitchen, the same helpless fear I had felt leaning against the door. It was electrifying terror in my arms, my legs, the palms of my hands. I whirled and looked wildly along the edge of the trees. A fallen branch flew upward as if flung or kicked by a powerful foot. There was nothing there.

"Who are you?" I screamed into the wind.

There was no answer, only the cold moonlight, the wind whipping my hair into my eyes, the freezing sweat on my back. I had my back to the water now, truly cornered. I looked back and forth again, back and forth, along the line of trees.

"What do you want?" I screamed, so hard I felt a painful rasp in my throat. I was bent almost double by the effort.

Again, it did not answer.

I was nearly sobbing now, I was so afraid. "*Who are you?*" I screamed again, my voice cracking and rasping this time. "Answer me!"

It listened. I knew it did. I took a breath to scream again, when something touched me. I jumped and let out a sound that was unholy, but it was a warm touch, a human hand on my shoulder. I turned, and Drew was there.

"Jillian," he said, grasping my shoulders. "We're getting out of here. Now."

"Did you see it?" I gasped. "Can you see it?"

He shook his head. His hair was damp. A sheen of sweat shone on his throat. "Move," he said, pulling my arm.

I let myself be pulled, but he stopped, stilled. He was looking at something behind me. His face bore no expression. I turned and followed his gaze back toward the water.

My footprints were there, in the dark sand. And Drew's were there, larger, coming toward mine. Behind both sets, just where the water lapped the shore, was a third set. It was unmistakably two human feet, standing still. There were no prints leading to them and no prints leading away.

The prints faced away from the water, toward me. It had been standing behind me, watching me as I screamed into the wind.

Drew moved closer, bent down. I was still locked in terror, but whatever it had been was gone. I jerked my legs into motion and followed him.

The surf was washing the prints away. Next to them were words, also being swallowed by the water:

MAKE M

The other letters were already gone. Water washed into the footprints, filling their hollows. I noticed the prints had a large,

V-shaped gap between the big toes and the others; then the foot-prints were gone as well.

Drew took my arm again, and I let him pull me. But the sight of those prints never left my vision as we made our way back toward the trees.

Sixteen

I washed my hands in the kitchen sink, letting the water run icy. I shook with exhaustion, and a kind of lassitude had come over me; the aftereffects, I supposed, of so much terror and confusion, the body and the mind draining themselves. The cold water brought my thoughts into reluctant motion again.

We had taken the track back through the woods and up the slope. I realized, once I was no longer in the grip of terror, that the path I had found must be a smuggler's track, cut deep into the earth so it would be easier for travelers to remain unseen. This must once have been the route used to haul cargo from the beach.

The woods had been quiet on the way back, cold and peaceful, the full moon peering through the treetops. Whatever had chased me on the downward journey had disappeared.

I twisted off the water now and turned to face Drew. He was leaning a shoulder against the kitchen door, where he'd pushed it closed, as if he'd momentarily lost the strength to go farther. Our eyes met for a second; then both of us looked away.

"Are you all right?" he said.

I realized my hands were dripping at my sides, so I picked up a rough towel and dried them, dabbing around the bandage on my thumb. "Yes."

He took my bandaged hand by the wrist. "I should check this. Change the dressing."

"What was it?" I said. "What was that writing? What was it trying to say?"

"I don't know." His hand moved up my arm. "You're freezing. Where's your sweater?"

I found my old men's cardigan hanging on the back of a chair and slid it on, wrapping it around me. Drew turned to leave, but on impulse I grabbed his arm and leaned into him, pressing my cheek into the wool of his sweater. I just inhaled him, feeling the warmth of his collarbone under my cheek as he put an arm around me.

"I told you not to follow," he said, after everything managing some frustration in his voice. "I told you to wait."

"You were gone too long. I was worried."

"It wasn't that long."

"An hour," I said.

That gave him pause. "Was it? It was so strange. I suppose I didn't track the time properly."

I pulled away and looked up at him. "What happened to you out there?"

He frowned. "Well, when I was in the garden I saw someone in the trees, or so I thought."

"Yes, I was watching you."

"Were you? Well, I thought someone was there, so I shut off my light and went to find him, calling out that I was the police. Then I saw the light—there was a light. Did you see it?"

"Yes. William mentioned a signal house, where the smugglers would signal the boats from the water. I thought that must be what it was."

"It's likely, yes. Though who was signaling from there, and why, I don't know. So I made my way toward it, to find whoever it was."

"I thought you might have. I went that way, too. But I got lost and went down the slope instead." I swallowed, thinking of what had hunted me down the path. "He followed me—Walking John did. Did you see him?"

Drew sighed. "I saw nothing but a lot of brambles and wet grass. There is a break through the woods, where you can get 'round to the other promontory without going down, but it's a hellishly dangerous path, and I had to go slowly. I never did quite get all the way; there must be a simpler path, probably hidden, that is best found in daylight. In any case, I got turned halfway down the slope myself, and then I heard you screaming."

"It was chasing me," I managed.

He gave me a long, searching look. "I believe you. Those footprints—my God. I came right down the beach and I saw nothing."

"Drew, I don't—" I was near tears with exhaustion and help-lessness. "I don't know what to do."

"Hush," he said. "It's gone now, whatever it was. Get some sleep; that's the first thing." If he was afraid, if he was uncertain, he gave no sign.

"You're going back out there," I said.

"In the morning, yes, early. I want to know what's going on in those woods—because something is. Someone was lighting that beacon."

"It may not have been a person." But the words from Toby's journal rang in my mind. *A person. At least I was not seen. I have no choice. . . .*

"We'll see about that," Drew said. "We'll see."

In my bedroom, I pulled my nightgown over my head. I thought of the sound of the creaking gate outside the window, of Sultana staring at that strange cold spot on the landing just outside the door.

I don't want to be alone, I thought, crossing my arms. But there was nothing I could do, nowhere I could go in the middle of the night. And to say those words to the man in the next room seemed like a very bad idea.

My body flushed hot and cold as I remembered how he'd kissed me. How I'd kissed *him*. That moment had been madness, the maddest thing I'd ever done. I pressed my toes into the cold floor and searched through my feelings, looking for shame. I had been raised to behave properly, after all.

And yet what came to mind was my mother's story of the day she'd met my father. *I took one look at him and I knew*, she'd told me. *I ran out like a madwoman the next day and bought sleeveless dresses. Even though it was March, I wore nothing but sleeveless dresses until he noticed me. I froze, darling, but it was worth it.*

But my parents had fallen in love; they were still in love more than twenty years later. And my father had not been a Scotland Yard inspector with other girls' notes in his pocket and plans to leave in the morning.

A knock at the door interrupted my thoughts. I opened the door as my insides somersaulted. "Yes?"

In the hall, Drew held a lantern brought up from downstairs, which he had relit. He raised it a little, and the light sent shadows playing over his face. "Are you all right?"

I kept my voice amazingly calm. "Yes, thanks."

"I'd like to check your room, if you don't mind."

I stood back and motioned him in. He twitched the blanket on the window and glanced out at the back garden, then looked around the room, holding up the lamp. "It was too dark in here before," he said. "I didn't notice the bed. Who moved it?"

He would guess, of course; there were marks on the floor under the window where the bed had been. "I did. After the first night."

"And the blanket on the window?"

"Me again."

He glanced at me, though I could not read his expression in the dark. "You should try to get some sleep."

I shrugged. "I won't sleep."

"Jillian, whatever was here is gone."

Two things, I thought. *There were two things, one outside and one inside. And we were right in between.* I wondered whether Toby would have been afraid. I wondered whether what he'd possessed was fearlessness or simply the will to go forward in the face of fear; those were very different qualities, and I suspected Toby had more likely had the latter. It made me admire him more.

I crossed to the bed and sank down on the edge. I wasn't Toby. I hadn't his courage, his passion for pursuing the dead. I hadn't any expertise in solving murders or making sense of things. I rubbed my hands over my face, my skin numb with exhaustion and the aftermath of terror.

The bed frame creaked and the mattress sagged as Drew sat next to me. His arm came around me, warm and strong, and as always seemed to happen with Drew, my body responded before my mind could protest. I leaned into him, seeking his heat, and I realized he was tugging me down, laying me gently on the bed, tucking himself behind me.

"Drew," I said, faintly alarmed through my haze of exhaustion.

"Be quiet" was all he said in reply. He pulled the cover over me. He stayed on the other side of the blanket like a gentleman, fully dressed even to his shoes. But I could feel his chest against my back, his knees behind mine, his solid arm pulling me closer, and despite the layers of clothes and blankets, the effect was anything but gentlemanly.

"Do you know what happens at a women's college?" I asked softly after a moment.

"No," he said, nuzzling my hair.

"Nothing. Nothing, ever. Remind me to be missish in the morning."

"I'll leave you a note."

"I'm a fool," I said as I closed my eyes. "You do this to all the girls."

He was still. For a long beat, his breath stopped against my neck. "No. I do not."

I opened my eyes again. I could see nothing in the muffled light as the moon outside began to wane. "I feel as if the earth has tilted. As if I'm seeing things through a glass. Or as if I've suddenly had a glass removed. I can't decide which it is."

His arm was heavy over the curve of my waist, his large hand resting on the coverlet before me. "It's been a long night."

"You don't seem shaken. It's as if you've seen something like this before."

"Like this? Jillian, no one has ever seen anything like this."

Something about the tone of his voice alerted me. "Not exactly like this, perhaps. But you've seen something. Haven't you?"

"I don't know what you mean." Then: "It was years ago."

The war, I thought. *It has to do with the war.* I took a breath. "Tell me."

"I don't even know how to describe it."

I knew the feeling. "Try. Start at the beginning."

He sighed. "In early 'eighteen, we fought a battle near Va-lennes. It's just a tiny French town, and the Germans had taken it in 'sixteen. We took the town back. I was air support, along with the other fellows—our job was to fight off enemy aircraft, strafe where we could, and spot artillery positions and infantry movements while avoiding the antiaircraft guns. You could get good at it if you lived long enough."

The words seemed to come easier the more he spoke, so I did not interrupt, but lay there and listened.

"We'd taken the town," he continued, "and I was flying back to base. I'd been knocked in the head—nothing bad, but I wasn't feeling right. I saw one of our bases and thought I'd land for an hour, get myself straight so I could fly again. I was descending low, almost all the way down to the makeshift runway on the airfield. I looked down and saw four officers leading a line of Ger-man prisoners below me, taking them to the holding cells. They had seven men—six in tight formation, three close rows with an English officer at the four corners of the square. The seventh pris-oner lagged behind. I thought it was strange that they'd let the seventh man go like that. There are certain rules when you've caught the enemy—but still, you don't turn your back on him for a march, even if you've disarmed him. Even a prisoner who has surrendered can be a problem. But they all just marched ahead of this fellow, and he was trailing them at his own pace.

"I got closer—when you landed one of those planes, in an open cockpit, you could see the heads of the daisies. I could make out that the seventh man was injured. The neck, it looked like . . . he had blood all down both the front and back of his uniform, as if he'd bled quite badly. Something in the way he walked both-ered me, too. An uneven gait, not like a man in pain, but a little like a man on two false legs, staggering one step after the other. But bloody determined—even from the sky I could see that. It was doubly strange that they'd just ignore an injured man like that. Enemy or no, that wasn't usually the way we treated our prisoners.

"It wasn't until an hour after I landed that I met one of the officers in the mess hall, and I remembered to bring it up. I told him he'd taken a hell of a risk, and he might not get so lucky with a lapse like that again. He gave me a funny look and asked what the hell I was talking about, and when I told him I'd seen his seventh prisoner and that the man should see a medic before being put on the train, he told me he'd only brought in six. There were six prisoners, and that's all he'd had."

Again he was quiet, and again I said nothing.

"I know what I saw," he said. "I knew it then. He was there plain as day. I was close enough to see the blood on him, for God's sake. I saw the color of his hair. I thought about going to the medic's tent to see if the seventh prisoner had been admitted. I thought of going to the prisoners' quarters to ask the other men, though I don't know a word of German. I thought of going back the way I'd come to see if the man had just fallen dead by the side of the road—God knew there were enough men on both sides who had done just that.

"But I didn't do any of those things. I got some headache pills and took off, even though I'd been planning to stay longer. I wanted to get out of there. I told myself it was just one of those things. But I think the reason I didn't ask about the seventh prisoner is that I didn't want to know."

In the dim light, I could see his hand curled in front of my body. It was a hand that had held guns, fired them. It was not easy to reconcile the war with the men I saw at home. One didn't want to think that the baker or the banker had shot other men from the air, had machine-gunned them on the ground, dropped bombs on men as they ran, used knives and bayonets and gas. That the man in bed with you had done such things. Sometimes it seemed as if the men had all put down their guns only a moment ago, washed the blood from their hands, and gone back to work.

"You see," he said, "by then, near the end, when things really started to go haywire . . ." He cleared his throat, and his voice sounded strangled. "By then I had started . . . I started to think I'd gone mad. I was forgetting things—simple things. I was hearing things, like my name when no one had said it. I had dreams that didn't feel like dreams, and times when I thought I was asleep, but I wasn't really sure. The men who went mad—they were despised. Everyone looked down on them as weak, and secretly everyone was afraid of them. And I thought it was happening to me."

"And then you saw the prisoner," I said.

"Yes. I couldn't admit what I'd seen to anyone. I buried it and tried to forget about it. I did forget about it, until tonight. I had to."

I thought of his ruthless competence, the focus that pushed him into wanting no connections, and I began to understand. "Working for Scotland Yard makes it better, doesn't it? It helps keep the memories of war away."

"Jillian, work is the only thing that keeps me going. The only thing. It's why I have no wife, no family, just a few phone numbers on slips of paper. Because if I stop working, if I let anyone in, if I let anything go, then I lose my grip completely."

A slice of pain, deft as a needle, went through my heart. But it had been a long night, and I ignored it. Instead I put my hand over his and squeezed. "I don't know how you bear it," I said. "The war. I don't know how you go on."

"You go on, that's all. You simply do."

"My father says the war was a cataclysm created by greed. He says it was a bunch of old men rattling their sabers and planning the deaths of thousands like pawns on a chessboard."

"Jillian." His voice had a note of pained amusement. "I don't give a damn what it was. All I give a damn about is that it's over."

But he tucked me closer. I felt the scratch of his rough cheek on my neck.

"Go to sleep," he said as I closed my eyes, "and I'll be back as soon as I can."

Seventeen

I awoke the next morning alone. Pale dawn light was just faintly visible around the edges of the sealed-off window. I lay staring at the ceiling for a long time, feeling the warmth dissipate from the bed beside me.

Through the quiet hush of early morning, I imagined I heard the faint hum of a motorcar starting and driving away. Drew had parked his motorcar down the lane to avoid suspicion. I closed my eyes, listening. Was it even possible to hear the car from here, or was it wishful thinking? He'd said he would go into the woods this morning. Had he already done it? I wished I'd been awake when he left, wished I could have asked him, wished I could have said . . . But I didn't know what I would have said.

Sultana leaped onto the bed beside me with silent precision and gave me a reproachful look. I rubbed a knuckle back and forth behind her ear. "I'm sorry," I said to her. "Your sleeping spot was usurped, wasn't it?" She closed her eyes and listened as I continued to scratch, but she was still too miffed to purr. "What should I do?" I asked her. "He didn't tell me why he was going to London, not really. And I don't even know if he's coming back. What do I do?"

She had no answer for me. She let me touch her a little longer, her soft fur a comfort, and then she leaped away, waiting to be fed.

I sat up and swung my feet to the cold floor. The light was growing stronger at the edges of the window. I could still feel Drew's body against my back, his arm around my waist. I could still feel that kiss, that incredible kiss that I suspected had shifted something in me.

I rose to draw a bath and find something for Sultana's breakfast.

"Well." William Moorcock leaned back in his chair. He hooked his thumbs in the armholes of his vest, his thoughts ticking wildly behind his gray eyes. "I don't quite know what to say."

We were sitting in the kitchen of his small house. It was a tidy room of lace-trimmed curtains, flowered wallpaper, and matching jars of sugar, flour, and oats lined neatly along the sideboard. The big dog, Poseidon, slept soundly in front of the fireplace—his habitual spot, obviously, even though there was no fire lit. The scene was cozy and snug, and the place looked nothing at all like a bachelor's quarters, though William Moorcock did not seem to have a wife.

"I came here for reassurance," I said. "If you're looking for something to say, 'You're not mad' will do."

He smiled at me. His narrow, clean-shaven face, under its short crop of dark brown hair, was unremarkable—except when he smiled; then it lit with what could only properly be called charm. "All right, then. You're not mad, and that story was simply *smashing*."

My mind caught on the word *story*. "It's true," I protested.

"Of course it is. And it's bloody fantastic." His gaze dropped down to the table between us. "I've neglected to eat my pie, I'm so enthralled."

There was, in fact, an untouched slice of pie on the table. I'd come there unannounced, finding his house from the directions he'd given me when we met, and I'd interrupted him just as he was sitting down to a treat he'd obviously been looking forward to. As I told him the wild story of what had happened to me the past two nights, he'd listened without eating. "I'm sorry," I said. "I've dumped my problems on you. It's most unfair."

"Are you sure you don't want some? My sister is a wonderful cook. She likes to keep me stuffed."

"I'm certain, thanks." I looked around. "Is your sister here?"

"No. She lives with her husband. He has a small farm, a little bit of livestock. They have no children, so she needs someone to fuss over. With Raymond gone, I seem to be the candidate." He picked up his fork, gestured with it to the room around us. "This was our parents' house; when they died, it came to me. I could never quite bring myself to redecorate it."

"What happened?" I asked.

His tone was thoughtful. "It was a car crash, while I was in France. They both died instantly. My mother cooked me breakfast in this room the day I went to war, and when I came home she was gone. I think that's why I've never really wanted it changed."

Somewhere at the front of the house, a clock gently chimed the hour. I couldn't think of anything to say. "How terribly sad."

"It is, isn't it? It's supposed to be the son who dies at war, not the mother. Raymond got that part right, of course." The last of his smile faded, and his eyes looked far away. "I sometimes think I'll see Raymond coming right through that door over there, asking what there is to eat. He was always hungry, Raymond was. Mother said she couldn't keep the kitchen stocked high enough for him. At least, that's how it was before he married Rachel. What he ate after that, I don't really know. There are times, in the evenings, when I think I hear his voice coming from another room, though I can never quite hear what he's saying. It seems so real sometimes." He noticed me again and shrugged. "I already told you I say odd things."

"It isn't odd," I said gently, "considering I just told you a story that was completely insane."

The ghost of a smile came back to his face. "I suppose we're even, then." He cut himself a bite of pie and ate it thoughtfully, then looked at me again. "The footprints you saw. Were they longish, and narrow? Prominent depressions at the bones just under the toes? A large gap between the first and second toes, shaped like a V?"

I stared at him, speechless.

He nodded. "Walking John. One of the old vicars drew a sketch of those prints back in the last century—Aubrey has it in his archives, I believe. You really should take a look at it."

"Is this . . . Does this happen all the time, then? What happened to me?"

He began to cut himself another bite. The pie seemed to be cherry. "No. He goes through long periods of quiet; I've no idea why. A few months or a year. I've never known what sets him off—probably nothing. This time of year the activity increases, but even then it isn't predictable. We had two ghost hunters come through here just after the war, while Walking John was in one of his retreats; they couldn't find a thing. They were nice fellows, too—a man and his assistant, both veterans. Gellis, the man's name was, a rich chap, and the other one was Ryder. He was moody, that one. They had some first-rate equipment, and I felt a little sorry our local ghost didn't give them a good show."

"You sound so casual about it," I said.

"I realize it's strange. It's easy for those of us here to forget. I grew up in Rothewell. I was born here, and so was my father. I spent all my life here, and I trained to be a schoolteacher so I could teach here. I've never really wanted to leave. There are a few of us left like me."

"You teach school?" I asked.

He smiled, with only a little bitterness. "No. I went off to war, and while I was away, they closed the school. There weren't enough children left for them to run it." He sighed. "I know I should go somewhere else, but I've never wanted to. So here I stay."

"I met Aubrey Thorne yesterday. He says you two grew up together."

"Oh, yes, we did. We even went to war together. What a time that was! We were trouble, I tell you. But Aubrey hasn't been the same these past few years. First he met that Enid woman and went mad to marry her. Then he went and became vicar." He laughed. "Aubrey, a vicar! What a disappointment."

"I don't know," I said, a little disconcerted that he would refer to his best friend's wife as "that woman." "He seems content with it."

"Perhaps." He shrugged. "It seems dull to me. How is your thumb?"

I raised my bandaged hand. "All right."

"Let me have a look at it."

I hesitated, but he insisted, and in the end I reached across the table. He had just taken my hand and leaned over the palm when a voice came from the front hall. "Will?"

"In here, Annie."

A woman appeared at the kitchen doorway. She was older than William, but she had his thin build and his narrow chin. Her look, when she caught sight of our pose, was a mix of distaste and alarm. "Oh. Hello."

William let go of my hand and made introductions. Perhaps I imagined it, but his joviality suddenly seemed a little forced. "Annie, this is Jillian Leigh, who is staying at Barrow House, collecting her uncle's things. Jillian, this is my sister, Annie Hughes, she of the wonderful cherry pie."

Annie turned her attention from me and looked at her brother, taking him in with a sharp, critical gaze. "Is she bothering you?"

My mouth opened; I had never heard such a rude question in my life. William only shrugged, not looking at his sister. "No, of course not. Her hand is hurt. She came by to talk about Walking John."

"That nonsense." Annie dismissed the local ghost with a snort and turned back to me. "I hope you're not encouraging him."

"I may be," I replied coolly.

Her eyes widened at that. "I see. And are you finished?"

If her intent was to rile me, it worked. I stood and pushed back my chair. "Thank you for the advice, William. I'll be on my way."

"Jillian," he replied softly. He tried a smile, but his good mood had deflated. "Have a lovely afternoon." He did not look at me as I left.

I walked out into the autumn afternoon. Somewhere on the other side of the house, toward the trees, a man whistled for his dog, but there was no answering bark. I started back to Barrow House, anger speeding my steps.

I was halfway down the lane when I heard my name called. I turned to see Annie Hughes hurrying up the path after me. "Miss Leigh."

I kept walking. She caught up.

"I need to talk to you," she said, "about William."

"It was a neighborly visit," I said. "There was no reason to chase me away. You needn't act as if I'm Mata Hari."

"Miss Leigh, I'm only protecting him. My brother is easily upset."

"Is he? He seemed just fine to me."

"With all due respect, my girl, you don't know him as well as I do."

I stopped walking and turned to her, suddenly tired. "It's none of my concern, of course."

Her eyes blazed; she was a woman on a mission. "That's true; it isn't. I'd appreciate if you stayed away from William in the future."

I shook my head, annoyed again. "You may rule his life, Mrs. Hughes, but no one decreed you would rule mine."

She followed me as I started walking again. "You don't understand. William was in the war. He had a fever."

"Fever?"

"Yes. He got sick while he was in the trenches—headache, chills. They thought he was faking. They didn't know how sick he was until one day he couldn't stand and they carried him to the medic. He doesn't remember anything, so we know only what the doctors said. They told us it was an infection that went to his brain." Her jaw set in a grim line, one I realized was born of endless months of worry. "He was . . . They said he didn't know where he was, or even who he was. He couldn't say his own name. He . . . saw things that weren't there. Delusional. They never told me in detail what he raved about, and I don't think I want to know. It's just merciful he doesn't remember any of it now."

"That's terrible," I said, thinking of the kind, lonely man I had just left. "I didn't know."

"They thought for certain he would die. He lay alone in some foreign hospital for months. Our parents had just passed, and I couldn't get a ship to France."

"Of course you couldn't have. There was a war on."

"Do you think I cared? I would have gone anyway and nursed him myself. He was my only living blood relative by then. If they'd let me on a ship, I would have gone. When they sent him home, he was different. Fragile. I had to tell him about our parents, about Raymond, because none of my letters had gotten through. I felt like he had just come home from war, and I had shot him myself."

Grudgingly, I had to admit that her rudeness warranted a little understanding. "You're protective of him; I see that."

"He tries, and most days he gets through. But he's never been able to work," she said. "It's too hard on his nerves."

I frowned. "He told me there were no jobs."

"Do you see what I mean? Of course there are jobs. He just can't do them. It's too much for him. So he tells people there is no work." She looked away.

Now I felt only pity. "I'm sorry," I said. "I'll be careful."

But she hadn't softened. "Just stay away," she said, and turned back down the lane.

<hr />

The sun had risen to a crisp midday brightness. I took my motorcar down the steep cliff again, following the winding turns at my customary coward's pace, my foot barely leaving the brake pedal as I descended.

There were a few people out, and they seemed to recognize me as I passed, Rothewell being a quiet town, and my motorcar conspicuous. One man, busy with a rake in front of his house clinging to the hillside, gave me a wave; a boy of about eighteen, riding a bicycle up the hill with a rucksack across his back, pulled aside and touched his cap as I hogged the road on the way down. Once I had passed he must have continued on the ridiculously herculean task of cycling up the road—something only a boy of eighteen would attempt.

I parked in my familiar spot off the end of the High Street and made for Rachel Moorcock's shop. A figure stood across the street, sitting on the wall where Rachel and I had first met, staring out to sea. It was a man wearing a woolen pea jacket and dark trousers. He wore no hat, and I paused for a moment, recognizing his wheat blond hair. It was the same man I'd seen in the pub on my first morning, watching me from the window.

I wondered now who he could be. Both times I had seen him alone. Was he a local? A tourist? It seemed a strange, cold holiday. He didn't turn as I passed, and I kept walking.

As I continued down the street, someone touched my arm. I turned to find an elderly woman, well over sixty, in an old-fashioned flowered dress, tendrils of her gray hair blowing in the salty breeze. "I beg pardon," she said, "but you are Miss Leigh, who is boarding at Mrs. Kates', are you not?"

"Yes," I said.

"I thought it was you. You don't know me, of course. I'm Mrs. Trowbridge, the postmistress. I was just about to send a boy up to you when I saw you walk by."

"Send a boy?"

"Yes, you've a telegram. It just came in. Would you like to come in and get it?"

I followed her into the quiet post office, where a teenaged boy sat behind the counter, reading a movie magazine. "Did you catch her then, Gran?"

"I did," said Mrs. Trowbridge, "and she's here. Find her the telegram, won't you?"

The boy promptly dropped his magazine and rifled through a pile of papers. I turned to see the older woman watching me, nearly staring, a curious expression on her face.

She shook her head when I caught her looking. "I'm sorry," she said. "It's just that you resemble someone."

"Oh? Someone you know?"

"Someone I used to know, yes. But I haven't seen her in years." She gazed at me again, moving a little closer, unable to hide the avid interest in her eyes. "My goodness. You really do look like her. It's quite something."

"Who do you mean?" I asked, taking the folded message the boy handed to me.

"Oh, she died a long time ago. I'm not even sure you'd have been born. Her name was Elizabeth."

The entry in Toby's journal came back to me like a chime. "Elizabeth?"

"Gran, you're embarrassing her," said the boy.

Mrs. Trowbridge shook her head. "I'm sorry. What foolishness. It's just that she was dear to me; that's all. Do you have your message? Well, then."

She paused, smiling at me expectantly, and I thought perhaps she wanted me to say something, or open the message as she stood there watching. By instinct I put the envelope in my handbag, unseen. "Thank you," I said.

She hid her disappointment gamely and turned away. I left and headed to Rachel's shop. I wondered who Elizabeth was, but the telegram overshadowed my curiosity. I meant to read it once I got inside and had a moment of privacy, but the second the bell tinkled over the closing door behind me, I knew something was wrong.

Rachel's son, Sam, was on his stool behind the counter, alone. This time he didn't slide off the stool and run away, but only sat watching me from eyes with dark shadows under them. His gaze tracked me as I wandered the aisles, looking for a few tins of cat food I could take back to Sultana, as if I were a predator closing slowly in on him.

The shelves hadn't been restocked. Over the usual musty smell of a dry-goods store was another odor, something sour that was difficult to place. I came to the counter, smiling at the boy, who looked even more terrified as I approached. There was something very wrong with a store that left a frightened nine-year-old boy in charge alone.

"Hello," I said gently, putting the tins on the counter. "It's Sam, isn't it?"

The boy bit his lip and nodded.

"My name is Jillian," I said. "I met your mother the other day."

He squirmed, obviously wishing he could escape as he had the first time I'd seen him. "Mother says I mustn't go to the back," he explained.

I wondered why in the world she would say such a thing. "Well, then. You must do what your mother says, mustn't you? If you'll just leave these here, I'll come back for them another time. Perhaps you could tell your mother I was here?"

"Sam!"

She came through the doorway, harried, her hair escaping from the messy bun she'd tied it in. She was dressed as unfashionably as before, in an off-the-rack dress she'd obviously not had altered and seemed to have just thrown on. She saw me and gave me a smile with some effort, though I noticed her eyes were very tired. "I'm sorry," she said. "I heard Sam talking to someone."

"He's doing a very good job."

Rachel touched her son's hair, gently, as he squirmed again. "Thank the lady, Sam, and sit still. She's just said something nice to you; did you hear?" He said nothing, and she sighed. She looked exhausted, and her shoulders sagged with defeat. "You must think I'm a terrible mother."

"No, but I'm worried about you. Are you quite all right?"

She dropped her hand from Sam's hair. "Yes, I'm all right; I'm sorry. Let me just ring these up for you, shall I?"

But she had hardly begun when a sound came from the back—a frightful crash, laced with the sound of glass shattering, and a great, rasping, carrying male voice began shouting curse words I had never heard in my life and could only guess the meaning of.

The three of us froze, and I reddened despite myself, glancing at Sam. He was looking steadily at the countertop. Tired humiliation showed in Rachel's face. "I'm sorry," she said yet again. "It's my father. He's particularly bad today. I must get back there. Just take these, will you, and pay me later?"

"Can I help?" I asked.

"Oh, no, no—really. I can handle it. It's just—"

But more sounds came from the back now, and she left her sentence unfinished as she turned and hurried away. I hesitated for only a moment, glancing at Sam again. Perhaps it was a private family problem, but my conscience simply wouldn't let me leave. No one should have to bear all of this without help. I skirted the counter and followed her through the door to the back of the store.

We came to a narrow hallway lined with a few empty crates and boxes of stock. The end opened into a dark storeroom, where I could see a bare light and chain hanging from the ceiling and shelves piled with goods in the gloom. Rachel opened the only door leading from the hall, and I followed her into a small room, perhaps meant as a second storeroom, now cleared out. It was furnished with a narrow cot, a plain bedside table, and an old sideboard holding a pitcher and basin. Heavy curtains covered the only window.

On the bed lay an old man, thin and withered as a stick. He had pushed the sheet from his body and was dressed only in an old undershirt and a ragged pair of men's shorts. He was twisted on the bed, his hips and pale old legs lying flat, while his torso and upper body were turned in the direction of the bedside table, toward which he reached his arms. The remains of a drinking pitcher and glass lay broken on the floor, tossed from where they had presumably been placed on the table at the bedside, with water spilled everywhere. The man seemed to be attempting to get up.

"Papa!" Rachel exclaimed. "You've broken it! Look what you've done!" She tried to calm him on the bed, while stepping over the broken pieces of pitcher, as he flailed his emaciated arms and shouted another string of curses. I stepped quickly back out into the hall and hunted until I found a broom and dustpan. When I reappeared with them, Rachel finally noticed I had followed her.

She reddened as bright as a tomato. "Jillian—it isn't necessary, really."

"Nonsense," I said. "Of course I can help. I can wield a broom as well as anyone."

But she took both the broom and pan from me and started to sweep the wet crockery. This left her father unattended on the bed, and he began to twist again, shifting his arms and legs in yet another attempt to rise. So I moved to the bedside and patted his shoulder. "Please," I said as soothingly as I could in the midst of chaos. "You must calm down."

He turned at my voice and looked up at me. His eyes were

shockingly sunken in his head, his mouth trembling, his chin covered in spittle and straggling white whiskers. His skin was a grayish yellow hue that spoke of a man very, very ill. But his gaze, when he took me in, glittered. "Elizabeth," he said.

I froze. "I'm sorry?"

"Elizabeth," he said again.

"No, Papa," Rachel said as she stood with the dustpan. "This is not Elizabeth. Do you hear?"

"Who is Elizabeth?" I asked her.

"I have no idea; I'm sorry. He's been so ill . . . and the pain medications they have me give him . . . His mind wanders sometimes."

"It's all right." How truly awful this must be for her, caring for both a sick father and a young son, all alone with a shop to run. "Your mother . . ." I said.

She bent to the dustpan again. "She died three years ago. Right before Papa got sick. I must empty this. I'll be right back."

I watched her go. This was why she lived here in this tiny place, tied here, unmarried. Why she looked older than her years.

"Elizabeth," said the old man again, this time touching my wrist, his skin hot.

Twice in the space of a few minutes, someone had thought they recognized her in me. "I'm sorry," I said. "I'm not—"

His grip tightened, and he pulled on my arm. He was not terribly strong, but the panic I saw in his eyes gave him a burst of energy. "She's gone. She's gone. You must help me."

"Please. You must calm down, Mister . . ." I realized Moorcock was Rachel's married name.

"I'm George York. You know that. You know me. You must help me." To my frozen horror, helpless tears ran down his cheeks. "I know I can trust you. I see them when I close my eyes, Elizabeth.

She doesn't know—my own daughter. I never told her. But I see the men when I close my eyes, drowning in the sea. The men . . ."

He was in such agony, I could only bend down in pity and say, "Of course, of course I will help, Mr. York. What men? What do you want me to do?"

"You always were a good girl," he said. "You look just as you always did. You've been away."

"All right," I said, leaving for the moment the fact that I had no idea who he thought I was. "What can I do for you?"

He seemed calmer now, though his grip did not loosen. "Listen. The boat. Just burn it. I should have done it long ago. You can't do it yourself, I know—you must find someone to help you. I don't know why I did it—I needed the money, and Ray had enlisted; he went away, and—I don't know. I shouldn't have. But I did. Please, Elizabeth, you must burn that boat."

"Yes," I said. "I will."

"It doesn't matter anymore. I hid it for as long as I could—I should have destroyed it. I know that now. No one can have it, not now." Tears ran from his eyes, dripped down his temples and onto the pillow. "Don't tell my daughter. For God's sake, please, it's the only thing I ask. I can't bear it. Don't tell her. Elizabeth!"

"Papa!" Rachel had come back in the room. "I told you! She is not Elizabeth!"

I straightened from where I had bent close to the old man. My cheeks flamed.

"You mustn't mind him." Rachel's mouth was set, and if she had heard any more of her father's words, she gave no sign. "You really mustn't. I told you." She leaned over the bed now, tucked the blanket around him as he lay looking up at her. "Papa, please relax. I'll get you another pitcher, I promise."

The old man touched her hand, then lay back on the bed, his eyes closed. He seemed to sink into the pillows.

We left the room, and she closed the door gently behind us. "Thank you," she said.

"I'm sorry about your husband," I said. "I truly am."

Her eyebrows rose in surprise. "Was that what he was talking to you about? He did love Ray. My husband died in Belleau Wood." She sighed. "Poor Papa."

I looked at her for a long moment. I should tell her everything her father had said. I knew it.

Inevitably, she asked, "What else did he say?"

He was an old man in a shadow world—that much was clear—and almost nothing he'd said had made sense to me. Still, I had promised. So I hedged. "He said something about a boat."

"A boat?" She shook her head. "What a strange thing for him to remember."

"Why? Whose boat is it?"

"Ours—it's a fishing boat. Papa used to be a fisherman. When he got too sick to do it anymore, he gave it up." She shrugged. "It's strange that he would mention the boat now. We need the money, so I put it up for sale two weeks ago."

Eighteen

The blond man had gone, and I sat on the low wall overlooking the sea. The encounter with the old man had rattled me. I turned the words over in my mind, trying to make sense of them, but nothing came. I simply had no idea what Rachel's father had been talking about or how I would even begin to untangle it. I watched the boats go by in the distance, unseeing.

Elizabeth.

I took a few deep breaths. Then I dug through my handbag and pulled out my telegram.

It was from the solicitor, Mr. Reed. It stated that he had important information concerning Toby's will, and he needed to impart it to me in person. He was coming from London the day after next.

I felt ill. Was Toby leaving me money? I had no need of it. My parents had plenty, which Toby must have known. I'd been here for days, and I was no closer to catching his killer. Whatever he had left me, I couldn't accept it.

Oh, how badly I wanted to leave in that moment. How terribly, disloyally, and childishly I wanted to drive away and disappear. I was afraid. It wasn't just a physical fear, though I felt plenty of that; it ran deeper: a fear of what lay ahead, of what my life was becoming, of the choices I would have to make. I was painfully, almost paralyzingly afraid.

Mixed in with the fear, I suddenly longed for Drew. I wanted his arm around my waist again, his chest against my back. I could practically hear my mother's voice: *Darling, you barely know him. He's handsome, I'll admit, but God made lots of handsome men. This one is going to hurt you.* And still, I wished for him with an ache that was nearly physical.

I allowed myself this blinding self-pity for perhaps twenty minutes, staring unseeing out over the water. I did not cry, but I wallowed satisfyingly for that short period of time and came out feeling as if I'd quite finished. Then I stood and continued on.

I called at the vicarage, but neither the vicar nor his wife was home. The teenaged day maid who answered the door said they had gone to Barnstaple. When I asked whether I could leave a message for the vicar, the girl's look turned blank and a little panicked, so I rummaged through my handbag for a piece of paper and a pencil. Crooking my foot on the doorstep, I flattened the paper across my knee and wrote on it, the same way my friends and I always did when we exchanged notes on the common; the maid watched this with what could only be termed a gawp. I wrote the vicar, requesting to see his historical archives of Rothewell at his earliest convenience, folded the paper, and gave it to her.

She took it solemnly, still gawping a little. I smiled. The melancholy that had come over me had now completely drained away, and in its place was a feeling of readiness, almost recklessness. I was the daughter of Charles and Nora Leigh, the world-famous chemist and his glamorous wife, and the only way to face fear was simply to face it.

"Tell me," I said to the maid. "Is there a path around the headland to Blood Moon Bay?"

The bay looked different in sunlight. Under the bright canopy of sky, studded with clouds making their way one by one across the sun, it almost seemed like a peaceful place. It should have had tourists walking the beach, perhaps, or having a drink at a little hut of a bar. It should have had fishing boats coming in and out, bringing their salty marine smells and the shouts of fishermen. It should have had locals bustling about, bringing the day's catch ashore, trading quips with the fishermen, laughing and talking and smoking in friendly knots.

But Blood Moon Bay was blank and silent. The water was icy, the waves choppy, daring you to navigate a boat or—God forbid—set your own foot in the water. Through the mouth of the bay I could see fishing boats going by in the distance, but there was no pier here; nor did any of the boats come close. It seemed Blood Moon Bay was too treacherous and remote a spot to risk a landing.

The beach was dark and rocky, cold through the soles of my shoes. The wind stung my cheeks and brought tears to my eyes, howling through the trees that signaled the start of the woods and the slope.

I walked along the curve of the shore, my hands in my pockets. I had not bothered with my hat, and my hair blew wildly in the wind, my curls knotting themselves in the salty air. I found the spot where I had stood the night before, but the beach had been washed smooth by the tide. There was no sign of the marks, of the message scrawled in the sand, as if it had never been.

It had a dark beauty, this place. I looked over the deep, dangerous waters to the entrance to the sea, and it was easy to picture it: a boat slipping silently through as if through an opened doorway, sailed easily and expertly by a man who had done the route many times. It slid through the water, bold as could be, its captain keeping a wary eye on the light coming from the signal house above, telling him the way was safe and clear.

Easy to see it pull up just off the shallow shore and weigh anchor in the last of the deeper waters; easy to see men move out in small rowboats, pushing them off the sand until they were wet to the thighs, then getting in and rowing the last of the way, pulling up next to the boat, practiced experts despite the treacherous current. Easy to see the cargo begin to be unloaded, the well-wrapped packages splashing into the water: rum, tea, silks, spices, the barrels glistening black in the moonlight. Riches beyond most men's imaginings, all for a night's work.

Easy to see a small boy, his clothes bravely pulled on over his nightclothes, wanting to follow his father, taking a step too far, unaware of the power of the sea at his feet—a thump, a cutoff cry, his head pressed under one of the unseeing boats, the blood in the water . . .

I turned away, shivering, turned my back to the water, and looked up.

The rocks and driftwood, the detritus of incoming and outgoing tides, ended at the edge of the beach where the trees began. From there I was at the bottom of a gently sloped bowl of woodland, dense and dark green, rising up to my left and before me. To my right, the lip of the bowl sloped off, as if the potter had ruined it on the wheel, and the great line of land continued down the coast, beautiful and tangled. It was impossible to go that way, where the land itself buckled and broke up, where no footpath could go and, even if one existed, it would go nowhere.

No, the footpath—and there was at least one, as I had walked it—went up through the trees, to the left up the side of the angry cliff—or perhaps there were others, dug into the earth straight up the lip of the bowl, where, presumably, the signal house stood. But from here I could see nothing. The paths had been dug deep so they would not show through the trees, and so that men climbing them, carrying cargo, could not be seen from the shore once they entered the woods.

The boat, Rachel's father had said. *Just burn it. I needed the money.*

And Toby's words: *I cannot write what I saw.*

Walking John had lived in the seventeenth century, and smuggling had died out not long after that lively century was over. What, then, had Mr. York done, sometime after his son-in-law had gone to war, that haunted him so?

I want to know what's going on in those woods, Drew had said. *Because something is. Someone was lighting that beacon.*

I brushed the stinging water from my eyes in the wind. Was the bay not the ideal place for something outside the law? Both Aubrey and Rachel said they wouldn't come through these woods at night for anything. Most of the Rothewell locals probably felt the same. What better cover, then, for an illegal operation than a place where no boats could dock, and none of the locals ever dared go?

But Toby had gone into these woods. What had he seen? What, if anything, had Drew found? Would he ever trust me enough to tell me?

A ghost would be ideal cover, but this ghost was not a foolish old legend. He was real, and Mr. York, for one, would have known it. What would have made him go ahead anyway, knowing the bay and the woods were haunted? What happened on those midnight excursions—assuming they existed?

Oh, Toby. What did you walk into? A few stolen goods would not have rattled him so. *I have no choice.*

Perhaps they had been lucky. William said that Walking John had quiet periods. Perhaps whatever an old ex-fisherman raved about had nothing to do with Rothewell's resident ghost. But I couldn't help but feel that somehow the two were related—and that all of it somehow circled back to Toby and the way he had died. If only I could see all the pieces of the puzzle.

Seabirds flew in lazy turns overhead, their cries echoing off the cliffs. Far out to sea, another tiny boat inched by, intent on its own business. The sun climbed in the sky, indifferent to another day on Blood Moon Bay. The cliffs looked down, unspeaking.

Whatever had happened here, the bay had nothing to tell me. I shook the circulation back into my chilled feet and began the return walk over the headland.

Nineteen

I arrived at Barrow House. While daylight still held, I went 'round the back of the house and fixed the shutter again. Then I went into the library and closed the heavy curtains. I never wanted to see that window again.

I dug up the stack of textbooks I'd brought from Oxford—I remembered carrying them in from the motorcar in the rain, worrying they'd get wet. It seemed a year ago now. But a stern stab of guilt pierced my conscience. In all my life I had barely gone a week without studying. I had to keep up, no matter what was going on. The thought had a comforting feel to it, as if, by reading by lamplight until I couldn't prop my eyes open as I'd done so many other nights, everything would go back to normal.

I opened the first textbook and glanced down at the page, but my gaze caught on something at the edge of the desk. A battered book, dog-eared and used. Toby's journal.

I wasn't sure how it happened, but the next thing I knew, I had pulled the journal to me and was reading it again, going through it passage by passage, trying to understand the man who had written the lines.

I was utterly absorbed, my textbook forgotten, when a knock sounded on the front door. It was Mrs. Kates, this time without her daughter, inviting me to tea the next day. I accepted, in the torrent of her words hardly knowing what I was agreeing to.

"I am amazed you're still here," she said, as usual her insulting words spoken with the best good nature. Today she wore fabric primroses on her hat. "Who would have thought it would take so long to pack up Toby's things? He didn't seem to me like the type who had many belongings. He barely had a few cases when he moved in. But then, what do I know, of course. As I said, it's paid to the end of the month, so take your time—though not to the first, of course."

"I like it in Rothewell," I managed, just to get something in, though I realized as I spoke that, despite everything, it was actually true.

She shrugged at that, her brows coming down as if there were no accounting for taste. "It's all right, I suppose, though of course I married here. We locals are rather close. I positively despair sometimes of Julia's marriage prospects, but there are a few fellows about. I do my best."

"Why don't you leave?" The words were out of my mouth before I could curb their nosy impertinence, but she did not seem to notice.

She pulled out a cigarette. "My dear, where would I go? My husband left me the house, you know, not to mention this place. The rents do help keep us going, though to be frightfully honest we get fewer and fewer tenants. Your uncle seemed such a good prospect. I wish he had stayed longer."

She sighed, and I stared at her, wondering whether she could have completely forgotten that Toby's rent payments had ceased because he was dead. I watched her light the cigarette, thinking of the cigarettes Drew had found on the cliff top. She smiled at me, and the idea of this lady, tiny and perfectly groomed, pushing my uncle to his sinister death was almost laughably ridiculous. *That explains why you're you*, Drew had said, *and I'm me.*

Still, if Diana Kates had killed my uncle and smoked a cigarette, she would certainly never have done it without lipstick.

I closed the door after she left and went to the kitchen to make a cup of tea. As the water boiled, I thought of the silly thing I had said to her—but in a strange way, I *did* like it here. The afternoon had clouded and the house sat under a blanket of quiet, the gray light coming diffused through the windows, and the only sounds the far-off rush of trees in the wind and the call of birds. Despite everything, I saw myself staying here, seeing the seasons change, writing books and papers perhaps, taking long walks, having tea with neighbors. There was something about the air here—the smell of the sea perhaps—that one could never quite get enough of. It was a pleasant moment's dream.

I took my tea back up to the library. I stopped.

The desk drawer was open. I had been sitting at that desk for two hours before Mrs. Kates came to the door; I knew very well that drawer had been closed until the moment I stood up. But it was now unmistakably open.

Cold crawled up my spine to the back of my neck. I thought back to the conversation at the door with Mrs. Kates, the long moments spent in the kitchen. I had not heard a sound.

My hand shook, and hot liquid spilled on my wrist. I put my cup carelessly on the chestnut sideboard, not looking where I placed it. There was definitely cold in the room now. My nose was chilled, and the sweat on my neck was icy.

I seemed to have stopped breathing, to have become one with the still room, waiting for something to happen. There was not a movement, not a breath of air.

I stepped toward the desk. The journal was open where I had left it, displaying the same page. I took another step, and another, the impetus coming from somewhere deep in my spine, out of my control. When I was within arm's length I leaned forward and placed my hand in the open drawer.

At first, I found nothing but bare wood; the drawer was empty. I moved my fingers, and a crinkle of paper met my fingers. I choked a sound back down my throat and pulled the paper from the drawer. It was a small slip of notepaper, folded in half. I unfurled it in my hands. It was a handwritten note, and I recognized the writing as exactly the same as in the notebook that lay open before me.

Beware, daughter of Rothewell.

Something came over me. I jumped, dropped the paper as if it burned. I backed away, bumped into something, backed away again.

Now I did make a sound, a pained, strangled gasp, and with clumsy feet I turned and fled the room. I ran straight through the front vestibule and out onto the gravel drive. Even then I couldn't stop my legs, and they kept going and going, down the road under the soft gray late-afternoon sky.

❧

The kettle sang on the hob, and William wrapped a tea towel 'round his hand to remove it.

"So," he said. "There is something in the house. Go on."

I was sitting in his kitchen for the second time that day. Annie was gone, and though I was mindful of her warning, I could think of nowhere else to go. In fact, he'd seemed happy to see me, as if he'd been worried his sister had chased me away.

I was bedraggled and out of breath, my sweater pulled around me, already feeling unreal in the warm yellow kitchen light. "It's difficult to explain. It sounds mad, actually."

"Yes, of course. What you've experienced is not possible, you worry for your sanity, et cetera, et cetera. I think we've established that I believe you?"

The words had a sting, but they were said with humor. I took a breath and stared down into the mug he'd set before me. The prickle of terror still worked in my veins, and the cold sweat was only beginning to dry on the back of my neck, but I felt rationality returning. "Something is in the house," I admitted. "There have been signs, but I've been ignoring them or explaining them away. I think it's time I told myself the truth. There is something in the house that moves things, that produces cold spots, that leaves items out for me to find when my back is turned."

William stirred sugar into his own tea, standing by the counter. He did not take the seat across from me. "Interesting. Who do you think it is?"

I shook my head. "I had a theory—I thought it so clever— that Walking John was trying to lure me out of the house because he couldn't get in."

"Yes, quite so. Walking John is not in your house, Jillian," said William matter-of-factly. "He keeps to the woods and the beach; everyone knows that. Did you think Walking John was the only ghost in Rothewell?"

I stared at him stupidly. "I don't . . . I hadn't thought of it. Who are the others?"

He shrugged. "Who knows? When I was a child, there was someone—a man, I'm quite sure—who used to whistle for his dog in the back lane by the woods there. Every night around sunset he'd whistle, and none of our dogs ever answered. But they'd always look funny and stand with their tails up, as if expecting something we couldn't see." He looked thoughtful. "I always did wonder who that fellow was. I still hear him sometimes. Aubrey had an old rocking chair that used to rock by itself when we were children, no matter where his parents put it in the house. We called that chair the Old Nanny; I don't know why. Eventually his father took the chair out to the woodpile with an ax and chopped it to pieces."

I was staring at him, memory dawning on me. I'd heard a man whistle for his dog when I first arrived in Rothewell. And again earlier today. "All those people . . ."

"Forgotten people, Jillian." He shrugged again. The deepening afternoon light created shadows on his face. "Just as we're all forgotten after we're dead."

My brother is fragile. I looked at him. He had always seemed cheerful and kindly to me, if a little awkward, but now I saw tired depths in his eyes, the etching of long-ago pain in his features. Perhaps I imagined it, or it was the end of a draining day. But now that I knew what had happened to him in the war, I couldn't help but see him differently than I had only hours ago.

He didn't know where he was, or even who he was. It's just merciful he doesn't remember any of it now.

Suddenly I was desperately sad, my emotions swirling into a dark abyss of panic. "William," I said, my voice cracking.

He looked down into his tea. "Yes?"

I swallowed. "We're friends. Aren't we?"

He glanced up at me, and his charming smile flitted across his face with an effort. "Well, you've visited me twice in one day."

"No. I mean it. Are we friends?"

The smile dropped slowly, and he nodded. "Yes. Yes, we are."

"Then listen to me." I leaned forward across my mug of tea. "I think you should leave this place. I know you grew up here, and I know it's beautiful, but there's something . . . there's something *wrong* with it." I glanced around me, at the house left him by his dead parents, the kitchen decorated by his dead mother. "This place isn't good for you. Rothewell, this house—all of it. You can be a schoolteacher anywhere. London, Edinburgh, even the Continent. This is the twentieth century, William. There are wonders of the world out there. You could truly live life. This place—it's as if it's stuck in time, looking backward, where everyone lives with the dead. Won't you leave?"

He was watching me speak, and I couldn't read his expression. He dropped his gaze to his cup again and was quiet for a long moment. "No one has ever bothered to say that to me," he said. "That I could go be something. It was Raymond who was going to be something, not me."

"But you can," I said. "I realize it's been difficult—the war. . . ."

"God, no." He looked surprised. "The war was the only time I was ever happy. It's strange to say that, I know, but it's true. It was exciting. Important. When I was fighting, I had a purpose."

He didn't remember, then, just as Annie had said. He had forgotten the pain, the sickness, the months in hospital, the delirium. "William, I don't know."

"No, I know you don't. Most people don't see, especially women. Some men are made for war, that's all. We're born for it. I thought I would be a teacher, but it wasn't until I enlisted—until the moment my feet hit the ground in France—that I knew why I had never really been happy. Even though it was terrible, even though I could have died and saw so many others die—I still knew I had a purpose. After I came home . . ." He frowned, a fleeting look of confusion. "Nothing was the same. Ray was gone, and Aubrey got married. I understood, then, a lot of things I'd never understood before."

He raised his eyes. At first he looked as he always did, but as

I watched, something changed in his face—his mouth slowly drooped; his skin sagged; his lids lowered with exhausted anguish. For a long, endless moment, he looked like a much older man, a man who was gazing upon something he could not contemplate, and it had made him so tired he could barely move.

And then, piece by piece, like a wilted flower that had been watered, his face came into itself again. His eyes regained their intelligent sparkle, his chin lifted, and the smile played across his lips. "It's nice of you to say those things," he said, and his voice sounded as it always did. "But you're seeing it the wrong way. I can't leave Rothewell. Someday you'll understand."

"William—"

"No, no, truly. I appreciate it. But it isn't quite as bad as all that, really."

"It isn't just the ghosts," I said. "It could be dangerous here. Inspector Merriken thinks there's something going on in the woods, and so did my uncle. I'm starting to agree with them."

He raised his eyebrows. "Now, that *is* intriguing. I have yet to meet this inspector, though I've heard much about him. Where is he, by the way?"

"Gone to London. The Yard called him back. He left this morning."

"I see."

Something in the tone of his voice made me realize I'd sounded too casual, too intimate. I felt my cheeks heat. So much for discretion.

The corners of his eyes crinkled, but he did not quite smile. "Ah, Jillian. Be careful, will you? I don't want to see you hurt."

"I don't know what you mean." My cheeks grew hotter, to my chagrin. "There's nothing to say."

"There never is," he said. "Never anything, until it's too late."

Twenty

Outside, the dark was beginning its slow reach over the water and under the eaves of the trees as the last of the sun slipped toward the horizon. I came out the back kitchen door of William's house, crossed the small now-dead garden, and let myself out the gate, closing it behind me. From here I could take the path behind the house, along the edge of the trees, back to Barrow House without having to take the main road.

There was no sound in the purpling dusk but for the wayward call of a few early-evening birds. At the edge of the path my step stumbled, my ankle turned, and I nearly fell. I felt my shoe come loose, and I knelt in the cool grass to rub my ankle and refasten the buckle.

As I knelt a sound came from the house behind me, the click of a door and, surprisingly, voices. I halted. William and I had been alone in the house. But it was certainly two male voices, talking low. They seemed to come from around the house, by the front door.

I don't know what possessed me to stop and make my way back to the garden gate. It was sudden suspicion, prickling and unsure. Perhaps the conversation I'd just had with William had unsettled me more than I realized. But instead of going back to Barrow House I moved quietly through the twilight, trying to get closer to the voices.

I had closed the gate behind me, but I reached over the low wall and unlatched it, letting it swivel open. I slid through the resulting crack and along the shadowed wall. At the garden shed I paused, taking shelter behind it, berating myself for a nosy fool, slinking around like a nighttime thief. I was stuck there now behind the garden shed, with no way of getting out without risking making noise and exposing myself; well, it was only as much as I deserved. With nowhere to go but onward, I peered 'round the shed and found I had a slanted view of the front of the house.

A beam of light spilled from the open front door and onto the stoop. It was broken by a moving shadow just inside the door. The voices were raised in tension and anger now, though they stayed hushed—two men arguing and trying to keep quiet about it. I realized I had come to William's door in a frightened rush, and he'd not said anything, but William had already had a visitor all along, who had moved into some other part of the house while we'd been talking.

The voices quieted, and a shadow broke from the doorway and resolved into the figure of a man. He stepped out onto the stoop into the light, and I clearly saw the tall frame and long features of Aubrey Thorne. From inside the door, William grasped Aubrey's arm, and he stopped and turned; apparently their conversation was not quite finished.

I couldn't hear everything, just a few words. Aubrey was upset about something and kept shaking his head. "Didn't you hear her?" he said once, and I flushed in my hiding place, knowing he must mean me. William said something, and Aubrey answered: "You're wrong." He said something else, related in a fierce whisper, and I heard the words "call it off"—but whether he was asking William to call something off, or arguing passionately against it, I couldn't tell. He pulled back, William's hand let go, and then

the vicar was gone. The square of light on the front stoop disappeared.

I was alone in the dark now. I detached myself from the shed
and moved slowly back toward the garden gate, taking care where
I placed my feet. My heart was thumping in my chest. Aubrey
had been hiding at William's for some purpose he had not wanted
discovered. And they wanted to—or did not want to—call something off. . . .

I halted my steps when I realized two things. First, the bright
yellow light of the kitchen window was shining over my path,
and if William looked out just this instant, he would see me; and
second, when I'd come back into the garden I'd opened the gate
and left it open. If William had heard me close the gate the first
time, and if he saw the gate open now . . .

No face came to the window, and there was no activity from
the house. I moved a little farther along, and now I could see
the back of William's head as he stood in the kitchen. From where
he was placed I guessed he was standing at the counter, rinsing the
used mugs of tea. There was nothing unusual about him at all,
and I counted my steps, praying that he would not turn and come
to the window. Just for another five seconds . . . four . . .

I moved out from the light of the window. He hadn't seen
me. Perhaps he hadn't heard the gate latch close the first time, or
perhaps he hadn't looked out at the unlatched gate since. If my
luck held, I could slip through the gate, shut it as silently as I
could behind me, and he'd never be the wiser.

The light spilling from the kitchen windows shut off.

My breath stopped. It was a coincidence; he'd finished in the
kitchen and shut off the light as he went. I must not think of the
fact that, in the pure darkness, he could be watching the gate
from the window even now, and I wouldn't be able to see.

There was nothing for it. I crouched low like a soldier and pushed through to the garden gate. I slipped through and on the other side I dropped to my knees, reached back, and hooked my fingers through the gate, closing it slowly and carefully behind me.

Despite my precautions, the gate shut with a click that seemed as loud as a gunshot to my ears. I rolled off my knees and sat full on the ground, my back to the cold garden wall, and waited.

The darkness brought a chill wind from the ocean, and I shivered. No one walked the paths; no neighbors appeared, going about their evening business, or shouting for their children, or raking the fragrant leaves. I should simply get up and walk away, as if I were out for an evening stroll.

And yet I couldn't move. William was observant and sharply intelligent. He would not have called Aubrey out of hiding unless he had heard the gate click shut on my departure. Instinct, deep in my spine, told me he'd seen the open gate, turned off the light, and gone to the window. If he hadn't seen me in the dark, he'd certainly heard the second click of the latch.

I could nearly picture him standing patiently at the window. I felt as if I could follow his thoughts. There were only two logical possibilities to that click of the gate: It had either been Walking John, or it had been me.

I closed my eyes. I wondered why I was now so frightened of a man whose house I had already come to twice for comfort. But every instinct I possessed told me to be still.

I knew what William would do mere seconds before he did it; our thoughts were that much in tandem. I hoped against hope that I was wrong, but just as I thought it, he opened the back door and let out Poseidon.

I heard an excited *whuff* of breath and the padding of the big dog's paws. I shrank myself smaller, but there was no hope he would not notice me; his sense of smell was unerring, and after a quick bounce 'round the garden, he headed straight in my direction.

I leaned 'round the wall and looked at him through the gate. He was standing, his ears perked, his tail raised and ready. I made a helpless gesture and shushed him in mime, begging him not to bark. *Now would be a good time for that ghostly man to whistle for his dog.*

He didn't, but luck was with me. Poseidon, it seemed, was not an excitable dog; he took me in with his brown, long-lashed eyes and, having cataloged and assessed me, gave his tail a single wag of approval and turned away, intent on his business. Apparently it had been agreed between us that we would share the garden.

William would be at the back of the house, watching his dog. I rose onto my hands and knees and crawled—literally crawled— on the ground along the garden wall, making my way toward the front of the house. The wall was only shoulder-high, and even a crouch would be risky, so I sacrificed my stockings until I was well away, hoping no nosy Rothewell villager would happen by and see me. I would, I thought, have to learn to mind my own business in the future.

But even as I got far enough from the house to rise onto my feet again, even as I slid into the shadows of the bushes and through them onto the road, my mood sank lower and lower. What a fool I'd been, warning William that it was dangerous here. He'd been lying to me, and so had the vicar. And now, after that little fiasco, William for one would no longer trust me. But I had no idea exactly what I was up against, and until I did, it would be unwise to make a move.

Best to wait for Drew to come back, if he ever would.

I brushed my hair from my face. I no longer looked like a

crazed fugitive, only like an innocent—if dirty—woman out for an evening walk. I tried to brush off my skirt and my knees, but there was no help for it. If anyone saw me and noticed my disarray, I'd say I'd tripped on the forest path and fallen.

Barrow House was quiet and dark when I returned. Sultana waited by the front door and slid past my ankles as I entered. The cup of tea was where I'd left it, cold now. The journal was still on the desktop in the library, the drawer open, the crumpled note still lying where I had dropped it on the floor.

I picked it up and read it again. Toby's handwriting was truly elegant, masculine and clear. *Beware, daughter of Rothewell.*

I supposed some part of me had always known, but it was time to acknowledge the ghost in Barrow House.

I cleared my throat. "Toby," I said.

There was no reply. It had been Toby who left me the pocket watch, Toby who had put the book in the oven. Toby who had rolled the torch down the stairs when the lights went out.

"Toby," I said again, louder.

Nothing. I glanced at the instruments on the desk, but they didn't move. Sultana wound around my legs, hoping for food. Walking John terrified her, but of the ghost in the house she had never been afraid; that night on the landing, she had merely looked at it, as if it were fascinating. I wished I knew now what she had seen.

"Who murdered you?" I said into the silence. "Write it in a note. Please."

I smoothed the note in my hands. I was not a daughter of Rothewell—I was the daughter of Charles and Nora, and I had been born in London. Still, the message was unmistakable. But who, or what, should I beware of?

Walking John was outside the house; Toby was inside. And

suddenly I wondered: What if it was Toby whom Walking John was trying to lure, not me? What if it was Toby he wanted? And what could Walking John possibly want of my uncle, alive or dead?

"I don't understand," I said aloud. "Help me."

When there was again no answer, I put the note in my pocket and started for the kitchen, to wash the stinging dirt from my palms.

Twenty-one

I woke from a dream in which I was drowning in Blood Moon Bay. I was in the middle of those cold, merciless waves, thrashing as they broke over my head and pulled me under. I was cold, my skin growing numb, my limbs becoming sluggish as I tried to stay afloat. The cliffs rose bloodred above me, lit by some uncanny light.

A figure stood on the beach, watching me drown. At first it was a boy; then it was a man, gaunt and dark, staring at me from the black eyes of its face. I opened my mouth to scream, and swallowed salty water, and then I woke.

Dim sunlight made its way through the covered bedroom window, the chill gray color of dawn. Sultana lay on the bed with me, curled up and unconcerned. I stared at the ceiling, the walls, wondering for that long, free-falling moment after the end of the nightmare exactly where I was. I had survived another night in Barrow House.

A hot bath restored me to sanity, and I was putting some breakfast together when a knock came on the front door. I opened it, trying not to notice the kick in the beat of my heart that meant I hoped it was Drew.

It was Edward Bruton, his ruddy face kind as he doffed his cap.

"I've just come to see how you are, then, miss," he said, "as I'm just ending my rounds. I hope you don't mind."

I let him in. He'd worried about me my first night here, and he'd checked on me every day since. It seemed to surpass mere neighborliness, and part of me wondered whether Drew's insinuation—that Edward was interested in me—was true. If so, what a mess it would be. How to appear friendly, but not encouraging?

I led him to the kitchen. He preferred coffee, so I busied myself making it; he had brought me some, of course, in his supplies. He sat at the kitchen table a little uneasily as I worked, perched on the edge of the hard wooden chair, running a hand through his thick red hair. Though he was well-kempt, he had the shadow of stubble on his face and neck—the kind of skin some men have that indicates a constant struggle to stay clean shaven. If he ever let it go, I thought, he'd have a bright red fiery beard that would be eccentric and unmistakable.

"I nearly forgot," he said after a moment. "The vicar gave me this for you." He pulled a folded note from his pocket.

Aubrey Thorne granted me permission to see his archives at ten o'clock this morning.

"Bad news?" asked Edward, seeing my expression.

I'd made the request in implicit trust, but now I knew I'd walked into some sort of game to which I didn't know the rules. "It's fine," I told him. "I've asked to see the vicar's archives, and he's agreed."

"Archives? You mean those musty old papers he keeps in the vicarage?"

"The very ones, I suppose. I know my uncle asked to see them. I'm trying to figure out what he may have been looking for."

"Ah." Edward's expression clouded a little, some of the

openness and pleasure gone. I handed him his cup of coffee and remembered that I did not know whom I could trust in Rothewell. "Your uncle didn't talk to me much," he said. "I don't think he quite liked me, to be honest."

I tried to picture Toby warming up to Edward, and couldn't. "You mustn't take it to heart. I don't think Toby dealt very well with people."

"Maybe not. I tried a few times, I did. He only ever really spoke to me once, and that was to ask me where I was born. Why would he ask a question like that, do you suppose?"

I sat in the other chair and looked at him across the table, puzzled. "I don't know. What did you tell him?"

"I told him I was born here, of course. I never left it for a day until I went to war."

"The war again," I said. "It seems to have affected everyone in the village."

He shrugged. "Every young man in Rothewell went, though only a few of us came back. I joined late, because I broke my hip when I was a lad and at first they wouldn't take me. They changed their rules soon enough, when things got bad. I drove an ambulance. I was still driving it on Armistice Day. Kept going until about six o'clock that afternoon; it took that long for the news to reach some of us. Then I came home and drove my father's donkey cart instead, and I was glad to make the trade."

I looked down at my cup, not sure what to say.

But Edward leaned toward me, the war momentarily forgotten. "Have you found anything? About what your uncle was doing, I mean?"

I sighed. "Edward, my uncle was a ghost hunter."

"Yes, I knew that. He did tell me. But I'm wondering what else you may have found. If you've seen anything . . . important."

I looked up at him, my eyes narrowed.

He seemed to have no subterfuge to him, only an interest that was strangely avid. "It's just that the question he asked me seemed to have a purpose to it," Edward went on. "As if he was putting something together. And I wonder if you've found out what it was."

I shook my head. If there was some other purpose to his question, Edward was a terribly good liar. "I wish I knew. I don't."

He leaned back again. "I'd like to know what was going on. I'd talk to the inspector again, but he left for London yesterday."

I blinked at him, keeping my voice steady. "You talked to the inspector?"

"Didn't he tell you?"

I was going cold, deep in my stomach. "Tell me what?"

"I thought he might. You seemed to be working together." His face reddened, the shade matching his hair. "I thought he might have said."

"Edward," I said, "what might he have told me?"

"I've blundered into it now." He stood up from the table, his cup forgotten, and paced the kitchen, distress written all over his face. I watched him, my hands icy, as he tried to sort it out in his mind. He moved back and forth, staring down unseeing.

Finally he gave up. "I'm no good at this," he said. "I knew I wouldn't be. I knew I should stay out of it, but of course I go ahead and just assume. The fact is, Miss Leigh, I have something to tell you."

"Please," I said, my teeth clenching now. "Go on."

"And now I'm at it, I don't know where to start." He put his hands in his pockets. He had stopped pacing and stood in the middle of the kitchen, still not looking at me, unable to sit down. "The thing is, I got back from the war. I told you I've lived in this place all my life. I got back from the war and something was different about Rothewell."

He shrugged. "At first I thought it was just me. War makes men a little mad, you know, and I wondered if I'd gone wrong in the head. But after a while I knew it wasn't me. There were lights in the woods at night—not the usual ones Walking John brings. Strangers would come to town for a few hours, then be gone again. I know every fishing boat that travels these waters, but I saw boats I didn't recognize—in the bay, going back and forth, or just sitting there—and I didn't recognize the men in them either.

"I didn't know what to do about it, not really. There wasn't any harm happening to anyone, and the sightings were so sporadic, only a few times per year. I thought my imagination was running away with me, and there could have been an innocent explanation. But I do my route up and down the hill every day, and it gives a man a lot of time to observe and to think. And then I saw something that I couldn't get out of my head."

"What was it?" I asked.

He still had his hands in his pockets, and now he recited carefully, concentrating as if trying very hard to get it right. "I had come down the hill one morning. I'd finished dropping off the supplies and was letting Henry—that's my donkey—take a bit of a breather before the journey back up. It was very foggy that morning, and there wasn't much visibility. I was just off the end of the High Street, by the edge of the headland. A boat came by out of the mist, a small one. I saw it clearly. The name on it was *Cornwall*. It seemed strange that it was out on its own in the fog so close to shore. One man was on deck, and he called down to another, whom I couldn't see. Sometimes fog plays funny tricks with sound, and from where I was standing I could hear him perfectly. He was calling to the other man in German."

"In German?" I asked. "On a boat called *Cornwall*?"

"I know it's strange. But I was over there long enough to know what German sounds like. It didn't add up, and I didn't like it. This is my home, Miss Leigh, the place I grew up in. I decided I had to do something."

Despite myself, my first thought was of the blond man I'd seen twice now. Could he have been German? It was hard to tell. "Is it possible you were overreacting? Perhaps they were tourists or hired hands. We're not at war with them anymore, after all."

"Maybe not, but they aren't our friends, either. So I did something I never thought I'd do. I wrote a letter to Scotland Yard."

I leaned back in my chair and crossed my arms. "Scotland Yard."

"That's what I'm trying to tell you." He glanced up at me. "That's why the inspector came. He came because of the letter I wrote."

"And my uncle died—"

"After I wrote the letter, yes."

I shook my head. "He came here because of my uncle. He came here to determine whether my uncle was murdered."

"Miss Leigh, I'm sure that's part of the investigation. Once Scotland Yard started investigating, I guess a man turning up dead at the foot of the cliffs seemed awfully suspicious. But a Scotland Yard inspector doesn't spend this much time on a single death that hasn't even been proven murder. They don't have the manpower for it."

I didn't want to hear it; I wanted to argue. "No, they don't have the manpower. That's why he's been sent back to London. He said he was going to talk to his partner, look into things on his own. . . ." I trailed off. Even I, in my stubbornness, had to admit it didn't make sense.

Edward, of all things, looked apologetic. "With due respect, Miss Leigh, he doesn't have to do anything on his own. He's still on the official investigation. The one into Rothewell."

"You're saying that Scotland Yard based an entire investigation on one letter talking about a few lights and a man speaking German?"

"I'm saying that after I wrote that letter, the inspector showed up so fast I thought he'd come to arrest me. And then he questioned me within an inch of my life, he and his partner. It wasn't the behavior of policemen checking out a local man's hunch. It was the behavior of two investigators already on a case."

"You're saying they already knew. That they were already pursuing something of their own when you sent the letter."

"Yes."

I stood and began pacing. I was angry at myself for being so stupid. Scotland Yard investigating a death that the coroner had already ruled an accident—it was an utter lie, of course. I had been completely naive, a fact that Drew had shamelessly taken advantage of. "But what? What is it?"

"I don't know. The only thing I can think of is . . . well, there have been rumors of smuggling along the coast."

"Smuggling? Now?"

"It's just rumors, of course. We've a lot of history here. But yes, even now. It would be farther up the coast, because no one can land in Blood Moon Bay. Walking John sees to that. But if someone in Rothewell is part of a larger scheme . . . it might explain Scotland Yard." He looked worried. "I don't like seeing you in the middle of it. I don't guess I can persuade you to leave?"

"No, you can't. When did the interview happen? The one with you and the inspectors?"

"The day after your uncle died."

It added up. *I got to Barnstaple shortly after you did*, Drew had said the first day I'd met him. I'd assumed he'd come from London. But in fact he'd come from Rothewell; he'd already been here, and he'd never seen fit to tell me. He'd never seen fit to tell me anything: that there was a larger investigation, that they thought my uncle's death was a part of it. I'd been shut out from everything that was going on, left to wander through the dark on my own.

I looked at Edward, who obviously knew exactly what I was thinking. "And this trip to London?"

"He's regrouping with the Yard, and he's pooling information with his partner. He's to meet with his superiors and give a progress report. He came to see me on the way out of town to tell me."

Just after he'd gotten out of bed with me. "Is that so?"

"I'm sorry, Miss Leigh. But you have to see that this is more dangerous than even you thought. Please let me convince you to leave Rothewell."

"That's what the inspector said," I told him. "What a fool I was. I thought he was just worried about Walking John."

"You're not a fool," he said softly. "And Walking John is not a small worry."

"He's wrapped up in this, Edward. I don't know how, but somehow he is."

"I think you're right. I'm used to seeing lights in the woods. I've been seeing them all my life. An outsider wouldn't understand, but that's just the way it is here—you see lights; you know Walking John is abroad; you close your doors and stay home. It's just what he does. But the lights I've seen recently are different. They come at odd times. Walking John's lights are always still, opening and shutting like lanterns. They're beacons. These lights move. They jump and jerk like men are carrying them."

The lights I'd seen had been still, opening and closing just as he'd described. I shuddered, remembering. "No one goes in the woods at night," I said. "No one goes to Blood Moon Bay. What better place to commit a crime?"

He shook his head. "You'd have to be desperate indeed to go through Walking John's land in the middle of the night. It isn't anything I'd do for love or money."

I made a sound that was almost a laugh. "I've already been, and you're right. I don't know who could bear to do anything out there—but that must be the answer."

"I don't like the way you're looking right now," he admitted. "It makes me worry. Are you going to be all right?"

This time I did laugh. "Is that why you've been checking on me so regularly? Because you've been worried I'd get caught up in all this?"

"Of course." He reddened a little. "I didn't think I was so obvious."

"I was starting to fret that you were sweet on me, you know."

Now he reddened fully, as embarrassed as I'd ever seen a grown man. "Miss Leigh . . . that is . . . not that you aren't a beautiful woman and all. You are very lovely. It hasn't escaped my notice or . . . that is . . . If I've given the wrong impression, I didn't mean to. I must apologize. I don't want to lead you to think—"

"You mean you aren't?"

He shoved his hands deeper in his pockets and looked as if he wished he were anywhere else in the world. "I don't—er. There is someone I am already promised to. Promised myself, that is, even if she hasn't said yes yet."

And suddenly I knew. "Rachel."

He didn't even seem surprised. "Yes. I don't have much money, not after my father lost everything. She has her boy to support, and her sick father, too. She was torn up when her husband died; for a long time she couldn't even think about remarrying. She hasn't agreed yet—but I've been working hard to rebuild my finances, and I've tried to get to know Sam, you know. Rachel won't marry any man her boy doesn't like. But I'm hoping she'll say yes. And I'm waiting. For as long as it takes, I'm waiting."

It was a moment before I could say, "She is a very, very lucky girl."

He shrugged. "I'm not much to look at; I know that."

"Is that what you're worried about? She'd be mad, absolutely mad. Grow your beard like a Viking, toss her over your shoulder, and carry her away. And please stop worrying about me—though I very much appreciate it."

"All right. I must get back to my rounds." He put on his hat. He stopped at the kitchen door just before leaving and looked back at me. "I'm not going to stop worrying, you know. So please be careful." He smiled, still shy. "But the Viking thing I'll consider."

Twenty-two

I know you're not a ghost hunter like your uncle was," said Aubrey Thorne. "But I've always thought that if any place was ever haunted, it must be the vicarage."

We were crossing the well-kept lawn, away from Thorne's ramshackle greenhouse. The church stood low and dignified at the end of the village, the small cemetery spread out before it like an apron. It was not a showy church, but it still assumed its place as the most prominent structure in Rothewell with the ease of a lady who knew she had centuries of breeding behind her.

"Have you ever seen anything there?" I asked.

"No, not at all. But the church dates back to 1544, and the vicarage shortly after. A building that old must have ghosts, don't you think? Sinners, penitents, mad old priests. Someone. When you see the inside, you'll see what I mean."

"I don't understand," I said. I was doing rather a good impression, I thought, of someone who didn't have grave suspicions about her conversational partner. "I thought the house you live in with your wife is the vicarage."

"They both are. We live in what's called the new vicarage—though it's not that new, really. The original vicarage is on the other side of the church, over here. It's terribly tiny and gloomy, but the vicar of Rothewell did in fact live there until the nineteenth century, when a predecessor of mine—I've looked him up; his name was Henry Thomas—had the current house built in 1801." He smiled at me from his long, friendly face. "Thank goodness for Henry Thomas, or so I fervently believe. When you see the old vicarage, you'll see what I mean."

The old vicarage was just past the graveyard, and it was long and low and built of stone. Leaves from the overhanging oaks rained down onto the slate roof, decorating it in yellow and brown, and piled in drifts by the walls. The old mullioned windows were thick and narrow, and the front door with its large, carved knocker was dark and imposing.

The inside opened onto a cramped front room into which very little light made its way. There was no furniture except a dusty old sofa, and an unused fireplace took up much of the outside wall. The air was chill and damp, smelling of something abandoned and unused. The wooden floors creaked under our feet.

"This is the common room, the one used to entertain," said Aubrey. "The other rooms down the hall are in even worse shape. Unfortunately, you'll have to abide one of them, as I keep my little archive in the library."

"Why here?" I asked, thinking of the librarians at Oxford, who would faint at the thought of putting even one of the Bodleian's precious books in this damp, moldy place.

"I've unlimited room in this building," he said, "that I don't have in the house. My wife, Enid, doesn't much like the dirt and the dust of all the old papers—not to mention the space they take. The greenhouse is too wet, and the church doesn't seem the right place somehow." He shrugged. "This just seems like the best location. I'm the only one who uses it; it's secure; it's dark. And if there were ever to be a fire, next to the church this would be the last place to burn."

"All right. I'll appreciate the benefits of your nasty old vicar-age." I shifted the bag I carried on my shoulder; I'd brought a notebook and pencil. "Where do I start?"

He laughed and picked up a candleholder on a low table by the door, along with a book of matches. I watched him as he lit the candle. His face carried nothing suspicious, no emotion but a pleasant willingness to help.

"Follow me," he said, and took me through the back of the room to a decrepit hallway. He opened one of the doors and showed me through to a room being used as a library. It featured a wooden table and chair, two bookshelves, and a mismatched cabinet. An unlit oil lamp sat on the desk. There was only one narrow window, shuttered, with muted, shady light barely coming through the slats.

"I don't suppose you know what you're looking for," Aubrey said.

"Not exactly, no."

"Well, these are the books over here—no one has yet written a history of Rothewell, but there are histories of the area and such. In here"—he gestured toward the cabinet—"are the origi-nal papers I've collected. Mostly letters, a great many from my predecessors in this office, as well as a few journals. There are photographs as well. Most of them I've identified and cataloged as best I can. There are a few wonderful old maps in there I think you'll like."

I tried to think of something polite to say. "You should write the history of Rothewell yourself."

His expression closed, and he looked away. "Yes, well, some-day perhaps. Do you have everything you need, then?"

"Yes, I think so. Where do you keep the parish register?"

"Ah. That's kept at the church. Would you like to see it?"

"Not today, no." The register was the real record of a place. It listed all births, deaths, and marriages in its official list. It was the vicar's job, as the one performing christenings, marriages, and funerals, to keep the records. I had wondered whether Toby had wanted to look at it for some reason.

"I'll leave you, then. I'll light the lamp. Please remember to douse it before you leave; that's all I ask. If you need me, I'll be in the greenhouse. Otherwise, I'll be back in an hour or two."

The door shut with a click behind him, and in the resulting quiet, alone amid the gloom with only an oil lamp for light, I began to see what he meant about ghosts. This was a perfect place for them: very old, abandoned, and run-down. Even in the low light I could see the stains of mold on the upper walls. Despite Aubrey's excuses, this was no place for a proper archive.

I waited a long moment, listening—and, perhaps, waiting to see whether the hairs on the back of my neck would stand up. They didn't, so I set to work.

I started with the bookshelves, reading the spines. The books were old and mostly dull. Still, Toby had been in this room, looking for something. I let myself read the titles one by one, letting the information sift, trying to see what he could have been seeking.

The only strange thing I found was a cheap, modern edition of the *Book of Common Prayer*, the gilt lettering on its cover flaking, the kind that could be bought at any common paperback stand, tucked on the shelf among all the old books. It seemed an unlikely thing to keep in a treasured archive, but when I opened it and leafed through the pages, I saw nothing unusual.

I moved to the cabinet next. There were journals, mostly belonging to past vicars, though not many; Aubrey's predecessors had not been great writers. A few bundles of letters were present, and I noted with horror that catalog labels had been pasted directly onto some of the fragile old letters with glue. Aubrey Thorne was not much of a historian.

I glanced through the letters, but they were also from past vicars and seemed to address the terribly everyday business of ecclesiastical life: weather; politely worded gripes to bishops about the lack of new candlesticks, or leaking ceilings; pleas for money to restore the churchyard or to replace an assistant. I was beginning to get frustrated when I found a bundle labeled, *Stephen S. Williams, vicar 1829–1835.* These letters were entirely different.

The vicar Williams, whoever he had been, was preoccupied with the problem of Walking John. He'd written the bishop complaining of nighttime noises frightening the villagers, damaged fences, barking dogs, and terrified chickens. He asked for ecclesiastical help, which the bishop—or the bishop's assistant—declined. I wondered what kind of help the bishop could be called upon to give. Church investigators, perhaps, or even an exorcist?

The pleas from Williams did not stop coming, however, and Williams seemed convinced his parish was being "most grievously harassed by a hellish spirit." Finally the vicar made his own brave expedition into the woods to Blood Moon Bay at night, in an attempt to gather evidence, which he then sent to the bishop in a final plea for help.

I admired the man's courage and his dedication to his flock. But the letter he'd written, with the evidence he'd collected, made me stop cold.

It was a drawing of the footprints I'd seen in the sand. I remembered William Moorcock mentioning that there was such a drawing in the archives. It was a remarkably good sketch, accurate and well drawn. The footprints were narrow, with a heavy depression at the base of the toes, and a large gap between the first and second toes. They were exactly the same as the ones I'd seen only the other night, almost a hundred years later.

But it was not just the drawing that left me staring, unable to believe what I was looking at.

It was the writing.

John Barrow had left his message ninety years ago, and that time, it had not been washed away.

The vicar had sent the drawing and the message to the bishop, claiming it proved the need for an exorcist to be sent right away. For the message, powerful in its simplicity, was written in three simple words: MAKE ME SLEEP.

My hand shook as I read the letter. John Barrow did not haunt Rothewell out of malevolence, or a wish for revenge, or an impetus of evil. John Barrow wanted to be with his son, to have someone make it end for him, to make it be over.

With sudden certainty I knew that Toby had found this same letter. Toby had learned what Walking John wanted. And Toby, being a ghost hunter by trade, would have looked for a way to give him rest.

Could that have been it? Could that have been why someone wanted to kill Toby? But how could that be?

After the last letter featuring the drawing and the message, Stephen Williams had been removed from Rothewell and given another living, and no exorcism had ever been performed. Most people in town moved into the center of the village, where the ghost didn't go. Over the years, the houses closest to the woods—with the exception of Barrow House—had been torn down. So had Rothewell made its uneasy truce with its resident *boggart*.

There were photographs in the cabinet, some pasted onto pages and labeled, others still in careless piles. The labeled ones were of Rothewell itself, dating back to the beginning of the century. There were pictures of the seashore, the High Street, the view down the steep road to the water. It seemed that someone, in those early days, had invested in a camera and gone shooting, and Aubrey had ended up with the photos, which he had assembled into a historical record.

The unsorted photos were of people. Either Aubrey didn't care to catalog people or he hadn't had the time to do it, for these were in a messy pile—part of a bequest, perhaps, or a collection he had bought. I looked through them quickly, taking in the ladies in their Gibson girl hairdos and high-necked blouses, the men in their severe whiskers and dark hats. Some were casually posed outdoors, others taken inside before a background of rough canvas in what looked like an amateur photographer's studio.

I stopped.

A woman looked out at me from the photograph I held, her black hair tied up demurely, her chin and shoulders uncertain, a pose that looked just a little reluctant. Her face was angled slightly away, and her large, dark eyes were hooded, as if, at the moment the shutter clicked, she was pondering something a little bit sad. She was pretty, young, slender, and seemingly unsure of herself.

She looked like me.

There was no mistaking it. Even with her different hairstyle and slightly longer nose, she looked very much like me. I flipped the photograph over, hoping for an inscription or any indication of who she was, but there was nothing.

Elizabeth, Rachel's father had called me. And Mrs. Trowbridge, the postmistress: *You really do look like her. She died a long time ago. Her name was Elizabeth.*

I hesitated for a long moment, then slipped the photograph into my pocket. Aubrey hadn't even cataloged these pictures; he wouldn't miss this one. I doubted it was a coincidence that the girl in the picture and I looked alike. She must be a relative, though I had never heard my parents speak of one. An aunt? A great-aunt? The photo was undated, but the girl's style put it only about fifteen or twenty years ago.

But if my resemblance to this Rothewell girl was no coincidence, it tugged at me uneasily that Toby's coming to this place—specifically to Rothewell—was not a coincidence either. He had written her name in his journal. *Elizabeth.* The pieces were beginning to fall into place, though I knew I was missing much of it. The answer was tantalizingly out of reach.

Drew could help, I thought, *if I could find him.*

As I put the letters back in the cabinet, I wondered how long I had been in here—not long, though it felt like ages. I wondered when Aubrey would return for me. I stood back and looked around the room, and then I noticed something.

The bookshelf was dusty. I had seen the dust as I had read through the spines of the books, but it was only as I stepped away and observed the shelf as a whole that I saw the pattern. The dust had been smeared and disturbed on every shelf, in front of every book, as if each had been removed and replaced one by one.

I'd removed only one of the books myself, the *Book of Common Prayer.* I thought of what Aubrey had told Drew and me: that when Toby had visited the archives a second time, Aubrey had left him alone. He hadn't known on that occasion what Toby had been looking for.

Perhaps my uncle had ransacked the books. But why?

Through the door I heard the distinct sound of a click.

I went to the door. It swung open easily, revealing the dark, empty hall. "Mr. Thorne?" I said. "Aubrey?"

I stepped out into the hall, blinking into the darkness. The oil lamp still burned in the archive room, and I had no candle. I moved down the hall toward the old sitting room, one hand on the wall to guide me and one before me like a blind person. The light grew as I came to the end of the hall, sunlight coming through the high windows of the room.

There was no one here. No other sound came, and there were only cobwebs to keep me company. I'd go back and get the lamp and get out of here.

I blinked. There was more light now, brighter light, harsher. It flickered against the gloomy wall.

No. I whirled and ran back to the archive room, which now emitted a reddish glow. A strangled sound came from my throat. The oil lamp was overturned, the desk burning. The flames were climbing up the bookshelf, consuming the dusty old books with hideous speed. Aubrey Thorne's archive was on fire.

I ran to the cabinet, which was still untouched, and wrenched it open. Perhaps I could save some of the journals and letters, the photographs—

I had pulled papers to my chest, clutching them like an infant, when I heard the door thump shut behind me.

Twenty-three

Part of me insisted it couldn't be real. As I struggled with the door, which refused to open, as the flames fed their way through the bookshelf and toward the papers I'd dropped to the floor, as my eyes began to smart and sting, part of me believed it wasn't happening. I simply could not be trapped in a small room that was on fire. Hadn't this happened in a serial I'd seen at the cinema?

The door was hopeless, obviously locked, though I'd never seen a key. I bruised my hands shaking it, jarring it, hitting it for all I was worth. I screamed and screamed for help. I was slick with sweat that ran into my eyes.

This would be the last place to burn, Aubrey Thorne had said. He was right; the room itself, the old stone walls, would not burn. But the books, the shelves, the old dry papers, even the wainscoting would burn quite merrily indeed. There was not a single vent for the smoke. I'd suffocate long before the fire burned itself out.

I turned to the window. It was high and narrow, the shutter nailed into place; I could do nothing with my bare hands.

My throat burned now, and screaming became difficult. Behind me, the table was aflame, the books, and now the cabinet. I could barely see for the smoke. I looked around me for a long moment in despair as my stomach turned and spots began to dance before my eyes. Past that window, just past the glass, was the copse of trees, the fallen leaves, the crisp, fresh sky. The world went about its business, unable to hear my screams through the thick walls of the old vicarage. *This is not happening.*

I tried the door again, but my hands were sweaty now and slipped off the knob. I looked wildly around the room through the black haze of smoke. I was coughing, unable to control it, each breath scraping painfully through my throat and sending me into another convulsion. I thought incongruously of Drew, far away in London, oblivious of me at this moment as I choked to death.

The table was nearly burned through now, the center falling in. I pushed it over with my foot, coughing again as it heaved to its side, cinders spiraling up to the ceiling. I kicked at it again and again. There were large spots of black in my vision now, but I kept kicking. I lost my balance and the room swung wildly, but I pushed myself upright, stars dancing in my vision. I thought I could hear thumping on the door. I was still screaming, but no sound was coming from my throat.

When the desk fell apart, I grasped one of the legs, pulling at it with all of the weakened strength left in my arms. It cracked with a sickening sound and came away in my hands, taking a narrow part of the edge of the tabletop with it. I now held a thick wooden club in my hand—or as close an approximation as I was going to get.

I set to the shutter. I had hacked at it with my makeshift tool for a few precious seconds before I realized, with sluggish logic, that I was wasting my time. Even if I could get the shutter off and break the thick glass, I had no hope of getting myself up and through the window. The best I could hope for would be a few breaths of air before I died.

The leg broke in two, and I fell to the ground. I stared at my ruined weapon. I didn't have the strength to get another one. My head hurt, each cough was painful, my chest hurt, and my brain wanted to shut down. My legs wouldn't get under me again.

I wiped my forehead. The remains of the desk were still burning, and the bookshelf and cabinet were aflame. The wainscoting was also on fire. The wooden door was burning.

The door was burning.

The top half of my table leg was a long, thin wedge, the wood lighter where I had splintered it away from the rest. I crawled to the door and peered at it through the flames. If the wood was weakened around the lock mechanism, then possibly I could break the lock and smash it out of the jamb. It was a long shot, but it was all I had.

I probed with the wedge of wood, the heat burning my fingers, and placed it just so under the metal plate. I waggled it, my mind stupid. It wedged in a tiny bit, giving me just enough purchase. Someone was definitely pounding on the door now, unless I was imagining it. I wondered vaguely who it was.

When I had the wedge placed, I took the heavier end of the broken leg and pounded it into the other piece of wood as hard as I could. I could barely breathe now, and my lungs were gasping hard, trying for oxygen. My vision blurred, and the piece of wood fell from my hands, disappearing in the smoke.

I leaned back on the floor and took off my shoe. Propping myself on my elbows, I set my stockinged heel against the widest part of the wedge. My chest heaved with coughs; my eyes watered. I stared at my foot and thought of tennis matches on the green lawns at Oxford, the summer breeze fragrant in the gardens. The way we girls had laughed and chased one another through the sunlight, our faces tanned, our legs flashing, not a thought in our minds except who would win the next match and what was for supper.

My partner had been Evelyn Matchhouse, a girl a year ahead of me who had incredible power in her shoulders and arms. She could have knocked a grown man off his feet, and she thought of nothing but tennis. *A single shot,* she had told me once, *well planned and well executed, can mean all the difference between winning and losing.*

I squinted through the smoke. I pulled back my heel and smashed it directly into the wood. The shock jolted straight up my leg. The lock splintered, and the door swung open.

There were shouts. Someone grasped me under the arms and dragged me from the room, the grip both gentle and forceful. *Those feel like Drew Merriken's hands,* I thought vaguely as I watched the fire recede from my vision. Then: *I wish I'd had more time with all those precious books and papers before they burned.*

The hands set me down. I rolled to my side and retched emptily onto the worn carpet, over and over, the ugly rose pattern dancing in the spots before my eyes.

When I had finished, or as near as I could, the hand touched me again and rolled me over. I was dimly aware of other shouts in the background, calls for water. I was defenseless, unable even to lift my arms, and a dim pulse of fear beat in my temples like a heartbeat. I had to get out. I had to run. . . .

"Jillian," came a familiar voice.

I looked up at him, and his face became clear in my watering vision. "Oh, my God," I managed, and then the blackness overtook me.

⚬⚬⚬

I came to on a hard sofa that smelled of old wool and something pungently rotten. It took a moment for me to realize I was in the front room of the old vicarage, with the cold fireplace and stains on the ceiling.

"Oh, good," said a voice. "She's awake."

It was a voice I didn't recognize. I turned my head, which seemed to be attached to my neck with rusty screws. Two men stood in the room with me, ranged along the opposite wall as if they'd been waiting for some time. They both wore overcoats and hats. One was Drew Merriken in his familiar black coat, tall and looming. The other man was fairer, with high cheekbones and an angular chin, his eyes a vivid light blue. From under his hat came a hint of wheat blond hair. The man I'd seen twice in Rothewell.

I stared at him. "You," I said.

He tilted his head. His mouth quirked; it was supposed to be a kindly smile, but it came across as wry amusement. "Scotland Yard, at your service," he said. "You were in a bit of a fix in there."

I looked back at Drew. I opened my mouth to speak.

"Miss Leigh," said Drew, before I could say whatever I'd intended. "How are you feeling?"

I blinked. His voice was impersonal, as if he were passing the time of day. "I don't know," I tried to say, but it came out as only a rasp.

"I'm Inspector Merriken," he went on, as if he hadn't heard. "If you remember. And this is my partner, Inspector Easterbrook."

I stared at him, my mouth quite likely agape. *If you remember?* He had kissed me, shared my bed. My sluggish brain turned the words over.

"You had a scare," Inspector Easterbrook chimed in. He had a voice of such clear, perfectly modulated alto tones, I had the incongruous thought that the Oxford choir would kill for him. "You're lucky you came out as you did. Breaking the lock was a clever move, by the way. We'd nearly given up on breaking the door in."

"How are—" My voice would not work. "How—"

"Please don't strain yourself." Drew reached to the mantelpiece for a pitcher of water and a cup. He poured me a glass and carried it over.

I looked up at him. I was glad to see him, and embarrassed—oh, God, I had retched as he held me. I tried to read his face for some sign—for anything that showed he knew me. From where he stood, handing me the glass, his back was to his partner. I looked for some secret communication.

"Please," he said blandly. "Drink this. We've sent for a doctor."

I took it from him, and he turned away.

Inspector Easterbrook's glance met his partner's, and now it was me who could not see Drew's face. Again came that smirk from the blond man, brief but unmistakable. The two men, it seemed, were sharing a joke at my expense.

I looked down at myself. I was lying on the awful old sofa, my shoes off, my skirt rucked up above my knees. My blouse was deeply unbuttoned, and I had lost my jacket. I rolled myself upright in alarm and put my feet on the floor, spilling some of the water. My head spun, and it hurt to breathe.

"Don't exert yourself," said Inspector Easterbrook, the smile gone from his face, but I ignored him and drank the water.

"Miss Leigh," said Drew, back in place now. "We have a few questions for you."

"If you're up to it," Easterbrook added.

I leaned forward, my elbows on my knees, and nodded.

"First." Inspector Easterbrook took a notebook from his pocket and opened it. "You were here looking at the vicar's archives; is that correct?"

My throat hurt, so I just nodded again.

"Right. Did you hear anything before the fire started? Notice anything at all?"

"If you're asking whether the fire was deliberately set," I managed, "it was."

The men exchanged glances again. Under my exhaustion and barely suppressed fear, anger began a slow, satisfying burn. I looked slowly from one man to the other. "May I go now?" I asked.

Inspector Easterbrook narrowed his eyes at me. Next to him, Drew stood mute, his gaze unhappy. "Not quite yet," said Easterbrook. "We have to wait for the doctor. Who do you think might have set the fire, and why?"

It was a trick question asked to make me look paranoid, his tone frankly unbelieving. *Who do you think is trying to kill you, Miss Leigh?* I did not dignify it with an answer. "Why are you here?" I asked instead.

Again Easterbrook glanced at his partner, but Drew's gaze stayed on me. "Why, we're here to look into this incident."

"No. You"—I pointed to Easterbrook—"were already in Rothewell. And both of you were already here when the fire started. Why were you here?"

That gave them pause, but only for a moment; Inspector Easterbrook laughed. "Ah, well. And I thought I was traveling incognito."

"We came to see the vicar," said Drew, ignoring him. "Can you think of anyone who would want to do this?"

I hadn't rebuttoned my blouse, and I was leaning forward, elbows propped on my knees. I'm not very large in the breast department, but both men would have been able to see the gap where my blouse opened, and the lace edging of my camisole. I glanced at Drew, but he was looking directly into my eyes, his expression inscrutable.

"I don't remember," I said.

Drew's expression darkened, but he said nothing. Next to him, Inspector Easterbrook smiled, pleased with the view, which he took advantage of without a second thought. "Do think about it," Easterbrook said. "Do. You'll excuse us for a moment, won't you?"

I nodded, but as they moved to the door, Drew looked back at me. "We'll return directly. Will you sit still for a few minutes?"

"Yes," I said. "Of course."

My hands started shaking before the door closed, and I pressed them together between my knees. I bent my head and took a few long breaths through my ragged throat. The anger drained away and left only panic and the barely suppressed instinct to sob.

The men were talking in low voices, probably about me. I waited until the sound of them retreated down the hall. Then I limped to the door in my bare feet, slid soundlessly through it, left by the front door, and ran as fast as I could for my motorcar.

Twenty-four

I have very little recollection of the journey back to Barrow House. I remember the strange feeling of my bare feet on the pedals, the cold penetrating the thin fabric of my skirt and blouse. I had lost my coat and handbag somewhere in the vicarage. I remember nothing about the drive itself. If anyone saw me pass, I must have looked like a ghost.

I got all the way to the door of Barrow House before I realized I didn't have a key. It was here that I understood, with a horrified detachment, that I was in the grip of a terror so immensely large I could hardly begin to understand it. I was like a man standing with his nose to the wall of Notre Dame cathedral, unable to see the edges of something so big. I rattled the front door helplessly; I paced out into the front garden. A strange mewling sound came from my throat, and only when my neck grew wet did I realize that tears were streaming down my face, though I was not sobbing. I paced back to the front door again, just as helplessly terrified in daylight as I had been at night with Walking John hunting me through the woods.

I had just thought to go 'round to the kitchen door in the back when my eye caught something gleaming on the sill of the parlor window. I walked barefoot through the damp loam of the garden and stretched up to reach it, the cold penetrating the sore bottoms of my feet.

It was a key. I took it in shaking hands, used it to open the front door, and went inside.

I locked myself into the house. I paced from room to room, checking the windows and latching them tightly. I rattled the kitchen door, making sure it was secure. When I was finished I went over everything again like an automaton, my breath choking in my throat. At some point Sultana emerged, sleepy eyed, and watched me. Then I ran up the stairs and pulled off my clothes.

I drew a bath. I was shaking so hard as I lowered myself in that I nearly slipped. Then I sat in the hot water, hugging my knees to my chest.

I turned off the tap, and without the rush of the water, quiet fell on the house. Late-afternoon sunlight came through the high, fogged window. Sultana padded through the half-open door and sat where my skirt pooled on the tiles, watching me with mild curiosity. The heat from the water seeped into me, and I felt the shivers begin to subside. I ached everywhere; in the mirror I'd glimpsed bruises on my arms and legs, my heel hurt where I'd kicked the latch, and my hands were raw and stinging. I hugged my knees harder, feeling the bands of pain around my body as I breathed, and didn't look down.

I had a strange moment of clarity. I saw the washroom in perfect detail, as if etched in my mind. I saw the coils of the old radiator against the wall, the mirror with its scrollwork about the edges, covered in steam. I saw the basin with the thin towel tossed over the edge, the tiles, my blouse and skirt and underthings on the floor. I saw the key shining dully in the faded light, protruding from the pocket of my skirt—and, beneath it, the corner of the photograph of the girl I'd taken from the archives. Everything went 'round and 'round in my mind, faster than I could catch it, some parts clicking together with hideous clarity, others hanging in mystery as fog hangs in the air. But I felt that at long last I was beginning to see. I had always been good at puzzles, after all.

My chest heaved, and suddenly I was weeping. These weren't silent tears of terror, but a real storm of grief. The tears fell unheeded into the bathwater, and no one heard my sobs except Sultana, who lowered her ears and gave me a look of disapproval for such an unseemly display.

I cried myself out as the water cooled. Then I washed the smoke from my hair and dressed. I put the photograph in the pocket of my fresh skirt, the action automatic, as if I could not quite bear to put it down and walk away.

I thought I had calmed myself, but I jumped when a knock sounded at the front door. Instinct screamed for me not to answer it; I couldn't stand to talk to anyone yet, least of all Scotland Yard. My throat hurt, and I was still shaking.

But through the window I could see it was Diana Kates and her daughter, Julia. A memory came upon me like a cold splash of water.

"I'm sorry," I said without preamble as I opened the door. My voice was barely more than a rasp. "I was supposed to come to tea, wasn't I? It's just . . . there was an accident. . . ."

"My dear! You mustn't worry. We know all about it. We came to check on you. Are you all right?"

The local gossip telegraph must have worked like lightning. I squeezed my trembling hand on the edge of the door and tried to sound normal. "I'm quite fine, thank you. It's kind of you to check."

"My goodness. If you don't mind my saying so, you sound a perfect fright." She patted my hand with her gloved one as Julia goggled at me. "The smoke, was it? How horrid. Let us come in and make you tea."

Us, of course, meant Julia. Diana Kates led us both to the kitchen, then waved her daughter in the direction of the teapot as she sat across from me. "Now, you simply must tell me *everything*," she said.

I almost died. Someone tried to kill me. I will have nightmares about it for the rest of my life. No, that wouldn't do. "There, ah, isn't much to tell. I was looking at the archives, and—"

"Oh, goodness, that awful old vicarage! I've always hated the place. Of course, Aubrey Thorne won't do much until his wife tells him to. She's not from here; I've never liked her. Have you met her?"

"Yes."

"Such an awkward girl! And older than Aubrey, too. I'm amazed she married at all, though it was only the vicar. Not that tea, Julia—the other one, over there. I always thought he'd marry Rachel."

I tried to follow. If I kept her talking, she might not ask me any more questions. "Aubrey? Why?"

"Well, she lost her husband in the war, so she needs to marry someone. She said she was in mourning, but really—she has a boy to raise. Edward Bruton has no money, so that leaves Aubrey or William Moorcock as the only men her age. She can't marry her own brother-in-law, and besides, everyone knows William came back from the war a little strange. So unless she wanted to marry a boy or an old man, it had to be Aubrey."

In her mind, it made perfect logical sense. "I see."

"At least he has a bit of money, or he has since the war. So does William. But Aubrey found Enid somewhere and married her, and that was that. He must be thinking twice about it, as they have no children, so she must be barren, and there's Rachel turning into an old maid. Thank you, Julia, that is just right." She smiled at me.

"Perhaps Rachel doesn't need to marry," I tried.

"Poppycock! Of course she does. The Yorks used to be a well-to-do family, you know, but not now. George was a fisherman, but he became ill after his wife died, and they don't have Raymond to support them. I hear now they're selling the boat to pay the debts. I wonder what Rachel will do after he goes. That store doesn't make much money, I'm sure. She's a nice enough girl, I suppose, but her luck has been hard, and she's missed her best marrying years now. I wonder if anyone will take her."

Marry Edward Bruton, Rachel, I thought, *and give this woman the shock of her life.* Listening to her unending gossip, I was gripped by a sudden compulsion. I wondered whether I would regret it, but I couldn't help what I did next any more than I could have helped rubbing my bruises to see whether they still hurt.

I pulled the photograph of the girl from my pocket and placed it on the table. "I wonder, do you know who this was?"

Mrs. Kates, sensing a story, looked avidly at the photo. "Yes, of course, that's Elizabeth Price, the girl who married the butcher. Why do you ask?"

"I found this in the archives. She . . . she looks like me, don't you think?"

Her eyes flickered between my face and the picture. Julia's eyes did the same. "Why, yes, I believe you're right. Perhaps it's a family resemblance? That's interesting, though no one knew anything about her people. She started as a servant, you know, at the Yorks', before she married."

So this was the girl Rachel's father thought I was. For some reason my throat was dry, and not from the fire or the smoke. "I think she died."

"Yes, she did. Childbirth. The baby didn't live either. I saw her once or twice in the butcher shop during that last pregnancy, and she looked terribly ill. It was sad. Price left town after she died. I heard he remarried. We all thought it a grand joke, a butcher named Price. How very interesting—I wonder how the two of you are connected. No one asks about servants, you know, except to get a character." Her eyes glinted. "You seem to be a respectable girl, I've noticed, even though you're a little odd. If you weren't respectable I wouldn't let Julia anywhere near you— she needs proper influence. Perhaps Mrs. Price was from quality but had fallen on hard times."

From the back garden came a single soft thump. I glanced at Mrs. Kates and Julia, but the mother was busy talking, and the daughter was sipping her tea in silence. I thought I knew exactly who it was.

"I'll make a few inquiries, if you like," Mrs. Kates was saying.

My attention snapped back to her. "Oh, no. You needn't."

But she smelled good gossip and was not about to let go. "It's nothing. How thrilling if you found a lost family connection. There now, we've had our tea after all, didn't we, and wasn't that a lovely chat? All's well that ends well, you know. Julia, please do something about these cups. I'm off to powder my nose."

She left the room, and I looked at Julia's silent back as she put the cups on the washing board. "Do you speak?" I asked.

"Yes," she said softly, without turning.

"You should try it," I said.

She shrugged, just a quick move of her shoulders under her boxy dress. "There's no point." She turned, and her eyes flickered to the doorway before coming back to me. "He had a picture of her, too, you know. Your uncle did."

"What do you mean?"

"The lady in the picture. Your uncle had a photo of her, a different one."

I stared at her. "Where?" I tried to control the excitement in my faded voice. "Where did you see it?"

"I came to see him one day. Mother doesn't know. He had it out on the desk, with those strange instruments."

When I looked more closely at her face, I realized it was impossible to tell how old she was. She was perhaps sixteen, but on a closer look, she could easily have been past twenty. Or maybe it was just the oldness in her eyes.

"I never saw it," I said to her. I wondered where the photograph was now. "Did you know her?"

"No. Mother didn't either, not really; that's why she didn't see that you look like her. She likes to pretend she knows everything, but that's because she's stupid."

I should have chastised her for speaking of her mother so, but instead I said, "Why did you come to see my uncle?"

For the first time she reddened, and looked uncomfortable. "I came to ask him things. He was a ghost hunter. I came to ask him to fix it—to fix this place." Her cheeks flamed even brighter as she spoke. "I know it's stupid. I do. But I hate it here. The ghosts are everywhere. I'm always afraid. I have nightmares all the time. I don't want to marry a man and live here, but Mother says I have to. And I just thought he might have the answers."

There was a furtive shuffling sound in the garden, but I ignored it. "Julia," I said gently, "I'm not sure this place can be fixed. Not in the way you mean."

"It can. Mr. Leigh said that Walking John wants to go away, and he knew how to do it."

"When was this?"

"Just before he died. He said—"

"Julia!" Mrs. Kates came back into the room. "What are you prattling about?"

I turned to her calmly. "She wanted to know how I make my hair curl."

"You foolish girl. She doesn't use anything; any ninny could see that, though she should be using Miss Pym's Hair Tonic for Young Ladies, like the rest of us with curls. And what are you doing asking about hair anyway? I can't get you to let go of that braid."

Julia looked from me to her mother. "I'm going to cut it."

"Heavens! It will frizz straight to the skies. Come, we'll discuss it on the way home. Good-bye, dear, and take some lemon and honey for that throat—you sound a little like a man."

When they had gone, I stood in the kitchen and waited, taking in the silence. After a long moment, I walked to the back door.

"Inspector Merriken," I whispered through the closed door, "get out of my back garden."

"Is that old biddy gone?" came a deep voice through the wood.

"Yes."

"Then let me in."

"No. I told you, go away."

"Jillian, I'm sorry," he said. "Teddy Easterbrook is an ass."

I leaned my head on the door and closed my eyes. I tried to remember what I had been angry about, but just his voice had my blood singing in my veins. "Yes, he is. I believe I'm finished with Scotland Yard."

"All right, I don't entirely blame you. But Scotland Yard is not finished with you."

"Does that line work on all of your girls?"

A single thump came on the door, of a frustrated man slapping it with one large palm. "Jillian." His voice was darker now. "For God's sake, let me in. I'll stand here all night."

I opened the door, ready to be brittle, ready to use my defenses, but I had no time. Drew Merriken walked in, kicked the door shut behind him, and threw his hat on the table. Then he took me by the shoulders, backed me against the door, and kissed me.

Twenty-five

I resisted the kiss for all of a second. But it felt good to be held, to be touched, and his kiss made me feel safe and fiercely alive. I gripped his flexed upper arms and let him press me to the wall, the heat of his body suffusing mine. I parted my lips, and he needed no other invitation. He tilted my chin and kissed me with raw, naked hunger until I couldn't breathe.

He broke off and cupped my face in his hands. "Are you all right?"

"Yes," I managed, my fingers curling under his lapels.

"Damn it, Jillian. Damn it. You just left before the doctor could come. I told you to stay bloody put. Are you hurt? Are you in pain?"

"Not really—just . . . my throat, a little. My chest hurts. And my hands."

He grabbed my hands and stared down into the palms, at their crisscrossed scratches, the red welt still running under my thumbnail. He was dressed like an inspector again, his collar crisp and his tie perfectly knotted, but his jaw was clenched and his eyes were wild. I was as liquid as a bowl of cream.

He gripped my wrists and raised his gaze to my face. "What were you doing in there?" he demanded. "Tell me. What the bloody hell were you doing in that place? Full of all those dry, dusty papers? What were you thinking? How the hell did you *knock over an oil lamp?*"

"I didn't knock it over. I told you. I thought I heard something, so I left the room. Someone went in behind me and knocked it over. The lamp was on the table, but the bookshelf was already on fire. Someone set it, and when I came back into the room, they locked the door."

"And that is supposed to make me feel better?" he choked. "That someone is trying to *kill* you? I think I'm losing my mind."

It was insane, it was ridiculous, but I watched his mouth and I wanted him to kiss me again. "You look all right to me."

He made a sound like a laugh. He let go of me, but he put his palms against the walls over my shoulders, still boxing me in, and leaned hard on them, looking at the floor. I could smell clean wool and starch and warm, faint shaving soap. "I've spent the last day beside myself with worry. I made up some ridiculous paper-thin story for Teddy Easterbrook about needing to talk to the vicar just to get back here. As if I give a damn about the vicar, or anything else."

"You did?" I said.

"Jesus, Jillian! I've barely been able to focus. And we were at the vicarage, of all places, and we saw the smoke, and you started screaming—" He looked at me, then leaned in and kissed me, swift and hard. "I didn't think I'd get that door open," he said when he finished.

I touched his face, ran my fingers along his cheekbone, touched his lip with my thumb the way he'd done to me. "I broke the lock myself. With a piece of table leg."

His gaze darkened at the contact, and I began to wonder just how deeply in trouble I was. "Yes, you did, you bloody brave, brilliant girl. I nearly planted Teddy a facer just for looking at you, you know. He's insufferable, even if he has his uses. I just couldn't let on."

"I may accept that. I'll think about it."

I thought he might kiss me again, but as I watched, he changed his mind. He seemed to make an effort to pull away from me, his expression settling into a semblance of professional detachment. He dropped his hands from the wall and stood straight, backing away.

"We need to talk," he said.

I stayed where I was, leaning against the wall, and waited.

"Why were you in the vicarage in the first place?" His voice was calmer now.

"I wanted to see the archives. My uncle had been to see them."

"And did you find anything?"

My gaze flickered to the table behind him. Sitting next to his hat, which he had tossed there as he came through the door, was the photograph of Elizabeth Price, her sad gaze staring into the distance. Drew hadn't noticed the photo.

"Walking John wants to be put to rest," I answered. "His message is, 'Make me sleep.' A previous vicar saw the full message in the sand and recorded it along with the footprints."

Drew seemed to take this in for a moment. I saw the memory of that night in the woods cross his expression, then disappear again. "Interesting. And what else?"

I looked away from the photograph and raised my gaze to his. "Would you like some tea?"

"Thank you, no."

"I want some," I said. "My throat hurts." I stepped forward and pushed past him, brushing alongside the table. I scooped up the photo and put it in the pocket of my skirt without looking down.

"Did you see anyone before the fire started?" Drew asked me.

"No. Aubrey let me into the vicarage; that was all."

"Did you see Mrs. Thorne?"

I swallowed, realizing for the first time that Aubrey's wife could have tried to kill me. "I didn't see her. Was she home?"

"They were both home. They claim to be horribly upset about what happened. Mrs. Thorne wanted to come here and see you, but we talked her out of it. Teddy is interviewing them now while I'm here interviewing you."

I busied myself preparing a cup of tea I didn't want and had no intention of drinking. My skin was still burning. Drew's idea of *interviewing* was an interesting one, but I let it go for now. "It doesn't make sense that Aubrey would burn his own archives. He spent years collecting the pieces. But it had to be one of them. It must have been."

"Not necessarily." He had turned and was watching me. "When you told us the fire had been set deliberately, I checked the building. If you were in the hall, no one could have come through the front door without your seeing them. But there was a back door as well as a side servants' entrance that came through the scullery. That means if you were facing the front of the building, someone could have come from behind your back."

I stilled. I had noticed nothing. The person, whoever he was, had been completely silent. He, or she, could just as easily have attacked me directly from behind—a bludgeon, perhaps, or a pair of hands around my throat—and I would have died none the wiser. Why bother with fire?

I gave up and put the kettle down without pouring. My hands were shaking again. "Were any of the doors locked?"

"Yes, but Thorne keeps the key ring in his greenhouse, hanging on the wall. And the greenhouse wasn't locked. If someone knew where the key was, he could have let himself in."

"So." My voice was barely a whisper. I tried to stay calm. "You're saying that anyone at all could have come in one of those doors and set the fire." I turned to him. "You're also saying you actually listened to me when I said it was deliberate."

He shrugged. "Teddy thought you were hysterical. But it seemed plausible enough to me."

"Because you suspect everyone of murder," I supplied.

He came toward me, and my heart thumped in my chest. "It's convenient sometimes, isn't it?" He was close to me now, and he reached out, his hand brushing my waist. "Now, perhaps we can make a deal that you'll tell me everything you found in that archive before it burned."

"I did tell you everything."

"I don't think so." His hand moved lower. I tried not to shiver. Then I realized he was sliding his fingers into the pocket of my skirt. He deftly withdrew the photograph and held it up. "You're a terrible liar, Jillian, and an even worse thief. Who is this?"

I felt my cheeks flame. I snatched the photograph from his hand before he could look too closely at it. For some reason I wanted to keep Elizabeth Price to myself, at least until I had a better idea of who she was. "That's none of your concern."

"My concern is that you're keeping things from me."

Now I was outraged. "I'm keeping things . . . ? I think it's the other way around. You've kept me in the dark about everything, including the true nature of your investigation."

His gaze shuttered. "Ah. That."

"Yes, that."

"I thought you may have learned something. I could see you were angry with me at the vicarage. Who have you been talking to? Or did your infernal intelligence figure everything out on its own?"

"My infernal intelligence failed me utterly, in fact. I talked to Edward, and don't you dare get him in trouble. He was torn enough as it is."

Drew sighed, ran a hand through his hair. "Jillian, this is a job. A rather important one this time. In a job, I'm not always free to say what I'd like to."

"And Toby's murder?"

"Your uncle's death is part of it, yes. I'm convinced of it. But I wasn't lying about that. I can't make a case for murder. The Yard doesn't work on hunches or circumstances. There isn't enough evidence."

"Drew." My voice would not quaver. It would not. "Someone has just tried to kill me. I don't know what I'm up against. There must be something you can tell me. Anything at all."

He put his hands in his pockets. I watched him wrestle with himself, with the weight of duty and the wish to keep me safe. He looked out the window, thinking. At last he turned back to me with a sigh.

"All right," he said. "The first thing we need is a map of England."

※

Drew shrugged off his jacket and placed it over the back of a kitchen chair. He loosened his tie, as if preparing for something physical. As I watched the line of his shoulders, he reached into his hanging jacket and pulled a piece of paper from the pocket. "Like so," he said.

He spread the paper on the kitchen table. It was a small printed map, England's distinctive shape in ink. "There's Plymouth there—see?—and there's Cornwall. Here we are, here. The tides are dangerous along this coast, and the coastline itself is a challenge, but if you can land a ship, it's ideal."

"Like John Barrow and his smugglers," I said.

"Yes, exactly. Most smuggling was based on the east coast, where the waters are better and the trip to France is much shorter. That meant that most of the policing was based there as well. No one much bothered with the west coast here, so many of the smugglers brave enough to try it didn't get caught. What killed the smuggling trade more than a century ago was the lowering of taxes on imports, which didn't make it a lucrative business anymore."

I crossed my arms. "Let me guess—that isn't quite the end of the story."

"Not quite, no. Wherever you have ships and traffic, you have the potential for illegal trade, and England is all coastline. Smuggling has never exactly gone away. This corridor, along here"—he pointed to the sea along our western coast—"is a major merchant corridor. In fact, it was one of the main targets of German U-boats during the war for that reason. They were trying to strangle our imports by sinking all our merchant ships."

"And killing all the sailors."

"It was war, and we were doing exactly the same thing to them. Since it ended, things have gone back to normal, or as near as possible. But since the war, we've seen an upsurge of smuggling in this area. It's only the goods that have changed."

"And what are the goods?"

He shrugged. "Tobacco isn't profitable anymore, and neither is tea, but there are other things. Alcohol is still shipped, as are jewels and precious metals. Certain drugs I have no intention of telling you about—those go for a high price."

"That sounds lovely," I said. "It also sounds like the dominion of Customs and Excise, not Scotland Yard."

"Be patient, my girl. I'm not finished. The war was hard for Customs and Excise; they were as understaffed as everyone else, and they were under the thumb of the War Office, which was too busy to administer it properly. They came out of the war and found that while they'd been looking the other way, a new network of smugglers seemed to have set up shop along the coast—a group that seemed not only coordinated, but also well organized.

"They weren't able to nab anyone, and last year the smugglers committed the idiotic act of killing a customs agent. Now they have murder on their hands, and Scotland Yard was called in. A number of us are working up and down the coast, trying to flush this group from the bushes."

I shook my head. "How stupid I am. You told me you were here to investigate my uncle's murder despite what the coroner said, and I believed it. You must have been laughing up your sleeve."

He regarded me steadily. "If you truly thought that, I'd still be out in the back garden. Besides, I do think that Toby's murder has something to do with this. And I do disagree with the coroner. None of that was a lie."

"You make it sound so reasonable. But . . . someone in Rothewell, smuggling jewels and drugs? It's outlandish. I just don't see it."

"Neither did I. Neither did anyone until your admirer, Edward Bruton, wrote us that he'd heard those German sailors. We traced the boat *Cornwall* to an owner near Plymouth, who'd sold it to an Englishman named Jasper Kipps, who claimed to be a lawyer processing the transaction on behalf of a client. But when we checked, no such lawyer exists."

"Perhaps they were just immigrant laborers. We're not at war with Germany anymore."

"Jillian. Edward saw those men, and two days later your uncle was dead."

I blinked. Tears welled up in my throat and behind my eyes, and I beat them back. How senseless that Toby—kind, shy, eccentric Toby—had been killed over someone's greedy, grasping scheme. I stared fiercely at the map until I was under control again. "What are you getting at? You think someone is landing illegal cargo in Blood Moon Bay, is that it?"

"That's exactly what I think—though the buying and selling goes both ways. Until now, we haven't been able to narrow down exactly where on the coast they've been weighing anchor. If they're smart, and they are, they have several chosen spots. When I heard that no one goes into the woods for fear of the local ghost, I figured we'd found one of those spots."

"Toby's notes said that he'd been ghost hunting in the woods at night. Setting up his equipment and doing tests." It was starting to make sense. "He wandered into Blood Moon Bay in the middle of the night and saw something he shouldn't have. But he doesn't describe it in his journal. He only says that it all makes sense."

"In a way," Drew said, "your uncle's death provided an opportunity for us to investigate. It's perfectly normal for the police to come after a man has died on the cliffs, to be seen around town, to ask questions. I was to gather information and take it back to London without tipping off anyone who might be in league with the smugglers themselves."

"And Easterbrook?"

"Teddy was supposed to wander about town, seeing what he could see, meeting people if he could. It was his idea, but since you recognized him so easily, it seems he made rather a hash of it."

"He's blond," I pointed out, "and there are almost no young men in Rothewell. He rather stood out."

"As I believe I've mentioned, he's an ass. But it wasn't completely a waste. He learned a few useful things in his travels."

"Such as?"

"Now, that I can't tell you."

I pulled out one of the kitchen chairs and sat down. Drew put his hands in his pockets again and regarded me.

"You've found more information," I said, "and you're not allowed to tell me, which once again leaves me in the dark."

He sighed. "Look—let's just say we have information that we shouldn't have. But our information tells us the Germans are about to purchase something they're rather excited about."

"Purchase?" *The buying and selling goes both ways,* he'd said. "What is it?" I looked at his silent face. "What in the world would anyone in Rothewell have to sell?"

"We don't know for certain, but we have our suspicions."

"What suspicions?" I blew out a breath in frustration. "Drew, this isn't fair!"

"Jillian, I can't tell you. I simply can't."

"When is this transaction supposed to take place?"

"Very soon. That's all we know. Jillian, I want you to be careful. Our evidence says that Thorne is the leader, or one of them. I don't want you going near him again."

Given that I had nearly been burned to death in the vicarage, I wasn't going to argue. "If Aubrey is the leader," I said, "then William must be his accomplice." And I told him, as briefly as I could, about what I had seen and heard outside of William's house the night before.

When I finished, Drew's face was grim. "When exactly were you going to tell me about the second time you almost got killed? How long was I gone, anyway? Twenty-four hours?"

I bit my lip. "Don't be ridiculous. William had no intention of killing me. He just had a brain fever during the war, and it's made him a little strange."

"He what? I had no idea. Teddy and I will talk to him. I'd like to know where he was this afternoon."

Aubrey and William had grown up together. Perhaps they were at odds at the moment, but they had been very close. It was quite likely William knew where Aubrey kept the key to the old vicarage. But my instinct told me it hadn't been William who had set the fire. He was confused, and perhaps off balance, but I thought he rather liked me. I couldn't see him setting a fire and locking me in with it to die.

I looked at the map on the table and for the first time I understood what Drew was risking for me. He had let me in on a countrywide investigation involving teams of customs and law enforcement experts; he had told me about their findings and their investigative techniques. Perhaps he could have told me sooner, and perhaps there were still things he had to hold back. But if his superiors found out how much he had just told to a civilian woman, he could well be disciplined by the Yard, or even dismissed. He was trusting me.

I touched the photograph in my pocket, where I had put it after snatching it away from him. I was being secretive, and I couldn't even say exactly why. Perhaps I could tell him about Elizabeth Price. Perhaps he could even help me. Perhaps . . .

There was a knock at the front door, and we froze.

Our eyes met in a swift glance. The knock came again, and a distinctive voice, perfect for singing in the Oxford choir, rang out. "Miss Leigh?"

Drew took up the map and folded it, shrugging at me. "He knows I'm here. You may as well answer it."

I nodded and stood.

"Jillian," said Drew, stopping me as I walked toward the hall. "I don't need to tell you not to repeat anything I've just told you. Do I?"

"No," I said. "I understand."

Inspector Teddy Easterbrook removed his hat when I opened the door, showing his distinctive hair again. "Miss Leigh," he said in his lovely alto tones. "I'm so sorry we have to disturb you. I believe my partner, Inspector Merriken, is here?"

"Yes, he is. Come in."

"Are you quite all right?" he asked me as he followed me down the hall. I could feel his eyes on me, and the effect was distinctly less pleasant than when I had felt the same from Drew. "That was quite a scene earlier."

"She's fine, Teddy." This was Drew's voice as we entered the kitchen. He was shrugging his jacket back on.

I watched Easterbrook's sharp blue eyes take this in, and observe Drew's loosened tie. "My, aren't we cozy," he said in a dry voice. "How goes the interrogation, Inspector?"

"Don't start," said Drew.

Teddy held up his hands. "What did I say?" He looked at me. "You mustn't mind Inspector Merriken, Miss Leigh. He has a way with ladies, or so I'm told. I find it a bit of a relief that he has at least one flaw."

Drew straightened his tie. "I have plenty of flaws," he said through clenched teeth.

"Do you?" Easterbrook turned and addressed me again. "Did you know, Miss Leigh, that the fellows at the Yard gave Inspector Merriken a nickname? We call him the Paragon. He thinks it would kill him to have a pint with the rest of us every once in a while. If it weren't for all the female phone calls he gets, we'd have to toss him in the Thames."

"All right, let's go. We have work to do."

"Back to the trenches, eh?" Teddy smiled at me. "Off we go. Not literally, of course. I did my time in the mud, and much thanks I got for it, too."

The openness had vanished from Drew's demeanor. He looked needled and frustrated—perhaps even a little embarrassed. He nodded formally at me as he put on his hat and said, "Have a nice afternoon, Miss Leigh."

I crossed my arms and watched them go, Drew's tall, dark frame leading Teddy's smaller, elegant one. The Yard came first, I realized. It always would. And I stood alone again in the kitchen.

I glanced out the window, at the sun high in the afternoon sky. I had nearly died today, the longest day of my life. I should rest and recover. I should pack Toby's things. I should let the two inspectors do their job finding Toby's killer and whoever had tried to kill me.

But my mind spun. I could no longer pretend I was just an Oxford student here on a lark. That I could walk away and none of this would matter.

I would wait until dusk, and then I had an investigation of my own to begin.

Twenty-six

I had never taken the slope down to Rothewell on foot. I stayed off the shoulder of the road, placing one step at a time over the uneven ground. No one passed by as I traveled. By the time I got to the bottom my legs were shaking, I wished heartily that I could have worn a man's shoes instead of my low heels, and I could not contemplate the climb back. But I had no choice, as the motorcar would have been far too conspicuous for what I planned to do.

I circled away from High Street, keeping to the trees and the high grasses, avoiding the few houses whose windows were beginning to light in the first gray of dusk. It was time for supper, and people were retreating to their homes. Despite the chill breeze coming from the water, sweat trickled down the back of my neck. I caught sight of the church's roof and headed toward it in as steady a line as I could, keeping off the roads. The ground was hard, and I moved quickly.

I stopped in a copse of trees from which I could see the new vicarage and its greenhouse at the rear. I crouched down so I couldn't be seen and waited, watching.

The sun had just dropped below the horizon, and the day's light was fading. Through the glass of the greenhouse I saw a tall figure moving to and fro. Aubrey Thorne was tidying up.

Mrs. Thorne—Enid—came 'round from the front of the

house. She wore a large sweater over a blouse and a straight skirt that flapped around her long legs. Tucking her hair behind her ears, she leaned into the doorway of the greenhouse and said something. After a moment Aubrey came out and shut the door behind him. I watched the two of them walk away, leaning close to each other, a perfectly matched couple who were deeply in love, and I wondered whether I owed my near death to one of them.

More important, I watched the greenhouse door. Aubrey hadn't stopped to lock it.

I let out a breath. I'd put a brave face on it, but if he'd locked the door, my plan would have been stymied. I'd banked on Drew's comment earlier that the greenhouse was left open. They didn't teach girls to pick locks at Somerville.

Once the Thornes had disappeared, I left my copse of trees and hurried toward the door, hoping I wouldn't be seen. *Someone else did this earlier today,* a voice whispered in my head. *Someone may have taken this exact path, looking for the key to the old vicarage.* Still, I was filled with queer excitement. I moved faster.

I tiptoed into the empty greenhouse and looked around in the fading light. Drew had said the key was left hanging on the wall. But he hadn't said *key*; he'd said *key ring*. A key ring meant more than one key.

It was hanging behind the door, next to a stack of unused pots that was nearly as tall as I was. I pulled it down and looked at it. There were four keys on it, lying in my scratched, bruised palms. One of them would be the key I was looking for.

This wasn't London. Rothewell was a quiet place, a trusting place. There was no crime here, and no reason to lock the doors. But one would think the vicar would take better care of his keys after today's fire—if, in fact, someone had broken into the old vicarage and he hadn't set the fire himself.

The half-burned shell of the old vicarage didn't interest me, however. I never wanted to see it again. I closed my fingers tightly around the key ring and headed for the church.

The largest key fit the church's main door, where the congregation would be let in. I felt exposed as I pushed it open, certain someone would see, but I had no time to circle the building, looking for other doors and trying the keys. I slipped through the main door and pushed it closed behind me.

Another key opened the door to the vestry. I couldn't risk a light, but it didn't take me long to find what I was looking for. The parish register was kept just where Aubrey had said it was, in the church, in a very old oak cabinet with impressive scrolled doors. I pulled the large, leather-bound book from its place and set it on the desk, trying to catch the fading light from the mullioned window.

I flipped quickly through the pages. Here was Rothewell's history, captured line by line—births, deaths, marriages. Despite my hurry, the book called to the historian in me, and I tried not to peruse the more interesting entries. I resisted temptation and found the more recent pages, written in a slanted script that changed to a smaller, more crabbed writing when Aubrey Thorne took over the living.

I was looking for a certain name, and it wasn't long before I found it. It was in the older, slanted handwriting.

Wed on this day, the fifth of March, 1903, John Price, butcher, aged twenty-nine, and Elizabeth Winstone, servant, aged eighteen.

Elizabeth.

My breath came short. Courage, I must have courage.

I held the page between my fingers. If I turned it forward, I had an idea of what I would see. But what if I turned it back? Would I see her name at all? If so, was I ready for what I would find?

Perhaps there was nothing. Perhaps the knot in my stomach was only foolishness. Perhaps what I was thinking—what I was wildly, madly thinking—was only my imagination. If it was, I would be unbearably relieved. And if it wasn't—I had to know.

I turned it back. I scanned first one page, and then another. And finally, there it was, her name in an entry from the previous year:

Born on this day, the seventh of June, 1902, to Elizabeth Winstone, servant, aged seventeen, a girl child, unnamed.

I ran my finger over the words. She'd had a child out of wedlock, and the local butcher had married her. Perhaps the child had been his, perhaps not. If the baby had died, it would have been noted. So the baby had lived—but she had not been named, most likely because as a bastard child born to a servant, she'd been given away.

I read the line over and over, my eyes watering in the growing dark. Her photograph burned in my pocket. Part of me had known from the second I had first seen the picture. I felt sick and light-headed. It was the kind of sudden knowledge that comes upon us, unasked-for and unwelcome, no matter how hard we fight it or explain it away. The kind of knowledge that tears down our carefully constructed lives inexorably, brick by brick, as we desperately grasp each disappearing brick with our fingernails.

I looked exactly like Elizabeth Winstone, a servant girl who had given away a baby girl. And June seventh, 1902, was my birthday.

I made a sound deep in my throat. Memories came to me, as fast and as unstoppable as rain. The fact that I looked nothing like my own mother. Toby's visiting Rothewell as a young man. Edward saying I looked like Toby; Aubrey taking me for Toby's daughter. Mrs. Trowbridge telling me I looked like Elizabeth. The way Toby had sat with me hour upon hour, too shy to speak. That day on the beach, our pleasure in each other's company. The telegram from the solicitor. Mr. York's delusion that I was Elizabeth Winstone in the flesh.

And the note placed in the drawer of the desk in the library, so clearly in Toby's handwriting. *Beware, daughter of Rothewell.*

It fit. I could make it fit.

It could not possibly fit.

And yet, if it didn't fit—if some small, hidden part of me had not suspected for longer than I wanted to admit—what had driven me here? Alone, on foot, risking capture in a place I had no business being, by someone who may already have tried to murder me?

I wiped my watering eyes and turned the pages forward. There was a single-line notice of the death of Elizabeth Price in 1908, "while giving birth to a child, a boy who did not live." She would have been only twenty-three.

Who does that make me? I thought. *Who am I? I don't know. I don't know.* Nothing was what it had been. Nothing was the same.

I closed the book and put it away. I locked the vestry behind me, locked the door of the church as I left. No one saw me as I slipped back around the old cemetery and into the greenhouse, where I put the ring of keys on its hook.

I had a long return walk. I lifted my chin, pushed my shoulders back, and began.

Twenty-seven

It was full dark by the time I reached Barrow House. The damp chill of night had set in, and the first stars were appearing in the sky. My legs hurt and my feet were in pain; the sweat of exertion turned icy on my face and neck. I was exhausted in both body and mind, tired of my own thoughts and weary, and if you'd asked me I would have said that nothing could have kept me from my bed. But it seemed that, after all, something could.

I noticed it when I came through the front door. It was light, warm and cheery, coming from the doorway to the library. Someone had lit a fire in the fireplace.

I froze. Whoever it was would have heard the door; there was no way I could escape without being heard. What kind of predator broke into a woman's house and lit a fire in the fireplace? Or did ghosts light fires? Was there anyone there at all?

There was only enough time for me to quickly eye the umbrellas in the umbrella stand—the only things within reach that looked remotely like a weapon—before a shape emerged from the library door. Even in silhouette, with the light spilling behind, I recognized him.

"I'm sorry," said Drew Merriken.

He put his hands in his pockets and leaned against the wall. My fear dissipated and my exhaustion was forgotten as I watched him. In their place something warm bloomed deep in my body, triggered by his long legs, his broad shoulders, the gentle and capable hands I could see so clearly in my mind's eye even when they were out of sight. I pulled off my hat and ran my hands through my hair, speechless, not wanting to come out of the darkness by the door.

"I would have waited in the back garden, just like before," he said, his deep voice reaching through the gloom to touch me. "But when I got there I found a key sitting on the back stoop. So I let myself in."

I hooked my hat on the hat stand. "It's all right."

"Where have you been?"

I shook my head. "Nowhere."

He tilted his head at that, and I could tell he was trying to examine me. Sultana emerged from the library and twined shamelessly around his ankles, the faithless hussy.

I took a step forward, then another. "What have you been doing?"

He rubbed a hand over his face, and I heard a faint rasp of stubble. "Waiting. Wrestling with myself."

"That doesn't sound very pleasant."

"It's exhausting."

"Have you come to any conclusions?"

"As a matter of fact, I have."

My heart was pounding. *He's come here for you, you fool,* said a voice in my head, *only for you. Tell him to go, or turn around and leave. You're not a girl who does this.*

But what kind of girl was I? I'd always thought I knew, but identity, as I'd learned in the past hour, was a flimsy thing. It had fallen away like tissue paper, leaving me with nothing to hold on to. Perhaps I *was* the kind of girl who would do this. Perhaps I always had been, somewhere deep down. Perhaps this girl, to-night, had always been possible.

I took another step forward. I could catch his scent now, warm and heady. I could see the reflection of the light on the planes of his face. He was looking at me, intent and still.

He pushed away from the wall, stood straight, and began to tug at his tie. In the half-light, my face reddened.

"What are you doing?" I said.

"I plan to take you to bed," he replied. "I should have done it this afternoon, but I was too gentlemanly. I don't feel gentle-manly now."

My face was hot, but I didn't stop him. I watched his fingers move, listened to the hiss of his tie against his collar as he pulled it off. "Why now?" I asked.

"I won't sleep. Will you?"

I shook my head.

"Jillian," he said. "Come here."

I took another step. Then he touched me, slid his hands un-der the collar of my coat and pushed the garment from my shoul-ders. It fell to the floor unheeded as every part of my body sang. He cupped my face and kissed me.

His hands held me firmly, and his kiss was deep; yet it was a gentle kiss that asked a question. I put my hands on his chest and tilted my face up to his and answered it. My doubts fell away as his touch moved down my back, his thumbs pressing lightly into my ribs. I was tired of being alone in fear and doubt, and I wanted him.

He broke away and shrugged out of his own jacket, then be-gan to unbutton his shirt. I stared at the hollow of his throat and chest with a naked longing I would not have thought possible. "You don't have much of a way of seducing a girl," I said.

"Be quiet and come to bed with me."

"You see what I mean."

He put his hands on my waist and leaned in, his breath hot on my neck. My every nerve ending followed his progress. He kissed my neck, hot and slow, then kissed it again, moving up toward my ear. The cloth of my dress rustled as he touched me. He gently bit the lobe of my ear, and the sting of it made me moan out loud.

"There is nothing," he growled, "wrong with my technique."

He slid down, hooked my legs around his waist, lifted me easily, and carried me down the hall toward the stairs, still kissing me. I kissed back, gripping him hard as we moved. Somewhere on the stairs he let me down and I stumbled backward, and I found myself sitting on a step, his body lowered over me, his knees on the step below mine. His hips pressed between my legs, rucking my dress up almost to my waist, and he kissed me even more, deeply and slowly, as we lay there entangled like a lovers' knot. It was complete surrender.

He pulled back, his eyes dark, his breath heavy as he ran one palm up the bare back of my thigh. "Get up," he said, "or I won't make it." I untangled myself and scrambled out from under him, but I pulled at his shirt as I went, desperate to feel his skin. In one motion he pulled the shirt off and tossed it over his head. He left it there on the stairs and carried me the rest of the way.

We made it to my little bedroom, the bed tucked against the wall, and he set my feet on the floor. His skin was hot. His shoulders were wide and muscled, his chest dusted with dark hair that narrowed in a line down his stomach. Without a word he dropped to one knee, ran his big hands up under my dress, grasped my satin underwear, and dropped it to the floor at my ankles.

My shoes and stockings followed. Now I was bare under my dress. His nostrils flared as he lifted the clothes from the floor and tossed them away. He slid one hand slowly up my thigh, taking the hem of my dress with it, his gaze intent on my skin with what looked like admiration, then kissing the flesh as he revealed it, his mouth rasping against me.

"Drew," I managed, my voice strangled and pleading.

He put both hands on my thighs and slid the dress up now, over my hips. I unbuttoned the bodice as he stood and lifted the fabric over my waist, then off over my head. My slip followed, and my cotton brassiere.

I stood naked before him, unafraid. The dark, lifted only by the moonlight coming through the blanketed window, hid me in shadows; still, I felt bold. I'd come close to death that day. I was a stranger to myself. The way Drew's skin burned as he touched me made me feel more alive than I'd ever been.

He pressed me back to the bed. He touched me urgently and reverently at the same time, guiding me and asking me at once. When I was lying on the bed he shed the rest of his clothes with a grace and quickness that astonished me, and then he climbed in with me.

The springs creaked under him. He dipped his head and kissed my stomach and breasts, the line of my collarbone. He seemed to have slowed for this moment, waiting for something from me. I curled my legs around his and he stopped, looking down at me. I lifted my arms over my head and realized I was shaking.

"I don't know much about this," I said.

He nodded.

"It's all right," he said, moving me under him. "I know everything."

And to my amazement, he did.

Sometime later, Drew Merriken traced a finger down the curve of my spine as I lay on my stomach on the bed. "You're keeping something from me."

I turned my head on the pillow. I was boneless and happy, but still the touch sent deep electric shocks of excitement through my body. "You don't know that."

"Yes, I do." His fingers moved down my back, then up again, and if he was aware of what it did to me, he made no sign. "My mysterious girl. Are you going to tell me?"

I leaned to the side and looked up at him. He was propped on one elbow, his hair mussed, his brow furrowed in serious thought. I could just make out his features in the shadows. I'd never seen a handsomer man in my life. I could feel the pull of him, and I could feel myself twisting, turning as I rode the current toward him, like a branch in a rushing river. It would be so easy to lose myself.

"I don't know," I said. "That would seem an awful lot like a connection."

He was silent for a long time, long enough for pain to begin deep in my chest. "Jillian, you know what I am. What I offer."

I know it isn't enough. "Yes."

"It wouldn't work. I'm in London. You're in Oxford. Are you saying you'd give up school?"

That was easy. "Never."

"Then you see what I mean." His palm was flat on my back, rubbing along my skin. "Sometimes the moment is all we have, and we have to seize it. I learned that when I thought every moment was my last."

I rolled over, ignoring the slice of pain his words gave me. We'd taken precautions so that I wouldn't have a child. "I understand. But that's why I won't tell you my secrets."

His hand, which had lifted as I moved, hovered in the air for a moment. Hesitation, perhaps, though I couldn't be sure. Then he lowered it and I felt heat through the thin blanket as he caressed my stomach.

"We seem to be at an impasse," he said.

My heart beat faster, temporarily dimming the pain. "What shall we do in the meantime?"

He hooked one finger over the edge of the blanket and pulled it slowly down. He leaned over me.

"I accept your terms," he rasped.

"And I accept yours." My breath came short. "For the moment."

Twenty-eight

I woke to bright morning sunshine trying its best to fight through the blanket on the window. I was alone in the bed but for a handwritten note on the pillow next to me.

Jillian—

I had to get back to the inn before Teddy noticed I was missing. He's an early riser, damn him.

We never found William Moorcock yesterday. He didn't seem to be home. We have to make a telephone call to the Yard this morning and go over our plans; then I think we'll try him again.

I expect I'll see you again. I expect I'll have to act aloof. If Easterbrook found out about us it would make a mess of this case. Just play along the best you can.

Also—prepare yourself before you look out the window. I didn't hear anything either.

D.M.

I washed and dressed. I made my way down the stairs to the hall. I walked into the kitchen. Then I took a breath, prepared myself, and raised my gaze out the window.

I stared for a long time, taking it in. An entire bush had been uprooted from outside the garden wall and lay sprawled in the garden, its roots exposed to the air; part of the wall itself was crumbled and flattened. Shingles had been torn from the roof, and lay around the house like petals. Worse, when I walked to the front of the house, I saw that the bonnet of my Alvis was raised, and automotive parts were strewn on the cobbles.

It was madness. I hadn't heard a sound. Was it possible that a human had done this, at least the motorcar part, and not the ghost at all? But who would want me to stay in Rothewell quite so badly?

How had I slept through it all?

I wandered out the front door and sat heavily on the stoop, contemplating my car and feeling completely unreal, as if I were in a dream. There were no strange sounds or movements in the panorama of destruction before me. The ghost was gone; he usually was by morning. My fear settled to a low level, though I thought I could still feel an electric charge in the air.

The day was cloudy and overcast, threatening rain. I wore the last clean dress I'd brought to Rothewell, one that hadn't been suffused with smoke, crawled in, or worn for a run through the woods. It was dark gray with a slender belt and a pattern of flowers in cherry red, the brightness of them almost glowing in the gloom. I wore my last pair of stockings that were in one piece, and heeled shoes with buckles at the ankles. I smoothed the skirt on my lap and looked down at my legs. Did I look different? I felt different. Would anyone be able to tell?

A familiar exhaled *whuff* came from around the corner of the house, followed by the heavy patter of four large feet. The dog Poseidon appeared, his ears perked in pleasure, excitement dancing in his big brown eyes. He trotted straight toward me and sat near my feet as if we'd known each other all our lives. He looked up at me, his tail shuffling in the dirt as he wagged it back and forth.

"What are you doing here?" I asked him.

The tail dragged through the dirt again. He wore no collar and no leash. He must have escaped from William's house and was now on a mischievous doggy jaunt, running around the neighborhood. He lowered himself over his front paws and lay full on the ground, emitting a little groan of satisfaction.

I would have to return him, but instead I leaned down and rubbed one large, silky ear. Something about petting a dog—the pure, ecstatic pleasure he takes in your company—brightens even the strangest situation. He didn't care who my parents were or where I had spent last night. I was running my damaged hands over the large, lumpy dome of his head when I heard a motorcar pull up in front of Barrow House.

I looked up. It wasn't Drew. I knew no one else with a motorcar, but the moment the door opened, I remembered. Toby's solicitor, Mr. Reed, had come for his promised visit.

When he approached, his steps clicking on the cobblestones, I was looking back down at the dog. I saw only the toes of his shoes come into the edge of my vision and stop. "Miss Leigh." In his voice I could hear the confusion of the picture he was no doubt looking at: the mess in the garden, the ripped shingles, the girl coatless on the front stoop in the gloomy morning petting a smelly dog. I wondered how he contrasted this with the rather different girl he'd seen at Somerville. "Are you quite all right?"

I looked up at him. He hadn't changed, a small, slim figure dressed in a well-tailored suit and coat. He carried a briefcase in one hand and his hat in the other. His dark hair was combed neatly down on his head.

"I'm quite all right, thank you," I said. I looked at the scene around me. "Rothewell's ghost is rather insistent."

The color faded slowly from his face, bleaching it white, and I felt remorse. What I'd said sounded as if I wanted to deliberately provoke, though I hadn't meant it that way. "Ah. I don't—" he began.

"I'm sorry. I'm not thinking what I'm saying. This looks rather strange, I know. It startled me, too. But you mustn't worry. He only comes out at night."

I had to give him credit; he merely cleared his throat and said amiably, "May I sit down?"

I moved aside on the stoop. Mr. Reed folded himself next to me as Poseidon shuffled his tail again, getting that particular appendage ever filthier in the dirt of the ruined garden. The dog looked at both of us, pleased to have more company, then lowered his head to his front paws.

Mr. Reed put his briefcase on his knees. He seemed to take a moment, looking out at the laneway, the trees still beautiful with their dying leaves, the sunlight filtering through the lowered clouds. The air carried its cool, salty smell and the cry of faraway gulls. As always, in the quiet when the wind was down, we could hear the rush of the sea.

"You've had," he said finally, "a rather difficult time of late, I believe."

I smoothed my skirt over my legs again. *Courage, Jillian.* "Mr. Reed, have you come to tell me about Elizabeth Winstone?"

He sighed, as if the topic gave him actual pain. "So you know, then. How? Was there some memento of hers among Toby's possessions?"

"No, nothing. I pieced it together myself. I found a photograph in the archives. The postmistress knew her. The old man she used to work for thinks I look like her. And I know she had a baby girl, born on my day of birth, that she gave away."

"That is correct; she did. That baby was you. Elizabeth Winstone was your mother. And Toby was your father."

The words hung in the air, blunt and looming with physical weight. "You knew," I managed. "That day at Somerville, you knew."

We were sitting side by side, looking out at the yard and the lane, not at each other. "As to that, if it matters, I've known for about six years, ever since I took over Toby's file from my father. Confidentiality can be the greatest burden of my profession."

"Then why tell me now? You sent me to Barnstaple to see his body. I've been blundering around here, figuring it out myself. Why did you wait?"

"Toby had very specific instructions," he replied calmly. "He had a sealed letter for you placed in his will. No one was to tell you anything until the will was read. There are legalities—certain matters to resolve—before the will could be officially read and the information given, so you had to wait a few days. But he did try. He wanted you to know, you see, in case he died before he had the chance to tell you in person."

"I'm twenty-two," I said bitterly. "How long was he going to wait?"

"Ah, well. I can't really comment on that in too much detail. But that had more to do with your parents than with Toby."

I had a cold stone in my stomach. My parents—my adopted parents—had not wanted me to know. "He wanted to tell me," I said slowly, "and they said no."

"More than that, actually," Mr. Reed replied. Overhead, a lark flew up from its perch in a tree, crying. "He wanted to take you back and have you live with him. Your parents refused outright. They fought rather bitterly over it, and it ended with Toby being forbidden to see you at all."

"That was why he disappeared from my life when I was fourteen."

"Yes, it is." He sighed. "It's a very difficult issue. Your parents were doing what they thought best. Toby was . . . eccentric, as you know. He had no intention of giving up his unusual living, even if he took you back. He wasn't entirely the best candidate to raise a girl."

I pictured myself being taken from place to place, year after year, looking for ghosts. "It doesn't matter," I said. "They should have *told* me. I should have been given the choice."

"You'll have to talk to your parents about that."

"Yes, of course. I'll pop over to Paris and do just that."

He ignored my rudeness; he must deal rather often with people upset beyond anything they'd ever imagined, and took nothing personally. "As it happens, your parents are currently in London."

I turned and stared at him. "London?"

"Just for tonight, mind you. Your father has a speaking engagement at the Royal Society, and then they're back to Paris. They're at the Savoy."

Mr. Reed didn't look at me as he spoke; he turned his gaze down into his lap, as if speaking directly to his briefcase. He knew that he was only making it worse by admitting he knew my parents' schedule when I did not, but this was—finally—a time for honesty, and he would honor it. "Thank you," I said, "for the information."

He nodded at his briefcase. "You'll need to read the letter. And then we'll go over the will."

"What happened?" I said. "Can you tell me?"

"Toby came here as a young man. He stayed for a time, investigating accounts of this Walking John." Mr. Reed raised his head and gazed around the yard, then looked down again. "He met Elizabeth Winstone while he was here, and they fell in love. I don't know very much about the relationship except that he was deeply in love with her, and he never stopped. She was the only woman he ever loved in all his life."

Oh, Toby, I thought. "Go on."

"Well, they were young, I suppose, and when he left she was pregnant. She wrote and told him. She was terrified of losing her position, of raising a baby alone while trying to live as a servant. No one would have hired an unwed mother; no one would still, in fact. She had no family and no other way to support herself. But she did not want to get rid of the baby."

He glanced at me and reddened, but gamely continued on. "Toby was, as I say, not a good candidate to care for an infant. But Charles and Nora wanted a child and couldn't have one. Toby came to them, and they agreed to take you."

"Why didn't Toby marry her?"

"I believe he would have, but she refused." Mr. Reed reddened again. "Toby never said much about that. I believe it was particularly painful for him. It had something to do with the fact that she did not want to leave Rothewell. And then she had, er, another offer."

"The butcher," I said. "He wanted to marry her."

"I believe she did marry, yes."

"So she threw Toby over."

I was being most unfair, requiring this poor man, who was only doing his hired job, to explain the many sins of my parents. I couldn't seem to help myself. "I'm not certain," he said, choosing his words carefully. "I think, if you look at it when you are calmer, you'll see that her choices were rather limited. But I never knew her, so I'm not entirely qualified to say."

"And before anything could be made right," I said, "she died."

"Yes, she died soon after, in childbirth. Toby tried to stay in your life, as much as he was able to. But he found it difficult being around you. He did the best he could."

"Mr. Reed," I managed after a moment, "you've turned my life upside down."

"I have," he agreed instantly. "I do apologize. Perhaps you'd like to read the letter now."

"Yes, thank you."

"Shall I leave you alone?"

I took the envelope he handed me. "There's no need."

"I'll just sit here, then." He reached down and rubbed a hand along Poseidon's back, and the dog raised his head, giving him a pleased look.

I looked at the envelope, its unremarkable cream paper, my name in Toby's distinctive handwriting on the front. *There's nothing for it,* I thought, and I tore it open.

> *Dear Jillian,*
>
> *If you are reading this, then I am dead, and someone has told you, probably Reed. I'm very sorry we lied to you. For we all did—Charles, Nora, and I. All I can say for us is that we did what we thought was best, from what we could see in our limited vision. Perhaps we were right, and perhaps we were wrong. It's too late to do anything about it now.*
>
> *Reed is a decent sort, so just in case he's fudged it in an effort to save your feelings, I'll put it bluntly: I fathered you when I was a young man, with a woman who was even younger, and as we*

didn't know what to do, and as neither of us was much fit to give you any kind of a life—and as my brother and his wife wanted you, and couldn't have children of their own—we gave you away. Thus in one neat transaction your father became your uncle Toby, and your uncle Charles became your father. It sounds very tidy when I put it like that, when it wasn't tidy at all.

As I write this, you are nearing the age of twenty. That is already three years older than your mother was when she had you, and one year younger than I at the time. If you think of it that way, perhaps what we did will make some small amount of sense. The fear we felt at the time was monstrous. I was perfectly unfit father material—I had no money, no permanent home, barely any possessions, and a disreputable career. Charles was always the responsible one. Your mother was a serving maid in a local home. I believe she was even more afraid than I, for she had even more to lose.

She looked exactly like you, and she remains the most beautiful woman I've ever seen.

You know what I do for a living. I saw it in your face when you were thirteen, though of course Charles and Nora wouldn't talk to you about it, and you were too shy to ask me. (That's my fault— I know nothing about children, and so our visits were always conducted in utter silence, which on good days I fool myself into thinking you enjoyed.)

I don't know what to tell you about ghost hunting, or why I do what I do. I remember *swimming in the river with Charles when we were children, the two of us immersed in the cold water on a sweltering hot summer day. We dunked each other under the water, and when we came up I saw a girl at the edge of the trees. She was barely seven or eight, if that, and her ribs showed under her ragged shirt. There were bruises under her eyes, and she looked at me. Then Charles dunked me under the water again, and she was gone. That was the first one I saw.*

I've seen a great many ghosts since then. It's a sensitivity, I suppose, the way some people have a wondrous sense of smell. I don't see them often, or I would have jumped in the Thames long ago. But at certain times, in certain places, I am aware. There is something about me that's visible to them, and sometimes—the good times—I can find what it is they want, what they're seeking that will lay them to rest.

None of them thanks me as they go, but it doesn't matter. I never saw the girl on the river-bank again. She was certainly murdered, and just as certainly whoever had done the atrocities that made her look as she did that day walked away with no one the wiser.

That is why I do what I do.

But I am nearing forty now, which is not so old, but on most days I'm beginning to feel over eighty. I realized at some point some years ago, after your mother had died, after watching you start to grow into a person rather miraculous and unexpected, as I suppose children do, that I have spent more of my life with the dead than with the living. It has made me weary beyond words. And so, selfish monster that I am, I asked for you back. Charles and Nora—I don't know why I ever thought differently—said no. And so I did great damage to my relationship with my only brother. We may not have had much in common, and he may have thought me a fool for much of his life, but he was my brother, and only after I lost him did I understand how much it truly mattered. I say this because you'll be angry with Charles now, and I advise you not to make the same mistake I did. Life is better with Charles than without him.

I've gone on and on in this letter, and I haven't told you much about your mother. I keep every memory of her close to me, folded and tucked away, jealously hoarded and unable to be shared. It seems odd to you now that I ever loved anyone and that anyone loved me. But she did love me, and it remains the only gift that has ever been given only to me, for me alone. My gift with the dead is only a duty.

What came after doesn't matter, not really. She wouldn't marry me, and she had to make her choices. She had to make a life for herself in Rothewell.

Rothewell was her place. It's a haunted place— that's what first drew me there, of course. I came across a ghost I didn't understand, and a place that was, perhaps, impossible to understand. Elizabeth could barely even read, but she understood it.

Rothewell is by the sea, and one day we sat there, on the rocks by the water, just sitting together. It was her half day off, and she had left work for the afternoon. She wore a pale blue cotton dress with a lace collar, her "good" dress, and her dark hair was tied back in a braid. She sat on the rocks in her low-heeled boots, her work-worn hands curled in her lap as if to catch something. She lifted her head and closed her eyes, and smelled the salty breeze with such a look of perfect, serene satisfaction on her face that I was almost jealous.

I asked her then why she stayed in Rothewell, where she cleaned up after a stranger's family, where the ghosts walked at night and scared the children. A place full of half-seen shadows and half-heard voices, creaks just around the corner, the faint thump of footsteps. Even then I knew there were too many ghosts in Rothewell, even for me.

"Because it's beautiful," she said simply, and then she opened her eyes and looked at me. "This place dreams," she said. "It dreams."

Well, there. I've given you one of my memories of her after all. You should have one, at least; please take care of it. The rest I will take with me when I die.

I'm sorry I can't leave you more.

I haven't the strength to read this letter over again, but if it sounds self-pitying, it isn't meant to. It's strange to think of you reading this after I'm dead. I don't know how I died in the end, but I do *already know why I was alive in the first place. I did some good in my life, and I eased some suffering, and I had you. And I find that is more than enough to justify all of it.*

Respectfully,
Toby Leigh

Twenty-nine

I folded the letter and put it back in the envelope with numb fingers.

Mr. Reed, seeing me finish, patted his pockets and produced the same clean handkerchief he'd offered me once before. I was about to refuse it when I realized that I did, in fact, need it this time. I dried my face and handed it back to him.

"Is there anything else?" I managed.

"There's the will," he said, folding the little square of fabric and carefully returning it to his pocket. "He's left you everything he has, as it happens. It isn't much. It may be for you to dispose of, as much as anything. But he did have some rather expensive ghost-hunting equipment, which is also yours."

"What am I to do with a galvanoscope?" I asked.

"Um. That is rather a good question to which I don't directly have the answer. He had a sum of money in the bank, no stocks or bonds, and no capital property. I don't want to give the impression that you're about to become an independently wealthy young woman."

"I understand," I said. My adoptive parents had always been perfectly able to take care of me—part of the reason, of course, why they had raised me in the first place.

"There is a photograph," said Mr. Reed. "This was specifically placed with the will." He held out another envelope. I opened it.

In the photograph it was a summer day, the sunlight bright on
the two captured figures. They stood in a field somewhere—off
behind the church, perhaps, though I couldn't be sure. Toby stood
on the left, young and slender, his hair combed fancifully back,
wearing a tweed coat and vest and a cap with a peaked brim. He
squinted a little into the camera, his eyes crinkling at the corners.
He was leaning toward his companion, his shoulder barely brushing hers, but his entire body slanted in her direction, as if she drew
him like a magnet. The smile on his face was purely happy.

Elizabeth Winstone was wearing a faded dress with a Peter
Pan collar and a line of pretty ruffles on the bodice, a dress she
had likely hand-sewn for herself, and it fit her perfectly. She had
thick dark hair, pulled back in a loose braid from which curls
escaped in the warm wind. Her hands were clasped demurely in
front of her waist, but the camera had captured the second her
attempt at a dignified expression had given way, and her features
had just loosened into the beginning of a laugh. Her shoulders
were flexed up slightly as if trying to keep it in, but her big eyes
were alight with joy and her beautiful mouth was breaking into a
headlong smile. Toby, I think, had just said something funny,
and she simply couldn't help it.

I looked at her for a long time, trying to peer into the mystery of her. I was beginning to make peace with the fact that
Toby was my father; I had known him a little, after all, and
I'd always considered him blood. But this young woman, this
seventeen-year-old near-illiterate maid, was a mystery, and she
always would be. What had she wanted? What had been her
hopes and dreams? Had she ever regretted giving up her child?
Perhaps the only thing I would understand about her was her tie
to this mysterious place, which seemed so alive, as if it had a will
of its own. *This place dreams.*

Mr. Reed was polite, but he was also human, and he was looking discreetly over my shoulder. "Miss Leigh, if I may offer some advice, I do suggest you talk to your parents as soon as you can. Find the nearest telephone and try to reach them. I think it will lay a lot of your trouble to rest if you do it."

I laughed, and it came out sounding less bitter than I thought it would. "Which parents? I have too many. I'd like to talk to all of them. I can't talk to these ones, but with this place, you never know." The thought triggered something that made me stop. "Wait. Wait a minute. Toby's journal." I looked up at the solicitor. "He mentioned her name."

"Did he?"

"Yes. He said . . . He said he had to admit that Walking John wasn't the only reason he came back. And then he wrote her name."

Mr. Reed blinked, trying to follow. "Are you saying he thought that perhaps . . . her ghost?"

He had never forgotten her; perhaps part of him had always worried about her, even in death. What if she was trapped here like the others and needed help to finally lie at rest?

But she wasn't here. Walking John still haunted the bay, unable to sleep. But Elizabeth, with her curly braid and her illuminating smile, was truly gone. It must have cost Toby dearly even to come here.

Mr. Reed took the photograph from me and looked at it thoughtfully for a long moment. His expression grew solemn, his gaze distant as he stared at the small square of paper. He seemed to collect himself before he handed it back. "My wife died in Malta in the war," he said. "She was nursing. She was killed by a shell. It was a week before I even knew."

"I'm sorry," I said, thinking of the first time I had met him, when I'd assumed he'd be going home to his wife and children. Assumptions are always so very, very foolish.

The solicitor nodded. "Nancy, her name was. She was so excited to go. Even after she'd seen war, cleaned up the bodies and lived in a tent with no water and driven ambulances through the mud—even then, her letters home glowed with purpose, an understanding of why she'd been put on this earth. I was stuck in an office in Athens at the time, of all places, trying to get supplies to our men in North Africa. I thought perhaps I'd get leave and we'd see each other. But it wasn't to be. At least it was quick, or so I've been told." He smoothed his hand along the crisp seam of his trouser leg. "I've often thought of going there since. Not to look for her ghost specifically, but for some trace of her. Anything at all. Just something of my Nancy. So, as strange as it is, I believe I understand why your uncle came here."

"Thank you," I said.

He looked at me and managed a smile. "We'll be in touch when you get back to Oxford, then."

"All right."

He rose and strode back through the debris to his motorcar, and I watched him go as I held the letter in one hand and the photograph in the other.

❧

I couldn't find anything to tie around Poseidon and use as a lead, but I didn't need one. When I started down the lane toward William's house, calling softly to the dog, he obediently got up from his spot in the garden and trotted along at my heels. I stuffed my hands in the pockets of the coat I'd put on and trusted him to keep following.

I felt different, and yet the same. My body certainly felt different, a change I noticed as I walked. My chest and legs still hurt from the fire, and my palms were raw. There were aches from last night that were a mixture of pain and pleasure, as well. And yet whoever had tried to kill me yesterday, whoever had killed Toby, had not been stopped. I kept my wits about me, my guard up.

The threatened rain had not arrived yet, but the air was wet and close, the wind an unseasonably warm breath. I watched the treetops move, the dying leaves flashing, listened to my footsteps on the damp earth of the lane, and thought, *I was born here.* I'd always thought I was a London girl, but I'd never felt the affinity for that place—or anyplace—that I felt for this one. I wondered where Elizabeth had lived after she married the butcher. Mrs. Trowbridge would know, if I had the courage to ask her.

A motorcar was pulled up in front of William's house, and two men were alighting from it: Drew Merriken and Teddy Easterbrook. They noticed me as I came up the lane.

"Good morning." Inspector Easterbrook was the first to greet me. "What brings you here, Miss Leigh?"

I found I was staring at Drew, and made an effort to look away. "William's—Mr. Moorcock's—dog wandered into my garden this morning. He must have gotten loose. I'm returning him."

"Can it wait? We have a few questions for him ourselves. In fact—"

"Teddy." This was Drew. Easterbrook turned to his partner, his brows drawing down, but when he followed the direction of Drew's unwavering gaze, he stopped.

I looked as well. The front door of William's house was standing open, showing the tidy and empty front hallway. There was no sign of William himself.

The three of us were still for only a second, staring at the open front door. Something about it gave me an uncanny feeling. It seemed out of place, as if it had been jarred loose. The two detectives felt the same, for I saw them exchange a glance.

Drew turned to me. "Stay here. And hold on to that dog. Teddy, around to the back if you would."

"Right." The two men moved up the walk to the house, Easterbrook disappearing around the side of the house, Drew's taller bulk taking the front door. I heard Drew knock on the open panel, heard him call out; then he disappeared inside.

I stood in the street, my heart beating in my throat. Poseidon gave a low moan and sat at my feet between my ankles, pressing close to me. He didn't look at the door of his master's house, but off down the street toward Rothewell, his gaze focused on the distance.

It seemed an age that I stood there, wondering what was wrong. Finally Drew reappeared at the front door and motioned toward me. I nudged Poseidon with my foot and came up the walk toward Drew.

"Nothing," he said in a low voice as I approached. "And I mean nothing. There's no one here. Do you know where he might have gone?"

I shook my head. "I thought it strange that the dog got out, but I assumed it was just a mistake."

"Well, the back door was wide open as well, and he isn't here."

I followed him into the house, silently agreeing. Not a thing was out of place. Freshly watered flowers stood in a vase by the front window, and a handmade quilt lay perfectly folded across the back of the sofa. The curtains blew in the wind that came through the open doors.

I moved back toward the kitchen. The dog wouldn't follow me, but instead stood on the front stoop, his tail lowered and moving back and forth apologetically. Eventually he sat just outside the door, and I had to leave him.

The kitchen was as neat as the rest of the house. Drew was standing at the back door, looking out at the garden. The teacups had been put away, the kettle cold and tidy on the unlit stove. The only dish to be seen was the empty pie plate from the last of Annie's pie, scrubbed clean and dried, left in the middle of the counter.

I was staring at the pie plate, which for some reason made me even more uneasy, when Teddy Easterbrook came back into the room. "Definitely nothing," he said, his voice breezy. "I thought for a minute we'd get a nasty shock, and I even checked the closets. If he's done for himself, I don't smell anything, do you?"

"For God's sake, Teddy," said Drew.

Teddy glanced at me. "I apologize. I can be a bit blunt. It comes with police work sometimes. It looks like all his clothes and things are in the bedroom, so he can't have gone far. Perhaps he just went to the store."

"And let the dog free and left both his doors open?" I said.

He glanced at me again, this time with just a little annoyance. "It's a little odd, I'll grant, but I hear he had a fever. Perhaps he's ill."

Drew looked at Teddy, a flicker of apprehension in his gaze. "Do we know where Aubrey Thorne is this morning?"

"You think he knows something about this?" said Easterbrook.

"I have no idea."

I thought of what I'd seen the other night, of Aubrey Thorne coming out of this house, of the two men debating. Was it possible their disagreement had escalated? If what Drew had said about the smuggling in the cove was true, there could be a lot of money at stake. Would it be enough to boil over, if the two men couldn't agree?

"It seems to me, then," Easterbrook was saying, "that the vicarage is our next stop."

"Agreed. I'll follow you out directly."

Easterbrook paused at that and looked from Drew to me. I tried to appear casual and not to flush; Drew simply shot his partner a look that would have sent any other man hurrying from the room. I felt all of our careful precautions go up in smoke at the smirk on Teddy Easterbrook's lips.

"Right, then," he said slowly. "I'll just be out front."

"That was hardly discreet," I said to Drew once Teddy had closed the door. "What possessed you?"

But now Drew had turned his gaze on me. He was well dressed and clean shaven, but I thought I could detect tiredness in his eyes. Still, the way he looked at me made me blush with memories of the night before. "I don't give a damn," he said at last. "It's too important."

"What is?"

"We've had some more information. The deal we're expecting is going to happen tomorrow night, in Blood Moon Bay."

My mouth dried. "The deal for the mystery item you can't tell me about."

"Yes. I want you gone by tomorrow morning, out of here to safety. I don't want you anywhere near here."

He was worried—I could see it. My girlish ideas evaporated.

"All right," I said.

"Do you mean it?"

"Yes." In fact, I did. "I don't have much desire to get myself

in the cross fire of some ugly, illicit deal. I'll get out of the way
and let the rest of you do the work. I only wish I knew what Toby
had seen, so I could help you. And now I wish I knew where William is. I hope he hasn't been hurt."

"Why? The last time you saw him, you were so afraid that
you hid behind his garden wall."

"That doesn't mean I want him harmed. He's kind, and a
little lonely." I glanced down at the pie plate again, the treat
baked by his sister that he had so enjoyed. *My brother is easily upset. It's just merciful that he doesn't remember.* "If he's done something foolish, then he deserves the weight of the law, but he
doesn't deserve worse than that."

"You've been crying," he said.

I laughed a little. "I've had something of a morning."

"Tell me what's going on."

I looked at him, and all I wanted was to go toward him, to
lay my cheek against him—on the woolen lapel of his coat, perhaps, feeling the warm strength beneath the scratchy fabric. I
wanted to tell him all of my burdens, laying them out one by one,
letting him take them from me.

It wouldn't happen that way. Drew Merriken didn't make
those kinds of connections—not with anyone. Teddy Easterbrook was outside waiting, and there was dangerous work to do.

But he had asked, for the second time, for me to tell him.
And suddenly I wanted him to know. I wanted him to be the first
person I shared this with, even if it meant I was sentimental and
foolish.

I took Toby's letter from my pocket, approached Drew across
the kitchen, and lifted the lapel of his coat. I slid the letter into
his pocket, letting my fingers linger slowly on the warmth of his
body just for a moment. Then I pulled away.

"Read that," I said, "when you have a moment."

Surprise flickered across his face, but he nodded. "We have to go."

"Whatever happened to William," I said, "he went out the front door and down the road toward Rothewell."

His brows lifted. "How do you know that?"

"Because Poseidon is his dog, and Poseidon is sitting at the front door, looking down the road. It's the last place he saw his master, and he's waiting for him to come back."

"Infernal intelligence," he said, and for the first time his voice softened a little. "It strikes again. Teddy and I are leaving Rothewell within the hour. We need to make it look like Scotland Yard has cleared out and gone home. But we won't be far; we'll be nearby, getting everything together for tomorrow night."

I followed him to the front door. As we came down the front steps, Rachel Moorcock appeared. She was riding a large bicycle, her long legs pumping under her skirt, her low heels jammed awkwardly in the pedals. Her grip on the bars had her hands nearly white, and wild, sweaty locks of hair stuck to her neck.

She stopped the bicycle. She looked directly at me and ignored Scotland Yard. "It's my father," she said. "I'm worried about him."

I took a step toward her. "Has something happened?"

"He's upset." Her face was red and her breath drew deep. "I haven't been able to calm him down. It started when he first saw you. He wants to talk to you again."

I could feel both inspectors watching me. "Me?"

"You." She shrugged quickly. "That girl he thinks you are. He keeps talking about his fishing boat, and something terrible he thinks he's done, but it doesn't make much sense. He's particularly bad this morning. He won't eat. I'm worried."

"I'll come, then." I looked at Drew and Teddy. "Would you mind giving me a ride into town? My motorcar is . . . indisposed."

"Yes," said Drew. He had regained his aloofness, though Teddy Easterbrook was avidly curious. "Of course."

"Wait." I turned back to Rachel. "You're all alone down there. Did you leave Sam and your father on their own?"

She shook her head. "It's all right. I left them with the vicar."

Alone with Aubrey Thorne. And William's strangely empty house sitting open behind me. I turned and saw an expression on the inspectors' faces that must have mirrored my own.

"What?" said Rachel to the three of us. "What is it?"

"We'll meet you down there," said Drew. "Let's go."

Thirty

We drove as fast as we could down the hairpin turns into Rothewell, with Drew in the driver's seat, but still Rachel beat us. She must have pedaled like the devil to have arrived so fast, spinning downhill at breakneck speed. She was flushed and windblown as she led us to the back of the store and opened the door.

"I've put up the Closed sign," she said. "I haven't been able to deal with customers this morning."

It was quiet inside. I didn't hear George York raving, or calling, or making any sound at all. Teddy touched Rachel's arm as she headed down the hall. "Please," he said softly. "Let us go first."

She looked at him in confusion and fear, but stepped aside. She motioned to the door to her father's room and watched them enter. I moved next to her.

"Thorne?" said Drew as he approached the door. "Are you there?"

There was a pause, then a low voice. "Yes. Come in."

The two inspectors exchanged a look of some kind of wordless readiness, and Drew opened the door.

Nothing happened. I heard no excitement, no raised voices. I followed and looked into the room.

George York lay on the bed, as he'd been the last time I saw him. His eyes were closed, and he had one hand folded neatly across his chest. The other hand was held between the large, long-fingered hands of Aubrey Thorne, who was sitting in a bedside chair, looking up at us. I stared at George for a long moment. *He looks dead,* I thought.

"Well, well," said Aubrey, and his voice was tired. "Scotland Yard is here."

"Papa!" Rachel pushed between us and ran into the room. "What's happened? Are you all right?"

My heart fell; then George turned his head as she touched his forehead and opened his eyes. "Dear girl," he said fondly.

"What's gone on?" Rachel looked up at the vicar. "What happened? Where's Sam?"

Aubrey looked at her, and his expression was utterly unreadable. "I've been sitting with your father, as you asked," he said. "He's calmed down."

"He was beside himself when I left!" Worry made her voice shrill, almost accusing. "What did you do?"

"Rachel, my dove," said her father. "This is the vicar. Do you know him?"

She looked down at him, making an effort to gentle her voice. "Yes, Papa. How are you feeling?"

"The vicar has saved me from Walking John."

For a second we were all stunned, taking this in. "Papa?" said Rachel.

"He saved me. Walking John came for me. But the vicar . . ." He smiled, his lips stretched painfully across his teeth. "He *saved* me. It's all right now."

"Thorne," said Drew. "What happened?"

Rachel's voice cracked. *"Where is Sam?"*

Aubrey looked at us, and for a moment I thought he was

going to tell us that Walking John had really come into the old storeroom, right there in daylight, and tried to take the old fisherman from his bed. Instead he put a hand on his forehead, rubbing slowly. I noticed his eyes were sunken with worry, dark circles beneath them. "Nothing," he said softly, and seemingly with effort. "Nothing happened. George thought . . . he thought Walking John was here. I told him I'd made the ghost go away. A little fiction, that's all. I sent Sam to see Mrs. Trowbridge at the post office."

"It was wonderful," said George. "You should have seen him go."

Rachel shook her head. "I don't understand."

"Neither do I," said Drew.

"There's nothing to explain," said Aubrey. He pitched his voice lower. "George was agitated. His mind wanders. He thought he'd seen Walking John coming for him. It was the only way I could think of to calm him."

"And you sent the boy off down the street," Easterbrook added.

For a second, fear flashed in Aubrey's eyes. "I didn't think Sam should see his grandfather like this, that's all. I thought it would be better if he left. Mary Trowbridge will take good care of him, I'm sure."

Rachel pressed her father's knobbed old hand. "Well, thank you," she said to Aubrey, still unsure. "Though I'll have to get Sam back. I don't like to impose on the neighbors. Sam is used to seeing Papa like this, anyway. Whatever happened, you seem to have calmed Papa."

"Elizabeth!"

George had caught sight of me. Everyone looked at me.

"Come!" said George, motioning to me. He tried to sit up in

the bed, but he was so frail, the motion was almost pitiful. "Come! Rachel, it's all right. Send the vicar home. Elizabeth will take care of me now."

He was agitated again, and I regretted having come into the room. I wanted to protest, but it seemed that would only excite him further, so I stepped forward. Aubrey stood, and I moved into his place. I sat down and took George's thin hand in my own. "Ah," I said. "Hello."

"I have much to tell you," he said, leaning toward me.

I patted his hand, unsure what to say, and he leaned back in his pillows. I felt everyone's gaze on me. No one in the room knew that the girl I'd been mistaken for was my mother. It must have seemed utterly inexplicable to them, but there was nothing for it. I patted the old man's hand again.

Aubrey moved to the door, but didn't yet leave. Instead, he said to me, "Miss Leigh, I must apologize."

I raised my eyes reluctantly to his. A rush of cold, tingling numbness came over me that I recognized as fear. It was instinctive, born of how close I'd come to death only yesterday, and it had nothing to do with the pain I saw in his face.

"I never had a chance to say how sorry I am about the fire," he said.

I made an effort to speak without screaming. *He can't hurt you, not with two policemen here.* "I'm sorry you lost your archives."

"It was just paper," he said softly.

I couldn't look at him anymore. If he knew who had locked me in that room—or if he had done it himself—he said nothing. He showed no guilt, no innocence. I turned away.

I heard him leave the room, and the inspectors followed. I looked down into my lap.

Rachel adjusted her father's pillows. He seemed to have melted back into the bed now, his bones nearly sinking into the mattress. I surmised I wouldn't have to sit here very long before he drifted off to sleep.

"I don't suppose you know what that was about," said Rachel. "What do a couple of police inspectors want with Aubrey Thorne?"

I tried to think of what to say. "William Moorcock seems to have disappeared."

She straightened and looked at me in shock. "Disappeared?"

"His house was found empty, the doors open, and his dog let go." I had put Poseidon back in the house before we left, though he had been reluctant. "Have you seen him?"

She shook her head. "And they think Aubrey—"

"They don't know. They just want to question him." I couldn't tell her about Germans, fires, and dangerous smuggling operations, but I couldn't leave her in the dark, either. "Rachel, you must be careful."

She was refilling the water glass by her father's bedside. "Of course. I'm always careful."

"No, I mean truly be careful. There are some strange things going on, and I'm not sure what it's about or what's going to happen. Please promise me you won't trust just anyone."

She gave me a look. "I've known Aubrey Thorne all my life, and William, too. Those two have always been best friends, inseparable, at least until the war came. It does make sense that if William has gone off somewhere, Aubrey might know where he is."

"You don't like William," I said.

"I didn't have much to do with him until I married Ray." She passed a tired hand over her forehead, tried to smooth the wisps of her hair. "I tried to like him."

"William said he and Ray were very close."

"Did he?" She shook her head. "William adored Ray; that much is true. And Annie dotes on William, though he barely notices her. That's how it went in that family. Annie adored William, and William adored Ray."

"And Ray?" I said.

"Ray wanted to get away from both of them. That's what he told me after we married—that he was glad to get out of that house."

George's hand twitched in mine, and I looked down at him. He was drifting off to sleep, his breathing shallow in his narrow chest. "I've been in that house twice," I said through the thickness in my throat. "Alone. With William."

"He had that horrible sickness during the war," said Rachel. "No one thought he would live. He came back different. He had always been calm and gentle, but when he came back he was wild, unsettled. Aubrey was the same. They both seemed so . . . disaffected, somehow. They'd come home when the war was still on—they'd been invalided out—and I think it bothered them to be at home while others were fighting. They didn't work; they said they wanted to have fun. They stole fishing boats and tried to race them, though neither of them knows how to drive one. They'd go up to the cliffs at night and drink until they passed out—one wrong step and they'd have gone over. William said he could swim anything, so Aubrey dared him to go into the ocean on the coldest day of winter. William swam until he was nearly unconscious, and two fishermen had to get in their boats and haul him out before he died. That sort of thing."

I swallowed. It didn't sound fun, or funny, to me. It sounded like the actions of men who wanted to die.

"Aubrey's parents were worried to death," Rachel continued,

"and Annie nearly had a breakdown. The war ended, and we thought it might calm them down, but it made no difference. Then Aubrey met Enid. She had an amazing effect on him. He stopped doing all those crazy things, quit drinking, and became vicar. Will calmed down as well, perhaps only because Aubrey did."

When I was sure George had fallen asleep, I gently slipped his hand from mine and laid it on the coverlet. Rachel slid into my place as I rose, a book in her hand. "In case he wakes," she said. "Reading seems to make him feel better."

"I'll come back later."

The smile she gave me when she heard this was heartbreaking in its pleasure. "Will you? I think he'd like that. I know he thinks you're someone else, but . . ."

"I know."

I left the room, closing the door softly behind me. Aubrey had gone, and Drew and Teddy were standing in the empty store, arguing under their breath.

"God," Teddy was saying. "How unbelievably frustrating to have to let him go. What I want to do is go to that vicarage and turn the bloody place upside down."

"It wouldn't do us any good," said Drew.

"It would put an end to it. I had a quick look at Moorcock's, but there could be lots of places in that little house where he's stashed it. What I wouldn't give to go back there and toss it."

"Teddy, we're leaving, just like we were told."

"And what if the information's wrong? What if nothing happens tomorrow, and they've gotten wind? Get the evidence now, I say. For all we know, that book burned up in the fire."

"What book?" I said.

They stopped and looked at me. Drew opened his mouth,

but Teddy spoke over him. "You needn't concern yourself, Miss Leigh."

I came toward them down the aisle. "I'd say I'm already concerned. I want to know. What book are you talking about?"

Drew held my gaze, but it was Easterbrook who spoke. "How thoroughly did you go through the books in the old archive before they burned?"

I didn't look away from Drew. His mouth became a hard line of resignation, but he nodded.

"I looked at them," I said.

"Closely?" Teddy went on. "Each one?"

I thought back, remembered. "I read all the spines."

"And you saw nothing out of the ordinary?" This was Drew. "Did you open them all? Look at the pages?"

"I didn't open them all, no. The only thing I noticed was the *Book of Common Prayer*. It was worthless, and it was stuck in the bookshelf with all the antiques."

"What about that one?" This was Teddy. "Did you open it?"

"Yes. It was truly the *Book of Common Prayer*."

Teddy gave Drew a meaningful look, and Drew said, "He moved the book, then. He put something else there to fill the gap."

"Unless they're lying to the Germans."

"Look," I said. "You may as well tell me. I know enough about it as it is. Perhaps I can help. What book are you looking for?"

Drew put his hands in the pockets of his overcoat. He loomed big in the dimly lit store, and I pushed away my memory of the muscles moving in his shoulders as they flexed bare under my palms. "We don't know for certain," he said. "There's no proof."

"For goodness' sake, what is it?"

Teddy glanced at Drew. "You tell her," he said. "I won't be

the one to spill a bloody state secret." He walked out of the shop, and we heard the back door close behind him.

Drew and I were quiet. From the other room I could faintly hear Rachel reading to her father, her voice soft and steady as she spoke the words. There was no movement among the tins and bags in the aisles.

"If I tell you," said Drew, "you must promise to leave. Tonight."

"I already told you I would," I said.

"I'm asking you again, and I'm making you promise. Tonight, Jillian."

"Yes. I promise."

"Very well, then. Yes, we think that the next transaction is going to be for a book. A codebook."

"Codebook?"

"We used code during the war for radio communication, especially at sea. The Germans did the same. That way, if the other side picked up reception of the signal, it would be meaningless and they wouldn't know what to do with it."

"I see."

"In order for everyone to know what code they were using, every captain was given a book. The codebook. So he could encode and decode messages from his fellow ships. When ships were taken or captured, the books were valuable, as you can imagine."

"If you had the book," I said, "you could decode the enemy's messages."

"Exactly. We got a number of the German books, but they never got very many of ours. The intelligence tells us that they're buying a thing they call Mercury, and they're excited enough to pay a lot of money for it. Mercury was the name of one of the codes we used that the Germans never captured."

"Do we still use it?" I asked.

"Yes. I don't know where this book has been since the war, or why it's surfaced only now. Our orders are to find the book and stop the transaction as a top priority, because a compromise in the Mercury code is a threat to our merchant ships."

"Now?"

"Perhaps now. Perhaps soon. We're at peace with Germany, Jillian, but not everyone in Germany is at peace with us. There are factions with ideas that would keep you up at night, and they're growing every day. The codebook in the wrong hands could be deadly."

I put a hand on one of the shelves, my fingers grasping a jar of mustard. "Wait," I said. "Wait. You're saying that *Englishmen* are selling their own code to the Germans?"

"Yes. It's treason, pure and simple, and we mean to catch them at it."

I was nearly dizzy. "Who would do such a thing? Put our own sailors in danger? Aubrey? William? I can't believe it."

"Teddy wants to search for the book," said Drew. "The problem is that finding the book now does us no good. Just having the book isn't enough. We have to wait for the transaction to take place, and catch them as they're doing it. That way we get all of them, and we get them cold."

I nodded, unable to say more.

"I'd like to know how they got their hands on the bloody thing as well." Drew's voice had gone rather dangerous. "But that's a conversation we'll have once we get them in custody."

I remembered the second visit Toby had made to the archives, the scuffs on the shelves. Toby's note in his journal: *If only I could find it.* Toby had searched the archives. He must have learned about the book somehow, learned what would happen.

That was why he couldn't do anything without proof. Why he had been more upset than he would have been over a few loads of smuggled goods. *I believe I can stop this.*

He found out about the book. And then he was dead.

I was in over my head. Drew was right: I had no place in a world of treasonous dealings and murder. I was a fool to think I could help, that there was anything I could do. Someone had murdered Toby over this deal, and they may have hurt or killed William as well. I tried to put my scrambled thoughts together. "I don't think . . . I don't think the book was in the archives."

"It was there," said Drew. "At some point it was there. The *Book of Common Prayer* proves it. Thorne hid it. But he moved it and put the other book in its place."

"I wish I had found it." I shook my head. "And I thought finding Walking John's message was so important."

"If Walking John makes an appearance, things will be interesting tomorrow night."

I felt cold. "Don't make light of it. You saw the destruction around Barrow House this morning. He'll appear, Drew. It's his most active time of year."

"That's why I want you gone, Jillian. Tonight. I'm not leaving you here alone."

"I'm going, I'm going." I didn't mention the small complication of my motorcar currently sitting in pieces in the front garden of Barrow House.

"Good." There was a long, tense pause. I kept my face tilted away, my hand gripping the shelf. He was leaving, and he'd catch his criminals, and I'd go back to Oxford and continue with my life. *No connections.*

I found the strength to look at him. I would not cry. "There's something I need before I can leave town, as you've repeatedly demanded I do."

"What is it?"

He was very close, looking down at me. I could have kissed him by just raising up on my toes.

But I took a step back. "I need someone to fix my motorcar."

Thirty-one

Sidney Corr was fiftyish, solidly built and nimble, with a salt-and-pepper beard and a paunch that pressed tightly against the knitted wool of his jersey, as if he'd just eaten a pumpkin. He had picked up the strewn pieces of my motorcar with barely a greeting and gone straight to work.

"Bit of a mess here, then," was his only comment after several moments of tinkering.

I shivered in the chill wind and pulled the collar of my coat closer, trying to forget my terror over the codebook and my misery over Drew. "Your ghost did it," I replied.

"Did he, aye?" His elbows moved as he worked. "It isn't his usual kind of handiwork, but then we don't have motorcars in Rothewell. And some of these pieces are upside down."

The people of Rothewell never ceased to amaze me. "Aren't you afraid?"

"Of Walking John? I steer clear of him, and I hope he steers clear of me. It seems to work well that way." He straightened and wiped his hands on a handkerchief he pulled from his pocket. "I don't go to Blood Moon Bay, if that's what you're asking, and I never did. Not even when I was a fisherman."

"You were a fisherman?"

"Oh, yes." His salt-and-pepper beard split into a grin. "For over twenty years. Did you think I fix motorcars for a living? I only know how to do it as I've fixed my boat so many times. A motor is a motor, even if it's in one of these newfangled things."

Sidney had been Rachel's idea; she knew him through her father. When she heard I needed my motorcar fixed, she'd said she knew exactly whom to ask, and Sidney had turned up barely an hour later. "I don't see very many boats in the water," I said.

"No, aye. There's not as much as there used to be. The waters here are deep and hard to fish, and no one goes to the bay. There are easier places to go. I thought my nephew would take it up after me, but he moved to London before the war, met some girl, and never came home to see his old uncle. So I retired and put my boat away, and I do odd jobs instead." He looked dubiously around my ruined yard. "Could be I could fix some of those shingles, perhaps, if you had a ladder."

I thought of George York, with no one to take over his trade, or his boat either. "Don't you miss it?" I said. "Fishing."

His wily eyes twinkled at me, and he turned back to the motorcar again. "Oh, yes," he said, loud enough for me to still hear. "Though it wasn't easy, as I said. The water was cold, and sometimes there were storms that made you wish you'd never been born. But there's nothing quite like it, I've always said."

I put my hands in my pockets, content to listen. He seemed to be settling in to talk.

"Of course, it got even more difficult during the war," he continued. "What with the U-boats and all."

My muscles grew taut as my every sense came alert. I remembered what Drew had said about German U-boats sinking our merchant ships. "Surely there weren't U-boats along here?"

"They were everywhere, or so we believed, and who can tell with a boat that sinks underwater like that? There's something wrong with it, in my opinion, putting a bunch of men in a tin can and sinking them into the sea. But no, we never saw anything directly along this coast. It was out to sea that was the worst, where all the big ships came along. God only knows how many ships they sank, and how many men died. To go in that direction, you'd never know quite what you'd find, and it was never pleasant. Broken bits of boats, torn lifeboats, burned pieces of furniture—even bodies, or so some said, though I never saw one myself. It takes a man's heart out of his job, it does, to have to navigate through that, and to be terrified of getting in the cross-hairs of a U-boat besides. I wanted to fish and make a living, not get in the middle of a war."

"That's terrible. But how far would you go? Surely where the ships were hit was several days' journey from here?"

"No, aye. Four hours, three and a half in a good wind. And the current carried the stuff toward you, so you'd meet it as you went."

And suddenly, just like that, my mind was spinning, spinning. "Are you certain?" I couldn't keep a strange note from my voice. "Are you certain about this? How many fishermen saw this?"

He shrugged, deep inside the car. "All of us, I suppose. You wouldn't have to go far down in the water out there to find sunken ships of a size you wouldn't believe."

"Did you only see . . . debris? Did you never see, say, the cargo?"

"A crate here and there, perhaps, but nothing so valuable, if that's what you mean." He straightened again and pulled out the handkerchief, looking down at the parts of the motorcar with a practiced eye. He seemed to be talking almost without thinking. "Though, of course, some of the fellows had stories. There were legends that some of the ships sank with gold on them and all kinds of valuables. One ship supposedly carried the Kaiser's secret plan." He looked up and smiled at me. "Me, I would have sold my boat for some sugar or flour under the war rations. Everything I saw was waterlogged anyway, and what sort of man would pick up cargo from a sunken English ship that could have been carrying his own son?"

I shook my head. "I don't know."

"Then I'll tell you. No one would do such a thing, no one. Even the other fishermen I knew, the ones who talked the biggest—no one would have picked up a single piece of coal." He shook his head. "I never thought I'd live to see a war like that. I was never so glad as the day it was over. But then, it hasn't really been the same since, has it?" He nodded toward the fallen shingles. "Walking John haunts the woods; sure he does. But what's an old haunt next to a betrayal like that?"

I shook my head. There had not been a single thing about any of this in Aubrey Thorne's archives—not a single newspaper article mentioning a sunken ship, not a single photograph or letter. "Mr. Corr, I have what may seem a strange question."

He wadded the handkerchief and put it back in his pocket, digging under his paunch. "Well, all right."

"Did you never—truly never—hear of anyone looting those merchant ships?"

He looked at me for a long, steady moment, but I gave nothing more away.

"Never," he said. "Never. They could not have done it in our sight."

"And if one were to do it," I said, "how would one go about it?"

Now he seemed almost offended, as if I'd accused him, but he gamely thought about it anyway. "Well, you wouldn't be able to, not really. Because you'd have to be there right when the ship was sinking, wouldn't you? And how would you know where to be, and when?"

"That's a very good question," I said. "I'd love to know the answer."

≪◦≫

Drew and Teddy had gone. I had no way to reach them. I threw Toby's few clothes into his empty suitcase, then went into the library and began to pack the instruments into their velvet cases. I put away the heavy galvanoscope carefully, wondering what in the world I would do with it.

Sultana wound around my legs. I would take her, of course; the landlady at my boardinghouse would have a fit, but she would just have to make do. I wasn't leaving my cat behind for anything. And what about Poseidon? What if William didn't come home?

I bit my lip and went into the kitchen to get Sultana something to eat, thinking furiously. If I could find Edward Bruton, I could ask him to take care of the dog. And perhaps he had a way to get in touch with Drew. I needed to tell him what I suspected—that somehow the smuggling ring had included looting merchant ships. I wasn't sure how it could help them, but they had to know. It could be how the codebook had come to light.

And I should talk to Diana Kates. Today was the thirty-first, so at least she'd be glad I was out by month's end, as I'd promised—though she wasn't likely to be very happy about the state of the house.

I put down Sultana's dish and looked around the kitchen for anything I'd forgotten. My eye caught on a book on the windowsill.

I'd completely forgotten about it. It was the book I'd found in the stove on my first day in Rothewell, *A History of Incurable Visitations*. It was lying on the kitchen windowsill, where I'd last put it when clearing the table for tea.

I picked it up and leafed through the pages. Toby had left this book out for me that first morning, opened. The section about *boggarts*, I recalled. I turned the pages until I found it.

Though possibly demonic, the account of the *grappione* at Sénanque also bears resemblance to the traditional Scottish haunt called a *boggart*, or sometimes *bogey*, a mischievous—sometimes vicious—manifestation tied to a single place, and often terrifying the inhabitants of the area in which it takes up residence. . . .

And the next page:

For *boggarts* of particularly vicious temperament and tenacious character, a certain ward or charm can be used for removal. A person who has been born in the place that ties the *boggart* to it must take six branches of hawthorn, lay them crosswise in the haunted place, and turn his back to it. He then tells the spirit that, as one born in this place, he now asks the spirit to leave, as he has become unwelcome. In some cases, the *boggart* will appear, but the back must stay turned; it is crucial to the completion of the spell. When the spirit sees that those who inhabit his place have turned their backs on him, he will depart. This charm is thought to originate in Rumania, though it is also known in France, Greece, and Ireland. . . .

I have Vizier's book here, Toby had written. *I will read until I fall asleep.*

I made a sound, and Sultana, startled from her supper, glanced up at me. I laughed.

"It's here," I said to her, holding up the book. "It's always been here. Toby showed it to me on the first day, but I didn't read the other page. Toby tried to tell me from the beginning." I lowered the book and looked around the empty kitchen. "I'm sorry," I said. "I should have understood sooner. You wanted to try it, didn't you? And now you want me to try it."

I set down the book and thought of the fixed motorcar, the suitcases.

I would leave Rothewell tonight, just as I'd promised. But I had one last thing to do first.

Thirty-two

I found the Kateses' house rather easily, as it was the next house along the lane. It had an elaborate garden, currently dead, that would be as pretty and as overblown in summer as one of Diana Kates' hats. The shutters were painted periwinkle blue.

I ducked around the side of the house, trying not to be seen, peeking in the windows one by one. I lucked out at the kitchen, where I spotted Julia slicing apples next to a large woman who was obviously the cook. When the cook left the room, I tossed pebbles at the window and waited.

Julia's plain face appeared soon enough, and her jaw dropped when she saw me. She stood still in the window in indecision, then disappeared.

A moment later she was at the back door. "What are you doing here?" she whispered in a high-pitched hiss that could have been heard at the neighbors'.

"I need your help with something," I said.

"Mother will see!"

"Hush—I don't want her to know. I don't want this all over town."

She glanced behind her, then drew closer to me, lowering her voice. "What is it?"

"Just read this and see."

I handed her the book, open to the page about *boggarts*. Her brow furrowed as she began to read. As she finished, her expression tightened, her skin paling. She looked up at me.

"You said you wanted to fix this place," I said. "You asked my uncle to do it. Well, this was what he found, only he never lived long enough to try it. Why don't we try it? You and I."

"But it's just an old folktale," she argued.

"It may be. How are we to know if we don't try?"

Wariness flashed across her face, as if she thought perhaps I was duping her. "I'd get in trouble."

"That's why you must sneak away. When do you think your mother wouldn't notice?"

"I don't know. She always takes a nap after supper. Five o'clock or so." Now she was calculating. "She closes her door and sleeps like the dead, and the cook goes home." She looked up at me, uncertainty in her eyes again, and the pain of deep shyness. "I'll be afraid," she said.

"So will I," I told her. "I'm completely terrified, in fact—too terrified to do it alone. But it will be less frightening, don't you think, with the two of us?"

"It isn't just that. You need to have me with you."

"What do you mean?"

"The charm." She nodded toward the book. "It says you have to have someone who was born here. I know I was. So that's me."

I nodded. "Yes. That's you. It's up to you, Julia."

She bit her lip, and then the corner of her mouth quirked just a little in a trace of a mischievous smile. "Tonight?"

I smiled back. "Tonight. Where shall we meet? In the woods?"

"I don't go in the woods at night. No one does."

"Julia, I have only one chance at this. It says we have to go to the haunted place. It's almost All Souls' night. He'll be there."

Her eyes were wide, but she nodded. "I'm not going alone.

We'll meet at a landmark and go down to the beach together. How about the signal house?"

"All right, but I don't know how to get to it."

"There's a shortcut. You go north instead of along the main path down to the bay. The turnoff's just behind William Moorcock's house. There's a track through the trees. It's less used than the other, but it's there." Behind her, a voice came from the hall, calling her name. "I have to go."

"Five o'clock?" I said. "Before it gets dark."

This time she smiled. "Five o'clock."

I melted back into the garden, behind a tinkling cherub water fountain and its seashell pool, and waited until Julia closed the door. Then I slipped through the back gate and away down the path by the trees.

჻

I had no idea whether the spell would work. It was an old folktale found in a book. But I had seen firsthand that old folktales were not always what they seemed. I was glad I'd enlisted Julia, because I truly was afraid. But still, it felt rather good to have a plan.

The postmistress, Mrs. Trowbridge, led me to the village's only telephone, which was placed in a tiny booth in the post office, with a folding door considerately placed for privacy. "Take your time," she told me with a smile. "We don't put much stock by telephones here, so I barely get one person in a day."

I looked at her for a long moment. She had known Elizabeth Price and had cared for her. But no. I wasn't ready, not yet. "Thank you."

I had the operator connect me to Scotland Yard. I told the person who answered that I needed to get a message to Inspector

Merriken; I was patched through to one person, and then another, and then another, then mistakenly disconnected. I rang through again and finally reached someone who told me that he wasn't entirely certain of where Inspector Merriken was, or whether a message could be gotten to him, but if I told him my message, he was game to take it down. I told him that I had information about the book and that I needed to speak to the inspector as soon as I could. I told him I'd be in Barnstaple in the morning and named the inn I'd stayed in before. I'd wait there for the inspector's call.

The man repeated it back to me, and rang off. Next I rang the White Lion Inn in St. Thomas' Gate on the chance that the inspectors hadn't yet left, but Mrs. Ebury—disgusted, of course, at yet another girl phoning for the popular Inspector Merriken—said they'd gone more than an hour ago. I sat in the telephone booth, staring at the receiver, wondering where else I could call to find him. I could come up with nothing.

I thought perhaps I'd leave then, nod to Mrs. Trowbridge, walk out the door, and keep going down the street. I saw all of that in my mind, but what happened was I picked up the receiver again and had the operator put me through to London—to the Savoy Hotel.

The front desk man confirmed that yes, Professor and Mrs. Leigh were staying there, and he'd put me through to their room right away. I listened to the clicks on the line, my heart in my chest, waiting for the voice to come on the other end.

It was my mother—my adopted mother, that was. "Darling!" she said. She sounded happy, but I thought I detected a high note of strain in her voice. "We're only here for such a whirlwind stay. It came up so quickly, and we knew you weren't at school. However did you find us?"

"Mr. Reed told me," I said.

There was a pause. "I see. So you've spoken to him, then?"

"Yes," I said, and suddenly I was tired. "I know everything now, Mother. I know."

The line crackled in the silence, and then I could hear the distinctive sound of my mother lighting a cigarette and slowly inhaling. "Well. You've been thrown for a loop, I'm sure. It was best, darling."

"What was best?" I asked. "Lying to me about my parentage, or keeping Toby away from me?"

"Both of them, actually. That girl was practically a child. And Toby—well, you know how Toby was."

"I don't," I said, unable to hide the bitterness in my voice. "I don't know how he was at all. Perhaps you could tell me."

She took another drag on the cigarette. She was keeping her voice carefully controlled, but my mother never smoked quickly unless she was quite upset. I knew her so very well. "Difficult," she said finally. "He was younger than your father, and quieter, but he was just as stubborn. We could never talk him out of ghost hunting—God, how we tried! We were at him for years. Charles said he'd get him a job at a bank or an insurance company, use his connections. A stable job that would make money. Toby would just nod politely and go his own way. What do you do with someone who actually *believes* in what he's doing?"

"Perhaps it was true," I said softly. "All the things he saw."

"Please don't say that, dear. He lived his entire life under that delusion. He couldn't possibly have raised a child. We were going to tell you everything; I promise."

"For God's sake, when?"

"Soon. Very soon. We should have known you'd find out if you went to Rothewell, if you talked to Mr. Reed. But Toby's death was so unexpected, and we were caught in Paris, and it's been incredibly busy, and we couldn't leave. You understand, don't you, darling?"

I pinched the bridge of my nose hard right between my eyes. "Mother, he was murdered."

"*What?*"

"It's true."

"That's madness. I can't imagine why anyone would want to kill Toby." Another pause, this one worried. "My God, I'll have to tell Charles."

"Is he there?"

"No, he went out to get a new tie; the one he has got ruined. He's taken Toby's death very hard, darling, harder than you'd think. This will only make it worse."

"If he's taken it so hard, why am I here alone? I had to identify his *body*, Mother."

"All right," she said slowly. "Yes, I'll admit we deserved that. We weren't thinking, I suppose. Your father . . . Charles wouldn't even hear of going home. I don't think your father quite understood how Toby's death would affect him. It's been hitting him slowly. And, God, he has a lecture tonight. What should I do?"

"Mother, listen." I recognized the tone of my own voice from long years of calming down my mother. "You have to tell him. Just tell him that it's an open case, and Scotland Yard is investigating. I'll update both of you as soon as I can."

"You're angry; I can tell. Darling, please don't be angry. And there's something else going on. What is it?"

There's a ghost, and Toby is haunting my boardinghouse, and someone tried to kill me. Toby was murdered over a treasonous plot, the Germans want to sink our merchant ships and we're trying to stop them, and I think I may have fallen in love with the police inspector who came to my house and took me to bed. . . .

"I'm handling it," I said. "I am."

"Of course you are." And I knew, with a sudden flash of perfect clarity, that she hadn't wanted to know. "I know you're angry with us. I do. And I'll admit that cutting Toby out of our lives was rather a mistake—that was your father's doing, I'm afraid. But Jillian, you were fourteen, and he came to take you back. You'll understand when you have children, but you're my *daughter*." A fierceness had crept into her voice that I recognized as the product of genuine anger. "You're my daughter, and anyone who wanted to take you would have had to kill me first. If you want a mea culpa, I can give you one. But I won't apologize for that. I won't."

The operator cut in and warned us that we were nearly out of time. When we were connected again, my mother had lit another cigarette. "All right, then," she said, her voice brittle. "We haven't much longer, and Charles and I are in London for only few more hours—we leave for Paris just after midnight. So I suppose we have to leave it." She exhaled. "Just tell me one thing, please, before you go. Tell me you forgive me."

I closed my eyes. I thought of Toby, of all the opportunities I'd missed, the chance to know him, to see whether he was like me. "I want to," I said honestly, "but I don't think I can. Not now. I just don't think I can do it."

"Darling." Her voice, even with the brittleness, even through the crackling line, was classic Nora Leigh—charming, magnetic, confident, and utterly without fear. "You are my daughter. I raised you from the day you were born. I gave you everything that was the best in me, and I know you better than you know yourself. The one thing I know is that you can do anything."

And before I could answer, the line went dead.

⟳⟲

Rachel's store was still closed, so I went 'round the building to the back door. I found her sitting at her father's bedside. She had stopped reading and was now only sitting, his hand in hers, her eyes hollow. It looked to be the last vigil George York would ever need.

"Go rest," I told her gently. "I'll sit by him for a while."

The smile that illuminated her features nearly broke my heart. "Would you? Do you mean it? I have Sam back, but he's upstairs alone. I don't want him here for this."

"Yes, of course. Go see to him. And get some sleep."

"It's just for a while."

"I know."

She stood. "Jillian, you're a good friend."

She moved to the door, but before she was gone I asked her one more question. "Rachel?"

"Yes?"

"Your father's boat. Who has used it since he got sick?"

She looked puzzled. "No one."

"No one at all?"

"No."

"Has anyone been on the boat? For any other reason?"

She thought about it. "Just William. I told him I was going to sell the boat, and he helped me. He went through it top to bottom to get it ready to sell." She shrugged. "He's the only one. Does that help?"

"Yes," I said. "I'll call you if anything happens. Now go."

She went, and I took her place in the bedside chair, the old man's hands in mine. He moved restlessly, and his eyes opened. "Elizabeth."

I turned to him, and this time I smiled. "Yes, it's me."

"I'm so glad you've come. . . ."

"Yes," I said. "I've come." I leaned closer to the bed. "I hear you have something to tell me."

Thirty-three

It grew dark early this time of year, and the faded sunlight had begun to vanish into twilight. The clouds were so low they seemed to scrape the rooftops, and there was moisture in the chill wind. I stepped out of Barrow House and watched the trees bow.

I hurried down the lane, tying the belt of my coat tightly around my waist, pulling the collar up to my chin. I hadn't bothered with a hat and gloves, and I wore my sturdiest low-heeled shoes. In my pocket I carried the second torch, which had suddenly reappeared in its case, just where it should be. I couldn't think of what else I would need to go ghost hunting.

I stopped first at William's house and knocked on the door, but there was no answer. I could hear Poseidon inside, restless and whining. The inspectors had left the door unlocked—almost no one locked their doors in Rothewell, it seemed—so I entered the quiet house to let the dog out. While Poseidon was in the yard I rifled through William's cupboards to find the dog's food. When Poseidon whined to come in again, I fed him and sat at the kitchen table, watching him eat, feeling uneasy and out of place in the silence. It was as if William had gone on a trip and asked me to watch his dog—that quiet emptiness and unaccustomed smell of a house waiting for its owner to return. I wondered whether

William were hurt, or dead. Perhaps even now he was lying some-where, where no one would find him.

I came out of my melancholy thoughts as Poseidon finished his dinner and lay in his accustomed spot by the unlit fireplace. He gave me a look of impossibly deep sadness, almost apologetic, from his beautiful brown eyes. *Something is wrong, and I know it, but I can't help feeling hungry and sleepy; I'm sorry. I'll just lie here and wait.*

I rubbed his ears and told him everything would be all right. He thumped his tail once, as if appreciating my effort. I won-dered whether Annie Hughes would like a dog.

Back outside, I skirted the edge of the woods, looking for the path Julia had told me was there. It took me some twenty min-utes, but eventually I found it, narrow and barely visible, a thin line through the trees. John Barrow would have taken this path on nights when the ships were due to come in; he would slip out his back door and through the dark woods to the signal house to send the message to the captain whether he should land. Two and a half centuries later, my own steps followed the same path.

It wasn't easy. The trail was overgrown, thick with brush, and it completely disappeared in places where heavy rainfall had washed in piles of debris. The still-full moon provided the only light. One section of the path was thickly lined with bushes crowned with particularly vicious thorns, and I had to move as gingerly as I would through a lion's jaws. The wind, cold and damp, howled in the trees, and I began to wonder whether I'd wandered into an enchanted wood from a fairy tale, and either a gnarled witch or a handsome prince would appear on the next bend of the path.

The way took me much longer than I'd thought it would. From the smell and sounds of the sea I could tell I was skirting

Blood Moon Bay, following the cupped semicircle of it across the complicated tops of the cliffs instead of along the windblown beach. I saw no sign of Julia along the path and wondered whether she was ahead of me or behind. I looked for a hawthorn tree as I walked, and when I found one, bare and denuded of leaves, I quickly pulled off six small branches and stuffed them in my inside coat pocket.

Finally I sighted a clearing off the side of the path. The trees thinned a little here, and the sound of rushing water was stronger. I picked my way through the brush as gulls wheeled and cried overhead. Before me was a rough wooden structure built low to the ground, with knotted planks for walls and birch shingles on the roof. It was about the height of a man and looked—I couldn't help but think it—just a little like a very old, rather decrepit privy. But what I found when I went through the narrow door was nothing like a privy at all.

A window had been cut into the wall facing the bay. There was no glass, and the wind blew sharply through the little enclosure. Leaves piled in the corners, and the ground—for there was no floor—was littered with decades of blown-in debris. I lowered my head to the opening and found a perfect view of Blood Moon Bay, the rounded expanse of the beach, the restless water, and the entrance to the ocean beyond. From this spot, the signalman could indeed look for approaching vessels, and even see individuals on the beach or at the edges of the woods. He could then lift his lantern—which was protected from wind and rain by the primitive hut—and give the agreed-upon signal. It would be a lonely outpost, but the long hours in the cold and damp would be worth it for the treasure brought by the incoming ships.

I stepped back from the lookout hole and gazed around the rest of the hut. There was barely room to move in there or to stand straight, for it had been built to be as small and hidden as possible. The only item I could make out in the gloom was a wooden box to be used as a chair. I sat on it and waited, listening to the wind and the water. A rustle on the primitive roof suggested that the rain was finally beginning. I rubbed my hands over my eyes.

George York had told me everything.

It had required a tight clamp of control for me to sit and listen as his weakened voice went on and on. Before she married, Elizabeth Winstone had nursed Rachel's mother through two miscarriages after Rachel's own birth, caring for the mother while looking after the little girl; she had been a trusted family confidante, a quiet girl who had never complained and never gossiped. In the wispy haze of his memories, George saw her as the final person he could trust, the only one left with the strength to withstand the truth—Rachel, of course, must be shielded—and the moral fortitude to understand it. Elizabeth's pregnancy, disgrace, and death had vanished from his mind, and I had sat there in my mother's place, wondering what she would think about the fact that this man's old age had granted her forgiveness.

I must tell you. I must tell you what we did. . . .

It weighed on me. I hoped fervently that my message had somehow made it to Drew. I'd go to Barnstaple in the morning and lay it all before him, just as it had been laid before me.

But first I would try my best to lay John Barrow to rest. These woods had been haunted too long, the bay left deserted. John Barrow begged for sleep. And tomorrow night's operation by Scotland Yard would go more smoothly without a ghost's interference.

But mostly I wanted to do it because this was what Toby had come here for: to put this ghost to rest, as he had helped so many others. To put some of his own ghosts to rest, as well. I couldn't help him heal, but I could do this one thing for him. I could do this as my father's daughter.

I moved on my seat, and it creaked beneath me, the wood bowing under my weight. I realized the box I sat on was hollow, and one side had a hinge—not a seat at all, then, but a container. I stood up and lifted the lid.

Metal gleamed dully up at me, and brass. A cold, heavy black square, it chilled my fingers as I lifted it from the box and examined it. My first thought was that it looked much like my father's galvanoscope. After a moment, I saw the headphones still in the box, and I realized it was a radio.

A crystal radio—my father, Charles, had one and had tinkered often with it in the garage, usually on rainy afternoons. *It's an incredible little machine*, he'd told me once. *If you have a clear signal, you can hear for miles.*

If you have a clear signal.

I turned to the little window and looked out. For miles, yes. Tonight was clouding over with cold rain, but on a clear night, it would be easy. Anyone sitting here with this little receiver would be able to get a radio signal, even from somewhere far out to sea.

They always knew, George York had said. *They'd come to my door early or late, and tell me we had to get the boat and go. I just followed. They always knew where they were going.*

And Sidney Corr, when I'd asked him about looting merchant ships. *You'd have to be there right when the ship was sinking, wouldn't you? And how would you know where to be, and when?*

I set down the radio. So they'd used this place, then. This little shack out in the woods had been part of their plan. I looked in the box again.

The radio's headphones were there, and something else as

well. A square, wrapped in oilskin. I pulled it out and unwrapped it, revealing a book the size of my hand with a thick leather binding. The pages were yellowed and damp. Stamped in the leather of the cover were the letters *Hg*.

For a second I blinked at the letters. They were familiar to me, but I couldn't place them; were they initials? My shocked brain took a painfully long time to whir into motion, to tell my eyes what they had seen so many times. My father was a chemist by profession. *Hg* was a symbol on the periodic table of elements. It was the entry for mercury.

I held Drew Merriken's fabled book in my hand. For the past half hour I'd been unwittingly sitting on England's Mercury code.

I gingerly flipped the book open and glanced through the yellowed pages. I could understand none of the columns of letters and symbols, but a code breaker, I imagined, could sit with a book like this for several hours or days, methodically building an understanding. He'd finish with a recipe to decode England's radio signals. I held treason in my hands.

I could burn it. If I could find a match, I could destroy the book entirely and be done with it forever. It would take only minutes. But that wouldn't put away the men who had stolen it and meant to sell it. Drew wanted the deal to go through so he could have arrests, trials. Justice.

A sound came from outside, the strike of a shoe in the dirt. Julia was here. I hurriedly wrapped the book again and put it in the box. I put the radio on top of it, where it had been before, and closed the lid.

I stepped outside into the growing dark. It was beginning to rain, just as I had thought, the wet mist coming down in cold drops that drummed on the roof. I put my hands in my pockets, ignoring the scratches of the hawthorn branches, and stared at the person who stood before me. I clenched my fingers and tried not to tremble.

For I knew who used the radio, and who hid the book. I knew who had killed Toby, and I knew what expression he had worn as he did it. It was a look of perfect calm, beautiful in its serenity, terrifying in its utter detachment. It was the expression he wore now, looking at me, as he put a cigarette to his lips and lit it.

Thirty-four

"Jillian," said William Moorcock, taking me in with his curiously blank eyes. "You look lovely."

My mouth was dry. There seemed nothing to say, so I said nothing.

He smoked the cigarette and squinted at me through the haze. "Did you find my dog?"

"Yes," I managed. "He—he came to me."

"I thought he might." He smiled a little, and just a spark of it reached his eyes. "I told him to go find a new owner. My dog has excellent taste in women."

"Where—" I made myself speak. It would not do to show how terrified I was, though he must have suspected. "Where have you been?"

"Were you worried?" At my expression, he nodded. "I see. Yes, I see. You thought perhaps I'd come to some mishap. I'm sorry to have worried you." He shrugged, looked around at the trees and the darkening woods. "I've been in the woods. In this place." His brow furrowed, then cleared. "I don't quite remember."

He was so unlike the William I'd last seen—the kind, friendly man who had listened to my troubles and told me tales. And yet, in a way, he was recognizable—without artifice, without his willingness to please. This man wanted nothing from me, nothing at all. I wondered whether this was the aftereffects of that awful sickness, with its forgetfulness and delusions. If so, he would be impossible to reason with. My fear dug a little deeper.

"William," I said, as gently as I could. "What happened?"

He sighed. He was wearing a lined coat of dark corduroy and a peaked cap, which he adjusted now. The cigarette burned between his fingers. "Everything has started coming down. Everything at once. Ever since I found the book on George's ship. Do you know he hid it for years, and I never suspected it was there?" He shook his head.

"But you found it," I said.

"I did. Rachel said she wanted to sell the boat, and I went over it from top to bottom. And there was the book, just sitting in the bottom of a locked trunk. It took me some time to figure out what it was. And when I did, you could have knocked me over with a breath of wind. George York, of all people!"

"He didn't know what it was," I said, "but he suspected it was important. He'd thought he'd keep it as insurance, at first, and keep you out of it. But he realized that without you he didn't know how to sell it. By then it was too late to tell the truth. And then he got sick."

"Well, I got it anyway, didn't I? I took it off the boat, but I had to hide it while I did some negotiations. Aubrey kept it for a while, in his disgusting old vicarage. He said we should destroy it, but I said no. Then he said he wanted no part of it. Aubrey continues to disappoint me." He dropped the cigarette. "I moved the book here, but your uncle followed me. We stood right in this spot, as a matter of fact—though he was the one standing here, and I was the one coming out the door."

"It was you." I couldn't help the crack in my voice. "It was you."

He shook his head. "I am sorry. If you saw it my way, you'd

understand. There's too much at stake. To his credit, he put up a good fight. But not quite good enough."

I took a step back. It was an involuntary action, clumsy, but William didn't notice, and I began to wonder whether I would be able to run. "He didn't have to die."

"Jillian, please. Of course he did. I hit him over the head, and then I carried him to the cliffs. He wasn't even dead when he went over, which is why the coroner couldn't tell. He'd have been bruised everywhere; a man already dead would not have been. I was very careful about that. What baffles me, however, is how he came to know about the book. I wish I'd had a chance to get that from him before he died. I've thought about it, and I think he may have overheard a meeting I had in St. Thomas' Gate with one of my German allies." He looked at me. "It seems your family has a penchant for eavesdropping. It was you in the yard that night, was it not?"

I shook my head.

"It's all right," he said. "I can't blame you, not really. I sent Poseidon out, but it did no good. Even my dog let me down."

"What about the fire?" My voice was nearly a whisper. "Was that you?"

"God, no." He seemed disgusted. "That was Aubrey."

"He burned his own archives?"

"A decent strategy, I admit, but my God! I told him it had to look like an accident, the same way I'd handled Toby. How was I to know he'd make such a ridiculous botch of it? You see what I mean—I can't do everything." He patted his pockets as if looking for another cigarette, then dropped his hands again. "You were going too fast, Jillian—that was what worried me. And now you have everything, don't you?" He glanced at me, and his eyes were canny, knowing.

Julia, I thought. *Where is Julia?* I prayed she was off in the trees somewhere, listening before coming any closer. Or, even better, already running the other way.

"It doesn't matter," William said. Irritation crossed his face, then vanished again. "It doesn't matter. Not after tonight."

My stomach dropped, and my hands turned icy in my pockets. "Tonight?"

William smiled at me now. "I'm glad you're here," he said. "We have a little errand to run in Blood Moon Bay."

Tonight. Drew and Teddy had left Rothewell, thinking to come back tomorrow. There was no help to be had. And the handoff to the Germans was happening tonight.

William was shaking his head at me. "I can see you're a little surprised. Never trust leaked information, Jillian. I could have told your blond inspector that. You never know when it's wrong."

I lifted my chin and met his eyes squarely. After a moment, he looked away.

I ran.

Fear gave me speed. I sprinted down the path, back toward town, my legs churning, my heart pumping in my chest. If I'd had any breath, I would have screamed; as it was, the only sound that came from me was a high, gasping whistle as I swallowed breath. I took the first curve of the path and swerved off into the trees, hoping beyond hope to lose my pursuer, whose steps pounded just behind mine.

It was no use; I was smaller and slower than he, encumbered with a dress and heels. William was on me as I'd barely disappeared into the trees. He grasped the collar of my coat first, jerking me back, then swept his leg under mine and sent me crashing to the ground. As I thumped to the dirt he came down atop me, his strong, slim body over me, his knees digging into my thighs, his hands pinning my wrists. The breath flew out of me for a nauseating instant, then came back into my lungs. This time I did scream, as loud as I could.

His cap had come off, and as the shrill sound came out of me, his face reared back in surprise. He pushed my wrists together and held them with one hand, his fingers locked around my wrists with cold, shocking strength. He pushed himself upward, his legs digging painfully into mine.

"Jillian," he said, his voice cracking.

I stopped screaming. There was something in his face, just for a second, that I couldn't put a name to.

Pain shot up my back and through my shoulders where he held my arms pinned. I opened my mouth and drew breath to scream again.

"It's only for a minute," he said, and his fist came down on my face, and I fell into darkness.

Thirty-five

Gulls were crying, and I was icy cold. I opened my eyes. Dark sky sprawled above me, the torn clouds crossing the moon. It rose low on the horizon, and I looked at it for a long moment, my vision blurring in and out as I wondered where I was.

Next to me came a creak, then another. "You're awake, then."

I turned my head. I was lying on damp, hard wood, my knees drawn up, my chin tilted back as I looked at the sky. As I moved, bolts of painful stiffness came down my neck and shoulders. The creak came again.

I struggled to sit up and realized my hands were tied together in front of me. I wiggled and squirmed in the damp. The world rose and fell, rose and fell, and the creak came again. I was on a boat.

I pulled up and looked around me. I was sitting on the bottom of a rowboat, bobbing in the waves of Blood Moon Bay. The wind blew icy this far out on the water, and spray came over the sides, misting my face and my freezing legs. Two feet away, William sat at the oarlocks, his back to me, rowing us steadily out to sea.

I stared at the shoreline, dark and narrow. "What are we doing?" I said, my voice a rasp.

William glanced over his shoulder at me, and away again. "You shouldn't have run."

I pitched forward, tried to balance awkwardly on my bound hands, and struggled to move my numb legs, to get my knees under me. "Of course I ran."

"I didn't want to hit you," he said.

I gazed back at the shoreline. It was too far to swim, the water too cold. "I take it we're meeting the Germans."

"They'll be coming by momentarily, yes."

"I'll scream."

He glanced at me again. That strange calmness was back in his eyes. His voice held no inflection. "Jillian, I can kill you now, or I can kill you later. It's up to you."

I tried to push my sodden hair from my face with my tied hands. "It's kind of you to give me the choice." Anger began to warm me now, overtaking the abject terror. "Perhaps I'll take your precious codebook and throw it in the water. It would be only fitting, since you stole it from the water in the first place. From the bodies of drowned men."

He paused rowing and turned to me, looking at me full for the first time. He'd not bothered to put his cap back on, and the wind ruffled his hair. "You've been talking to George."

"He's still alive. It seems you missed committing one murder as you went down your list."

A spasm of angry disgust crossed his features. "I didn't miss it. Or I wouldn't have, but for Aubrey. I told you, it's all gone wrong. And it was George, I'll remind you, who took the book from the sea."

A picture came into my mind as clear as a photograph: of Aubrey Thorne sitting at George York's bedside, the old man's hand in his, a look in his eyes of unutterable exhaustion as he watched us come into the room. *Well, well, Scotland Yard is here.*

And George York smiling up at us. *The vicar has saved me from Walking John.*

We'd been so afraid, seeing Aubrey alone with the old man like that—afraid he'd do some kind of harm. But that hadn't been why he had been there at all.

"You tried," I said to William now. "And Aubrey stopped you."

"Aubrey," William spat, "has never been the same since he married that woman and decided to reform."

"The old man thought you were Walking John." I thought of Aubrey sending Sam away, telling him to go down the street to the postmistress. Had he done it as he heard William coming to the door, knowing the boy would be in danger?

"Did he? At least that's a compliment. He's an old man, for God's sake. A pillow on his face and we'd be done in minutes. Who would know or care? But Aubrey wouldn't let me. He said he'd call the police. The *police*!"

"He wouldn't let you kill your only witness."

"Don't paint Aubrey the hero. It was he who set that fire, though I had to threaten him. Now he claims he's consumed with guilt over it, but I know Aubrey. I think he's just scared of Hell."

I couldn't speak. I thought I was going to be sick.

"We were partners, friends," William said. "We've known each other since we were children. He owed me some loyalty." He turned and began to row again, anger powering his movements. "It was my idea when we came back from the war—to look for sinking merchant ships. It was simple enough to do. Aubrey thought like I did in those days—we missed the war, the thrill. We didn't want to be a part of normal life anymore. Going after the merchant ships was a risk like no other, and incredibly profitable. We didn't even need to find gold or silver—just rationed items, coffee, cotton, silk. It was worth plenty of money on the black market. George was desperate, and he had a fishing boat. We used Blood Moon Bay because everyone was too frightened to go anywhere near it. Walking John was the perfect cover."

"How did it go?" I said. "You'd pick up a distress signal on the radio, and the two of you would go rouse George York. You'd put to sea in his fishing boat, and you'd . . . you'd . . ." I struggled with the words.

"Say it," he said simply.

"You'd find the ship that had put out the distress call. A ship that had been in battle, or had been torpedoed. You'd catch up with it in your little boat as it was sinking, as the men were dying. And you'd take your boat through the wreckage, collecting loot."

"There's a long tradition on this coast," he said without turning to me, "of wreckers scavenging sunken ships. The legends say that in some places they even put out false signals on their lighthouses to lure ships to the rocks."

"But that isn't what you did, is it?" I cried. "You robbed your own countrymen—merchants bringing in supplies, and fighting sailors. Men of your own Royal Navy! You went to their graves, where they'd fallen in battle, and you robbed them."

"We stop here." We had nearly reached the mouth of the bay. He set down the oars and reached for me. For a second I flinched, but he just grabbed my roped hands and began tying them to the oarlock. We were rocking up and down now, as the rain whipped the water and the crosscurrents tossed the boat, but William held steady, his knees braced on the seat.

"And what about since the war?" I said. "When the ships stopped sinking, and the black market dried up. What did you do then?"

He looked at me for a long moment, then turned away. I wanted to scream. I was wet with rain and sea spray now, my coat nearly soaked through, and I was shivering. I pulled on the ropes that held me to the boat, and my eye scanned the line of beach behind us, now almost impossibly far away. There was movement there, in the trees. A person, or more than one.

"This place is beautiful, isn't it?" said William, as he looked out to the bay. "Do you know, when I came back to Rothewell, the first thing I did was go into the woods and lie on the ground for an entire afternoon, just looking at the sky." He looked up. "The sky is different here, I think."

Drew, I thought. *Please be Drew.*

It was impossible to tell from here who it was, or whether it was a man or a woman. But my eyes didn't deceive me when they saw the moonlight glint off metal in a slow, dull flash.

William was looking up; I hoped he wouldn't notice. He was sitting tall in the seat of the boat, smoking a cigarette, his hands resting on his knees. He lowered his gaze and looked for the German boat to come.

"I'd made contacts to sell the goods," William said at last, "and after the war, they started calling *me*. They wanted to use Blood Moon Bay, and they needed a signalman. I knew the woods, and none of their men would go anywhere near the signal house. I did it, of course. For a hefty fee."

"What about Walking John?"

"I told you, he had quiet periods. I'd wait for one, and I'd get them a message. I don't know how big the operation is, or who runs it. I just know I'd send a message, and I'd signal the boat that it was safe to come in. And then I'd get my money with no one the wiser."

"What about Aubrey?"

"Aubrey found God. And Enid. He wanted nothing more to do with it. But he couldn't exactly blow the whistle, could he? If it all came out, what we'd done, he'd lose everything. And he suddenly decided he cared."

A dull crack sounded. Six feet short of the boat, a thin line of water splashed upward. Another crack came, and another splash. I crouched down to the bottom of the boat.

William turned, but he didn't duck. He scanned the shore, his eyes narrowing, the cigarette balanced between his lips.

"I think that's your inspector," he said, as the third shot came.

I couldn't bear it. "William, please turn around. He's going to kill you."

He glanced at me and took the cigarette from his mouth. He still sat straight as an arrow. "How good a shot is he, do you think?"

I didn't know, but I could guess. "Very good, I think."

"Do you?" Another shot came, this one only five feet from the boat, and to the left. "He must like you a great deal."

"William, please—"

"He's mad, though. He can't possibly hit at this range, with the sea as choppy as it is. And with the two of us so close together in this little boat." His eyes glinted. "Why, he could easily hit you."

I stared at him as the wind tore my sodden hair and froze my hands to ice, and for the first time I understood exactly what was going on. I'd been assuming that when the deal was over, he'd threaten me if I were lucky, or kill me as his latest silenced witness, in his plot to get away.

But William was sitting straight in the line of fire in a flimsy rowboat. He had no gun, or any other weapon. He was going to meet the Germans unarmed. And he was going to kill me, but it wasn't in a plot to get away. William was not planning to get away at all.

I now understood the lack of concern on his face, the strange distance in his eyes. It was the look of a man who had come to a perfect resolve that he was about to die, and after this night he would never have to worry about anything again. I thought of the clean, empty house, the pie plate on the counter, the opened doors. *I told my dog to go find a new owner.* I had walked into the middle of his determined, well-planned suicide.

The thought struck me with such panic that I wanted to thrash at my ropes and scream. I had no chance. This was the last hour of my life, there was no escape, and the man who brought me could not be bargained with.

Another shot came, and he looked at me. He must have seen something in my eyes.

"Please," I said. "Don't do this."

He looked away, toward the shore again. "It won't hurt."

"William!" Now I did thrash, pulling on the ropes, kicking with my legs. "For God's sake—you're ill. Please!"

"We'll go together." A dreamy note entered his flat voice. "I was going to go alone, but when I saw you tonight . . ." He sighed. "I can't leave you behind. It's best."

"Why?" There was warmth on my face; I may have been weeping, though in the rain I couldn't tell. "Why are you doing this? For money? *Why?*"

The shots had stopped. He reached up and scratched his head, as if thinking of what to say. Finally he turned back to me. "Do you know how my brother, Raymond, died?"

I said nothing. His face convulsed with a spasm of emotion, and he rubbed his hand over it, as if scrubbing the memory away. "He took a shot to the face. It blew off half his lower jaw. He lived for three days like that. *Three days.* My brother died in agony, without me, and I never even knew."

You go on, that's all, Drew had said. *You simply do.* "William, it was terrible. Everyone suffered. But it's over."

He lunged and grabbed me, his hands gripping my shoulders. "That's just it," he said, furious, his face close to mine. *"It's not over."*

"Yes, it is. It is."

"You don't *see*. I was there. They say I had a fever for months. But what I had . . . what I had was a revelation." His eyes were alight now. He reached down and grabbed the codebook, still wrapped in its oilskin. "If it's over, why do the Germans want this?" He tossed it to the floor of the boat. "What we call peace, they call an insult. Germany is defeated, but she is *seething*. She has not lain down and died. Every corner is alive with unrest. It will happen, Jillian. Germany will rebuild, rearm, and amass a new army. The seeds of it are already planted. And it will happen all over again."

I shook my head. I felt sick. "That isn't possible."

"It is. It was shown to me while I was in that filthy hospital waiting to die. The angels told me. They said there would be no true armistice. That the war would only start again. I had to live with that knowledge, and I've suffered for it. But when I found the book, I knew. It was a sign. A sign that I could do something to stop it."

"William, you're not making any sense!"

"Read the newspapers, Jillian. The German people are already humiliated. They're already angry. It's not only possible; it's already begun."

"No!" I cried. "There's no way we'll go to war again. England won't stand for it. Someone will stop it. Someone will make sure."

"Wake up, my girl. No one is going to stop anything. There is no justice, no sense of right. It's going to happen, and when it does . . . it's going to be worse than anyone has ever imagined. It's going to be so terrible—I lie awake at night, thinking about it. I can't go through it again—I can't. And I don't want you to, either."

"What if you're wrong?"

But he only shook his head. "My little brother died in agony. They buried him somewhere in the mud over there, and they never even shipped him home. And he died for nothing. *That* is your wonderful twentieth century." He looked away. I couldn't tell whether he was weeping, just as I couldn't tell whether I was. The rain was coming down too strong.

I shivered in the bottom of the boat, sick and miserable. "But why loot ships? Why sell the code to the Germans? Why commit treason?" I said. "For money?"

"I send all my money away," he replied, tired now. "There are forces in Germany—new organizations that are struggling against the power. They need money. Have you heard of the Nazi Party? I doubt you have. Everyone underestimates them, believes them mad. But they are fighting for a new government, and they are gaining ground. I send all the money to them. When I found the Mercury book, I knew they would want it, even though the war is over. Because the war isn't over for them." He turned to me. "And I'm not selling this book to the Nazi Party. I'm giving it to them as a gift."

"But why? You've said you could stop the war. Why commit treason to start it?"

"Because if this new regime comes into power, if they overthrow the corrupt old government, then perhaps we'll have peace. And if not . . . if they have the codebook and the advantage on us, if they have already won . . ." He shrugged, hopelessness in the gesture. "Perhaps we won't fight."

I opened my mouth to say something, but two things happened at once. First, a boat appeared out of the rain.

And second, another shot rang out, and William fell.

Thirty-six

The rowboat jolted, and I lost my balance, landing hard on my elbow. William had gone down on the other side of the seat, and I couldn't see anything but his crumpled legs. I dared not raise my head to go to him, so I called his name.

Above us, the boat William had been waiting for came out of the misting water. It was a fishing trawler. As it approached, I could see its peeling paint, the coils of rope on the deck, the water rushing past the hull. A man in a dark sweater and watch cap stood on the front deck, his back to us, gesturing to one of the crew I couldn't see. He waved his arm once, twice.

I looked back at William's legs, and for a wild moment I thought the Germans had shot him from the trawler. Then another shot hit the hull of the trawler, sending up a shower of splinters, and the man in the watch cap dropped to a crouch, his shouts faint over the sound of the engines and the ceaseless rush of the water.

I gingerly lifted my head. The shots were far too close to still be coming from the beach. I could see nothing.

The Germans were moving now. The ship began to turn.

I called to William again. I slid over the seat, crouching as low as I could, rolling to accommodate my tied hands. "William!"

He moved then, twisting onto his back, trying to get up. I

struggled, wishing I could keep him down, even though he'd kidnapped me, even though he wanted to die. His coat was soaked with rain, and in the dark I couldn't see blood.

"Are you hit?" I called to him.

He swore, seemed to come to himself again, and pushed himself up. "Where are they? Where are they?"

I thought he meant the shooters. "I don't know," I said, but he meant the Germans. Their boat had fully turned now and was steaming away. I could see the word *Cornwall* painted on the hull.

William shouted at them to stop until his voice was hoarse, but it was for nothing. The Germans, it seemed, had no interest in being shot at. In minutes they had receded out of range, and soon after that they were gone.

He sat heavily on the seat of the boat. His face was ashen. He hung his head for a long moment, his hands braced on his knees. Now I could see a darker stain spreading across the front of his coat, just under the breastbone.

We'd been drifting for too long now without anyone at the oars, and the boat was pitching wildly. We'd turned so the side of our hull went into the waves; the water sprayed over us with each assault, soaking us with freezing spray. The current was carrying us toward the mouth of the bay. We were headed toward the open water, where, even if I could get free and pick up the oars, I had almost no chance of fighting my way back to shore.

If I was to get free, I had to do it now. "Please," I said to William, making my best attempt—ragged, I'm sure—to sound rational and sane. "Let me help you. Untie me."

"I don't want help," he said, not looking at me.

I opened my mouth to try again, and then I stopped.

Over William's shoulder, past the end of the boat and across the water, I was now facing the rocky shore at the outer edge of Blood Moon Bay. It was the jumble of overgrown, impossible terrain that I hadn't thought anyone could navigate. Incredibly, there was a rowboat in the water there, and two figures pushing off.

This, then, was where the second volley of shots had come from—farther up the coast toward the ocean, in much closer range to our boat. Having hit William and chased off the Germans, the marksman and one other—I had my money on Drew and Teddy Easterbrook—were making their final play. They were coming to get me.

I glanced at William. He was struggling to raise his head, his breathing growing harder. He hadn't seen them. I thought quickly. The men must know that William wasn't armed; if he had been, he'd have shot back at them already. They must also see that the boat was drifting farther and farther out of the bay. They were coming in their own boat, betting on the fact that William was shot, that he was unarmed, that if he threw me into the sea, they'd get close enough to catch me before I drowned. It was far from a foolproof plan, but to wait until our boat disappeared was no plan at all.

They needed to get as close as possible before William saw they were there. I looked at the sick grimace of pain on my captor's face and couldn't help but think that if they got close enough, fast enough, Drew and Teddy could save him as well.

I tore my gaze from the oncoming boat before William could look up and forced myself to concentrate. "Please," I said, making my voice sound as it had a moment before. "You're hurt. You need help. If you'll just untie me . . ."

"You haven't been listening." He looked up at me now. "I don't want help. He's done me a bloody favor."

"It doesn't have to be this way. You could reconsider. Or you could just let me go. I wouldn't tell the police; I promise." I was babbling to keep him distracted, but his brows came down in bemusement. Why would he care what I told the police after he'd killed himself? But fresh terror was making its way up my spine, robbing me of the ability to make sense. Behind him, the other boat had hardly made any headway at all. If I botched this now, before they even got close . . .

"Listen," I tried again. "Listen—" But I had no chance to say more, for suddenly the boat rocked as something hit it from underneath. I fell against the side, my arms wrenching, and William was jolted off his seat.

I tried to get my legs under me, but the boat rocked again, harder, banging as if some strange leviathan were under the water, a white whale or a kraken or a—

I froze.

William pulled himself up and smiled at me. His nose was bloody, but he gave me a wide grin, almost beatific in its joyousness.

"Walking John!" he cried.

Something hit us again, and the boat rocked nearly sideways, creaking ominously as it rose from the water. I nearly slid over the side, my feet dipping into the icy bay to my ankles before we righted again. My arms were being wrenched nearly from their sockets, and my hands had long ago lost their feeling. My scream was carried away by the wind.

William's hands were on me, pulling me up. He was still smiling. "It's Walking John!" he said again, and suddenly he was jerking the rope from the oarlock, freeing my arms, though not untying my wrists. Blood from his nose dripped onto the rope as he worked. "He's come. He's come for both of us. Now we'll see—"

The boat rocked again, and this time it arched up, rising over us into the moonlit sky, water spraying from the hull. I was paralyzed with terror, just as I'd been that night in the garden, just as I'd been that night as I ran through the woods to the beach. It was the terror that always accompanied the presence of Rothewell's resident ghost.

The boat rose, rose over us. We tumbled back into the water. It sucked at me in an icy grip. I felt it hit my back, the back of my head, and then I went under.

The cold was unlike anything I'd ever felt, so shocking it no longer had anything to do with temperature, but was more like a slap or a clap of thunder in my body. I thrashed, kicking as hard as I could, winnowing upward with my tied hands. I could feel the current pulling me, and the cold, and— *What was that?*

Panic pushed my body to the surface. The boat was a few feet away, righted and half-filled with water. I had just enough time to realize I couldn't see William anywhere when another wave overtook me and put me under.

Again I pushed to the surface, focusing on bending my legs and kicking them out. I couldn't use my arms, but I pointed them upward, as if that could pull me further. Bend and kick. Bend and kick. Again I broke the surface.

I couldn't keep this up. Already my body was slowing, my thoughts beginning to fog in the cold. I had to get to the boat. I focused on pushing myself toward it—bend and kick, bend and kick—as the waves thrashed me and I swallowed water. *I will reach the boat,* I said to myself. *I do not want to die.*

I could barely grip the side; my hands, already awkward, almost completely refused to work. I levered myself just far enough to hook my elbows over the edge, then thrashed with the last of the strength in my legs, pressing my face down into the water-

logged bottom of the boat and hauling in the rest of my body. I
gasped for air, curling into myself, trying futilely to get warm.
The boat tossed under the dark, rainy sky.

I pushed myself up. I was shaking now, my teeth chattering.
The boat with Drew and Teddy was still coming; it was closer
now, and—though I half thought it was my imagination—I
heard a shout.

Something came out of the water.

It was some twenty feet away. It lifted from the waves, a long,
dark head, featureless in the shadows of the water. I got an impression of long hair, sodden, and narrow shoulders, a pointed
nose and a smooth, black brow. It faced me, though I couldn't
see its eyes, and for a long moment it protruded perfectly from
the water, utterly still as the waves crashed around it. I was
speechless with fear, my throat closed. Then it lowered itself and
was gone.

Closer to the boat, a hand came from the water. I crawled to
the side and leaned over. The hand came again, and this time I
grabbed it.

William's face appeared, his eyes half-closed, his lips blue.
He came to the edge of the boat. I helped him grasp it—he
couldn't grip it any more than I could—and then I leaned forward, clutching his coat with my tied hands. I pulled and pulled.
I was frantic to get him out of the water, away from the thing I'd
seen. I couldn't lift him in.

"Jillian," I heard him say.

"Just try," I said. "I can pull you in. I can!"

"Jillian."

"William, the ghost's in the water somewhere! For God's
sake!"

He was looking into my face. His arms were hooked over the

edge of the boat, the rest of him in the water. He laid his cheek against the wood and looked at me.

"Don't be afraid," he said. "It's just his nature."

"It isn't over," I heard myself say, though now I could barely feel my own face. "I won't let it be."

"He wants to sleep," said William. The words were staccato, broken by the chattering of his teeth. "It's all he wants. You saw the drawing. He asked to sleep."

I tried again to grip him, but my hands wouldn't work. "It'll be all right."

"Mind what I told you. You must mind it. It's important. Jillian . . . it's coming."

When I realized he'd closed his eyes, I tried to shake him. "William!"

"It's just his nature," he said again.

"William!"

And then he was gone, slipped through my numb fingers, the fabric of his coat sliding under my numb palms. I tried to grasp him, tried to find some purchase, but there was none. He went under without a sound and disappeared.

I screamed. I howled into the wind, the sound from my throat unearthly. I hovered my useless hands over the water, waiting to grasp him as he came back up, willing him to surface again. He didn't. I merely hung there, making a mad sound, as birds cried in the sky overhead.

He had kidnapped me, hit me, tried to kill me. I shouldn't have felt anything but triumph. But all I could think of was how heavily it must have weighed on him all these years, believing as he did that another war was coming. It had suffocated him so much he had been desperate to die. No one deserved to suffer so.

Then the boat jerked, and I was flung back, landing hard in the water on the bottom. Walking John was coming again.

I shouted something foolish—*Stop*, perhaps, or, *Please*—and then I heard other voices in the wind. I pulled myself up to see Drew and Teddy's boat rise from the water, just as mine had, and lower again. As the boat came up I saw that chilling black figure for just a second before it slipped under like a fish. The boat was so close now I could make out Drew's big, broad body and the smaller, lighter-haired Teddy Easterbrook. They gripped the side of the boat as it came crashing down, as a wave came over the side.

Walking John was going to take us all.

My icy brain began to work. I still had my coat on; I twisted and shoved my hands in the inside pocket. There, incredibly—having survived this wild boat ride and a freezing dip in the water—were the small hawthorn branches I'd picked on the path on the way to the signal house, seemingly a year ago. My fingers closed over them and I yanked, snagging them on the lining of my pocket as I jerked them out.

I tried to keep my balance in the swaying waves as I set down the branches. With shaking hands, I put them on the rowboat's seat—for the bottom was filled with nearly half a foot of water—and arranged them crosswise. I tried to remember stupidly what the book had said. Was there another rule? What was I supposed to do?

The wind and the waves wanted to wash my branches away, but I held them firmly in place until the boat came to a lull. Then I turned my back, folding my knees under me in the water. Over my shoulder I heard more shouts as Walking John again attacked Drew and Teddy's boat.

For a second, the words utterly deserted me, as they do to an actor with stage fright. I blinked furiously, my mouth open, nothing coming forth. Then I remembered.

"John Barrow!" I shouted as clearly as I could. I prayed the branches had stayed in place behind me. "As one born in . . . in this place, I tell you now that you must leave. You are unwelcome here."

I waited. Was that all of it? Was I supposed to say more? The shouts from the other boat had stopped, and I heard nothing. *The back must stay turned*—I remembered that much. I would not turn around.

There was no sound from the boat behind me: not a step, not a creak. But my breath stopped in my chest, and the sodden hairs tried to stand on the back of my neck. I gripped the side of the boat, fighting the urge to jump out, to do anything to get away. *In some cases, the* boggart *will appear. The back must stay turned.*

My arms shook; my hands burned; I knelt braced, locked in terror. He was behind me. I could *feel* it, the icy presence, the dangerous disturbance of the air. Walking John's presence was like a knife slicing through the atmosphere of everything you knew, cutting it open. You looked through and you saw nothing but sadness, nothing but fear. And you had to look.

I found a breath. "Please," I said, my voice unrecognizable. "I am Toby Leigh's daughter. He would have helped you if he'd lived. So I'm doing it now. I am Toby Leigh's daughter. It's time for you to sleep."

The boat rocked, but it was just the waves. I thought I heard breathing.

Don't turn around. Don't turn around. . . .

And then it was gone.

I let go and fell to my hands and knees in the water. Still I didn't turn. I closed my eyes.

I had no idea how long I stayed there, waiting. Eventually something hit the side of the boat. It was a gentle thump, wood on wood. My boat creaked in response.

The sound of feet—human feet—hitting the floor of the boat. "Jillian!"

I opened my eyes and pulled myself up. Drew Merriken splashed toward me, wearing a dark sweater and trousers, his hair tangled with salt water. He leaned over me and held out one large, strong arm. "Take my hand," he said.

I would have smiled, but my lips wouldn't move. I raised my hands and placed them in his, and he pulled me from my knees.

Thirty-seven

———— ∞ ————

It hurt when they cut the ropes from me. I moaned helplessly when Drew rubbed my hands, the blood slicing back into them like arrows.

"Jesus, Teddy," I heard Drew's voice say. "Row faster."

"Believe me," came Teddy's voice, "I'm rowing as fast as I bloody can."

"She'll have hypothermia in a second. Jillian, can you hear me? Come here."

I pushed my face into his neck, my cheek against his soaking-wet sweater. "You shot him."

He rubbed my shoulders, my upper arms. "I'm sorry."

I pressed closer; I couldn't get warm. "Who was shooting from the beach?"

"That was my work, I'm afraid." Teddy was rowing hard, but he still managed an arrogant edge to his voice. "Gave you a bit of a fright, did it? It's an old trick, really. Put the enemy off guard, get him looking in the wrong direction. Get him to empty his gun at you, if you can, and distract him from your comrade, who's sneaking 'round the other way."

"You could have shot me," I said.

"I couldn't have, at that. But I do apologize for scaring you. When you're up against it, you go with the best plan you have. We assumed he had a gun."

I closed my eyes as Drew kept rubbing me, his hands big and strong through my sodden clothes. Everything hurt, I was freezing, and I never wanted to move again. "Did you see him?"

Both men were silent for a long minute. I wondered whether they were looking at each other, or if each of them was looking away.

"There was something," Drew said finally, his reluctant voice rumbling in his chest where I leaned against it. "It was hard to be sure."

"Yes," said Teddy. "Definitely something. And you can put that on my gravestone—*definitely something*—because that's all I'll ever say. If I have to go to Tahiti, I'm rowing in the other bloody direction as fast as I can."

"It's all right," I heard myself say. *It was just his nature.* "I may have gotten rid of him. I think he's gone."

We were silent for a long moment. "Drew," I said at last. It was becoming harder to speak.

"Yes."

"The book was in the boat. The codebook."

"I know, sweetheart," he said. "Now stop talking."

<hr />

I opened my eyes. It was still daylight, so I couldn't have slept long; I suspected I had just dozed after the doctor had left.

I was in my little bedroom at Barrow House. Every quilt from the closet had been piled atop me, and a cup of cooling tea was placed next to the bed. I pushed the covers aside and sat up, swinging my feet to the floor.

Pain shot everywhere through me—my arms, my knees, my face where William had hit me. But my hands were the worst. My wrists were wrapped in red, angry welts, and I still had trouble moving my fingers. The doctor had said the pain and stiffness would go away in time.

I stood on shaky legs. They were bruised and scraped from knee to ankle from my encounters with the bottom of William's rowboat. I was wearing one of the nightgowns from my suitcase. I'd been put in a bath as soon as possible, and now, though a chill still moved through me, I was at least a little warm and clean.

I limped to the tiny washstand, where a glass of water and an old pitcher had been set out. I had barely taken two swallows down my ragged throat when the door opened. It was Julia Kates.

It was Julia who had drawn me a bath, Julia who had found my nightgown for me, Julia who had fetched the quilts. I smiled at her now.

"You're awake," she said, in her blunt way.

"I am. I'm feeling a little better now."

"That's good." She hesitated at the door, as if unsure whether she should leave. "Do you want food?"

I hadn't thought of it, but suddenly it sounded good. "I'd love some. Whatever you can find in the larder."

"There's lots. I can do a sandwich, or . . ." She hesitated again.

"Julia." I set down the glass. "Were you in the woods?"

She looked away. "Yes." Her face reddened in distress. "I heard voices. When I heard William . . . I didn't know what to do. I hid in the trees, and I ran. I was almost all the way down the path when I heard you scream." She dropped her gaze to the floor, and I realized she was deeply ashamed. "I'm sorry."

"Whatever for?"

"I should have *done* something. I ran like a coward."

I took a step toward her. "Julia, there was nothing you could have done. Besides, when you came out of the woods you found Inspector Merriken, didn't you?"

"I didn't mean to," she argued. "I was running home because I thought I'd tell Mother, and he was banging on the door of Barrow House, calling your name."

"So you told him what you'd seen and what you'd heard."

"Yes, I had to, didn't I?"

"Then you saved my life," I said gently, "and I thank you for it."

She shook her head, unappeased. "Mother says there was always something strange about William Moorcock. She says she always knew he'd turn bad someday."

"Yes," I said. "I'm sure she does."

She glanced shyly at me, then away again. "I'll get a sandwich."

I heard her steps clatter halfway down the stairs, then stop.

"Is she awake?" came another voice.

"Yes. I'm getting food."

"Leave it outside the door."

I stood frozen as that voice rang through me. My nightgown suddenly seemed entirely too small.

He came into the room, closed the door behind him, and waited for me. I turned and looked at him.

He'd changed into clean, pressed trousers and white shirt-sleeves, though he wore no jacket or waistcoat. He leaned on the door with one arm, his shoulders impossibly broad, his beautiful face regarding me with an intent expression that contained, I noticed, just a touch of improbable humor.

"I liked the trousers and sweater better," I said. "You should wear those more often."

"I," he said simply, "like that gown."

Blushing, I realized, was a good way to get heat back into one's body.

"Why did you come back?" I tried to change the subject. "You were planning to stay away until tonight."

"I read this." He pulled Toby's letter from his pocket and held it up. "I came back to talk to you. Jillian—what you must have been going through. Why didn't you tell me?"

I shook my head. I had a lump in my throat. "I didn't know what to say. I didn't know how to feel."

He handed the letter back to me. When he brushed his thumb across my cheek, his touch was gentle. "And how do you feel now?"

"I'm still confused." I bit my lip. "But I think . . . proud. Proud that they were my parents."

His thumb skimmed my cheek again. "I knew something was wrong the minute I got back here," he said gently. "This place was empty, and Moorcock's dog was howling so loud you could hear it down the street. I would have searched until I found you."

"But you didn't have to, because Julia came along."

"Yes."

"You came back with Teddy?"

He shrugged. "We have one motorcar. Where I go, Teddy goes. Unfortunately. He knew I wasn't giving him a choice. He's been onto us from the first."

Us. My eyes stung with tears as a sweet, slicing pain twisted through me. I looked up at him, at the man I was so in love with, and I smiled.

"Sweetheart," he said, "don't cry."

"I'm so happy to see you," I whispered.

He leaned down and kissed me. I rose up on my toes and wrapped my arms around his neck and pulled him close. There was so much passion between us—so much that was madly intoxicating and deeply bittersweet. I never wanted to let him go.

He broke the kiss and touched the bruise on my face where William had hit me, then ran his fingers gently over one of my ruined wrists. "I'm glad he's dead," he said hoarsely.

"Don't be," I said. "It was awful."

"Are you ever going to tell me?"

"He should have died in the war. It was a soldier's death."

"I'm sorry I had to shoot him. I told you killing isn't much of a talent." His gaze searched my face. "What did he say to you?"

I thought of telling him all of William's ravings, his prediction for another war, but I couldn't bear to think of it, so I shook my head. "Nothing that made any sense. The fever had affected his mind. He was more ill than anyone thought." I looked him in the eye. "It was all just the talk of a madman."

"All right," he said. "They want me back in London, but I can put them off for a few days. Just to make sure you're all right."

Tears stung my eyes again, and I took a breath. "No. You won't."

He frowned. "What do you mean?"

I raised my eyes to his as my stomach tied in knots. *Courage, Jillian.* "Drew, you need to go. You need to leave."

"What are you talking about? Why?"

Because I'm in love with you. Because if you ask me to go to bed with you again, I'll say yes. Because I can't bear to look at you and know you'll never be mine.

"Because I want . . . more," I said. The tears were on my cheeks now, and I didn't stop them. "I want a connection."

Understanding dawned in his expression, and a strange, tired panic. "Jillian, we've had this conversation. You know how I am. You know why."

"I do. And in a way I even understand it. But I want *more*, Drew. I can't live half a life, watching and waiting for you. It isn't . . . it isn't just that I can't. It's that I shouldn't. And I won't."

He touched my hair. "You deserve better." His jaw was set, and his expression grew hard. "I won't argue with that. You deserve better than me."

I made a sound that was almost a sob. "That isn't what I meant, and you know it."

"Jillian, if you think this is going to change me—if you think this is going to change my mind . . ." He shook his head. "I went through a war. Even after they tell you it's over, it doesn't end just like that."

"No. But you didn't die, Drew. And neither did I. I don't know how it would work, with you in London and me at school. But I know I want to try to find a way—and you don't."

He took a step back. He took a long look at me, but the shutters had closed on his expression, and his thoughts were buried, far from where anyone could see them. Without another word, he turned and left the room.

I waited until I heard his footsteps retreat. Then I made my way to the bed. I lay down, pulled my knees to my chest, and let my tears fall to the pillow.

Thirty-eight

The doctor suggested I rest for several weeks before going back to school, but in this I disobeyed. I prepared to store Toby's things and return to Oxford. I was far enough behind in my studies as it was.

It took me two days before my motorcar was fully packed, my good-byes given to Rachel and Edward. Aubrey Thorne had been taken away by two police constables; Edward had witnessed it on his rounds and offered to describe it to me, though he knew I'd refuse him. I didn't like to think of the church unattended, the greenhouse empty, the happy confidence gone from the vicar's wife. I'd wanted no charges laid in the setting of the fire that had nearly killed me, but even in this Aubrey left me no choice, for he confessed to it, claiming he could not live with the guilt of having attempted murder as a man of God.

Drew and Teddy went to London to put the case together and make a report to their superiors. I wondered what the repercussions would be in the Home Office as to the loss of the Mercury codebook and the attempt of the Germans to seize it. The book had never been recovered from William's rowboat, which had been lost out to sea.

I'd never know, of course; the government didn't keep university students informed of such developments. Still, I wondered what conversations were even now taking place in the hushed halls of Parliament.

I took down the window cover in Toby's old room and the one in my own as well. I took my courage in both hands and moved my bed back to its former spot under the window. I slept like a child both nights and heard not a single sound. Rothewell was as quiet as any other English town. I wondered, though, whether the ghostly man still whistled for his dog.

Mrs. Kates was unhappy about the torn shingles, the damaged fence, and the overturned bush, but as I'd nearly been killed, even she couldn't bring herself to say much about them. She compressed her lips and made a few comments, none of them about ghosts. I let her fume; it didn't seem that she'd have this problem again.

She did cheer up just as she left me the last time, when she spotted something in the middle of the kitchen table and picked it up. "My key!" she exclaimed. "This is the one I lost weeks ago. Where did you find it?"

"I didn't," I said. The key had appeared in the same spot as the pocket watch had.

"Well, you must have found it somewhere—it's right here!"

"I don't know," I said. "Perhaps I did, and I've forgotten."

"How foolish of you," she said in that way that somehow never seemed an insult. "You're just as bad as Julia right now. She's as absentminded as can be, and her chores are suffering awfully. I swear, I don't know what to do with that girl."

"If I may suggest," I said, "you should send her to school."

"School! My goodness—she'll never marry there. Only old maids come out of school. Present company excluded, I'm sure. No, Julia needs to stay home. I saw her looking at that Scotland Yard inspector, the blond one—and I didn't like that look at all.

The last thing Julia needs is an awful fellow like that. At least we're proper here. I'll just tell her what's what, that's all."

Don't listen, Julia, I thought. *Don't.*

There was no inquest into William Moorcock's death, as two Scotland Yard inspectors had seen him drown. The coroner declared that no one could be certain any shot had in fact hit William, and thus the entire affair was put to rest. His body was never found; I heard much later that Annie erected a gravestone for him in the Rothewell churchyard, alongside the graves of their parents. The headstone for their lost younger brother, Raymond, lay a few yards away on the plot Rachel had bought for him. And so Annie had only two empty graves where her brothers should have been.

I saw Raymond's headstone on my own visit to the Rothewell churchyard. I passed it as I walked the tidy rows of graves on a cold, sunny afternoon with the wind coming salty off the sea. I didn't look up at the church that now had no vicar, or over at the burned ruins of the old vicarage. I looked only at the graves, reading them one by one until I found the one I sought.

Elizabeth Price

Beloved wife and mother

1885–1908

And next to it, a small square with no markings, indicating the baby who had died with her.

I knelt and traced the letters with my fingertips. What would have happened if my mother had chosen differently? What if she had married Toby, and kept me? Would she be alive? Would Toby? Would we have been happy? Would I have turned out the same way I was now? Or worse? Or better?

"It doesn't matter," I told her softly, still touching the stone. "You chose. You thought it was best, and you chose." I laid my palm flat, warming the stone. "Thank you."

There was no sound as I left but that of the wind rushing through the grass. A restful, somnolent sound. I left the churchyard sleeping behind me.

Eventually I did make it back to Somerville. The incident had only briefly made the newspapers, and my name had never been mentioned, so I simply told the concerned girls in my boardinghouse that I'd foolishly gone boating and gotten myself in an accident. That explained the bruise on my face and the colorful injuries on my legs and knees. As for my wrists, which still pained me, the weather was cold, so I wore long sleeves, even to bed. I looked at them only when alone in the bath, where I stared at the ugly red welts, so slow to heal, and flexed my fingers over and over. When I thought too much of how it had felt to be tied to the oarlock in the heaving water, waiting for my death, I drained the bath and got out again.

I put Toby's belongings in rented storage, including the ghost-hunting equipment. I had become very fond of the equipment, even the galvanoscope, and I couldn't bear to part with it. They had been Toby's possessions—his cherished, beautiful possessions—and now they were mine. I kept his pocket watch in the drawer next to my bed, and carried it with me sometimes. The book, too—*A History of Incurable Visitations*—I kept with me, with Toby's letter and the two photographs tucked in the back, one of Toby and Elizabeth, and the photograph of Elizabeth alone. Sometimes, at night when the other girls were asleep, I read the book's strange pages by lamplight.

I brought Sultana back to Oxford with me, unwilling even to consider life without her. Caroline, my flatmate, took to her instantly and became Sultana's most adoring fan, a fact that the cat took in her stride. Our landlady was upset at first, and threatened to turn me out, but the combined campaign of both Caroline and myself, as well as the natural and obvious perfection of Sultana, eventually won her over. Sultana was soon the pet of the entire house, though it was only my bed she slept on at night, and only I was ever allowed to brush her tail.

Some weeks after my return to university, I wrote Charles and Nora a letter. I told them what had happened, though briefly, leaving much out, and under the strict caveat that I was in fact completely fine, and they were not to worry. I told them that I did, in some ways, understand the choices they'd made, and that they had acted with the best intentions. I told them I loved them and that someday I would very likely forgive them, but I needed time. I asked them not to visit for a little while and said that I wouldn't be coming home to visit them. But they could write me if they wanted, and I'd always read their letters and reply.

I got at least one letter every day after that. Many were in Nora's dramatic scrawl, but some were from Charles, short little missives in which he described the weather over and over, as if unable to bring himself to speak of anything else. My landlady remarked on the frequency of the letters I was getting; I merely thanked her, took my daily missive, and, once I read it, added each to the stack in my drawer. It wasn't a reconciliation, but it was something.

After I had written Charles and Nora, I wrote Mrs. Trowbridge in Rothewell. I told her that, as she might possibly have guessed, I was Elizabeth Price's daughter. I told her that I was not quite ready to hear everything about my mother yet, but that I would be soon—and when I was ready, would she share her memories with me? She wrote me back kindly, offering to come to Oxford anytime I wished. *What a lovely girl you turned out to be,* she said. *Elizabeth would be so happy if she knew.*

Rachel Moorcock wrote me, too. Her father had died peacefully in his sleep. Edward Bruton had helped her, she said, after it finally happened. He'd visited her frequently to make sure she was all right, and he'd assisted with the arrangements. He had also taken in Poseidon, as Annie hadn't wanted the dog, and was spoiling him rotten. Poseidon now came on Edward's daily rounds with him, running alongside the donkey, bounding into the bushes after rabbits, and wagging his tail.

In a shy postscript, Rachel wrote me that Edward had proposed, and she had told him she'd consider it. *Take him,* I wrote her back. *Let someone care for you for once. Let yourself be happy.*

Mr. Reed wrote, wishing me a healthy recovery and giving me the details of the very small sum of money Toby had left me.

I received exactly one hurriedly written missive from Julia Kates, saying she'd applied to a course in shorthand and typing in London, and if accepted she was going to run away—but I mustn't tell her mother, and if she was all alone in London, might I write? I mailed her five pounds and told her to buy the train ticket, and of course I would write.

I received no letters from Drew Merriken.

I told myself it was only to be expected. He had made himself clear. As I lay in bed at night, alone but for Sultana, I sometimes tormented myself with doubt. I should have accepted anything he offered. I should have simply said yes.

But when daylight came again and I looked at the spires of the university that still filled me with awe, when I read the letters from everyone who cared about me and I wrote them back, I knew I had made the only choice I could. There were people who could live a life of no attachments. I wasn't one of them.

I read and studied, sometimes in the library in the early dark, sometimes in the study room at the boardinghouse, wrapped in my men's sweater with a cup of tea by my side. I worked day and night to catch up on the time I'd missed. I went to lectures and tutorials. I spent laughing evenings with Caroline and the other students, indulging ourselves in smuggled sweets, or listening to the landlady's wireless radio. At night, I never dreamed of ghosts.

It was December, and the day had turned gray and very cold, the smell in the air promising snow. I had just been out shopping; I'd picked up tea to keep in my room, and yet another pair of stockings to replace all the pairs I'd ruined, and a pretty scarf I thought Nora might like for Christmas. I was just heading to the stairs with my parcels when my landlady stopped me.

"It's starting to snow!" she exclaimed. "I just saw some of those big flakes come down—you know, the really pretty ones. Here's your mail, dear."

I set down my parcels and took the stack. My daily letter from Nora, and one from Charles as well. One in Rachel Moorcock's handwriting—I hoped she was telling me she'd accepted Edward. And one in handwriting only vaguely familiar.

"This has no postmark," I said.

She peered over my shoulder. "So it doesn't. That's awfully strange. It was in the stack the postman handed me; that's for certain."

"But it wasn't mailed."

"It must have been, if the postman handed it to me, mustn't it?"

I stared at the letter again. The writing was a man's. I tore it open.

Jillian—

You shop beautifully. Women with legs like yours must never become Oxford dons.

Are you wondering how you got this letter? I'm not going to tell you. I think I'll leave you wondering.

I've come to the conclusion that I'm a fool. I haven't done much since I left you except wish I were wherever you are. It's terrible to realize that you love someone after you've been as big an idiot as I have—to realize there just isn't much else in life that really matters. The only thing I can do is ask whether you'll see me, just this once. Then you can tell me anything you like, and at least I can look at you as you say it.

I was going to write properly, but I've done one better. I'm currently standing somewhere behind the back garden of your boardinghouse in a well-hidden spot, and though it's a prediction at this point in time, I believe I'm freezing.

Rid yourself of your well-intentioned landlady and hurry. You needn't bring anything. I require only your beautiful self.

Did that sound like courting? It was.

One chance, Jillian. Will you give it?

D.M.

"Jillian," said my landlady after a long moment, "are you quite all right?"

"I'm—" I tried to breathe. "I'm going for a walk."

"But you just got back!"

"Yes, I did."

"But your parcels!"

"I'll bring them up later."

"Your handbag!"

I stared at her stupidly until I realized I'd dropped it, un-heeded, as I'd read the letter. It sat at my feet. If I were really going for a walk, I would bring it.

I smiled at her as joy bubbled up inside me. "I'll be back for it later."

"In this weather! Are you sure?" she called after me, but I was already gone, running down the walk as the large flakes of snow began to fall.

Author's Note

One of the many pleasures of writing novels is the opportunity to take historical fact and elaborate on it with one's imagination. In short, I get to make things up.

Though many British merchant ships were sunk by German U-boats during the First World War, there are no accounts of any merchant ships being looted. That is purely the result of my author's "what if?" storytelling process. However, the British Navy did in fact use galvanoscopes to detect the approach of U-boats. A galvanoscope was a simple device that measured the electric current generated by an object's magnetic field. Ghost hunters today use similar technology, but the portable version owned by Toby Leigh in 1924 is fictional.

Naval codes and codebooks were in use by both sides during the First World War, and captains of sinking ships destroyed these books as part of protocol. The capture and decoding of enemy books played a large part in the outcome of many naval engagements. The Mercury code itself is fictional, and the Nazi Party did not acquire any naval codebooks during the 1920s.

The Nazi Party was in existence in Germany and gaining a growing following in 1924. In fact, as this story takes place, Adolf Hitler was serving a prison sentence for his part in the failed "Beer Hall Putsch" of 1923. He used his time in prison to write *Mein Kampf* and re-formed the party in 1925 with himself as leader.

Photo by Adam Hunter

Simone St. James wrote her first ghost story, about a haunted library, when she was in high school. Unaware that real people actually became writers, she pursued a career behind the scenes in the television business. She lives in Toronto, Canada, where she writes in her off hours and lives with her husband and three spoiled cats.

Turn the page for a preview of Simone St. James's new novel, set on a remote estate-turned-hospital in 1919 and featuring a courageous young woman who encounters more than she bargained for:

SILENCE FOR THE DEAD

Available in April 2014 from New American Library in paperback and as an e-book.

England, 1919

Portis House emerged from the fog as we approached, showing itself slowly as a long, low shadow. I leaned my temple against the window of the motorcar and tried to make it out in the fading light.

The driver watched me crane my neck. "That's it, for certain," he said. "No chance of confusion. There's nothing else around here."

I continued to stare. I could barely see cornices now, the slender flutes of Grecian columns just visible in the gloom. A wide, cool portico, and behind it ivy climbing walls of pale Georgian stone. The edges faded in the mist, as if an artist's thumb had blurred them.

"A good spot, it is," the driver went on. My silence seemed to make him uncomfortable, had done so for miles. "That is, for what they use it for. I wouldn't live here myself." He adjusted his cap on his salt-and-pepper head, then stroked a thorny finger through his beard. "Table's low here, so it gets wet. These fogs come off the water. It all ices over terrible in winter."

I pulled away from the window and tilted my head back against the seat, watching through the front windshield as the house came closer. We jolted over the long, muddy drive. "Then why," I asked, "is it a good spot?"

He paused in surprise. I tried to remember when I'd spoken last since I'd hired him at the train station, and couldn't. "Well, for those fellows, of course," he said after a moment. "The mad ones. Keeps 'em away from everyone, doesn't it? And the bridge from the mainland means they've nowhere to go."

It was true. The bridge was long and narrow, exposed to the wind that had buffeted us mercilessly as we navigated its length. Any man who attempted to reach the mainland on foot would be risking his neck. I wondered if anyone had tried and fallen to his death in the churning ocean below. I opened my mouth to ask, then shut it again.

The driver seemed not to notice. "It wasn't built as a hospital, you see. That's what I mean. It was built as a home. Family named Gersbach. Lived there until the war. Children, too. God knows how they did it out here. Four hours on the train from Newcastle upon Tyne to town, and then over that bridge—no place for a child, I say. No one saw them much, and no wonder; it was all they could do to get supplies from the mainland, and they never could keep servants for long. I guess there's no explaining the rich. I hear they were standoffish folk. Typical for Germans."

We were drawing up to the house now, and he steered the motorcar around the drive, headed for the front portico. We circled a stone fountain in the center of the lawn, unused, sitting dry and stained in an empty garden bed. Patches of mist moved across it, sliding soundlessly over the carved, sad-eyed Mary as she opened her blessing arms over the empty basin, blank-faced cherubs flanking her on either side.

"You mustn't worry." The driver stopped the motor before the front steps. "It's remote—that's certain—but I've never heard of anyone being mistreated at the hospital. Your fellow is probably just fine. It'll be too late for me to come back tonight, but they've nice guest rooms here, for family. I'll just come by tomorrow morning, then, shall I?"

I looked at him for a moment before I realized he thought I was a visitor. "I'm staying," I said.

For a second his eyebrows flew upward, as if I'd said I was checking myself in. Then they lowered in consternation. "A nurse? I thought—" His gaze flicked to the rear compartment, where my valise lay. It was small enough to be an overnight bag. When he looked back at me, I met his eyes and watched him understand that the valise contained everything I owned.

"Well," he said. The silence sat between us for a moment. "I'll just get your bag for you, then."

He got out of the car, and I opened my door before he could come round, pulling myself from the painfully hard seat. He flapped his hands in frustration and retrieved my small bag. "Be careful," he said as he handed it to me, his friendly tone gone. "These are madmen, you know. Brutes, some of them. You're just a tiny thing. Young, too. I had no idea you were coming to nurse, or I would have said. Most of them don't last. It's too lonely."

I handed him payment. "Lonely is what I want."

"I get called out here to pick the girls up sometimes when they leave. They're quiet as ghosts, and we never see the nurses in town. Maybe they're not allowed. I'm not even certain they get leave."

"I don't need leave."

"What kind of nurse doesn't need leave?"

Now he sounded almost annoyed. I turned away and started up the steps.

"It's just that you don't seem the type," he called after me.

I turned back. "You needn't worry about me." I thought for a moment. "It isn't a German name, Gersbach," I said to his upturned face. "It's Swiss." I glanced past his shoulder to the fountain again, at Mary's slender, draped shoulders, her elegant arms. Then I climbed the steps toward the front doors of Portis House.

⁓✣⁓

"Katharine Weekes." The woman glanced through the papers in her hand, shuffling them deftly through her long fingers, the corners of her mouth turned down in concentration.

"Kitty," I said.

She glanced sharply up at me. We were in a makeshift office where perhaps the butler or the housekeeper had once sat, tucked in the back of the building, the room furnished with only a scabbed old desk and a mismatched wooden filing cabinet. Out the window, the fog drifted by.

She was a tallish woman, with square shoulders, her hair cut in a blunt fringe that was almost mannish. She wore a thick cardigan over her uniform and a pair of half-glasses that she didn't bother to use dangled on a chain around her neck. Her eyes narrowed as she looked at me. "You will not be called Kitty," she said. "You will be Nurse Weekes. I am the Matron here, Mrs. Hilder. You will call me Matron."

I filed this piece of information away. It was stupid, but I would need it. "Yes, Matron."

Her eyes narrowed again. Even when I tried, I never had an easy time sounding obedient, and something must have slipped through my tone. Matron would be one of those women who never missed a hint of insolence. "It says here," she continued a moment later, "that you come from Belling Wood Hospital in London, where you worked for a year."

"Yes, Matron."

"It's a difficult hospital, Belling Wood. A lot of casualties came through there. A great many challenging cases."

I nodded mutely. How did she know? How could she know?

"We usually prefer more experienced nurses, but as you were at Belling Wood, it's to be assumed your skills are higher than would strictly be required here at Portis."

"I'm sure it will be fine," I murmured. I had carefully placed my hands on the lap of my thick skirt, and I kept my eyes trained on them. I wore my only pair of gloves. I hated gloves, but I hated the sight of my hands even more. At least the gloves hid the scar that traveled from the soft web between my thumb and fingers down to the base of my wrist.

"Are you?" Mrs. Hilder—Matron—asked. Something about the careful neutrality of her tone set a pulse of panic pumping in the back of my throat.

I risked a glimpse up at her. She was regarding me steadily from behind a gaze that gave nothing away. I would have to say something. I quickly searched my memory.

"Belling Wood was exhausting," I said. "I was hardly ever home. I began to think I couldn't really make a difference." Yes, this I remembered hearing. "I was tired of casualty cases, and I had heard of Portis House by reputation."

A bit thick, perhaps, but I felt it had been called for. Matron's expression didn't change. "Portis has no reputation," she said without inflection. "We opened only last year."

"I hear that the patients are well treated," I said. Also true, even if I had only heard it from the taxi driver twenty minutes ago.

"They're treated as well as they can be," she replied. "You also have a letter of reference here from Abigail Morris, Belling Wood's head nurse."

I watched her extract the page and read it carefully. Her eyes traveled down the handwritten paper, then up again. Sweat beaded on my forehead.

It was a lie, all of it. I'd never set foot in Belling Wood. My London flatmate, Alison, had worked there, and in her few hours home between shifts, she'd told exhausted stories of what it was like. It sounded like hard work, but hard work didn't bother me, and I wanted a job. Washing bandages and emptying a few bedpans didn't seem like much compared to the factory work I'd been doing, and when I was let go, I found myself with no way to pay my half of the rent.

Ally'd had two nursing friends over one night, and as I sat in my tiny bedroom, I listened through the thin walls to their talk. One had a pamphlet from Portis House advertising for nurses and was thinking of applying. She was sick of London and the work sounded easy—just a few shell-shocked men, if you please, far from the blood and the vomit and the influenza in the city. But the others said the place was so far away she'd likely go mad. Besides, rumor had it Portis House couldn't keep staff past a few weeks, though no one could say why, and they were desperate for girls. Who wanted to give up a good London job and go all that way to a place that couldn't keep nurses? Best, all the girls agreed, to stay in London and hope for a promotion—or, even better, a husband.

I'd sat on my thin bed listening, hugging my knees, my heart pounding in excitement as they'd tossed the idea away, and after they left I'd fished the pamphlet from the trash bin. It was the perfect solution. A far-distant place, desperate for girls, and all I'd have to do was wait on a handful of soldiers. I'd sent off an application claiming Ally's experience as mine, complete with letter of reference from the head nurse. Ally had talked about her often enough; it was simple to change my handwriting and use the woman's name. Who would check too closely in these days of chaos, with the war just over?

I'd received a reply within a few days—an acceptance sight unseen, accompanied by travel instructions. I'd told Ally a made-up story about getting another factory job and packed my bag, leaving her none the wiser. If it doesn't harm anyone, I'd always thought, it's fair game.

Matron folded the paper again and put it on the desk. The pulse of fear in my throat slowed.

"This all seems in order," she said.

I swallowed and nodded.

"Conditions here can be challenging," she went on, "and our location is isolated. It isn't easy work. We have a hard time getting girls to stay."

"I'll stay."

"Yes," she said. "You likely will." She tilted her head and regarded me. "Because Abigail Morris happens to be my second cousin, and that isn't her handwriting at all."

My heart dropped into my stomach. No. *No.* "I—"

"Be quiet." Her voice was kept even, and her eyelids drooped over her eyes for a brief moment in what almost seemed an expression of triumph. "I should not only turn you away. I should report you to Mr. Deighton, the owner. A word from him to your next employer and you'd be out on the streets."

"But you brought me all the way here." I tried to speak calmly, not to sound shrill, but it came out a croak. "You can't just turn me away. Why did you bring me here?"

"I didn't. Mr. Deighton did. I was away for several days, and your application fell to him. Believe me, if he'd waited to seek my counsel, none of this would be happening." She sounded a little disgusted, as if the slight was a frequent one. "But now it's done."

What did that mean? I waited.

Matron leaned back in her chair and examined me. "Have you had measles?" she asked.

"Yes."

"Chicken pox?"

"Yes."

"Do you have varicose veins?"

"No."

"Susceptible to infection?"

"I've never been sick a day in my life."

"Are you capable of holding down a man who is thrashing and calling you names?"

Steady. She was trying to throw me, but I wouldn't let her. "I don't know about the thrashing, but I've been called every name in the book and then some."

She sighed. "You seem awfully confident. You shouldn't be. You're a pert one, too, and don't think I can't tell. I don't care for your attitude." She glanced down at the papers before her again, then back at me, and now her jaw was set. "I don't know what you're up to, Miss Weekes, and I don't care to know. As it happens, I'm in dire need of a nurse. I haven't been able to keep a girl past three weeks, and it's put the work far behind. Frankly, I'm about to lose my position over it."

I blinked. I hadn't expected candor. "I'll stay," I said again.

"I'll thank you to remember you said that, and not come crying to me."

"I don't come crying to anyone."

"You say that now. Another thing—I keep rules here at Portis House. Show respect to myself, to the doctors, and to Mr. Deighton when he comes for inspection. Cleanliness and neatness at all times. Always wear your uniform. Shifts are of sixteen hours' duration, with two hours of leisure time in early afternoon, and one week's night shift per month. You get a half day off every four weeks only, and no other leave will be given.

Curfew is strictly enforced, and no fraternizing with the men. Breaking of the rules is immediate grounds for dismissal. Do I make myself clear? And for the last time, you're to call me Matron."

I couldn't believe that this was happening, that I would be staying. That my wild plan had worked. *This place is perfect, so perfect. I'll never be found.* "Yes, Matron."

"I will not discuss your background, or lack of it, with anyone for now. But you are expected to perform all the duties of a nurse, to the level of your fellow nurses. How you do that is your problem. Is this fully understood?"

"Yes, Matron."

"Fine, then. I'll have Nurse Fellows show you around the place." She stood.

I stood as well, but I didn't follow her to the door.

"Well?" she said irritably when she opened the door and turned back to see me standing there. "What is it?"

"Why?" I said. "Why did you accept me, really? You don't like me at all. Why didn't you turn me away?"

I could see her deciding whether to answer, but her distaste for me won out and she went ahead. "Very well. Because I think the only girls who stay here will be the ones who have nowhere else to go," she said bluntly. "Normal girls haven't worked, but someone desperate might do." She shrugged. "And now I've found you." She turned to the open doorway. "Nurse Fellows, please show Nurse Weekes to her quarters."